EVERY TIME
I THINK OF YOU

TRACEY GARVIS GRAVES

EVERY TIME I THINK OF YOU
COPYRIGHT © 2014
TRACEY GARVIS GRAVES
All rights reserved. No part of this publication may be reproduced, distributed, or transmitted in any form or by any means, including photocopying, recording, or other electronic or mechanical methods, without the prior written permission of the publisher, except in the case of brief quotations embodied in critical reviews and certain other noncommercial uses permitted by copyright law.

Cover Design by Sarah Hansen at Okay Creations

Interior design and formatting by Benjamin Carrancho

*For Agnes Garvis and Margaret Parker
Because no two greater grandmothers ever
existed, at least not in my world.*

CHAPTER 1

THREE-YEAR-OLD ELLIOTT DISTEFANO hid underneath his mother's bed when the shouting started. He didn't understand what the raised voices coming from the living room meant, but instinct told him to hide.

No one ever yelled in his house. Sometimes they used a different tone with him, firmer. "Stop climbing everything, you little monkey," his mama would say, or "It's time to pick up your toys and get ready for bed," Nana would announce. Most of the time he would do what they said, although sometimes they had to ask him twice, especially if what he'd rather do was play a little longer. But they never spoke to him in such a harsh way, and they never told him to shut up like the man in the living room just did to Nana.

Elliott clutched his favorite green army man tightly in his hand. His nana had given him a bath after their early dinner at five and asked if he was ready to put on his pajamas. "I can do it myself," he'd told her, and she'd smiled and walked out of the bedroom he shared with Mama, closing the door behind her. She'd promised they could watch a movie and that Elliott could have one of the cookies they'd baked earlier that day for his bedtime snack. But then someone knocked on the door and now there was yelling and no movie and no cookie.

The man's voice was scary and mean. Nana sounded like she was crying, and as Elliott's fear grew, he began to tremble. The yelling got a little louder, followed by a crash and a thud. Then nothing. Was the bad man still there? What if he'd left but planned to come back? Elliott could no longer hear Nana's voice, and he wondered where she was. Did she leave? Did she go with the man? He curled himself into a tight ball and began to cry silent tears.

He had no way of knowing how much time had passed. It was dark under the bed and the crying had tired him out, so he rubbed his stinging eyes and took a little nap. When he woke up, he desperately needed to go to the bathroom. His mama and Nana had been so proud of him when he stopped wearing diapers, and he hardly ever had accidents, but he couldn't risk leaving the safety he'd found under the bed. The minutes ticked by, and though he tried his best to hold it, he peed in his pajamas, soaking himself from the waist down. He started to shiver.

It was quiet for a long time, and then someone banged on the door and shouted something, but Elliott didn't know if that was bad or good. He heard voices in the living room, not yelling, just talking, but he remained hidden. Mama would be home soon, and she'd know what to do. Elliott decided to wait for her under the bed.

More voices, drawing closer. The door to the bedroom opened. Elliott froze, wondering if it was the bad man coming to get him. He didn't make a sound as a pair of legs wearing dark blue pants with a stripe down the side came into view. If he didn't say a word or make any noise, maybe the person would leave.

No one would have known he was there if he hadn't coughed at that very moment. It was a bit dusty underneath the bed, and Elliott already felt a little wheezy, like he might need another dose of his medicine. The legs bent as someone crouched down to look under the bed and Elliott squeezed his eyes shut, terrified of what he might see.

"It's okay," the man said, speaking softly. "I'm a policeman. I'm here to help. Can you come out from under there?"

Heart pounding, Elliott didn't answer. He couldn't.

More footsteps. More dark blue legs. Elliott stayed put. No one was yelling, but Elliott's heart was still beating fast, and his body felt like Jell-O.

A lady wearing a dark blue uniform lay down on the floor next to the bed. "What's your name?"

She sounded a little like his mama. Her smile was nice like Mama's, too. He didn't think a bad person would smile at him, so he answered her.

"Ewiott," he whispered.

"My name is Officer Ochoa, but you can call me Regina, okay?"

He nodded.

"How old are you, Elliott?"

Using the hand not clutching the army man, he held up three fingers.

"Three, huh? That's a good age. I want you to know that you're safe and no one will hurt you. Can you come out from under there? Here, take my hand."

She stretched out her hand to him, and he hesitated but finally touched her palm with his fingers. She urged him gently toward her. Once he was close enough, she reached in and grabbed him by his pajama top, pulling him the rest of the way out.

Elliott blinked and let his eyes adjust to the light. One of the officers noticed his wet pajamas and his shivering, and they wrapped his Thomas the Tank Engine comforter around him, speaking in low, soothing tones.

"I want Nana and Mama," he said.

They could barely hear him.

"What is your mama's name?" they asked.

"Daisy." He knew this was true because it was the name other people called her when they said hello. And it was easy to remember because it was the name of a flower, and he liked flowers.

"Do you know your last name?"

He nodded. He and Mama had practiced saying it. "DiStefano," Elliott said. Maybe it didn't come out as clearly as it sounded to him, because they repeated it back like a question and he nodded.

The officers exchanged a glance and one of them said, "Got it." The officer who spoke scribbled something on a pad of paper and left the room.

"We're going to take you to the police station, and we'll call your mom so she can come get you," Officer Ochoa said. "Okay?"

He wanted his mama more than anything, so he said okay, and when she bent down and scooped him up, comforter and all, he put his arms around her neck. She hurried down the hallway, and just before they got to the door, when he would have tried to look for Nana to make sure she was coming too, Officer Ochoa pulled Elliott's head down to her chest and all he could see was the dark blue of her uniform.

CHAPTER 2

DAISY

THE SANTA ANA winds were howling in from the desert the day my grandmother died. Looking back, I can't help but wonder if this was an omen of sorts. A harbinger, if you will. My parents and older sister had died on the same kind of day: hot, arid, unforgiving. At least that's what my grandmother told me when I was old enough to hear the details of their demise.

I left the hospital around seven fifteen that evening. As I walked toward the parking garage, the blast-furnace wind sent the hair that had come loose from my ponytail swirling into my eyes. Blinking, I bent my head and quickened my step.

I should be used to the weather by now. I'm thirty years old and I've lived in Southern California my whole life, in the dying desert town of Fenton, located near the halfway point between Los Angeles and Las Vegas. My first six months were spent in a medium-size, split-level home. I've seen pictures of it: the light blue paint with white trim and shutters, the colorful flowerbeds, the well-tended patch of Bermuda grass out front. When my parents and sister died, my grandmother took me in, becoming both a mother and a father to me. For the longest time, it was the only family dynamic I'd ever known. Elliott and I moved back in with my grandmother about a year ago, to the same small apartment where she raised me. It's where we fled when my marriage went south, and Nana welcomed us with open arms. The house Scott and I had been living in before I left him was only a rental, but I'd worked hard to make it a home for us, especially after Elliott came along.

I tried not to think about the fact that the only two times I've ever lived in a house, things ended very badly.

Hopefully that was just an unfortunate coincidence.

The parking garage stood adjacent to the hospital, and upon reaching the shelter of the concrete structure, I hurried up two flights of stairs to my Camry. Once inside, I cranked the engine and turned the air conditioner on high. While I waited for the air to blow cold, I punched buttons on the radio until I found an upbeat pop song. My twelve-hour shift had been emotionally draining, and I needed something to lift my spirits. One of my patients—a young man in his early twenties—was in the late and final stage of kidney failure. I'd spent several hours that day preparing the family for what was coming. This was the part of being a nurse that I hated, and in the eight years I'd worked at the hospital, I'd never been able to overcome the feeling of hopelessness that surrounds an impending death, never been able to compartmentalize it as just part of the job the way some of my fellow nurses could. In some ways, I hoped I never would.

Traffic was light as I drove home. I didn't stop at the grocery store or the Thai restaurant to pick up a takeout order even though I'd worked through lunch and my stomach was growling. The gas gauge on my car hovered near a quarter of a tank, but I didn't stop to refuel either. Elliott was in good hands with Nana, but if I hurried I could make it home in time to read him a book before his eight-o'clock bedtime. I could look into Elliott's blue eyes, cuddle him in my arms, and shake off the blues that clung to me like the world's saddest perfume.

The flashing lights caught my eye when I neared the entrance of our apartment complex. Widowed at forty-nine, Nana had traded her home for an apartment shortly after my grandfather died because she didn't want the hassle of taking care of a yard and no longer needed so much space. There were a few times growing up when I'd longed for grass and a swing set and a sandbox like some of my friends had. But my grandmother had taken me to the park frequently, and I was doing the same with Elliott.

As I drove closer, I registered the emergency vehicles with only mild worry. Many of the building's residents were elderly, and the presence of an ambulance was, unfortunately, not that rare. But then I noticed not just one police car but several. Yellow crime tape. Barricades, and behind them people huddled together at one end of the parking lot. Agnes Beardsley had her arm around Margaret Parker. Margaret was our across-the-hall neighbor and one of my grandmother's closest friends. She looked like she was crying.

I scanned the onlookers for my grandmother and Elliott and felt the first stab of fear when I didn't spot them. Pulling up to the curb, I parked haphazardly and jumped out. My heart beat faster, fluttering in my chest like the wings of a tiny hummingbird as I tried to figure out why my grandmother and Elliott weren't standing outside with the others. I set my sights on the entrance of the building where a policeman stood and rushed forward.

"Ma'am! You'll have to stay back."

When I tried to go around him, he put out his hands to block me.

"I need to find my son. I need to find my grandmother." My frantic voice caught the attention of the onlookers, and heads turned in our direction. "This is my building," I said. "I live here!"

"Ma'am, no one is being permitted inside. Please go over there," he said, motioning to the far end of the parking lot where the others stood.

There had to be a reason why my grandmother and Elliott weren't standing outside with everyone else. Maybe they were still inside? But even I knew that wasn't the case. It looked like every resident of the building was standing in the parking lot.

Except for my grandmother and Elliott.

I tried to calm myself by taking a deep breath, but instead I gasped and gulped at the air like a goldfish that had flopped out of its bowl. This must be what Elliott felt like when his asthma flared up. My pulse raced and I shivered despite the scorching wind. I didn't walk toward the others, afraid of what they might tell me. If there was bad news coming, and I felt deep down in my bones that there was, I was still on the good side of it. The side that allowed me to hope that my grandmother and Elliott weren't a part of whatever had happened.

Then why aren't they standing in the parking lot with everyone else?

Trapped in limbo, the uncertainty flooded my body with adrenaline, and my shivering turned to shaking. Panic, swift and dark, threatened to overcome me. I needed answers. If this involved my family, I had a right to know.

Before I could approach the officer again, a man exited the building. He wasn't wearing a uniform, but he was followed by a policewoman who was holding something in her arms. They walked quickly toward a waiting ambulance and disappeared inside.

It's doubtful that many of the onlookers would have known what she was carrying, but I spotted that Thomas the Tank Engine comforter and my whole world shifted. The relief I felt was incomprehensible, immeasurable, bottomless. For a split second I stood there and simply *reveled* in the sheer joy of knowing where my child was, and then I took off at a run.

This time, before anyone could stop me, I pushed my way through the people gathered at the back of the ambulance, tears streaming down my face. "That's my child!"

Elliott wriggled free and leapt into my arms. "Mama, Mama!"

I'd never seen Elliott cry so hard, not even when he was nine months old and fell off the kitchen chair after he climbed it when my back was turned.

He clung to me and I held him tight, sobbing uncontrollably, which was the wrong thing to do because it probably scared him even more, but I couldn't help it.

"Are you okay?" I let go long enough to assess him. "Let me see you. Does anything hurt?" Before he could answer, I drew him near again, muffling his hiccupping cries with my shirt.

"Ma'am? Are you Daisy DiStefano?" someone asked.

I looked up. *They know my name.* "Yes." It hit me then, suddenly: my grandmother was missing. Not Elliott and my grandmother. Just her. "Is it my grandmother?"

"Yes," one of them said. "I'm very sorry."

Elliott had raised his head and was listening.

"Is she… gone?" I whispered.

"Yes."

"What happened?"

"We don't know yet, ma'am. The detectives are upstairs now. We need you to come down to the station and give a statement. I'm sorry. You won't be able to return to your apartment tonight."

Why in the world would they bring in detectives? Why would they need a statement? Nana was eighty-four years old, and there had been some setbacks in her health recently. Some heart trouble that had me worried. Dizzy spells that seemed to be increasing in frequency. She'd fallen and broken her wrist six months ago, and it still pained her. I feared it was only the beginning, and I'd begun preparing myself for what lay ahead. My grandmother's passing, while devastating to me, wasn't a complete surprise. "I don't understand."

The officer glanced at Elliott. "This was not the result of... natural causes."

My eyes went wide when the meaning of his words finally sank in. Someone had killed my grandmother? Is that what they were telling me? That someone committed murder in our apartment while I was at work? It was so far outside my realm of comprehension that my brain had simply failed to connect the dots. "Where did you find my son?" I asked, barely able to form the words.

"He was hiding under a bed. We didn't realize anyone else was in the apartment at first. He shows no sign of injury, but we want the medics to give him a quick once-over, okay? Then we'll take you down to the station."

I couldn't get the image of Elliott, alone and hiding and terrified by whatever was happening, out of my head.

The officer put his hand on my shoulder. "Ma'am? Are you okay?"

No, I am not okay.

"I'm fine."

"Is there anything you need from the apartment?"

"My son has asthma. I need his medicine and nebulizer. They're on the kitchen counter."

The female officer, the one who had carried Elliott outside, smiled and said, "I'll get it. I'll grab some dry pajamas, too."

She gave me a knowing look and I instantly comprehended what that meant. Poor Elliott.

"Thank you," I said.

I waited anxiously as the EMT listened to Elliott's heart and took his blood pressure with a child-size cuff. He looked into Elliott's eyes and asked him to follow a light from side to side.

"Is your hand okay?" the paramedic asked when he saw that Elliott was holding his left hand around his tightly clenched right fist. "Can I take a look?"

With a little coaxing from me, Elliott unclenched his fist. He'd been holding a small green army man so tightly it had left indentations in his palm.

"He keeped me safe from the bad man," Elliott whispered. "Don't no one take him away, pwease."

My eyes filled with fresh tears. "Of course not." Gently, I wrapped Elliott's hand around the toy. "But you're safe now, and I don't want you to worry about anything. Okay?"

"Okay, Mama."

When the medic proclaimed that Elliott was fine, I lifted him back onto my lap and held him tight. "What will happen at the station?" I asked the officer who was standing nearby.

"They'll need some information from you and they'll take a statement. Ask you if you have any idea who might have done this."

I shook my head. "I don't know anyone who would want to harm my grandmother."

I rocked Elliott in my arms and when Officer Ochoa returned with the medicine and pajamas, I handed her my car keys so she could retrieve Elliott's car seat. Once we were settled in the back of the squad car, she and another officer drove us to the police station.

CHAPTER 3

BROOKS

I TRIED TO AVOID looking in the rearview mirror on my way out of town so I wouldn't have to watch the San Francisco skyline as it slowly disappeared with each mile I put behind me. It wasn't for fear that I'd change my mind and turn around, because it was way too late for that, but I preferred to catch my next glimpse of the city I called home as I was driving toward it, not away.

Besides, it wasn't like this was good-bye in the traditional sense. I might have been reluctant to leave, but there was no need to mourn a city in which I still had a permanent address. San Francisco would be waiting for me when I returned. So would my apartment, my favorite corner bar, and the coffee shop I stopped at every morning on my way to work.

Even my job, if I was lucky.

I let my thoughts wander, listening to my iPod and switching over to the police-scanner app on my phone when I got tired of music. Two hundred and eighty miles later, I exited the 5 and stopped at a gas station in Bakersfield to fuel up and stretch my legs. The desert heat shimmered up from the asphalt and seeped into my skin as I filled the tank, making me wish I was wearing a T-shirt and shorts instead of a long-sleeve dress shirt, pants, and tie. I hadn't even reached my final destination and already I missed the fog and chill of San Francisco. I pushed those thoughts aside, feeling guilty for having them, and bought a cold drink when I went inside to use the restroom.

I merged onto the 15 and stayed on it until the Fenton exit came into view. Once I reached the surface streets, I drove for another two miles into town, past fast-food restaurants, gas stations, and strip malls with several vacancies. A restaurant called DiStefano's still had the same sun-faded Sorry We're Closed sign hanging on its front door that I remembered from my last visit home.

I pulled into the parking lot of the *Desert News* and parked my Jeep in the visitor spot. The squat, one-story building was a far cry from the *San Francisco Chronicle*, which had been my employer for the past eleven years. I retrieved my suit coat from its hanger on the hook in the backseat, slipped my arms inside, and tightened my tie. Overkill maybe, considering most of my fellow reporters had long since ditched their suits in favor of khakis and button-down shirts, but the way I dressed told witnesses I was legit, and that had opened more than one door for me when it came to making people feel comfortable. Plus, I believe what they say about first impressions. This position might have been a step backward career-wise, but I had every intention of making the best of the situation while I was here.

The lobby looked as tired and dusty as the town, and the receptionist barely mustered enough energy to hand me a visitor badge and buzz me back to the newsroom. At least Paul, my new publisher, was happy to see me, if the smile on his face as he walked toward me was any indication.

"Brooks McClain," I said, smiling and reaching out my hand.

"Nice to meet you, Brooks," he said, pumping my hand up and down. "Welcome to the *Desert News*."

Paul had been so desperate for a reporter that he'd hired me over the phone, and his sigh of relief upon meeting me in person was probably louder than he intended. Hiring someone without the benefit of a face-to-face interview was a real gamble, and Paul had dodged a potentially unpleasant bullet.

"Nice to meet you, too," I said.

"Let me show you around."

As an investigative reporter, I would be covering crime and breaking news. The *Desert News* also employed a couple of editors and one other reporter who would be covering everything I wasn't. Paul attempted to introduce me to my counterpart, a young woman—blonde, midtwenties, attractive—but she was on the phone and could only mouth hello and wave in our general direction.

"That's Maggie," Paul said. "She's smart, enthusiastic, and has a ton of energy. She's very happy to see you because she's been carrying a double load since Tom retired. It's getting harder and harder to find good help. I was just about at the end of my rope when your résumé came in."

That wasn't totally true. Thanks to newsroom cutbacks, there were plenty of talented reporters who needed jobs, but few would be interested in reporting the news in a town that appeared to lack anything that was remotely newsworthy. I would probably spend most of my time trying to spin breaking-news stories out of nothing and reporting on petty theft and DUIs.

"If you've got a moment, I'll issue you your laptop and phone," Paul said.

"Sure."

Paul returned and handed me a cell phone, which I pocketed. He gave the laptop a cursory check and zipped it back into its case; I slung the strap over my arm. "Your e-mail address is already set up—it's your first and last name at DesertNews.com. Let me show you your desk."

The newsroom had apparently engaged in a potluck recently and must have decided that Tom's empty desk would make a great place to set all the food. Crumbs littered the entire surface along with a sticky smear of something that looked like barbecue sauce. The layer of dust on the computer monitor made me wonder just how long Tom had been gone.

Paul picked up an empty Crock-Pot, which appeared to have held meatballs sometime in the past twenty-four to forty-eight hours, and swept the crumpled chip and cookie bags into the overflowing garbage can. "Don't worry. We'll get someone to clean this up. It'll look much better tomorrow."

"Great," I said, smiling with a level of enthusiasm I didn't quite feel.

Paul reached out and shook my hand. "See you in the morning."

*

The house I was raised in sat on a corner lot at the entrance of a quiet street. The homes—well-maintained two-stories built in the 1970s—were the type couples stayed in long after the kids had grown up and moved out, despite how the stairs hurt their knees and the fact that they no longer needed so much room. They stayed because they'd been there so long it was hard to imagine leaving, and besides, the next step seemed so daunting, so final. First it was a condo or townhome and then maybe an assisted-living facility. If they were really lucky, one of their kids would insist they move in with them even though that came with its own set of challenges.

There were certainly more desirable places to spend one's golden years than Fenton: Florida, Arizona, maybe the Carolinas. It didn't matter, though, because my parents had waited too long and now they couldn't do anything about it even if they wanted to. They had stayed and so I had returned.

I pulled into the driveway and turned off the engine. I waited a few minutes, delaying the moment when all of this would become real. Feeling ashamed for sitting in my car like a coward, I finally got out and walked along the sidewalk to the front door. It was unlocked. Silence greeted me when I stepped across the threshold and into the entryway.

"Mom, Dad?" I called. "I'm home."

My dad came around the corner, wiping his hands on a dish towel. He looked older than he should, as if he'd aged a year in the three months since I'd last been home. He smiled, but I could see the relief on his face. Reinforcements have a tendency to buoy anyone's spirits almost immediately.

We hugged and my dad clapped me on the back. "How was the drive?" he asked.

"Fine. No problems. Traffic wasn't too bad."

"Do you need some help bringing in your things?"

"Sure. That would be great."

I didn't know exactly how long I'd be staying with my parents so I packed my Jeep to capacity with clothes and the personal items I didn't want to be without for too long. The one time my dad and I had tried to talk about it, he'd broken down and cried.

It took us two trips to the car to bring everything in. Once we had it all inside, we began climbing the stairs to my bedroom, which was the first room on the left. My dad flicked on the light switch and it was like being plunged into a time capsule that contained all the greatest hits from my youth: the dresser, desk, and full-size bed, all made out of dark pine. A few football and baseball trophies sat on the bookshelf in the corner, along with my old yearbooks and the stack of paperbacks I'd left behind. A leaning tower of CDs. My old plaid comforter, faded from years of washing, covered the bed and matched the curtains that would let in way too much light. The blackout shades in the bedroom of my apartment in San Francisco would be sorely missed.

"We have a gal who comes every other week now," my dad said. "She vacuumed and dusted in here yesterday. Changed the sheets. Everything's clean."

"It's fine, Dad. Thanks."

It wasn't fine, not really. My entire being rebelled against being there, which I told myself was normal. No one wants to move from their adult apartment back into their childhood bedroom. It defied the natural order of things.

"Where's Mom?"

"She's in the bedroom, watching TV. I was about to make her dinner."

Mom had always done the cooking in our house, and I wasn't sure while I was growing up if my dad even knew how to make a sandwich. "Do you need some help?"

He waved me off. "I can handle it."

"I'll get these work clothes hung up," I said. "I can unpack the suitcases later. I want to see Mom."

After I hung my suits and dress shirts in a closet that formerly held nothing more substantial than jeans and T-shirts, I walked down the hall to the master bedroom. The door was ajar. "Mom?" I said, as I pushed it open a little wider and stuck my head in.

"Brooks." The look on her face—a combination of adoration,

relief, and pride—hit me harder than I was expecting. To deny my mother anything at that moment would have been unfathomable.

It was the reason I came.

"Hi, Mom."

I crossed the room and my mom gathered me into her outstretched arms, as if I were still a child. Her grip was so weak that she couldn't hold me for more than a few seconds before her arms flopped down onto the bed. I remained seated next to her.

"How was the drive?" she asked, her words so slurred that it took some effort to decipher them. Our most common method of communication during the past year had been e-mail, and it wasn't unusual for her to send a message to me at the newsroom every day. She hadn't sounded that bad the last time I spoke to her on the phone, which had been about a month ago. She'd deteriorated so rapidly since my last visit. Observing her now, I wondered if I should have been called sooner.

My dad entered the room carrying a tray, and he smiled when he looked at my mom and me. I could only imagine what he must be feeling: happiness at seeing his family together mixed with the acute sadness of what had brought us here.

The tray had a bowl of soup on it and I left my mom's side so my dad could set it down on the nightstand. He took the spot I vacated and started spooning the soup into my mom's mouth, which surprised me. I knew her motor skills were failing at an alarming rate, but I had no idea she was no longer able to feed herself. No wonder my dad had seemed so upset.

She didn't swallow more than five or six spoonfuls of soup, but my dad seemed pleased with it. The act of eating must have tired her out, because she closed her eyes and seemed on the brink of falling asleep.

"Do you want to go to the bathroom first?" my dad asked.

She opened her eyes. "Yes."

We weren't an overly formal kind of family, and I'd never felt the need to hide things that were uncomfortable or embarrassing from either of my parents. But knowing that my dad had essentially become my mom's nurse, attending to her most personal of needs, made me feel like I'd violated their privacy in some way.

I stood quickly. "I'll go unpack the rest of my things." Before my dad could help her out of bed, I crossed the room and gave my mom a kiss on the cheek. "I'll come back after you wake up."

"I love you," she said softly.

Her smile had been replaced by such a pathetic expression that I felt like crying for the first time in years.

"I love you, too."

I unpacked my suitcases, placing items in the dresser and hanging up the rest. Seeing the condition my mom was in had helped me gain a bit of perspective, and my living arrangements no longer seemed like such a hardship.

I decided to wait for my dad in the living room. Maybe we could find a baseball game on TV. The empty dining room caught my eye when I walked by, and I did a double take. My mom's antique dining table and matching sideboard—two of her most treasured possessions—were missing. She had always chosen a special tablecloth for each holiday and would spend hours at Christmastime setting out platters of food on the sideboard for a buffet dinner. Now there was nothing but window coverings and a polished wood floor. The room wasn't that big, but it suddenly seemed cavernous.

I turned around when my dad entered the room. "Where'd everything go?"

He cleared his throat. "It's been moved into the garage. I ordered a hospital bed. It should be here soon."

"Why can't Mom stay in the master bedroom?" I asked. "Wouldn't she be more comfortable there?"

"Yes, but she's having trouble walking down the stairs and won't let me carry her. She's afraid I'll drop her," he said, shaking his head. "That's ridiculous. She weighs nothing."

I pictured my dad carrying my mom down the stairs and both of them falling. He was in good shape for sixty-eight, but carrying another adult down a flight of stairs, no matter how little they weighed, was too risky. What if he tripped?

"Have you thought about hiring a nurse, Dad?"

"Yes," he said. "But I think I can take care of her a little longer. It's the least I can do."

I nodded and looked away. "I understand." I walked into the kitchen with him following me. "Are you hungry? I thought I'd run out and pick up a pizza."

"Sure. That sounds good," he said.

Before I left the room, my dad reached out and gave my shoulder a squeeze. He couldn't quite look me in the eye when he said, "Thank you for coming."

"You don't have to thank me. Of course I would come."

"It means a lot just the same. Especially to your mother."

I swallowed hard, feeling a lump form in my throat as I walked out the front door and got into my car.

A grown man of thirty-six would not willingly give up a job he loved in a city he never wanted to leave. A grown man would have zero desire to move back into his childhood home with his parents, and he'd definitely chafe at sleeping in the same bed he'd slept in since he'd outgrown his crib.

But as the only child of a mother who was dying of Lou

Gehrig's disease and living on borrowed time, I had just proven that I would most certainly do all those things.

My phone rang shortly after we finished our pizza and one glance at the display told me I'd grabbed the wrong one. Fumbling, I pulled the phone Paul had given me out of my other pocket. "Hello."

"Homicide at the Sunset Vista apartment complex," Paul said without preamble. "Maggie heard it on the scanner and a source has confirmed it. Try to get enough to file something for tomorrow's edition. I need it no later than midnight."

"I'm on my way," I said and disconnected the call. I stood and brushed the crumbs off my pants. "That was my boss. I have to go."

"Already?" my dad said.

I nodded. "I might be out late. Tell Mom I'm sorry and that I'll see her first thing in the morning."

"Of course," he said. "Go do what you have to do."

There was nothing quite like a homicide to get all my cylinders firing, and I felt the same spark of excitement I always did when there was breaking news. The desire to get the story that everyone wanted. To convince the witnesses, the bystanders, and the victim's family that they should talk to me first. I'd left my suit jacket hanging on the back of a chair in the kitchen, and after I slipped my arms into it, I grabbed the laptop Paul had given me. The glove compartment and console of my Jeep were stuffed with pens and notebooks.

I turned to my dad and said, "Don't wait up."

CHAPTER 4

DAISY

AT THE POLICE station, Officer Ochoa led us past the reception desk to a hard bench outside a small office. The door to the office was closed.

"A detective will be with you soon," she said. "Can I get you anything while you wait?"

"Where's the nearest restroom?" I asked. I needed to get Elliott out of his wet pajamas, and his fussing told me he was already overtired. I hoped that after he was dry and comfortable I could soothe him to sleep on my lap.

"It's just down the hall, on the right."

I hoisted Elliott onto my hip. Once we reached the restroom, I cleaned him up using damp paper towels and then dried him off and dressed him quickly. He was so tired he didn't push me away and insist on dressing himself, the way he would have at home. His tears had smudged the lenses of his glasses, so I took them off and polished them with my shirt. After he was squared away, I took a moment to splash cold water on my face. My eyes burned and my head throbbed. I wanted nothing more than to be alone so I could let the tears fall and grieve in peace. Later, I told myself.

Then I remembered that we wouldn't be permitted back into our apartment tonight. I would need to call Pam. She and Shane would have to come pick us up.

I blotted my face dry and blew my nose, then lifted Elliott into my arms.

He laid his head on my shoulder. "I so tired, Mama."

"I know you are, honey. Close your eyes and go to sleep."

We'd just made it back to the bench when a harried-looking man walked up to us. Blond hair, tall, midforties. He wore dress slacks and a white button-down shirt that might have been crisp this morning but was now crisscrossed with wrinkles. His tie was loose and he made a halfhearted attempt to tighten it when he spotted us.

"I'm so sorry to keep you waiting," he said as he opened the door to the office and motioned us inside. "There were a few things I had to take care of first. Please sit down. Can I get you something to drink?"

"No thank you," I said. "But do you have a plastic bag?"

He rummaged around in the drawers of his desk and produced a wrinkled Walmart bag. I shoved Elliott's damp pajamas inside, knotted the bag, and tucked it inside my purse with the nebulizer and medicine. There was barely room, and the sides bulged.

"My name is Jack Quick. I'm the detective assigned to this case. I'm very sorry for your loss. I'll make sure someone from our victims' advocates program reaches out to you. They can help answer any questions you might have throughout this process."

Ever since he was a baby Elliott had fallen asleep when I stroked his hair, so I ran my fingers through it and listened to his contented sigh as he snuggled closer, his eyes already half-closed.

"The preliminary report shows that there was no forced entry into the apartment, which means the perpetrator may not have been a stranger. It doesn't mean he or she wasn't, though. There are many ways to gain entry into someone's home, especially if they're caught off guard. I need the name of anyone you think might have been capable of such a crime."

"Everyone loved my grandmother. I can't think of anyone who would want to harm her."

"What about you? Is there someone out there who might wish you harm? Maybe they thought you'd be home but confronted your grandmother instead?"

It was true that I didn't know of a single person who would ever want to harm my grandmother, but I knew one person who was capable of just about anything if it came between him and his next fix. "My ex-husband is a drug addict."

"What's his name," Jack asked, pulling a notebook from his pocket.

"Scott DiStefano."

"What's he addicted to?"

"Meth." Though I had no reason to be, I always felt ashamed when asked about Scott's drug use. Thankfully, Detective Quick spared me the look that said *How did a nice, wholesome girl like you get messed up with a meth head?*

"When's the last time you spoke to your ex-husband?"

"About six months ago. When our divorce became final."

"Do you have an address for him?"

"Yes." I gave Detective Quick the last known address I had for Scott, which I'd been told was a house in the desert that he shared with several men of equally dubious character. "I don't know if he's still there."

"Why do you think your ex-husband would want to hurt your grandmother?"

"I don't know that he would. They got along fine. My

grandmother raised me, and Scott always treated her well and with respect. But that was before he stopped caring about anything other than drugs."

"Did your grandmother have anything of value?"

"Not that I know of. She was a bit old-school when it came to her finances. She never really talked about that sort of thing."

I'd never pressed her in that regard, not even when I got older and began managing my own finances. My parents had left behind an adequate life-insurance policy, and I had also received a monthly social security payment until I reached the age of eighteen. My grandmother had managed this money, and she'd done a good enough job that I never wanted for anything. There had been enough for clothes and dance lessons and school trips. Even a spring break vacation to Mexico with Pam's family during our senior year of high school. My college tuition had been paid for in full, which pleased my grandmother immensely. She told me I had my whole life to work and that I should concentrate on studying hard and earning my degree.

"Will you talk to my ex-husband?" I asked.

Detective Quick nodded. "Absolutely. We'll bring him in. Get a statement."

"Okay."

"Is there anything else I should know about? Strange phone calls. Threats?"

"No, nothing."

"How communicative is your son? He wouldn't tell us anything, and we didn't push. He might have heard something but blocked it out. Or he may not want to talk about it at all because it was a stressful situation. Don't force it, but if he opens up to you, see if you can draw a little more out of him."

"I will."

"We hope to have you back in your apartment by tomorrow afternoon."

"I don't want to go back there." There was no way we could stay in that apartment. I'd never feel safe again.

"That's understandable," he said. "Under the circumstances, it might be a good idea to find a new place to live."

"Do you think we're in danger?"

"It's hard to say at this point," he said. "The crime might have been completely random, but it's always a good idea to err on the side of caution."

"How did… how did she die?"

"We won't know until the autopsy has been completed, but it looks like blunt-force head trauma."

"Someone hit her?" I asked. The thought was absolutely horrifying to me.

"She was found on the floor near a coffee table. She might have been shoved and then hit her head on it when she fell. It wouldn't take much if she landed hard, especially at her age. I assure you we'll do everything we can to find out who did this."

Elliott was snoring softly. I was exhausted and wanted nothing more than to escape the depressing confines of the small office.

"Can we go now?"

He gave me a sympathetic smile. "Of course. Do you have somewhere to stay tonight?"

"I have a friend I can call." I dug my phone out of my purse, trying my best not to wake up Elliott.

"I'll give you some privacy." He plucked a business card from a plastic holder on his desk. "If you think of anything else or if your son mentions something, no matter how inconsequential you think it is, give me a call."

"Okay. I will."

After he left the room I took a deep breath and called Pam. I tried to hold it together as I told her what had happened and where I was calling from, but I broke down and started crying again. It was hard to believe she could even understand me.

"It's okay," she said. "Shane and I will leave right now. Just sit tight."

I hung up and once again gathered Elliott in my arms and found another bench to wait on, this one located near the entrance of the police station. It was fully dark by then, but I could see the parking lot through the glass doors. Feeling miserable, I shivered, wishing someone would wrap me up in a comforter and hold me tight. My eyes stung, so I leaned my head back against the wall and closed them.

As I sat there waiting for Pam and Shane, I thought about my grandmother. Detective Quick hadn't said whether her death had been fast or slow, and I hadn't asked. I held tightly to the hope that it was quick, because knowing that the woman who raised me had suffered for any length of time before she died would have been more than I could take. The fact that my son had been spared would forever be the great miracle of my life.

What I didn't know then was that another miracle would occur, but it would come much, much later.

CHAPTER 5
BROOKS

THE CRIME SCENE was already bustling with activity. When I arrived, the TV stations were setting up lights and preparing to go live with a breaking-news update. Policemen milled about, keeping everyone behind the barricades. Unfortunately, it looked like most of the key witnesses had already been transported to the police station for questioning or to give a statement, and many of the residents were being allowed back into the building, which didn't leave me much to work with. I had the additional frustration of not having any contacts on the police force. I'd spent years building relationships with patrolmen and detectives in San Francisco—people I could go to directly for information—but here I knew no one.

I spotted two elderly women standing apart from everyone else, lost in their own conversation. One of them was patting the other on the back. I might not learn anything crucial, but I could get enough to inject a little color into the story that would run with my byline tomorrow morning. They stopped talking when I approached them.

"Please excuse me for interrupting," I said. "I was wondering if I could ask you a few questions."

"Are you with the police department?" one of the women asked.

"I'm a reporter with the *Desert News*. Did you know the victim?"

The woman who seemed less upset answered me. "Pauline was our friend. She was one of the nicest ladies you could ever hope to meet," she said, dabbing at her eyes with a tissue.

I pulled out my notebook and pen. "Pauline..."

"Thorpe. With an *e*. I'm Karen Rose." She motioned to the other woman. "This is Dixie Buchanan."

"It's nice to meet you. Do you know how old Pauline was?"

"Eighty-four. We just celebrated her birthday last month. I remember because we play bridge with Pauline every week, and one of the women in our group brought a pie."

"Pecan," Dixie added. "Because pecan was Pauline's favorite."

"What can you tell me about Pauline? Were you close? Did you know her well?"

"We weren't as close to Pauline as Margaret was," Karen said.

"Who's Margaret?" I asked.

"She lives across the hall from Pauline. She was the one who called the police. They took *her* to the station," Dixie said, as if a trip down to police headquarters was an enviable outing.

"What's Margaret's last name?"

"Parker."

I jotted it down in my notebook. "Tell me about playing bridge with Pauline."

"She always played fair, and she never showed up without a baked good," said Karen. "Not something she picked up at the supermarket, either. Homemade."

"And if Daisy was working—she's a nurse—Pauline would bring Elliott with her. He'd draw us pictures while we played," Dixie said. "I have all mine taped to my fridge."

"Who are Daisy and Elliott?" I asked.

"Daisy is Pauline's granddaughter and Elliott is Daisy's son. Pauline raised Daisy. Brought that girl up right, too. Oh, how Pauline loved that little boy. He was in the apartment with her! If something had happened to that precious child..." Dixie burst into tears and produced a crumpled tissue from inside the sleeve of her cardigan, like a magician pulling a scarf out of a hat. She dabbed at her eyes and Karen comforted her, saying, "There, there."

A child was in the apartment at the time of the murder? Now *that* was newsworthy.

"Are you sure Elliott was there?" I asked.

"I saw them bring him out and put him in the ambulance," Dixie said.

"Daisy and Elliott live with Pauline," Karen said. "They moved in after Daisy and Scott got divorced. Pauline watches Elliott while Daisy's at work."

I wrote it all down in my notebook: Daisy—nurse, granddaughter, single mother—lives with Pauline. Elliott— great-grandson. "What are their ages?"

Dixie had completely lost the battle with her tears, and her sniffles had morphed into giant honking sobs.

Karen took over as official spokesperson for the duo. "Daisy is thirty. I remember because Pauline mentioned it was a milestone birthday. Elliott recently turned three."

I added the information to my notes. "What do you want people to know about Pauline?"

"I want them to know how kind she was," Karen said. "How

helpful. She wouldn't turn her back on anyone, even if they didn't deserve her help. And I think she'd want people to remember how much she loved Daisy and that little boy." Karen's voice had gotten softer and her lip began to quiver. It wouldn't be long before she joined Dixie in an emotional meltdown, and I could only hope her cardigan came equipped with its own supply of tissues.

I had what I needed, for now at least. "Thank you, ladies. You've been very helpful. Please accept my sincere condolences."

A representative from the police department gave a short statement to the crowd, naming the deceased as Pauline Thorpe, which meant that the next of kin had been notified and I could include the name of the victim in my story. I jotted down the other confirmed details in my notebook: eighty-four years old, cause of death to be determined. I had enough for a brief story, which was all Paul would be expecting. A glance at my watch told me that I still had a few hours before my deadline.

Plenty of time to drop by the police station to see if I could get someone to talk.

CHAPTER 6
BROOKS

WHEN I'D APPLIED for the job at the *Desert News*, I'd done some research and learned that the Fenton Police Department serviced twenty square miles and employed approximately nine officers. Violent crime was up almost twenty-five percent. Assault was the most common offense, followed closely by robbery and rape. There had only been one homicide so far that year; Pauline Thorpe was the second.

I arrived at the police department around nine o'clock, long after normal business hours. I didn't expect to get far and my hunch was correct.

"Brooks McClain, *Desert News*," I said to the uniformed officer manning the front desk. I reached into my pocket for a business card and then remembered I didn't have any yet.

Great.

"I'd like to speak to Jack Quick." It was imperative that I identify a contact and start building a relationship as soon as possible. A quick online search had told me a detective named Jack Quick should be at the top of my list. He would have returned to the station by now to begin interviewing witnesses or anyone who might have information about the crime.

The desk sergeant wrote down my name. "Can't promise anything, but I'll let him know you're waiting."

"Thanks."

I was walking toward a bench to wait for Detective Quick when I spotted her. She was holding a child on her lap, and I could see the top of his blond head poking out of the comforter he was wrapped in.

"Daisy and Elliott live with Pauline… They moved in after Daisy and Scott got divorced."

Her head was resting on the wall behind her, and her eyes were closed. The child appeared to be sleeping.

"Excuse me," I said, speaking softly so I wouldn't startle them. She opened her eyes and looked at me. She was wearing short-sleeved yellow scrubs and goose bumps dotted her slim arms. If I hadn't already been told she was thirty, I would have guessed she was younger. There was nothing flashy about her, no heavy makeup, no complicated hairstyle. Her face was lightly tanned, as if she spent a considerable amount of time outdoors, and her blond hair was pulled back in a ponytail. A quintessential California girl. Despite her tearstained cheeks and swollen, red-rimmed eyes, it was hard not to notice that she was extremely pretty.

"I'm sorry to bother you. Are you Daisy DiStefano?"

She nodded.

"My name is Brooks McClain. I'm a reporter with the *Desert News*. I'd like to talk to you for a few minutes about your grandmother."

"Okay," she said, sounding a little unsure.

"I'm very sorry for your loss. I had the chance to meet a few of your grandmother's friends tonight, and they spoke very highly of her. I'll be mentioning some of the things they said about her in my story. It would be great if I could include a picture. Do you have one I could use?"

She looked dazed, and it took her a moment to answer. "Yes." Taking one hand off the comforter, she dug her phone out of her purse and scrolled through it. "I don't have many of her alone, but this is a good one. It's recent." She showed me a picture of an elderly woman wearing a blue dress and holding a little boy with blond hair. They were both laughing. "Could you crop it so that it's just her?"

"Of course."

"Where should I send it?"

"You can text it to me." I gave her the number and she keyed it in.

"Do you need a ride," I asked. "Or I could call you a cab if you'd prefer."

"My friend and her husband are on their way."

"I'd like to talk with you again in a day or two, when things have calmed down a little and you're back in your apartment. Would that be okay?"

"Sure." She leaned her head back and closed her eyes again.

I took a seat on the bench farthest away from Daisy and Elliott. A few minutes later a man and woman walked through the door. The man lifted the sleeping child into his arms and the woman embraced Daisy and rubbed her back.

"I'm so sorry," she said.

Daisy started to cry and her friend grabbed the car seat that was sitting on the bench and led her by the hand through the door, down a short sidewalk, and to the back door of an SUV, which they'd parked in front of the building. After they pulled away, I opened my laptop and began writing about Pauline Thorpe's murder. I finished quickly but didn't send the story, hoping I might still get something from Jack Quick that I could add. An hour later, my back aching from sitting on the concrete bench, I'd all but decided to go ahead and file the story. But then I heard footsteps approaching and noticed a man walking toward me at a face pace. I could spot the wrinkled shirt and loosened tie of a detective from a mile away, so I stood.

"Jack Quick?" I asked.

He didn't stop walking. "Yeah?"

I matched his stride and caught up to him. "Brooks McClain," I said. "*Desert News*. Do you have a minute?"

"Nope," he said and walked out the front door of the police station, not bothering to hold it open for me.

Thanks, asshole.

I was a senior reporter for the *Chronicle* and hadn't been treated this badly in a long time. I had so many contacts in San Francisco that I no longer cooled my heels on hard benches; I picked up the phone and made a call. So Jack Quick had either had a bad relationship with my predecessor, was a dick in general, or was tired and in no mood to talk to the new guy.

I returned to the bench and hit Send on my story, then rubbed my eyes and yawned as I walked out to my Jeep.

It had been a long day and all I wanted to do was go home, even if I wasn't sure at that moment where home actually was.

CHAPTER 7

DAISY

SHANE CARRIED ELLIOTT into the house and deposited him in the spare bedroom bed. I had nothing but the clothes on my back, so Pam fussed over me, pulling a T-shirt and sweatpants out of her dresser.

As I walked toward the bathroom to change, she said, "Let me make you something to eat. Or some tea."

"I'm too tired," I said. "I just want to sleep."

Pam had set out a fresh towel and a brand new toothbrush, still wrapped in plastic. I washed my face and brushed my teeth.

She was waiting for me in the hallway when I came out. "I don't have my first client until eleven. I'll make a big breakfast in the morning. Maybe you can eat something then."

"I will. I promise." I hugged her, feeling her baby bump press against my stomach. "Thank you for everything."

"Of course, Daisy. Shane and I will help you with whatever you need."

I slipped into bed next to Elliott and fell asleep seconds after my head hit the pillow.

My respite was short-lived. I slept fitfully and each time I woke up it took me a minute to figure out where I was and what had happened. The events of the evening would eventually come rushing back, and disoriented, I would remember that my grandmother was gone. I'd lie there, calmed by Elliott's soft breathing, until I fell back to sleep. Then the cycle would start again.

The digital clock on the nightstand read 6:03 a.m., which was when I quit trying to fall back asleep and instead started making a mental list: call work, make funeral arrangements, daycare for Elliott, new apartment. Overwhelmed by the thought of everything I had to do, I got up and walked into the kitchen.

Shane was already up and sitting at the table drinking coffee. "Hey, Daze." He rose and poured me a cup.

"Thanks," I said.

He offered me a sympathetic smile as I sipped my coffee and tried to clear the cobwebs from my brain.

By now, the thought of my grandmother's death had left me numb, or maybe I was all cried out. I'd started to compartmentalize things because I had other problems to solve. Making sure Elliott and I were in a safe place was at the top of the list.

It was almost as if Shane had read my mind because he said, "You can't stay in that apartment."

"I know." I'd never feel safe there, not until they found the person responsible for my grandmother's death. How could I return to my normal life, never knowing if someone would show up on our doorstep again? How could I be sure I was keeping Elliott safe?

"You're welcome to stay here as long as you want," Shane said. "You know that, right?"

Pam and Shane's home had three bedrooms. They used one of the bedrooms as an office, and Pam had big plans for turning the bedroom Elliott and I had slept in into a nursery. She was almost six months along and eager to start preparing for the baby's arrival. They'd ordered furniture, and Pam had sounded so excited when she'd called me two days ago to tell me the crib and dresser had shipped and would be delivered next week. They'd picked out the room color and Shane was supposed to paint the walls this weekend. There was no way I'd stand in the way of their plans, no matter how much they protested.

"Thanks, Shane." I took a sip of my coffee. "I appreciate the offer, but I'm going to call around today and see if I can find another apartment. We'll stay until I can sign a new lease, but hopefully that won't take more than a few days. If you know of anyone who would be willing to help us move on short notice, I'll gladly pay them."

"We'll get it handled," he said. "Don't worry about it."

When Pam woke up, she cooked the big breakfast she'd promised, and the four of us were gathered around the small kitchen table by eight. I fixed Elliott a plate and poured him a small glass of juice. He hadn't let go of his army man, not even in his sleep or when he went to the bathroom after he woke up. I didn't dare ask him to put it down.

"I want to go home and see Nana," he said.

Stricken, I looked at Pam. She looked equally unsure about how to handle the situation. Ordinarily when faced with a child-rearing issue I was unfamiliar with, I'd reach for one of my parenting books or go online to find a solution, like when Elliott suddenly became afraid of the dark and I had to buy a special nightlight. Though I'd known my grandmother wouldn't live forever, I wasn't expecting to have this conversation so soon, and I'd done nothing to prepare for it.

I pulled Elliott onto my lap and improvised. "Nana won't be at home, sweetie. She isn't going to live with us anymore."

"Why?" he asked.

"Her body stopped working the way it's supposed to and she died."

"She didn't say good-bye," he said, his eyes filling with tears. "She didn't kiss me."

I wiped the tears that ran down his face, wishing I could let my own flow freely but knowing it would only make the situation worse. "There isn't always time for that," I said, my voice catching.

I'd already decided that Elliott was too young to attend the funeral, but maybe I could find a way to give him some sort of closure. "If you draw Nana a picture, I promise to make sure she gets it."

"Okay, Mama."

I set him back in his chair and he picked up his fork and began eating his scrambled eggs, sniffing occasionally.

Drinking two large cups of coffee on an empty stomach had made it churn. At Pam's urging, I ate enough to settle it, nibbling on a piece of dry toast and eating most of my eggs. Physically I felt better, but my grief simmered just below the surface, threatening to boil over at any minute. I pushed it aside because the number of things I had to take care of seemed staggering, and there was no one but me to handle them.

At nine o'clock, Detective Quick called. "You can return to

your apartment any time after noon. The cleaning crew is there now, but they should be done in the next hour or so."

I left the room so Elliott wouldn't hear my side of the conversation. "Is it safe to go home?"

"It's doubtful that whoever did this is anywhere near the scene now, but do you have someone who can accompany you?"

"Yes." Shane had the day off and had assured me it would be no trouble to drive us home so I could pack a suitcase with enough clothing and personal items to get us through the next several days.

"Don't hesitate to give me a call if you think of anything I should know," Jack said.

"I won't."

Next I called Jenny Nicholl, my supervisor at the hospital. Today was Thursday and I wasn't on the schedule because I normally worked three twelve-hour shifts per week, on Monday, Wednesday, and Friday. I'd need at least a week off in order to complete everything on my list. I rarely called in sick or asked for time away from work, and I had plenty of vacation hours saved up if I needed them.

"I saw it in the newspaper this morning, Daisy," Jenny said when she answered my call. "I'm so sorry."

"Thanks, Jenny."

"The story didn't say much. Do the police have any idea who did this?"

"Not yet." I struggled to keep it together because I really didn't have time to break down. "I need some time off. Elliott and I are going to have to move. We can't stay in that apartment. I also have to make funeral arrangements and find someone to watch Elliott while I'm at work."

"You take all the time you need. And I'll ask around. See if anyone knows of a good daycare."

"Thanks. I appreciate that."

"You take care of yourself, okay?"

"I will."

Next I called the funeral home. I'd never made arrangements before, but I was sure they'd have someone to walk me through it.

The funeral director I spoke with told me that my grandmother's body hadn't been released yet. "As soon as we receive it I can give you a call. It may be a day or two."

Of course. I'd forgotten to allow time for the autopsy to be completed. "Thank you. I'll wait until I hear back from you."

Feeling like I was spinning my wheels, I opened the browser on my phone and looked up the phone numbers for the apartment complexes I deemed appropriate for a single mother to consider. I had no interest in living in a building that catered to a bunch of loud-partying twentysomethings or one that was known for drug deals of any kind. That didn't leave me with much.

I narrowed down the list to three family-friendly options. The first two I called were full—and I worried I might have to expand my criteria—but the third building had a two-bedroom apartment available for immediate rental. It was a hundred and fifty more per month than I wanted to pay, but I couldn't put a price on our safety. I made an appointment to stop by and see the apartment that afternoon.

Elliott was in the living room with Pam. He was sitting on the floor putting together a wooden puzzle when I got off the phone.

"I called work and also made an appointment to see an apartment this afternoon. I can't do anything about planning the funeral until probably tomorrow, at the earliest." I sighed. "I feel so overwhelmed."

"I can only imagine," Pam said, sitting down on the couch beside me. "It'll be okay. I know it's a lot to deal with. We'll help you get through it."

"I don't know what I'd do without you and Shane."

"You'd do the same for us."

"Of course I would," I said. "Are you heading to work soon?"

Pam owned her own business, a hair salon located near the town square.

"In about a half hour. Shane said he was going to take you to your apartment."

"Yes. I'll grab enough to get us through the next few days."

Pam glanced at Elliott and lowered her voice. "Do you think Scott had something to do with this? Maybe he got himself into trouble again."

Her question didn't surprise me. If there was one person familiar with my marital history and its problems, it was Pam.

"I don't know, but he was the first person I mentioned down at the police station. He was the only person, actually. But if Scott *is* involved, why would he do it? For what gain? He of all people should know that my grandmother didn't have anything worth stealing."

"But if it wasn't a robbery, then what was it?" Pam asked.

"I don't know. But I'm scared that whatever it was, it was supposed to involve me."

*

Shane drove us to the apartment. One end of the crime-scene tape had come loose from the side of the building, and it fluttered in the wind. The place that had been my sanctuary not long ago was now tainted, and I was filled with a sense of foreboding.

"Don't be nervous," Shane said. "Whoever did this is long gone by now."

On a rational level, I agreed with him. And besides, it would be hard not to feel safe with Shane by my side. He was six feet tall and built like a linebacker. I'd grab our things and we could be in and out quickly.

"Mama?"

I turned around to see what Elliott wanted. "What is it, honey?"

"I don't wanna go in. The bad man might be there."

Shane glanced at me and turned off the radio so we could hear Elliott better. I kept my voice even. "What bad man, Elliott?"

"The one who said mean things to Nana. He telled her to shut up!" Elliott started to cry.

I opened my door and slid into the backseat, placing my arms around his trembling shoulders. "Shhh, it's okay."

"Mama," he said, running his fingers over the surface of his army man. "I want to stay in the car. Pwease."

"Of course," I said, stroking his head. "You don't have to go in there."

"Let me go in and make sure everything's okay," Shane said. "Then I'll come back out and sit in the car with Elliott."

Elliott nodded. "I stay with Shane."

"Yes, you can stay with Shane."

I handed my key ring to Shane and he got out of the car. "I'll be right back," he said.

I unbuckled Elliott's seatbelt and cuddled him, stroking his hair. He clung to me, but soon he calmed down, and I wiped his tears and kissed his forehead.

"Have you ever heard that man's voice before, Elliott?"

"No." He avoided eye contact and continued rubbing his fingers back and forth over his army man.

It had only been an occasional toy before, and I couldn't even remember where it had come from, but it appeared to have been elevated in status. Part comfort item and part talisman, it certainly worked well to calm him down.

Shane returned a few minutes later and handed me my keys. "Go on in. I'll stay here with the little guy." He turned toward Elliott. "Can I get a high five?"

Elliott smacked Shane's palm.

"You wanna rock out to some tunes while we wait for your mom?"

"Okay."

"How about Led Zeppelin?"

"I don't know 'bout Wed Zeppwin," Elliott said.

"Then it's high time I taught you." Shane hit a button on the stereo, and as the first notes of "Rock and Roll" filled the car I made myself open the door. "You'll be fine," Shane said. "They did a good job. Lock the door once you're inside, and then get what you need." He pointed at his cell phone in the cup holder. "Call me if you have trouble."

"Thanks, Shane."

The apartment looked just like it had when I left for work on Wednesday morning. The toys were picked up and my grandmother's knitting basket sat on the floor next to the couch. She always woke up early on the days I worked, and she'd tell me what activities she had planned for Elliott while we drank coffee at the kitchen table. When I walked back in the door after work around seven forty-five, Elliott would be bathed and fed and ready for me to read him a book before bed. The routine that I counted on, that I appreciated more than my grandmother had probably known, was about to change, which only added to my worry.

I walked into the bedroom I'd shared with Elliott and pulled down our suitcases from a shelf in the closet. The silent apartment felt eerie to me, and there was a sterile smell I couldn't place. Maybe it was the absence of the scented candles my grandmother liked to burn or maybe it was the cleaning supplies that had been used. Packing quickly, I zipped the suitcases and carried them down the hall.

In the living room, the carpeting had obviously been scrubbed because there was an area near the coffee table that was lighter than the rest. When my brain processed the reason for it, my stomach rebelled and it took everything I had to keep my breakfast down. I thought about what my grandmother had endured and how scared she must have been. It wasn't fair. Anger replaced some of the helplessness I felt at the injustice of it all, and I swore I wouldn't rest until the case was solved. My grandmother deserved at least that much.

I picked up the suitcases and locked the door behind me.

When I got back to the parking lot, Shane's SUV was rocking slightly as he and Elliott enjoyed their little dance party.

"You're going to make a fantastic father, Shane," I said when I opened the passenger-side door.

"Thanks. You know I'm always happy to help out with Elliott. He needs a man's influence. Not that you're not doing a great job on your own," he said quickly, "because you are. There are just some things that you shouldn't have to teach him." He smiled to soften the point he was trying to make. "Like girls, and rock and roll."

His words might have stung if I hadn't completely agreed with him. My grandmother had been both mother and father to me, and she'd done a wonderful job, but after I married Scott I'd been so happy that Elliott would grow up in a household with both parents. Yet here we were, right back in the same situation I'd grown up in, one person taking on the role of two.

"Thanks. I'll leave the musical influencing up to you. Just watch the volume and steer him away from rap, okay? Too many bad words."

"Deal," he said.

Shane drove across the parking lot to where I'd left my car the night before. I transferred Elliott's car seat from his car to mine while Shane loaded our suitcases into the trunk.

Then I buckled Elliott in, slid behind the wheel, and followed Shane home.

CHAPTER 8

DAISY

I CALLED DETECTIVE QUICK as soon as we got back to Pam and Shane's after digging his card out of my wallet. When he answered, I identified myself.

"You said to call if I thought of anything," I said.

"Absolutely," he said. "What is it?"

"It might be nothing, but when we went to the apartment to pick up some of our things, my son became quite upset and said he didn't want to go in with me. He said he was afraid the 'bad man' might be there. Does that help at all? I asked him if he recognized the voice but he said no."

"A neighbor confirmed it was a man's voice she heard, which isn't surprising. A man would fit the profile for this type of crime more than a woman. What we've found with children is that they block things out. Often they'll give you bits and pieces either as they remember or as they become more comfortable recounting the trauma. It usually takes time, so don't push too hard. But continue listening to what he says."

"I will. Do you have any new information?"

"Not yet," he said. "But it's still early in the investigation.

We're following up on every lead. If I have anything to pass along I'll be sure to call you."

"Thank you," I said.

"You're welcome, Ms. DiStefano. Take care."

*

After I took a shower and bathed Elliott, Shane and I went to the new apartment complex to meet the manager. The location would make my drive to work a few minutes longer, but that didn't really matter. The grounds were well maintained and Elliott pointed excitedly when he noticed the wrought-iron gates surrounding a small pool.

"Wook, Mom!"

"Yes, I see it." Our old complex didn't have a swimming pool. Elliott loved playing in the water, and I crossed my fingers that the apartment would work out.

The apartment manager was a kind-looking, older gentleman. He produced a lollipop for Elliott and grabbed a ring of keys from a desk drawer. We followed him to a stairwell that smelled slightly of lemons and walked up one flight. Then he led us to an apartment three doors down.

"This is one of our nicest two-bedroom units." He unlocked the door and swung it open.

There was a small entryway which opened directly into the living room. Short hallways on both sides each led to a bedroom. The larger bedroom had its own bathroom, and the smaller one had a bathroom directly across the hall. The kitchen wasn't overly large, but the appliances looked new and everything was very clean.

Though it was an older building, in many ways it was a nicer apartment than the one we'd been living in. Elliott and I had shared a room for the past year, which wasn't ideal but actually bothered me less than I'd thought it would when we moved in with my grandmother. I could have rented my own apartment and dropped off Elliott on my way to work, but my grandmother had assumed we would live with her, and I didn't have the heart to tell her otherwise. Now Elliott would have his own space with more room for his toys.

But the thing that sold me on the apartment was the peephole. We didn't have one in our old apartment, which meant my grandmother had probably opened the door without knowing who was on the other side. She wasn't a gullible woman, and she'd always had good common sense, but as she got older she seemed less aware of the problem of rising crime, as if she was somehow exempt from it. Maybe it was simply a byproduct of her generation, when the likelihood of danger appearing on your doorstep was less prevalent than it was today. Whatever the reason, I vowed to make it much more difficult for someone to cross my threshold.

"How soon can we move in?" I asked.

"If you fill out the application before you leave, I'll get the ball rolling today. I'll need the first and last month's rent and a deposit, but I'll prorate since it's the middle of the month. How's your credit rating?"

"It's excellent."

"Good. Once you're approved, I'll give you a call and you can move in any time after that. I should be able to get back to you first thing in the morning."

"That would be great." I crouched down until I was eye level with Elliott. "Would you like to live here? Go swimming in the pool?"

He looked hopeful. "With Nana?"

His question was like a knife to my heart. "Just you and me, honey."

"Okay," he whispered.

We stopped in the rental office, and after I filled out the paperwork, I mentally crossed 'find safe housing' off my list.

"Ready?" Shane asked.

I was about to answer him when I glanced over at the manager's desk and came face-to-face with a picture of my grandmother on the front page of the *Desert News*. I'd forgotten all about the reporter and the story he was writing. We subscribed to the newspaper, but I hadn't thought to grab my copy when Shane and I were at the apartment.

"Would you mind if I looked at your newspaper for a moment?" I asked the manager.

"Take it," he said. "I've already read it."

I quickly folded it so Elliott wouldn't see the picture and shoved it into my purse. When we got back to Pam and Shane's, I made Elliott's lunch, and while he was eating I smoothed the newspaper out on the kitchen counter.

San Bernardino County, CA
Local Woman Slain
By Brooks McClain

Police in San Bernardino County are investigating the homicide of an elderly woman. Authorities were called to the Sunset Vista apartment complex Tuesday evening after a neighbor heard shouting and called 911. When they arrived, they discovered the body of Pauline Thorpe, 84. Officers secured the apartment complex and transported several residents to the police station for questioning. Police have not released any information about the cause of death and have not revealed whether there are any suspects in the case. Sources at the crime scene confirmed that the deceased's three-year-old great-grandson was home during the attack but appeared to be unharmed.

"Pauline was one of the nicest ladies you could ever hope to meet," said Dixie Buchanan, a resident of Sunset Vista. Karen Rose, who also lives at the apartment complex, said that Pauline "wouldn't turn her back on anyone, even if they didn't deserve her help." According to sources, Thorpe enjoyed playing bridge and spending time with her family. Police are urging anyone who might have information regarding this case to call the station. Thorpe is survived by a granddaughter and great-grandson. Funeral arrangements are pending.

    I read it twice. After taking one last look at my grandmother's smiling face, I folded the newspaper and tucked it back into my purse.

CHAPTER 9

BROOKS

MY MOM'S FIRST indication that something wasn't quite right came when she had to ask my dad to open a container of orange juice for her. The muscle weakness seemed to affect one hand more than the other, so for a while she coped by switching to the opposite hand, admitting later that she hadn't mentioned it because she didn't want to worry us over nothing.

My dad had worked for the railroad for forty years and had made a list of all the places he wanted to travel to someday with my mom. "It will be one long vacation," he promised her. He was only two months into his retirement when my mom had trouble opening that juice. An illness would put a damper on their travel plans, so she continued to hide it, hoping the weakness would go away on its own. Other parts of her body weakened over the next several months, and one day my dad placed a worried call to me after my mom fell down at home.

"They've referred us to a neurologist," he said. "I have no idea what that means. I'm afraid it might be something serious."

One month later, they received the official diagnosis of ALS, also known as Lou Gehrig's disease, which carried with it an average life expectancy of two to five years. There is no cure.

It's been three years since my mom's symptoms first appeared, and my dad and I have known from the beginning that her condition would continue to deteriorate until she died. But we'd always talked about her disease in the abstract, both of us carefully sidestepping the reality. Her symptoms were manageable for a long time, and she remained in good spirits. It was possible to fool ourselves into thinking that things were going okay. Some ALS patients lived with the disease for many years, far outliving their projected life expectancies. Maybe Mom would be one of the lucky ones.

Then my dad called on a rainy day three weeks ago. "Your mom isn't doing well," he said.

Before his call had come in, I'd been sitting on the couch in my living room, watching ESPN and eating pizza. Not a care in the world. When he started crying, I grabbed the remote control and hit Mute, my heart pounding. My dad, who had never shed a tear or gotten choked up in my presence—ever—could hardly talk. I barely understood him when he said, "I don't think she has much time left." I pictured the days my mom had left like grains of sand suddenly pouring from one side of an hourglass into the other at breakneck speed.

That's when I blurted out, "I'll come home. I'll take a leave of absence. I want to be there for her."

He didn't even try to talk me out of it, and that's when it finally sank in that my mom was going to die.

*

I had breakfast with my mom the morning after Pauline Thorpe's murder. My dad had still been up when I returned home from the police department, but my mom had slept straight through until morning. I wasn't expected in the newsroom until nine, so I told my dad I wanted to be responsible for breakfast duty.

"You don't have to do that," he said. "That's not why you're here, Brooks."

"I know that," I said. "But I don't mind."

My mother had been devoted to my upbringing in a way that I only appreciated in hindsight, the way most people do when they grow into adulthood and realize the sacrifices that had been made on their behalf. There'd never been a time when she wasn't there for me. She'd been a homemaker until I went to college, and then she took a job working part-time at the library.

"I'll be bored out of my mind sitting at home all day," she'd said. She'd volunteered at the community center two days a week and become involved in several projects. She'd always stayed busy and she seemed happy. Though she'd never said anything to me, the only thing she might have wanted that she didn't have was a grandchild.

When I knocked on the bedroom door, my mom's voice sounded weak when she said, "Brooks? Come in." She was sitting on the edge of the bed, fully dressed. She would be sixty-two on her next birthday, and she'd stopped coloring her hair sometime in the past year. It was shorter now, completely silver and reaching only to her chin. It suited her. She wore pants and a loose cotton T-shirt. My dad had already laced up her tennis shoes, so I helped her stand, grabbing the sweater that was laid out on the bed and throwing it over my arm.

"I thought I'd join you for breakfast," I said.

"That would be wonderful." The slurring of her words didn't seem as pronounced, and I wondered if it was worse at the end of the day, when she was tired.

She gripped my arm tightly as we made our way down the hall. She hesitated at the top of the staircase, waiting for me to put my arm around her waist before she took a tentative step.

"It's okay, Mom. I've got you."

She clung to me as I half-carried her down the stairs, and I made a mental note to ask my dad how long it would be before the hospital bed arrived. The stairs were an unnecessary risk none of us needed.

My dad was in the kitchen making scrambled eggs and fried potatoes.

"Morning, Dad."

"Brooks." My dad smiled. "Would you like some coffee?"

"I'll get it," I said, grabbing a mug from the cupboard.

"I want you to try to eat all this, Mary," Dad said as he carried the plate toward the table. He sat down beside her and began spooning the eggs and potatoes into her mouth, much like he had the night before with the soup. No matter how many times my dad insisted he didn't mind taking care of my mom, this had to be hard on him.

It would be hard on anyone.

"I can feed Mom if you want to eat."

"Thanks, but I'll eat later." He continued urging my mom to eat, giving her enough time to swallow—which seemed to take her longer than usual—but not enough to lose the momentum. He'd confessed last night when I returned from the police station that making sure she got enough to eat was one of his biggest worries. If he couldn't get enough calories into her, the next step was the insertion of a feeding tube. "I add butter and mayonnaise and cheese to everything I can," he said, "but I still feel like I'm losing the battle."

I decided that if my dad was going to focus on making sure

my mom had everything she needed, then I would make sure he had everything *he* needed, including as many breaks as I could give him.

When he was satisfied that she'd eaten enough, I poured him a fresh cup of coffee and told him to eat his own breakfast. "We'll be outside," I said.

He'd probably never admit it, but the grateful look I saw on his face as he cracked fresh eggs into the bowl told me how he really felt and how draining Mom's illness had been on him.

I settled Mom into her chair on the front porch and sat down next to her. I worried that she might want to talk about my decision to come home. I didn't want her to thank me or tell me how sorry she was that I'd had to disrupt my life and return to the town she knew I had no desire to ever live in again. Preparing my rebuttal, I decided I would tell her that none of that mattered, even though we both knew it did. I would tell her what a wonderful mother she was and how much I appreciated the way she'd always been there for me. I would insist that I *wanted* to come home. She didn't say anything, though, and I felt relieved. She knew I wouldn't want to talk about it and spared me the uncomfortable conversation. She'd always been one of the most giving people I knew, and dying hadn't changed my mother one bit.

"I haven't read the newspaper yet, but your dad told me someone was killed."

I was already becoming used to her speech because I understood everything she said.

"Yes, it happened sometime in the early evening. A woman named Pauline Thorpe. Did you know her?"

"No, the name doesn't sound familiar."

"She lived in an apartment with her granddaughter and great-grandson. The child was there when it happened."

"Oh, my," she said. "How old is he?"

"Only three."

"Was he hurt?"

I thought about the little blond boy wrapped in Daisy's arms. "Thankfully, no."

She turned to me and smiled. "Good." She took a deep breath. "The fresh air feels so nice."

To me, the September air felt heavy and oppressive and would only grow warmer as the day went on. The sky was overcast and daily temperatures would start falling as October approached, but highs were still in the nineties, which seemed stifling to me. But maybe I would view the weather in a more positive light if I had fewer days remaining to experience it.

"Do you see my sunflowers?" she asked. They grew in clusters in front of the house, their stalks standing tall, the petals unblemished.

"They look great," I said.

"Your dad has been taking care of them for me. He knows how much I like to sit out here and look at them. That whole area used to be a big patch of dirt. When you were two years old, you had a dump truck and you spent hours moving the dirt around. You were so mad when I put in those flowerbeds. I had to watch you to make sure you didn't dig everything up."

I laughed. "I don't remember that."

"It was a long time ago." She paused and then said, "You'll have to make sure your dad takes care of the daisies when they bloom next spring." Her unspoken words hung in the air. *Because I won't be alive to tell him myself.*

"I will. I promise."

One of the worst things I'd read when I researched Lou Gehrig's disease was how hard it was for people stricken with it to remain positive. No one should have to bear the heavy load of losing all physical control while their minds remained as sharp as ever. Patients often became depressed, and who could blame them? My mom knew exactly what was heading her way.

"Can you take me back inside, Brooks? I'm getting tired."

"Of course."

When I helped her up from her chair, we both pretended not to notice the tear that rolled down her cheek and the fact that she was no longer able to wipe it away on her own.

*

Before heading into the newsroom, I decided to pay a visit to Margaret Parker, Pauline Thorpe's across-the-hall neighbor. According to Dixie Buchanan, Margaret had placed the 911 call. When I arrived at the Sunset Vista apartment complex, I took the stairs to the second floor. Pauline had lived in apartment number twelve; I knocked on the door of number eleven, directly across the hall.

"Who is it?" a voice shouted from behind the door.

"Brooks McClain. I'm a reporter with the *Desert News*."

"Slide your business card under the door," she said.

"I don't have a business card with me." I wondered if anyone had even *ordered* my business cards yet. "I'll give you my driver's license." I dug it out of my wallet and slid it underneath the door.

"This says you live in San Francisco!"

Yes, I know.

I pinched the bridge of my nose and exhaled slowly. "I do, but I'm living here for now. I just want to ask you a couple of questions about Pauline. I was told you're her best friend."

The door cracked open an inch. I could make out about half of Margaret's eyeball as she squinted at me.

"I am her best friend," she said. "Or at least I was."

She opened the door the rest of the way, and I could see that her eyes were filling with tears. Though it came with the territory when interviewing the families or friends of victims, I still felt uncomfortable anytime a woman cried, feeling as though it was my fault for showing up and asking questions.

"I'm very sorry," I said. "May I come in?"

"Yes."

Margaret handed me my driver's license and I followed her into the living room. "Please sit down," she said. "Can I get you a cup of tea?"

"That would be nice." I hated tea, and nothing sounded worse on a hot day. But I always drank whatever was offered, within reason, because accepting hospitality put people at ease.

"I'll turn up the heat on the kettle," she said.

When she came back into the room, she was dabbing her eyes with a Kleenex.

"Were you the one who called nine one one?" I asked.

"Yes."

"Can you tell me what you heard?"

"It was a man's voice," she said. "He was shouting something. I don't hear very well and I wasn't wearing my hearing aid because it hurts my ear. I was on my way out and if I hadn't been standing in the hallway, I might not have heard him at all. I feel so bad that I didn't do anything sooner!" Margaret was wringing her hands and when the teapot whistled a moment later, she jumped, making me aware of just how tightly she was wound.

"Are you okay?" I asked.

"I'm fine. I'll just get the tea," she said. "Would you like milk and sugar?"

"Plain is fine."

When she returned, I accepted the cup and saucer and took a small drink, trying not to grimace at the bitter taste. "Did Pauline normally have male visitors?" I asked after I set down the cup.

"No, never. I saw her every day, usually after lunch. Sometimes if Elliott was napping we'd play cards at her kitchen table."

"She watched Elliott during the day?"

"Yes. She loved taking care of that little boy. I can't believe that poor child was in the apartment when Pauline was killed."

"When you heard the man shouting at Pauline, could you understand any of the words he said?"

"He just sounded angry. Agitated, more than anything. I thought about knocking on the door, to see if Pauline was okay, but I got scared, so I went back into my apartment and called the police."

"Did you hear anything else? Like maybe a door slam?"

"I don't remember hearing anything like that."

"Is there anyone you can think of who might be responsible for this?" I took another drink of my tea. I should have accepted the milk and sugar.

She shook her head slowly. "I don't know anyone who didn't like Pauline. But there was that trouble with Scott."

I leaned forward. "That's Daisy's ex-husband?"

"Yes."

"What kind of trouble?"

"It's sad, really. That boy had such a bright future, but he fell in with the wrong crowd down at the restaurant. Drugs," she whispered. "He stole some money from Pauline once. It broke her heart. She just couldn't believe it."

I'd lost count of how many crimes I'd reported on that had drugs—or the money to buy them—as their motive. Margaret's disclosure immediately elevated Scott from person of interest to top suspect.

"Thank you for your time," I said. I ripped a page from my notebook and wrote down my name and number. "Please call me if you should think of anything else. We rose and walked toward the door. "Oh, and one more thing."

"Yes?" she said.

"Please don't open your door for anyone the way you did for me."

Margaret wrung her hands and looked frightened. "I won't."

"Do you have someone who can install a safety chain on your door? Or maybe a peephole?"

"My son is rather handy. I'll ask him."

I nodded. "Good."

I knocked on nine doors and spoke to six more people. They all said the same thing: Pauline was a wonderful person, everyone liked her, and wasn't this just a horrible tragedy?

Tragic, yes. But if Scott DiStefano wasn't responsible, the sheer absence of any reason why someone would want to intentionally harm Pauline Thorpe would lead me to believe that the homicide was every bit as random as it seemed.

CHAPTER 10

SCOTT

SCOTT DISTEFANO PLACED a few shards of crystal meth in the bowl of a spoon, added water, and stirred the mixture with the plastic cap of a syringe until it dissolved. His movements were those of a seasoned drug user. There was no fumbling, no hesitation. Just the habitual following of the necessary steps. If only he'd maintained the same precision, the same devotion, in other areas of his life—work, home, family—he would have had so much more to show for his thirty years.

But he hadn't.

He'd made mistakes.

Lots of them.

Thinking that he could outsmart and resist the pull of addiction had been the biggest one of all.

He pulled a small piece of cotton off the end of a Q-tip, dropped it in the bowl of the spoon, and then placed the tip of the needle into it. He drew back the plunger, making sure to get all the liquid, and then set the syringe aside while he made a fist and tied off with the tourniquet. It took a while for him to find a usable vein, but finally he stuck the needle in and slammed the hit home.

He coughed and choked.

His eyes watered.

And then… the most righteous high. There was nothing that even remotely compared to it.

Not sex.

Not money.

Not love.

Not family.

Nothing.

The high was just so *goddamn perfect*.

Especially when it was delivered straight into his vein by a needle.

No hit would ever compare to his first high off of crystal meth, but that would never stop him from chasing the possibility. He couldn't. He craved it, and one day he would find it again.

Every now and then, he thought fleetingly of his wife Daisy. She hadn't been able to convince him to quit, though God knows she'd tried. Meth was the only lover he had time for, and he gave it to her freely and willingly. His son, Elliott, hadn't been enough to sway him either. His loyalty lay firmly with his addiction, and he spent every dollar—and every waking moment—in the pursuit of it. Unlike coke, meth was a cheap and powerful high. But without a steady source of income, even cheap was often out of reach.

The door burst open and Dale entered the room.

"Can't seem to get that knocking thing down, can you?" Scott said, but he was feeling too good to get really fired up about it.

"I told you I don't have to knock," Dale said.

Dale owned the house and claimed he had the right to barge in whenever he felt like it. Scott was convinced that Dale was trying to catch him in the act. Of what, Scott wasn't sure, because the only thing he ever did in his room was get high.

With its cramped quarters and ever-present smell of unwashed bodies and lingering chemicals, the residence was hardly enviable. When Scott bothered to sleep at all, it was on an old, stained mattress on the floor that had been left behind by the previous occupant. Dale was by far the worst landlord and roommate Scott had ever had. He'd been using meth a lot longer than Scott and was prone to fits of drug psychosis and paranoia. He'd started carrying a gun, which he kept shoved down the front of his pants. One of these days, he was going to blow his balls clean off. But if it were not for the room he rented from Dale, Scott would have been forced to live in his truck.

Dale spotted the used rig on the floor. "Where'd you score?"

"The Tap. A guy owed me some money. I leaned on him and he paid up."

Dale's eyes narrowed. "How much?"

Scott didn't really want to tell him. The meth he'd bought was more than he'd had in his possession for months, and he didn't want to share. His habit required constant hustling, foraging, and—if necessary—stealing. If he was careful, this amount could last him a while.

"Eight ball," he finally said.

Dale's eyes lit up. "Fix me a shot."

Rent was due in three days, and Scott had no idea where he was going to come up with the money since the eight ball had set him back two hundred and fifty dollars. He could usually track down an odd job or two and make enough to cover his room, but lately he'd been having trouble finding work, and he was starting to sweat. Scott knew Dale was flat broke and tweaking, having burned through the last of his stash on a binge that spanned the previous three days. Scott figured Dale might be pretty desperate right about then and open to a little negotiation.

"I'm gonna need more time on my rent this month."

Dale visibly twitched, and his face hardened into a sneer. He'd inherited the house from his dad, and he counted on Scott's rent money, and the money he collected from various other tenants who came and went, to pay the utilities and keep himself in drugs.

"I told you if you don't pay, you're out."

"Then I guess I better get down to the Tap and sell the rest of this."

It would be three days before Dale would see rent money from anyone, which meant three days without drugs.

"Fine," Dale said.

"I have until the fifth to pay my rent."

"Yeah, whatever," Dale said. Thinking only about his impending high, he was no longer listening.

"You got any clean rigs?" Scott asked.

"I'm out."

Of course you are. Dale was always out. And unlike Scott, Dale didn't really care if the needle was clean. Scott grabbed a paper bag on the floor and pulled out a clean syringe. No way in hell was he sharing needles with Dale.

Scott tapped out more meth into the spoon and added water. "Where were you?" he asked. Not that he really cared, but Dale spent an exorbitant amount of time on the couch watching porn. He hadn't been home when Scott returned from the Tap, and Scott was curious about what had finally prompted Dale to leave the house.

"Nowhere," Dale said. He tied off and waited for Scott to finish loading the syringe. "Oh, that shit's good," he said when the needle hit home. He smiled, and it was truly a gruesome thing.

Dale's teeth were in horrible shape and he'd been picking at his skin again.

He looks like a ghoul.

Jesus Christ. I hope I never look like that.

Scott pushed those thoughts aside and smiled back as two addicts found their common ground.

CHAPTER 11

DAISY

TWO DAYS AFTER my grandmother died, I made arrangements with the funeral home. Pam and Shane both had to work, so I had no choice but to bring Elliott with me. One of my friends from the hospital—a nurse named Kayla whom I'd worked with for the past three years—had kindly offered to watch Elliott later that afternoon so I could go to my old apartment and start packing, but I didn't feel comfortable foisting him off on her for the whole day. My grandmother had always been there to watch Elliott—she'd insisted on it, in fact. I wasn't used to arranging for childcare, and I hated having to rely on other people. Finding someone to watch Elliott, especially with my work schedule, wouldn't be easy.

The funeral director shook my hand and spoke to me in calm, soothing tones undoubtedly honed from years of dealing with family members as they made arrangements for the burial of their loved ones. He was good at it too, because I instantly felt less anxious.

He led us into a room and pulled out chairs for Elliott and me. Settling into his own chair on the other side of the table, he fanned out a number of glossy brochures. "Do you know anything about your grandmother's wishes for burial?" he asked as I handed some crayons and a piece of paper to Elliott.

I was ashamed of how little I had pushed my grandmother to discuss this type of thing with me. If I didn't feel comfortable pressing her about her finances, I certainly hadn't been comfortable asking her what she'd like me to do when she died.

"Due to the circumstances of my grandmother's death, I've only been back to the apartment we shared long enough to grab a few things. I'm going there this afternoon, and I can look through her personal belongings. I'll see if I can find a will, or a directive of some sort."

I didn't even know if she had a will. When I'd given her a copy of mine, she'd thanked me and that had been the end of it. Another opportunity for a discussion that I hadn't taken advantage of.

"That would be fine," he said. "We can still make the preliminary arrangements and adjust accordingly if necessary."

"Many of my grandmother's friends are elderly and no longer drive. I'd hate for them to have to come out twice. Could I have a combined visitation and funeral service?"

"Absolutely," he said.

"Do you know approximately how much it will cost?"

"We have a range of options available. Do you have a budget in mind?"

"Not yet. I'll try to come up with one by tomorrow."

"That will be fine. For now we'll plan on a combined visitation and memorial service, with burial immediately afterward. Would Saturday work for you?"

I had so many things on my mind, so many things I was trying to balance, but I needed the closure of my grandmother being laid to rest. I felt like I hadn't spent enough time reflecting on her life or honoring her memory. I would put everything else on hold the day of her service so I could say a heartfelt good-bye.

"Yes," I said. "Saturday will be fine."

*

After I dropped off Elliott at Kayla's, I drove to the apartment to start packing. I chastised myself for feeling so apprehensive. This was still my home, for a few more days at least. I would lock the door behind me and concentrate on the task at hand, which was to get everything boxed up before Shane and his friends arrived on Sunday to move all our belongings to the new apartment. I walked down the quiet hallway, but instead of sticking the key in my own lock, I knocked on Margaret's door instead.

"Who is it?" she asked.

"Margaret? It's Daisy."

She fumbled with the lock and then threw the door open. "Oh, honey," she said. "I'm so sorry." She burst into tears and I threw my arms around her.

"It's okay," I said, patting her gently on the back.

"I'm sorry," she said again. "I should be comforting you."

"We'll comfort each other."

"Come in," she said, grabbing my hand and leading me into the living room.

I sat down on the couch. "I wanted to thank you for calling the police, Margaret. You don't know how much it means to me that you tried to help my grandmother. It was a brave thing to do."

Margaret wiped her eyes. "Pauline was a good friend to me. I'll miss her dearly."

I took a deep breath. "Elliott and I are moving. We can't stay in that apartment. It would be too painful and I don't know that I would ever feel safe there again. I'm going to miss you so much."

"I'll miss you and Elliott, too. But I understand. My son called this morning. He wants me to move, but I told him I'm too set in my ways. This is my home and I'm not afraid. He's angry with me, but he's coming over today to install a safety chain on the door."

Looking at Margaret, her back slightly hunched from osteoporosis, her bones brittle as old parchment, I was again reminded just how nondiscriminatory evil could be. Whoever had killed my grandmother didn't care that she was elderly and unable to defend herself. The fact that someone was capable of killing a woman like my grandmother, like Margaret, was unfathomable to me. And yet it had happened.

"I can understand why he's upset," I said.

"I can, too," Margaret admitted. "That reminds me. There was a reporter here yesterday. He told me to be careful about who I open my door to. He asked me lots of questions."

"I spoke to someone from the newspaper when I was at the police station."

"Was he handsome? This man was quite handsome. He had dark hair. Very tall. A little older than you, maybe."

"I don't remember what he looked like." I'd been so out of it I barely remembered speaking to him. I stood up. "I better get started on the packing. The visitation and funeral will be Saturday. Elliott and I are staying with Pam and Shane, but I'll come by and pick you up. I'll let you know what time as soon as the details are finalized."

"Thank you, dear. I would love that."

She walked me to the door.

"You were such a good friend to her," I said, reaching out to give her a hug. "I'll see you soon."

*

In the apartment, I flipped on all the lights and made sure the door was locked behind me. It was too quiet, so I switched on the small radio in the kitchen and turned it to the easy-listening station.

Deciding that my grandmother's room was the best place to start, I pushed open her door. She had insisted that Elliott and I take the bigger bedroom when we moved back in, and her furniture and belongings barely fit into the smaller space. The double bed was pushed up against the wall, and there was just enough room for her nightstand to be placed beside it. Her dresser sat adjacent to the bed, and other than a small walkway between the bed and dresser, every inch of the room was used up.

Feeling overwhelmed, I began by going through the nightstand. Shane was going to drop off some boxes later that afternoon. In the meantime, I decided I'd separate everything into piles on the bed: stay, toss, donate.

The nightstand was virtually empty. I found a roll of cough drops, lip balm, several pictures of Elliott, a tube of hand cream, a children's picture book, and a magnifying glass. Next, I went through each of her dresser drawers but found only clothing, all of which would go into the donate pile.

In the closet, my grandmother's shoes were lined up in a neat row, and her clothes—mostly polyester pants, cotton shirts, and cardigan sweaters—were grouped by item.

There was a high shelf that ran along the length of the closet. I spotted some cardboard boxes with lids and pulled down the first one. My grandmother had bundled her canceled checks by month—dating back fifteen years—and then secured them with rubber bands. Her bank statements were stored beside them in stacks and were also wrapped in rubber bands. Two more boxes held more of the same. The fourth box contained some old photo albums, the kind where you had to glue or tape the pictures in. I was more than familiar with the pictures in the albums. There was a time during my early teen years when I'd spent hours looking at the photos of my parents, trying to discern whose nose I'd inherited or if my straight hair had come from my mom or my dad. I definitely had my dad's eyes, but my smile was absolutely my mother's. I looked a lot like my sister, Danielle, so much so that we could have been mistaken for twins. I couldn't look at pictures of her for very long because I would start to feel sad and hollow. Guilty, as if the earth had only been able to hold one of us and I was the lucky one.

Underneath the photo albums was a policy for life insurance.

So she did have one.

The face amount of the policy was fifteen thousand dollars, and I was listed as the sole beneficiary. A scrap of paper was clipped to the front.

I want to be buried in my blue suit and I'd like daffodils, if possible.

I smiled as tears filled my eyes. If she wanted daffodils, I'd make sure she had them.

In the last box, I found a few personal items. I picked up a pair of clip-on earrings and remembered how I used to beg to wear them when I played dress-up as a little girl. They'd hurt my ears terribly, though I never admitted it. I found a string of pearls that I didn't remember ever seeing before, but when I rubbed them against the front of my teeth, their smooth texture told me they weren't real. Even if they had been, my grandmother was part of a generation that kept their valuables close. Maybe not in jelly jars buried in the yard, but not necessarily in a safe-deposit box, either.

It had taken me less than thirty minutes to sort through my grandmother's possessions. If she were alive, I knew what she'd say: *Things aren't important, people are. You and Elliott mean more to me than material things.*

Even so, I sat down on the edge of her bed, blinking back tears and feeling defeated when I thought about the utter unfairness of it all.

CHAPTER 12

BROOKS

THE PARKING LOT was full when I arrived at Daisy DiStefano's apartment complex. I knocked on her door and listened to the sound of approaching footsteps.

"Who is it?" she asked.

"Brooks McClain from the *Desert News*."

"Do you have a card?"

Well, no.

"I spoke to you the other night at the police station. You texted a picture of your grandmother to my phone."

She didn't say anything else, but a few seconds later my phone rang.

I smiled. Pretty *and* smart.

I answered the call. "You're very resourceful."

Daisy opened the door. "Sorry. I just wanted to make sure."

"No need to apologize. I hope I'm not bothering you."

She shook her head. "It's okay."

"I was hoping I could talk to you for a few minutes if you have time."

"Sure. I was about to take a break anyway. We're moving into a different apartment on Sunday, and I was going through my grandmother's things. Detective Quick wanted me to check and see if anything was missing." She exhaled as if the very act of it had exhausted her.

After she closed the front door, I followed her into a small living room.

"Please sit down," she said, motioning to the couch. "Would you like something to drink? I think there's soda and bottled water in the fridge."

"Water would be great," I said.

When I'd spoken to Daisy the night her grandmother died, her eyes had been red and swollen; now I noticed how blue they were. There were faint circles under them, which told me she probably still needed more rest than she was getting, but she seemed calmer and more in control. Not as shell-shocked. Her blond hair was once again pulled back in a ponytail, but her cheeks were no longer blotchy with tears, and her skin was clear and bright. She was wearing jeans and a lightweight, long-sleeve shirt. No jewelry. She was the kind of woman you might overlook in a dark, crowded bar, but the first one you'd notice when the lights came up.

In other words, she was exactly my type.

She returned holding two bottles of water. She handed one to me and sat down on the chair across from the couch and opened her water. "What would you like to know?"

I pulled my notebook from my suit pocket and uncapped my pen. "You and your son lived with your grandmother?"

"Yes. My grandmother raised me. When I got divorced a year ago, it was kind of a foregone conclusion on her part that Elliott and I would live here. She watched him while I was at work."

"What do you do for a living?"

"I'm a nurse at the hospital in Barstow."

"Do you have any idea who might have done this? Could it be someone you know? Someone you work with?"

"The only person I can think of who might be capable of something like this is my ex-husband."

I kept my expression neutral, remembering the comment Margaret had made about Scott using drugs. "What can you tell me about him?"

"He's an addict. That why we got divorced."

"What's his drug of choice?"

"Meth. He smokes it." She looked away as if she was embarrassed, and I could only imagine what traveling down that road must have been like for her. "I told Detective Quick about Scott. He said he would look into it."

"Can you give me his address?"

"You're going to talk to him?" She sounded surprised yet hopeful.

"Yes." It might have been a cliché, but if there was an ex-husband in the picture, he was usually the first person everyone wanted to talk to.

"I can give you the last address I have for him. It's the same one I gave to Detective Quick." She scribbled it down on a piece of paper and handed it to me.

"Do you think your ex-husband might have come here looking for money?"

"It's possible. He has a history of stealing anything that wasn't nailed down if he thought he could sell or pawn it. But like I told Detective Quick, Scott would know better than anyone that there was nothing in this apartment for him to steal. It's not like my grandmother and I kept cash around, either. We both learned that lesson the hard way."

"Have you noticed anything missing?"

"Not yet. I've only been through my grandmother's room so far, but everything seems to be accounted for. She really didn't have anything of value."

"No jewelry?"

"A few costume pieces, but it's all there."

Her phone rang and she shot me an apologetic look after she glanced at the screen. "I'm sorry. I really need to take this. It's about the move."

"No problem." I pulled out my phone and Googled Scott DiStefano. There were several hits, mostly local articles about a restaurant called DiStefano's, the one I had passed on my way into town that had the sun-faded Closed sign on its door. The image search showed a blurry picture of a man wearing a suit while cutting a ribbon during the grand reopening ceremony. Interesting. How long had it taken Scott to go from restaurant owner to addict?

"I'm sorry," Daisy said again when she hung up the phone. "I'm trying to coordinate the funeral and the move, and I'm just… overwhelmed." She rested her head in her hands for a moment and then looked up. "Where were we?"

"Since nothing appears to be missing, the motive may not have been robbery. Do you know of anyone who might be holding a grudge against you or your grandmother? Family member, scorned acquaintance?"

"No. Everyone loved my grandmother. I'm worried—" She stopped abruptly, as if she'd changed her mind about saying whatever she'd been about to say.

"What is it?"

"I'm worried that it was supposed to be me and not her."

"Why do you think that?"

"Because of my ex-husband. Nothing seems to be missing, but Scott is the only link I can come up with."

"Is there a specific reason you feel that way?"

"Just a hunch." She wouldn't look me in the eye, which told me that she probably *did* have a reason but wasn't ready to tell me.

"This apartment is severely lacking in security features. You're going to have to take some additional steps to ensure your safety once you move. It's just… you're incredibly defenseless." I rarely shared my thoughts when interviewing a victim's family members, and I didn't want it to seem like I was talking down to her, but there was something about a single mother, a young child, and an unsolved murder that had stirred my protective instincts in a way they'd never been before.

"The new apartment has a peephole and I'm going to install a safety chain." She rubbed her temples as if she felt a headache coming on. "I just need to get through the next few days."

"Can I get your new address? I'll let you know if I was able to speak to your ex-husband."

"Sure," she said. She gave it to me and I wrote it down on the same piece of paper she'd written her ex-husband's address on and put it in my pocket. "We should be moved in by Sunday. I hope to be back to work by Wednesday, but otherwise I should be there."

"Please call me if you think of anything else." I stood and followed her to the door. Before she opened it, I said, "I want you to be very careful."

She turned around and looked up at me, her expression a mix of gratitude and surprise. She blinked rapidly and looked away. "That's very kind of you. I will."

She opened the door, and before I walked out I said, "Take care, Daisy. I'll check on you again soon."

CHAPTER 13

DAISY

BY THE TIME Shane came by with the boxes, I'd organized most of the kitchen and half of Elliott's toys, placing everything into piles much the same way I had in my grandmother's room. He put the boxes together and I filled them, and then we sealed them shut with packing tape and labeled them with a Sharpie.

"A reporter came by about an hour ago," I said. "He asked me some questions. He said he's going to talk to Scott."

Shane whistled. "He's really gonna open that can of worms?"

"That's what he said."

What I didn't say was that the reporter's concern for my well-being had made me want to burst into tears. I expected Pam and Shane to care about me; they were my closest friends. But when a total stranger warns you to be careful, it really drives home just how alone you are. What I wouldn't give to have a partner, someone to navigate these rough waters with me.

But I didn't have anyone.

"I need to ask you something," I said as I labeled another box.

"Sure," Shane said. "What is it?"

"Do you have a gun?" The thought had come to me briefly while I was going through my grandmother's things, and after the reporter came right out and mentioned how defenseless I was, an idea started to form. At first it seemed ridiculous, but the more I turned it over in my mind, the more I embraced it.

He looked surprised. "I have shotguns for hunting. You know that."

"Yes, I know. Pam stockpiles all the chick flicks you won't watch and we have a movie marathon whenever you're out of town on one of your hunting weekends."

He grinned. "You have no idea how much I appreciate that, Daze."

"Happy to do it," I said. "But I'm not talking about shotguns, I'm talking about a handgun."

"Why are you asking?"

"Because I want to buy one."

His expression turned wary. "Look, I know you feel vulnerable, but that doesn't mean you should run out and buy a gun."

"I don't *want* to buy a gun, Shane. I can think of lots of things I'd rather buy. But I want to feel protected, especially in my own home."

"Gun ownership comes with a lot of responsibility."

"I know that. Believe me, I do. My biggest concerns are safety and that I don't know how to use a gun, not yet. I'll have a lot to learn."

"I'll tell you something, Daisy. If you don't know what you're doing, you run a high risk of someone using your own gun against you."

"Which is why I'll take a class," I said. "And I'll spend time at the shooting range so that I'll feel comfortable using it."

"You'll have to apply for a permit to carry it."

"I can do that."

"It's your right to carry a gun if that's what you want to do."

"This isn't about my right to carry it, Shane. This is about feeling like I have a choice. If I'm armed, I have some say in whether or not I'm going to be a victim. And if Elliott's life was in danger, I would have no problem pulling that trigger. I can't imagine any mother out there who would."

"Don't get me wrong," he said. "I don't think it's a horrible idea. I just hate the thought that it's come to this."

"I'm not thrilled about it either. But I hate feeling defenseless even more. Do you think you could help me pick one out?"

He groaned. "Pam is going to kill me."

"She'll understand," I said. "Eventually."

After Shane and I filled all the boxes he'd brought, I walked him to the door. "Thanks, Shane," I said. "For everything."

"You're welcome. See you in little while."

Next, I picked up Elliott. "How did he do?" I asked Kayla as I lifted Elliott into my arms.

"He did great," she said. "He drew a picture for his nana."

I kissed Elliott's cheek. "Can I see it?"

He nodded and wriggled out of my grasp.

"He seems really attached to that army man," Kayla said, lowering her voice.

"He was clutching it the night my grandmother was killed. He carries it everywhere."

"Bless his little heart," Kayla said.

Elliott returned with his picture and handed it to me.

"I'll make sure Nana gets this, okay?"

He nodded somberly.

"Have you found anyone to watch Elliott yet?" Kayla asked.

"Not yet. I need someone I can trust, and I'm worried about how Elliott will adjust. He's only used to being with his nana."

"I've put in a few calls. I'll let you know if anything pans out."

"Thanks." I reached out and gave her a quick hug. "I really appreciate it."

"It's no trouble, Daisy."

"Are you ready to go eat pizza with Pam and Shane?" I asked Elliott.

"Yeah!"

"Let's go, then. Tell Kayla thank you."

"Fank you," Elliott said.

"You're welcome. You come back and see me again sometime, okay?"

"Okay."

*

"Are you insane? You *cannot* carry a gun," Pam said as soon as we'd walked in the door and Elliott was out of earshot.

"I see you've had a chance to talk to Shane," I said.

"You're going to get yourself killed."

"I'm no expert, but I think that's actually the opposite of how guns are supposed to work." I raised an eyebrow.

She sighed. "You know what I mean, Daisy."

"Believe me, I do."

"I thought you said you were afraid of guns?"

Well, she had me there. "I am, but mostly because I don't have any experience with them."

"Shane said you're going to take a class to learn how to handle the gun."

"I'll sign up as soon as the funeral is over and we get moved in."

"It makes me nervous."

"That makes two of us."

"You don't have to move at all," Pam said.

I could tell by her tone that she was sincere. If we stayed, she'd make it work and I'd never hear a single complaint out of her.

"We can't stay here forever. Besides, you've got major nesting to do. That baby will be here before you know it." Tears filled my eyes and I blinked them back. "I'm scared, Pam."

She put her arm around me. "Things will get better."

"I hope so," I said. "Because I don't know how much more I can take."

CHAPTER 14
BROOKS

SCOTT DISTEFANO LIVED in a run-down shithole ten miles outside town. Potholes punctuated the dirt road, and by the time I turned into the driveway a thick layer of dust covered my Jeep. The house was surrounded by weeds and rusted-out vehicles up on blocks, as well as several stereos and TVs in various states of disassembly. A tweaker's paradise. I was just thinking that all it lacked was a junkyard dog when I heard the low growl and spotted the large, Cujo-esque mutt chained to a post in the front yard.

Great.

Hopefully the chain wasn't long enough for him to reach the front door.

I knocked and waited. No footsteps. No sound coming from within. I knocked again, harder this time. The man who finally opened the door had a lit cigarette hanging from his mouth and a gun shoved down the front of his pants.

Cujo instantly became the least of my worries.

"What the fuck do you want?" His rotten teeth were visible when he spoke, and the open sores on his face made it look like something had been chewing on him. But most alarming to me were his eyes, as dead and cold as any psychopath's. The pupils were dilated and the sockets were surrounded by purple rings so dark they were nearly black.

I met his gaze without flinching, the way you stared down a wild animal to let it know you weren't afraid.

"Scott DiStefano," I said. "I need to talk to him."

"DiStefano," the man yelled. He glared at me and walked away, leaving the door open.

The crumbling teeth and picked-at skin were a cautionary tale, but so many people in San Bernardino County had ignored it. It wasn't the meat-packing plant or the railroad or the outlet mall that kept the local economy buzzing, it was the drug trade. Especially if you were willing to deal meth. Knowing how to cook up a batch was even better. The fact that the kitchen might blow up before you were done was no more a deterrent than the gruesome effects of meth on your personal appearance. Easy money has a very strong appeal.

While I waited, I sniffed the air. I detected no smell of rotten eggs, which would indicate the presence of anhydrous ammonia. Other than the gun, their security was pretty lax, and the dog seemed less ferocious watchdog and more neglected pet; he was chained too far from the house to be much of a threat. The kicker was the cigarette. You'd have to be insane to smoke in the presence of all those flammable chemicals and fumes.

When Scott DiStefano finally made his way to the door ten minutes later, my patience had worn thin. He was around six feet tall and probably twenty pounds underweight. His blond hair reached his collarbones, giving him a California-surfer look that seemed oddly out of place in the high desert. His skin had a yellowish tint, but he hadn't started picking at it yet. It wasn't unfathomable that a woman who looked like Daisy would have once been married to him, because he wasn't an ugly man. But he was doing his best to ruin what was left of whatever handsome traits he'd once possessed.

He looked at me indifferently and said, "You a cop?"

"I'm a reporter with the *Desert News*. I'm here to ask you some questions about Pauline Thorpe."

"Shiiiiiit," he said, drawing the word out as if he had better things to do.

I got a good look inside his mouth. His teeth had started to rot.

"You must have known her well, considering you were married to her granddaughter, Daisy."

His eyes flickered with recognition when I said Daisy's name. "What's it matter if I know Pauline?"

"It matters because someone killed her."

He leaned against the doorframe. "That cop wanted to know where I was and I told him. I got nothing else to say."

I studied him, wondering what he'd done to Daisy before she left him. She said he'd stolen and pawned their things. Had he also abused her in some way? Roughed her up a little?

"Somehow I don't believe you. And if I feel like you might have something else to tell me, I'll be back. You can count on that, Scott."

He slammed the door in my face. I stood there for a moment, teeth clenched, doubting that Scott DiStefano was as innocent as he wanted me to believe. There was something that connected him to Pauline Thorpe's murder, but I didn't know what it was. At least not yet.

I walked back to the car, and after beeping open the door with my remote, I reached in and grabbed the water bottle I'd been drinking from on the drive there. It was three-quarters of the way full. The dog growled at me as I approached, but when I crouched down and filled the dusty, empty bowl, it eagerly lapped at the water until it was gone. I refilled it and when the dog had gotten its fill, it flopped down on the grass and made a contented sound.

"I'll try to remember to bring you a burger next time," I said, because something told me that I would be back. I scratched the dog behind its ears and then got in my car and drove away.

*

The newsroom was crowded when I returned, or as crowded as it would ever get with such a small staff. Maggie was typing furiously while talking into a headset, and one of the copyeditors and Paul were deep in conversation. When I reached my desk, I turned on my computer and typed in the web address for a search engine dedicated to finding people. By plugging Scott DiStefano's address into the reverse-lookup feature, I was able to determine that a man named Dale Reber, age thirty-four, owned the home. A Google image search of that name revealed a picture of the man who had answered the door. In the photo, he looked a few years younger and not quite as strung out, but it was obvious that it was him. Next I searched court records under his name but came up empty-handed, which surprised me. Either Dale Reber was smarter than the average tweaker, or he was very lucky.

Scott had mentioned he'd told the police his whereabouts at the time of Pauline's murder. It was time to pay a follow-up visit to Jack Quick, and this time I wouldn't leave until he talked to me.

*

Jack only kept me waiting for twenty minutes. He didn't seem all that happy to see me, but he didn't seem like he minded, either, which meant I was making progress.

"Brooks McClain, *Desert News*," I said.

"Yeah, I remember. Follow me," he said, leading me down the hallway to his office.

The remains of his lunch—a deli sandwich by the looks of it—were scattered across the desktop. Jack swept the crumbs and a few errant shreds of lettuce into the garbage can and took a drink of his soda, crunching the ice in a way that made me wince.

Without waiting to be directed, I sat down in the chair opposite his desk. "I understand you've questioned Scott DiStefano?"

"Yep."

"And?"

"I know that he was drinking cheap beer at the Desert Tap at the time of Pauline Thorpe's murder. A bartender by the name of Chase Arroway vouched for him."

"Has Scott been eliminated as a suspect?"

"Pretty hard to keep him on the hook with an alibi and no physical evidence."

"You believe the bartender?"

"Not necessarily, but I've got no way to prove that he's lying. For all I know, Scott *was* sitting on that barstool, just like he claimed."

"Have any other leads panned out?" I asked.

"Off the record, no, so if you've got anything to add, I'd be happy to hear it." Jack had just revealed the real reason he'd deigned to speak to me. "How did you know we questioned Scott?" he asked.

"I paid him a visit at home about an hour ago."

Jack leaned back in his chair and looked at me with mild interest. "Really? What was that like? I didn't actually go there myself. I sent a patrolman to bring him in."

"Rundown house in the desert. A man named Dale Reber

answered the door. He was armed. I could tell by his appearance that he was a heavy meth user, and I'm sure his paranoia meter is off the charts, which explains the gun. Frankly, I'm surprised anyone even came to the door. They're not cooking, though. I detected no anhydrous and security was way too lax. If you had a warrant, I doubt you'd find meth in any significant quantity. I'd venture their financial situation is somewhat precarious, which means their supply is, too. That can make people do really stupid things."

Jack looked at me appraisingly. "What's your take?"

"At this point, I'm not sure. When I questioned Scott about Pauline Thorpe, he denied all involvement. According to Daisy DiStefano, there doesn't seem to be anything missing from the apartment, but she seems pretty convinced that her ex-husband is somehow involved. She told me she's worried that she was the target, not her grandmother."

"I'm inclined to agree with her," Jack said.

"I think I'll have a chat with that bartender."

"You sure about that? I avoid the Desert Tap if at all possible, and I'm a cop."

I stood. "What can I say, Jack? I'm in dire need of some excitement."

He slid a business card across the desk. "Stay in touch."

I pocketed the card and decided not to acknowledge his request. As far as I was concerned, he could do the waiting this time.

"I'll see you around," I said and showed myself out.

*

The Desert Tap was like something straight out of *Deliverance*. The men all looked related and like they lived in tents. Meth is especially unkind to the fairer sex, and the women who were present looked haggard and old, regardless of their true age. There were plenty of tweakers in San Francisco, but the sheer size of the population meant that the users were spread out. Here, they all seemed to congregate in one place. I doubted there was a single person in the room who wasn't currently enjoying a meth high, which—according to anecdotal evidence—is vastly superior to just about everything, including food, sleep, and sex.

The big draw, in addition to the Pabst Blue Ribbon which was currently on special for happy hour, were the two pool tables, judging by the people playing continuously, burning off their drug-fueled energy.

I couldn't have been any more conspicuous if I'd tried, considering I was the only man in the joint wearing a suit. I also had all my own teeth, which only served to further differentiate myself from the clientele. Heads turned when I sat down at the bar, their eyes narrowing with suspicion.

The bartender looked down his nose at me and sneered. He appeared to be in his early twenties. Full-sleeve tattoos on both arms. Stained wifebeater. Pockmarked skin. Longish hair that probably hadn't been washed in days.

Judge me, loser. *I dare you.*

"What do you want?" he asked.

"Give me a beer."

Silently, he poured PBR into a visibly dirty glass and waited for me to pay. I pulled a five-dollar bill from my wallet and laid it on the bar.

"Are you Chase Arroway?" I asked, taking a drink and hoping I didn't contract anything that couldn't be cured with a round of strong antibiotics. Inwardly, I grimaced; I hadn't tasted beer that bad since quarter-draw night in college.

"Who wants to know?" he asked.

"I do."

"Who are you?"

"Brooks McClain."

"What do you want?"

"I want to ask you a few questions."

"You a cop?"

Wow. Twice in one day. Must be the tie. "I'm a reporter."

He snorted. "That's worse than a cop. You ask questions, but you got no power. Only thing worse than a reporter is a lawyer."

"Nice to know my place in the hierarchy."

He looked confused. "The what?"

"Never mind." I pushed the beer away. "I've been told you corroborated Scott DiStefano's claim that he was here on the evening of September fourteenth."

"Huh?"

I felt the beginning of a headache. "That means that when the police asked you if Scott had been here, you said yes."

"Yeah. So?"

"Well, was he actually here at that time?"

"Yeah. He was."

"Do you remember what time he showed up? What time he left?"

"Look. I told the cops he was here because he was. I'm not sure of the exact times. I'm not his babysitter. He was here for at least an hour in the early evening. That's all I can tell you." He turned away to help another customer and then moved to the other end of the bar where he struck up a conversation with an old man playing video poker.

Scott's alibi wasn't airtight, but it was probably strong enough to prohibit further questioning unless the police were willing to arrest him on suspicion of murder, and I doubted they had enough evidence to do it.

"I know where the garage sale is," a voice said beside me.

I turned to see who had slid onto the stool, recoiling when I got a good look at him. His age was indeterminable, somewhere between thirty and sixty. He'd been badly burned on his face and hands; his fingers were rounded stumps. I wondered how close he'd been to the meth lab when it blew.

"Jesus," I said. "Where'd you come from?"

"I know where the garage sale is," he repeated.

Garage sale? "Yeah, I don't know what that is," I said. "And I'm not looking for it."

He leaned back his head and laughed, a horrible cackling sound.

"Stop it," I said.

He picked up my glass with his stubby, scarred fingers and drained it. "For twenty bucks and a pack of cigarettes, I'll tell you." The grin he gave me was wide, toothless, and horrifying. The stuff nightmares were made of.

I stood. "Sounds like a bargain, but like I said, I'm not looking for the garage sale."

Suddenly his eyes went cold and he pulled a short, rusty knife from his pocket with more speed than I would have thought possible considering the condition of his hands. He jabbed it at me, narrowly missing my torso, and not one person in the bar stopped what they were doing. I reached out and grabbed his wrist, squeezing until the knife clattered onto the bar. His strength was surprising. Feeling unnerved, I walked backward toward the door so he wouldn't have the opportunity to stab me from behind.

Outside, I squinted as my eyes adjusted to the bright sunlight. One glance at my watch told me it was only four thirty in the afternoon. It didn't matter, because I was officially done with this day. When I reached my Jeep, I started the engine but didn't pull out of the small lot behind the bar where I'd parked. Curiosity got the better of me, so despite my resolve to leave Jack Quick hanging for a while, I found myself texting him instead.

What's it mean when a meth head talks about a garage sale?

His answer came thirty seconds later. *You bring in an item and they pay you in meth. Almost everything has been stolen. Mobile. New location every day. Motherfuckers.*

Thanks.

I drove out of the parking lot and headed home, feeling some nostalgia for the freaks of San Francisco.

CHAPTER 15

SCOTT

DALE HAD BEEN thoroughly pissed off after the reporter left, flying into a rage as soon as Scott closed the door.

"This is the second time a cop has shown up at this house looking for you," he said.

"Relax. He wasn't a cop." Scott was two hours into his high and feeling argumentative, but he decided not to feed Dale's paranoia by mentioning that the man was actually a reporter. "He's just some guy nosing around about Pauline Thorpe. I told him the same thing I told the cop: I had nothing to do with it."

Dale started pacing. His hair was thick and curly, and as he walked around the room, he ran his hands through it so that it stood on end, giving him the look of a mad scientist. "You can't keep drawing attention to us. Don't you know they're watching?"

"Who?" Scott asked. He was in the middle of prying apart an old MP3 player, and Dale's ranting was starting to get on his nerves.

"Them," Dale said.

Scott rolled his eyes. "Actually, they're not."

"Maybe they're not watching *you*, DiStefano. But they're

watching me. And if you fuck up my chance with Brandon, I'll kill you."

Dale often threatened Scott and the other occupants of the house with bodily harm, but since he rarely followed through, they mostly tuned him out. But Scott's curiosity had been piqued.

"Who's Brandon?" he asked.

"He's a dealer. Pretty well known, too. The guy who used to sell for him went and got himself arrested, so Brandon needs someone to take over his customers until he gets out of jail."

"And he asked you? Really?" Scott started laughing. A person would have to be out of their mind to willingly enter into any kind of business relationship with Dale. It's true that he knew everyone in town who was holding or using, but he'd never been able to get his own operation off the ground. He could usually find the drugs, but his business skills were nonexistent. He'd rather play mind games: come through with the drugs, tell you it didn't matter when you paid, and then—when whoever he'd gotten the bag from started leaning on him—announce that you had one hour to come up with the money. It made him feel important.

It made Scott want to punch him.

"I don't know why that's so funny," Dale said.

"Of course you don't." Scott might have lost everything, but he still held himself in higher esteem than Dale. He was a lot smarter, too.

Scott had thought about dealing, but none of this middleman shit Dale took part in. Often, when he was on a binge, he'd come up with elaborate business plans about how to build the biggest drug operation in San Bernardino County. But his addiction had grabbed him so fiercely, and so quickly, that he'd never been able to put a plan into action. Never been able to look beyond his next high or set aside enough money to get started. Listening to Dale ramble on, Scott realized he'd finally found the way to make it happen. No more scrambling every few days for drug money. No more scrounging for something to steal and sell.

"So what do you have to do?" Scott asked.

"Brandon's going to front me an ounce when his next shipment comes in. I'll have one week to pay him."

It was a test, and Scott knew exactly what would happen: Dale would skim off the top like he always did and the chance of him selling enough to pay Brandon back was negligible at best. He was more likely to go on a binge to end all binges and would probably end up dead. Scott couldn't care less whether Dale lived or died, but he didn't want this opportunity to slip through his fingers.

"I want in."

Now it was Dale's turn to laugh. "Why the fuck would I give you a piece of this?"

"Because I know how to run a business, and you don't. And if you think selling drugs means you can ignore basic business principles, you're wrong. If you want to make this work, if you want to turn a profit, you need my help. That's what I'm contributing."

"No way," Dale said, but Scott knew the wheels in his head were already turning.

"Suit yourself." Scott shrugged and went back to his MP3 player, engrossed in the intricacy of the tiny pieces.

"You better know what the hell you're talking about," Dale said. "This ain't no restaurant. We aren't peddling little plates of fancy food. I got ideas, too. I know people."

Scott set the MP3 player down. "For once just shut up and listen," he said. "This is what we're going to do."

CHAPTER 16

DAISY

I DISCOVERED I WAS different when I was four years old. My preschool teacher organized a tea and we spent one whole day in the classroom making invitations. I was so excited that I used extra glitter on mine. I loved my preschool teacher and my classmates, and couldn't wait for my grandmother to sit beside me while we sipped lemonade and ate cookies. I wore a special dress and my grandmother rolled my long hair onto sponge curlers the night before so that it hung in perfect spirals down my back. When the teacher told us our guests had arrived and would be joining us in a minute, I beamed with pride. I couldn't wait to show my grandmother the special placemat I'd made for her and the place card at her seat, the one on which I'd drawn a bunny rabbit.

But when everyone filed in, no one referred to their guest as Grammy the way I did. They called them Mommy, Mama, or Mom.

"What do those words mean?" I asked my grandmother.

"A Mommy is someone who gave birth to you or adopted you," she said.

"You didn't do those things?" I asked, not really sure what either of them meant.

"No," she said. "But I love you as if I had."

By the time I was in second grade, I learned not to say the word *Grammy* in front of my classmates. Sometimes I would even refer to my grandmother as my mother so as not to attract unwanted attention. Every once in a while one of the girls or boys would make fun of my grandmother when she came to pick me up, asking me why her hair was gray or why she had wrinkles on her face. I would see her walking slowly up the sidewalk toward me, wearing a big smile, and I'd feel like crying although I really didn't understand why. She was only sixty-two then, which doesn't seem so old to me now. But when you're eight, it seems ancient.

My grandmother finally told me what had happened to my parents and sister when I was ten. She said they had died on a hot and windy September day. The Santa Ana winds had been blowing and a Red Flag warning was issued late that afternoon. After dinner, my parents dropped me off at my grandmother's apartment and took my two-and-a-half-year-old sister Danielle out for ice cream. I was six months old at the time and my parents wanted to take Danielle on an outing alone so they could shower her with some of the attention that had recently been diverted my way.

A man who had been gambling and drinking all day in Las Vegas had been on his way home. He'd taken the exit ramp off the interstate and had executed a U-turn and tried to reenter using the same ramp. He hit my family's car head-on. There were no survivors at the scene.

When I tell people this story, they look at me in shock while they wait for me to tear up or break down. There's an awkward silence when I do neither, and I've learned that the best way to handle it is to change the subject quickly and move on. It's not that I don't possess the capacity to exhibit strong emotions, because I do. It's just that I was so young when it happened. It's horrible, I know that, but the tragedy exists in a vacuum in which I have no frame of reference. When I grieve, it's not because I miss my parents and sister. It's because I never got the chance to know them at all. The only time I ever really lost it was in college. For some reason, seeing all those couples on Parents' Weekend while my grandmother stood off to the side alone brought me to tears. I started sobbing when she hugged me, not caring by that time who witnessed it or what they thought.

When I married Scott and we had Elliott, I swore I would give him the family I never had, but when that hadn't worked out, Elliott and I had gone straight back to square one. My son would be the one without two parents on Parents' Day. The child who has no dad to make a card for on Father's Day.

I held out hope that someday I could break the cycle.

*

At ten o'clock on Saturday morning, I stood in line and greeted guests as they filed by my grandmother's casket. I had spent every penny of the life-insurance policy on the funeral and burial plot, and for a private luncheon in one of the reception rooms at the funeral home after we returned from the cemetery. There were daffodils on the altar and a large spray of them covering the casket.

They had dressed my grandmother in her blue suit. Applied a dusting of peach to her cheeks and styled her hair. Before they closed the casket, I slipped Elliott's drawing inside.

"You did a wonderful job raising me, and I'm going to miss you terribly," I whispered. "Elliott and I love you so much."

In the future, when I tell people my family history, this is the part where I'll break down and cry.

The turnout was small, which was to be expected when you'd outlived almost everyone. A few of my friends and fellow nurses attended, and so did several of my grandmother's friends, including Margaret Parker, who had ridden to the funeral home with Elliott and me, and two other ladies who lived in our building. They sniffled their way through the service and the scent of their perfume clung to me after numerous hugs, cloying yet comforting.

When most of the guests had gone and it was just Pam, Shane, and me, I had one last good cry. I wanted to get it all out of my system before I picked up Elliott at Kayla's. Afterward, I dried my eyes and took a deep breath, feeling bone-tired and weary. Onward, I told myself.

Right before the funeral, Pam had given me the greatest news I'd received in a long time.

"Elliott's got a spot at the same daycare our baby's going to be attending," she said.

"How did you pull that off?" I asked. In the few spare moments I'd had between packing and finalizing the funeral arrangements, I'd called a list of daycares. Any center with a decent reputation was not only full but also had a waiting list. Thanks to a tip from a friend about an opening, Pam had secured a spot at an in-home daycare months ago, which is what I really wanted for Elliott because I worried that a large center would overwhelm him. The woman who ran it was a former teacher who had decided to open a daycare in her home when she had her first child. There would only be four children total.

"Don't get too excited," she said. "I'm giving you my spot, but only until the baby comes. With a little over three months until my due date and another twelve weeks for maternity leave, you've got about six months to find a place for him somewhere else." Pam looked worried. "She can't do weekends, Daisy. She can keep Elliott until you get off work—she'll feed him dinner and give him a bath and his medicine so that he's ready for bed when you pick him up—but weekends are for her family."

I wouldn't be able to pick up any extra weekend shifts like I often did, but I didn't mind. Knowing I had someone trustworthy to watch Elliott was the only thing that mattered.

"I completely understand," I said, throwing my arms around Pam as the relief at having one more of my problems solved washed over me. "I don't know what I would do without you and Shane."

There were times when I felt like the drama that seemed to follow in my wake was a drain on the friendship. Pam and Shane had helped me move almost everything I owned the night I left Scott—under cover of darkness and with little advance notice, no less—and Pam had provided a literal shoulder to cry on while I was going through the divorce. I had tried to find ways over the past year to give back to them, whether it was a homemade meal delivered at the end of the day so they wouldn't have to cook or looking in on Shane's mom every day for a week after she had back surgery. If I spotted something at the mall I thought Pam would like, I bought it, and every time I made cookies for Elliott, I doubled the batch so I could bring some to Shane. But in the past week I couldn't help but feel I'd depleted every bit of the goodwill I'd tried to replenish. I hated that I was once again taking more than I was giving.

Pam hugged me tight. "Shane and I have a lot more family than you do. We have people to call on when we need help. You don't have anyone, Daisy. We know that. Besides, when this baby comes, we're going to need someone to watch it so Shane and I can have a date night every once in a while. I'm going to need your expert advice the first time the baby gets sick and I'm freaking out. And don't be surprised if Shane calls you someday because I'm not home and the baby has had one of those giant shitty-diaper blowouts. You know how delicate his gag reflex is," she said, laughing. "So you'll pay us back eventually."

I wiped my tears and smiled. "I love you, Pam. You and Shane are my family."

She hugged me again and said, "I love you too, Daisy."

CHAPTER 17

BROOKS

I KNOCKED ON THE door of Daisy's new apartment. There were footsteps followed by a delay, which I assumed was her looking through the peephole. The metallic scrape of a chain sliding back soon followed and she opened the door.

"Hi," she said. Her smile seemed genuine, as if she was happy to see me.

"Hi. I was in the neighborhood, so I thought I'd drop by." I didn't tell her that when I was on the job I almost always dropped by without calling. I had a better chance of a witness talking to me if I showed up at their doorstep; calling first made it easier for them to find a reason to say no. Not that Daisy had any reason not to talk to me, but after so many years it had become a habit.

"Sure. Come on in." She closed the door behind me, clicked the deadbolt, and slid the chain into place.

"I'm glad to see the safety chain on the door," I said.

"I installed it yesterday."

"Really? I'm impressed."

She waved off my compliment. "Don't be. It wasn't that hard."

"I hope I'm not interrupting anything."

"It's okay. We just finished eating lunch, so this is a good time."

Elliott walked into the room then.

"Hey, sweetie," Daisy said. "This is Brooks. He came by to talk to Mama."

He was a cute kid. Blond like his parents. Little bluish-gray plastic-rimmed glasses.

"Hi," I said.

"Hi," he whispered in that shy way kids have around someone they don't know well.

My experience with kids was somewhat limited, and I had no idea what to say to him. He appeared to be clutching something. "What's in your hand?" I asked.

"My army guy." He opened his palm but then closed it right away, as if he was worried I might take it from him.

"Is that your favorite toy?"

Elliott nodded. "He keeped me safe."

"Would you like to color in your coloring book while I talk to Brooks?" Daisy asked.

"Okay."

"Which one?"

"*Wion King.*"

Daisy set down Elliott's coloring book and a box of crayons on the coffee table in the living room. He began pulling them out of the box and lining them up next to the coloring book.

Daisy opened the book and pointed to a picture of a lion with two cubs. "I would love it if you could color this one for me."

He pushed his glasses up higher on the bridge of his nose. "Okay, Mama. I will do it."

"Thanks, buddy."

When Daisy returned, she said in a low voice, "He was

clutching that toy the night my grandmother died. The paramedics could hardly pry it out of his hands."

"He must have formed quite an attachment to it," I said.

"Yes. I don't dare take it away. It's obviously a comfort to him."

"It certainly looks that way. When do you go back to work?"

"Tomorrow. It's also Elliott's first day with his new babysitter. I'm nervous," she said. "He's never been in daycare before. He has asthma, so if he catches a cold, it could trigger a full-blown attack. He's probably going to get sick a lot at first, but hopefully his immune system will catch up eventually…" Her voice trailed off as if she was imagining all the potential illnesses he might come down with. "I'm sorry, you didn't come here to talk about that."

"It's okay. I don't mind," I said, hoping she could hear the sincerity in my voice. "I can understand why you'd be apprehensive."

She glanced at Elliott, who was engrossed in his coloring book in the living room. "We can sit at the kitchen table."

I pulled out a chair and sat down across from her. "I was able to have a brief conversation with your ex-husband."

"Really?" She looked surprised, which made me wonder if she'd doubted me when I told her I'd speak to Scott. Suddenly I wanted her to know I was the kind of man who kept his word, who followed through on things.

"He was at the address you gave me. The house is owned by someone named Dale Reber. Does that name ring any bells?"

"No. But I don't know the names of any of the men Scott associates with these days, and I don't want to." She looked puzzled. "I tried to have Scott served with papers at that address a few months ago. The person who answered the door said he didn't live there anymore."

"What kind of papers?"

"I was attempting to terminate his parental rights."

"Sounds like he might not have wanted to sign them."

"He didn't want to sign the divorce papers either. God knows he can probably spot a process server from a mile away by now."

"Has Scott ever harmed Elliott? Neglected him?"

She looked absolutely horrified at the thought. "No, but I never left Elliott alone with Scott after I discovered he was using. We have joint custody, but according to the custody agreement, all visits are to take place at my residence when either I or my grandmother would be here. I told Scott he had to come alone, and if he showed up high he'd have to leave."

"Did he comply?"

"He never came. Not even once. Thankfully Elliott was too young to really understand what was going on. I don't think he would even recognize Scott at this point. It's been a little over six months since our divorce became final and longer than that since Elliott has had any contact with his dad."

"Why do you want to terminate his rights?"

"If he can't be bothered to be a part of Elliott's life, then I want to be the only one who can make decisions on behalf of our son. And if something were to happen to me, I don't ever want Scott to have Elliott."

"Does Elliott have a guardian?"

"My best friend Pam and her husband Shane are Elliott's godparents. I've also appointed them his legal guardians. But I doubt the courts will let them have Elliott if Scott still has parental rights. I'll call my attorney and tell him to try to serve Scott with the papers again. But even if they're successful this time, it's no guarantee Scott will sign them."

"Does he pay child support?"

She shook her head. "No, he never has. Scott loves Elliott, I do believe that. And in some strange, twisted way, he still thinks he can be a good parent. But he never *shows* me that he can." She paused and looked away. "How did he look?"

"Not good. He's underweight. His teeth are starting to rot."

She was quiet for a moment, like she was processing what I'd said. "Has anyone close to you ever had a drug addiction?"

"No."

"When Scott's abuse turned into full-fledged addiction, Elliott and I became the second and third most important things to him. Addicts don't care about anything but their next fix. Meth is particularly insidious. I picture it as this malevolent mist that surrounds a person until it seeps inside them, replacing everything they love. Their moral code ceases to exist because all they care about is feeding their addiction."

I looked at Daisy, thinking of everything her ex-husband had given up. I couldn't wrap my mind around a drug being more important than a man's wife and child, especially *this* woman and *this* child. It seemed unfathomable to me, yet I knew what she said was true.

"I'm sorry," I said.

"It happens," she said. "But it's heartbreaking to me that Elliott won't grow up knowing his father."

"Do you have any contact with Scott's family? I would think they'd want to see Elliott."

"His parents moved to Florida when they retired. His mom died about a year ago, but his dad is still alive. When I first discovered Scott was using drugs, I called them to ask for their help in getting Scott clean. I thought maybe Scott would listen to his parents."

"Were they able to help?"

"They didn't believe me. They said I must be mistaken. Their son would never do drugs. And they were right: the son they knew wouldn't. But they didn't watch it happen like I did. By the time they finally figured out that what I'd told them was true, it was too late. Then Scott's mom died and I think his dad just wiped his hands of everything, including Elliott and me."

"Have you thought about what you're going to do next?"

"I don't want to raise Elliott here. I wouldn't have left my grandmother, but I knew that someday, when she was gone, I'd take Elliott and we would go. Unfortunately, Scott left a financial mess in his wake. I found out that he'd opened a couple of credit cards in both of our names, forged my signature, and run the balances up until he hit the credit limit. He drained our accounts—we'd been saving for a down payment on a house—and I was humiliated one day when I tried to buy groceries on my way home from work and my debit card was declined. I opened new accounts in my own name and didn't tell Scott."

She sighed and looked away, and as much as I wanted her to keep talking, I knew I might make more headway if I kept quiet.

A moment later, she continued. "Anyway, I'm paying off the balances of those credit cards. I track the payments on a spreadsheet, and I know exactly how long it will take me to pay it off. I have excellent credit, and I can't allow anything to jeopardize that because I'll need a good credit rating someday when I go to buy a house. My grandmother wouldn't allow me to pay rent or give her any money for watching Elliott, no matter how much I protested. She knew what Scott had done, and that was her way of helping. I used to pick up all the extra weekend shifts I could, but I won't be able to continue doing that because I have no one to watch Elliott. I have rent and daycare to pay now, too. In light of what's happened, it might be smarter to leave as soon as I can, but I have a good job and I don't want the uncertainty of trying to find another one, plus the expense of relocating and starting over. Not until I have Scott's debt paid off. But once I do, we'll go. I'll be happy to leave this town behind." She looked at me as if she was embarrassed. "Once again, I'm telling you way more than you probably wanted to know."

I admired her resolve. Installing a safety chain was probably a walk in the park compared to what she'd been dealing with. "I don't mind," I said. "You seem to have a really solid plan."

"Detective Quick told me they questioned Scott but don't consider him a suspect at this point."

"He claims he was in a bar at the time of your grandmother's murder. His alibi seems to have checked out."

"So what happens next?"

That was a hard question to answer. Unless someone made progress with the case, not much would be happening at all. "Hopefully the police will have a lead that pans out. Maybe a witness will come forward or someone will call the hotline. Has Elliott shared anything else with you? Something he might have heard while he was hiding under the bed?"

"No, and I haven't pushed him."

"That's probably a good idea. I imagine he'll talk if he feels like it." I glanced at my watch. "I need to get going." I stood and Daisy followed me toward the door. "Don't hesitate to call the police for any reason. Pay close attention to your surroundings. Keep your door locked. Don't ever open it without the chain on." I paused, once again struck by how alone she seemed. Was anyone watching out for her? "Listen, I don't mean for this to sound as sexist as it's going to, but is there a guy around?"

Rarely did I ask such a personal question, especially when the answer was absolutely *none* of my business.

And I'll admit to being more than just professionally curious as I waited for her answer.

"There was, but not anymore," she said. "It's just Elliott and me. We'll be okay. When someone knocks, I look through the peephole. If I don't recognize the person, I leave the chain on when I open the door. I also bought a gun."

She said that last part with such nonchalance that it took me a second to process it.

"*You what?*" I probably said it with a little more force than I should have.

She looked taken aback. "Shane helped me pick it out."

I was speechless. "I'm sorry, but you don't—"

"Look like the type of person who would own a gun?"

It was hard to argue with that statement when it was *exactly* what I was going to say. "Yes."

"I didn't buy the gun because I wanted to. Frankly, I would rather not own one. They scare me," she said. "But I bought one anyway because the thought of looking something evil right in the eye and knowing that I'm more than likely going to come out on the losing end of it terrifies me. The fear that I'll be assaulted, or raped and left for dead, or worse yet, that someone will try to harm my child, is the reason I have this gun. That's the type I am."

I saw her then, really saw her. Five foot seven, maybe, but small-boned. She was wearing a fitted V-neck T-shirt that emphasized her slight build. I could see the prominent ridge of her collarbone and the deep hollow at the base of her throat that I suddenly couldn't stop looking at. She'd be no match for anyone. If she wanted a gun, I was hardly in a position to tell her she couldn't have one.

"I'm sorry," I said. "I was out of line. It's really none of my business what you do."

"It's okay. Pam reacted the same way you did. But I'm doing everything I can to be a responsible gun owner. I've signed up for the safety class so I can learn how to handle the gun. How to shoot it. I'll apply for the permit as soon as I have my certificate. I'll go to the shooting range, and I'll practice."

Taking her to the shooting range was something I could do to help her. It would also give me a chance to spend time with her, which was something that was becoming more appealing by the minute. I could feel the boundary between witness and reporter starting to blur, but I really didn't care. It had been a while since a woman had sparked my interest the way Daisy had. "You don't have to justify anything to me. It sounds like you're doing everything right," I said. "I'll let you know if I hear anything on the case."

"I would really appreciate that."

Elliott put down his coloring book and ambled across the room.

Daisy lifted him into her arms. "You look tired, buddy. Are you ready for your nap?"

"I'm not tired," Elliott said, yawning and rubbing his eyes.

"Oh, my mistake," Daisy said, smiling at him. "I think we'll try a nap anyway, just in case." She looked at me. "Thanks for stopping by."

"It was no problem. I'll see you soon."

As I stepped into the hallway she said, "Brooks?"

I turned around. "Yes?"

"Maybe I'm reading this wrong, but you seem to genuinely care about my safety, and I want you to know that I appreciate it. I need all the help I can get."

I met her gaze and held it for a moment. "You aren't reading it wrong at all. Take care, Daisy."

She smiled and it illuminated her face, making every feature even prettier. She closed the door, and I made my way down the hall.

It was true that I cared about Daisy's safety. Maybe Scott DiStefano had never abused or neglected Elliott, but Daisy's decision to arm herself made me wonder what he'd done to *her*.

CHAPTER 18

DAISY

THE CALIFORNIA HANDGUN-SAFETY course was held in a small room at the community center. There were seventeen of us all together, twelve men and five women. There was a girl who barely looked old enough to attend the class, although I knew that wasn't the case because you had to be twenty-one to apply for a permit to carry a gun. Her black yoga pants said Pink! across the butt and her T-shirt had Hello Kitty on the front. Another woman was at the other end of the spectrum; I'd have guessed her age as late sixties. Her hair was gray and she was wearing a housecoat and a pair of Nikes. The remaining two women obviously knew each other because they took seats close together and began conversing. Both wore wedding rings.

The male representation seemed especially disparate, which surprised me because I'd expected them to all look the same: young and brash, full of false bravado and itchy trigger fingers. I couldn't have been more wrong. There was a man in the corner wearing a three-piece suit who would have fit in perfectly down at the bank. The man beside him wore wire-rimmed glasses and a heavily starched button-down shirt and jeans. He lined up his pencils and a notebook, then folded his hands in his lap and waited patiently for the class to start. The man two rows back wore pressed khakis and a polo shirt; he looked a lot like the accountant who does my taxes. There were a few younger men, and the room probably boasted more than the average amount of ink per the number of people who had showed up for class, but the tattoos seemed to be of the trendy variety more than anything. I couldn't help but wonder what they all thought when they looked at me. Maybe they assumed I'd entered the room by mistake and was really looking for the cake-decorating class down the hall.

I pulled a notebook out of my purse and stifled a yawn with the back of my hand. I'd only been back to work for two shifts, and while I was grateful for the support of my coworkers, the sheer volume of questions I'd fielded had been exhausting. Maybe I still hadn't caught up on my sleep, because my shifts felt longer, more grueling. I wanted to be at home, cuddling on the couch with Elliott, not spending the evening of my day off trying to cram more information into my already overtaxed brain. And there would be additional hours of classroom and shooting instruction to complete before I would be able to apply for my permit to carry a concealed weapon. But I knew how important this was, so I took a drink of the iced tea I'd brought and hoped the caffeine would help me power through.

At least the transition to daycare had gone more smoothly than I'd expected. There had been a few tears (mine), but Elliott had handled the drop-off with an ease that surprised me. Celine, the woman who operated the daycare, encouraged me to call on my breaks to check in, which I would have done anyway. She gave me a full report when I picked up Elliott at the end of my shift. There was another little boy who was close to Elliott's age, and Celine said he and Elliott had bonded instantly. They must have played hard because Elliott fell asleep in the car on the way home and slept straight through until morning. "Did you like going to the babysitter?" I'd asked him at breakfast the next day.

"Yes," he said. "Want to play again."

Everything seemed to be looking up, and I felt empowered because I was taking steps to protect myself and Elliott. In addition to gun safety, the course description promised to cover basic self-defense. The time I spent here would be well worth it.

Tonight's session was classroom instruction only. I would also take a hands-on class at a range where I would learn how to safely handle and fire a gun.

My gun.

The one which now resided in the fingerprint safe next to my bed. The only way it would open was if I placed my fingers on the sensor.

"What is that, Mama?" Elliott had asked when he spotted it.

"Just a place for me to store important things," I'd told him.

The instructor asked everyone to take their seats and introduced himself. "My name is Steve."

He looked to be in his early forties, and as he gave us his bio, his relaxed demeanor put me at ease right away. He gave us a handout which listed the topics we would cover during the four-hour class, everything from the storage of firearms to the laws pertaining to carrying one.

"It is up to you to know the laws of the state you're in," he said. "Saying you aren't aware of them is not a valid excuse. But because we're in California, those are the gun laws we'll learn about today."

Steve clicked on the first slide of the PowerPoint presentation and proceeded to go over the general rules of firearm safety. "The two major causes of gun accidents are ignorance and carelessness," he said. "Always treat all guns as if they are loaded. Keep your finger off the trigger until you are ready to use the gun. Don't point a gun at anything you aren't willing to destroy. Know what you are shooting at and what is behind it."

Next Steve talked about the storage of firearms and how both safety and accessibility needed to be considered. Of course I wanted to store the gun in the safest way possible so that there was no way Elliott would ever see it, let alone pick it up. But what Steve said about accessibility really hit home with me. If I wasn't willing to store the gun where I could get to it quickly, there was really no reason to have it in the first place.

When Steve talked about choosing a gun, he stressed that it needed to be reliable and no more powerful than we felt we could handle. He told us we would perform better under stress if we were comfortable with the gun we chose. Shane had helped me select a gun that fit my grip, with a recoil he thought I could handle. I wasn't comfortable yet, but I would be.

After a short break, Steve showed us several options for holsters. Although I understood their importance, I wasn't sure I wanted to wear one. I worried that it would feel odd, unnatural. My gun would always be locked in the gun safe when I was at home. I had my own locker at work, with a padlock, and my gun would remain there during my shift. However, I wanted it with me when I walked into, or out of, work. I raised my hand.

"What about carrying the gun in your purse?" I asked. That's where I'd planned on putting mine when I wasn't at home or work.

"I really don't recommend that you do that," Steve said, "and I urge you to consider a holster. But if keeping the gun in your purse means you'll carry it, then I'd rather you do it your way. Just keep an open mind. You may find that you actually prefer to wear a holster."

"I'm going to carry my 9mm in this," a female voice said, and I turned around. It was Hello Kitty girl. She held up her purse. "See the side pocket? It's got a compartment designed specifically for a gun. I bought it online. But I have a holster, too. It's tucked beneath the underwire of my bra. I keep my Glock in it."

Who is this girl?

Maybe I wasn't the only one wondering, because every head had turned toward her.

"I was assaulted a month ago. It won't happen again."

She said it with such conviction that the room remained silent for a moment as the meaning of her words sank in. I'm fairly certain everyone could guess the type of assault she had probably endured. Then the clapping started, and it was the gray-haired older lady in the housecoat who put her hands together first. I joined in.

When the noise died down Steve said, "Okay, okay. I understand how keeping the gun in your purse might appeal to some of you. But let me go on record as saying I'd prefer you wear a holster."

Despite what Steve said, I knew right then I'd buy the purse. It wasn't that I didn't believe him, or that I was trying to go against his advice. But knowing the gun was safely stored in my purse seemed like the right choice for me. And Steve had said if we were comfortable we'd be more confident.

We took another short break, and after I used the restroom and returned to my seat, Steve began explaining our rights when it came to defending ourselves by using force.

"There are four things you need to think about," he said. "First of all, is the person a threat to you? If they're unarmed, there is considerably less danger than if they have a weapon of some sort. Two, are they close enough to you to do harm? If there's a guy who looks threatening but he's standing way down at the end of the street, don't go down there." Steve looked around the room, making eye contact with each of us. "Take a different route. Three, are you in immediate danger? It doesn't count if there is *potential* danger.

You need to have reasonable fear that your life is in danger or that you will suffer great bodily harm. And lastly"—he leaned forward—"there has to be no other safe option. If all four of these elements are present, you are justified in using your weapon in self-defense."

It was a lot to consider. Could I make the decision to defend myself quickly and under great stress?

We spent the last part of the class period talking about general self-defense and awareness, and I picked up several things that seemed helpful. I learned how important it was to recognize, as early as I could, the presence of danger. I needed to be aware of my surroundings at all times.

"As a gun owner, you are not carrying a firearm so that you can be careless in other aspects of your safety," Steve said. "A gun is your last resort, not your first. There's one more thing I want to mention. If an assailant wants to move you to another location, do not go with him. Do not get in his vehicle. Do not go with him to an abandoned area. Do not go to his house. He may promise that if you come quietly, he won't hurt you. But if he wants to move you, it's because he wants to do something to you that he can't in your current location, and I guarantee you it will be worse than what he's already doing. Run if you can."

By the end of the class, I'd gained new respect and understanding for the concept of self-defense. Even so, as I waited in line for Steve to sign the form verifying that I'd completed the first four hours of classroom instruction, it was my resolute hope that I'd never find myself in a situation where I'd have to employ any of the knowledge I'd gained.

But I thought about the girl in the Hello Kitty T-shirt and told myself that if my life, or Elliott's life, was ever in danger, I would.

CHAPTER 19

BROOKS

I'D BEEN EATING breakfast with my mom every day since I'd been home, but when I went in a few mornings later to see if she was ready to go downstairs, she told me she didn't want to eat.

"You have to eat, Mom. You know how important it is."

"I can't," she said.

"I'll be right back."

She didn't answer me.

My dad was in the kitchen, leaning up against the counter and staring out the window while he drank a cup of coffee.

"What's going on with Mom? She said she can't eat breakfast."

He turned around. His expression was grim, and I braced myself. "She's having a lot of trouble swallowing. She's afraid she'll choke. I am, too. She could aspirate food into her lungs, which would put her at risk for developing pneumonia. I called the doctor. They want to move forward with a feeding tube while she still has the ability to withstand the procedure."

Relieved that the news wasn't as bad as I'd thought it would be, I said, "So the feeding tube is a good thing. It'll help her get enough to eat, safely."

"Yes. She'll be more comfortable, and there's nothing I want more for her."

"Then why do you seem upset?"

My dad set down his coffee cup. "She may ask at some point that we stop feeding her altogether. When her condition started to deteriorate, I made a promise to her that I would honor her wishes, even if what she wanted meant that she'd die. I agreed. How could I not?" He looked away. "The hospital bed will be here tomorrow. I hired a nurse to start coming every day, too. She can administer medicine, painkillers… whatever it takes to keep your mom comfortable."

"Of course," I said. "Whatever she needs."

"The feeding tube will be placed sometime this week. It's a surgical procedure, so she'll be in the hospital for a day or two." He blew out a breath. "I feel so powerless. There's absolutely nothing I can do to help her."

"You *are* helping her. You're doing everything you can. Take a break. Please. I'll go sit with her for a while before I head in to work."

He nodded, looking utterly defeated.

My mom's eyes were closed when I walked back into the bedroom. "Mom?"

"I'm not sleeping, Brooks. I'm just resting my eyes. Tell me how things are going. How is your job?" Her speech seemed like it was deteriorating a little more every day; it was hard to understand some of her words.

"It's going fine. I'm not as busy as I was in San Francisco." What I told her was true. I'd noticed a significant decrease in my professional stress level. Paul had stopped by my desk to let me know how happy he was with my work, and my coworkers couldn't have been easier to work with. It had taken moving from the *Chronicle* to the *Desert News* to see just how crazy my daily life had become in the past eleven years. The long hours I'd spent chasing stories. My complete and total submersion in work.

"Can you turn on the TV?" she asked.

"Sure." I picked up the remote from the nightstand and clicked it on. A little boy, two or three years of age, was chasing a dog. A woman off-screen was laughing and cheering him on, and I recognized my mother's voice at about the same time I realized the little boy chasing the dog was me. My dad had taken all our old home movies somewhere so that they could be transferred onto DVDs. My mom must have been slowly making her way through them because there was a stack of DVD cases on the nightstand and another small stack on the floor next to the bed. Suddenly, my mom's image filled the screen, and she beckoned me to come closer. I stopped chasing the dog and ran into her arms. She'd been in her late twenties then, and absolutely beautiful.

"How old are you?" she asked me.

I held up six fingers and said, "Free!"

She laughed and said, "You're not three. You're two. But you'll be three next week."

We watched in silence as I kissed her and ran after the dog again. At one point I sat down in the yard, threw my arms around the dog, and let it lick my face.

"Do you remember any of this?" my mom asked.

"No. Is that the dog you and Dad got when you were dating? Rex?"

"Yes. He died shortly after this was taken. Cancer. It broke my heart. Yours, too. You couldn't understand where he'd gone. Your dad brought these movies up from the basement for me. They make me so happy. I feel like I get to experience your childhood all over again."

My mom had seemed to accept the fact that it would be a while—if ever—before she could expect any grandchildren from me.

Now it was too late.

My ex-wife and I had been waiting for things to slow down a little before we started a family. Actually, Lisa was the one who had done all the waiting. I was mostly oblivious. I should have needed earplugs to drown out the sound of her ticking clock, but somehow I'd missed it. This was especially troubling considering I am, by virtue of my profession, the type of man who notices things.

The thing is, my job would never have slowed down. There was constant pressure to get content online. To decide which stories I'd expand upon for the next day's print edition. The interviews to complete for those stories. My work hours were brutal, and I was essentially on call twenty-four hours a day, seven days a week. The news waits for no one. I'd thrived on the pressure, the thrill of being the first one to get the story. But the whole time I was chasing the news, I'd completely missed the fact that Lisa was waiting patiently at home to make some news of our own. My mom would have loved having a grandchild to videotape, new memories to capture on film and add to the collection.

When the DVD ended, I ejected it and grabbed the next one from the top of the stack. My mom's eyes were closed when I turned around.

"I put a new disc in," I said. When she didn't respond, I thought she might have actually fallen asleep this time.

But then she opened her eyes and said, "Dying is the hardest thing I've ever had to do."

How in the hell are you supposed to respond to something like that?

I had no idea if it was right or wrong, but I reached out and took her hand. "I know, Mom," I said, squeezing it gently. "I know."

CHAPTER 20

DAISY

I WAS LOADING THE dishwasher when someone knocked on the door. The sound still filled me with anxiety, but after hesitating for a moment, I quietly approached the door and peered through the peephole. My insides fluttered a bit when I saw Brooks standing there.

I opened the door. "Hi."

"Hi," he said. "I hope I'm not interrupting."

"No, it's fine." I would have definitely pegged him as the call-ahead type, but once again he'd shown up unexpectedly. "Come on in."

I barely remembered talking to Brooks the first time I'd met him, down at the police station the night my grandmother was killed. Our second conversation hadn't been very memorable either. I'd been so preoccupied with the move and planning the funeral that I hadn't paid him much attention.

It was only during his last visit that I'd noticed how incredibly attractive he was.

He was tall, six two or three, and his presence filled the room. He appeared desperately serious most of the time, but his brown eyes were warm and inviting. His dark hair was short on the sides and back but slightly longer on top, which made it ideally suited for a woman to run her hands through it. Maybe it was because he was always dressed in a suit and tie, but there was something very dashing and chivalrous about Brooks that I found quite appealing. He seemed like the kind of man who would hold the door, an umbrella, a woman's hand. When I combined this with the fact that Brooks had admitted to caring about my safety, I was pretty much a goner.

It was not as easy to be around him now. I was more aware of my appearance, the things I said. If I'd known he was coming that day, I might have changed out of the tank top and shorts I'd worn to take Elliott to the park, and maybe I would have opted for something different than my standard ponytail. I told myself that this line of thinking was foolish. Brooks was only here because he was trying to do his job and probably couldn't care less about the way I styled my hair or what I was wearing. Even so, it was hard not to lose myself in the fantasy where Brooks charged in on his white horse, kissed me senseless, and slayed all the dragons that might be lurking nearby.

"Would you like something to drink?" I asked.

"Water's fine. Thanks."

Brooks was already sitting on the couch when I returned with two bottles of water.

"Did you hear something about the case?" I asked.

"I spoke to Jack Quick this morning," he said. "The crime lab is still processing the forensic evidence. They'll deliver their findings to him once they're done."

"But they haven't found anything really useful yet, have they? It seems like if they had, Jack would already know about it."

"Not necessarily. The crime lab has a lot of evidence to comb through. It just takes time."

"It's been almost three weeks since my grandmother died. Maybe I've been watching too many crime shows on TV, but I thought things would move faster."

"Murder investigations can drag on for a long time. That doesn't mean they'll never catch the person who did this."

"But in the meantime, whoever did this is still out there."

"Yes."

He didn't say anything else but made no move to leave. I wondered why I'd never seen him around town before. I was pretty sure he was older than me, but certainly I would have remembered running into him.

"Have you always lived in Fenton?" I asked.

"I grew up here, actually," he said. "I left after I finished college. I just… I couldn't imagine staying." He must have realized how that sounded, because the second the words left his mouth, he followed them with, "Not that it's a bad place or anything. It just wasn't for me."

"No need to apologize," I said. "I'm not exactly a huge fan of Fenton, myself. I stayed because of my grandmother. I couldn't see myself leaving her. Then I met Scott and we got married and had Elliott. You know the rest." I took a drink of my water. "Did we go to school together?" Our town had only one district, but I had no recollection of knowing him from school, either.

"I'm thirty-six. I would have already graduated by the time you entered high school."

"So if you don't like Fenton, why did you come back?"

"I actually work for the *Chronicle*, in San Francisco. I took a leave of absence so I could stay with my parents for a while. My mom is sick. She has ALS."

My heart sank. ALS was a devastating diagnosis, for both the individual and their family. "I'm so sorry to hear that. How long has it been since her diagnosis?"

"A little over three years."

If Brooks had come home, it must have meant his mother was entering the end stage of the disease. "Do you have any siblings?" I asked.

He shook his head. "No."

"So you left everything behind and moved here?"

"Well, it's only temporary, so it wasn't that hard to coordinate. Getting my leave approved was the biggest hurdle."

"Do you have a family in San Francisco?" During his last visit I'd noticed he didn't wear a wedding ring, but that didn't necessarily mean anything.

"No. It's just me."

"I'm sure it means everything to your mom to have you here."

"It does," he said. "I'm glad I came." He stood. "I'll let you know if I hear any updates. Please keep me posted if you think of anything I should know. Keep in touch with Jack Quick, too."

I walked him to the door. "I will."

"Where's Elliott?" he asked.

His question made me smile. Not everyone would care enough to ask. "He's asleep. He's almost outgrown his naps, but he's been playing so hard on the days he goes to the babysitter that he's been extra tired lately. We went to the park this morning, too. He was worn out."

"I'm glad everything is going well. You mentioned you were worried about sending him to a sitter."

I couldn't believe he remembered that. "I'm definitely feeling a little more settled now."

"I'll see you later," he said, but I got the sense I wouldn't see Brooks again anytime soon.

Though he'd tried to be encouraging, I knew my grandmother's case was growing colder by the day. There was really no reason for him to stop by unless I could give him something to follow up on or the crime lab suddenly discovered a perfect, overlooked fingerprint that just happened to have a match when they ran it through their databases.

"Good-bye, Brooks." I closed the door behind him and locked it, feeling once again like I was on my own.

CHAPTER 21

DAISY

I DROPPED OFF ELLIOTT at Kayla's and drove to the shooting range to meet Steve. I could have participated in a group class, but I'd paid extra for one-on-one instruction. Handling a gun made me nervous enough; I wasn't sure I wanted anyone watching me until I knew what I was doing.

Steve was waiting for me in front of range number four when I arrived.

"Hi, Steve," I said, reaching out to shake his hand. "Daisy DiStefano."

"Hi, Daisy. Ready to shoot?"

"I think so."

"You don't sound very sure."

"I've never shot a gun before."

"What do you have?" He pointed at my carrying case.

"Beretta Nano."

"Nice," he said. "That's a good choice. Easy to handle. You'll be fine, I promise."

I followed Steve through the doorway and he shut it behind us. He laid a large duffel bag on the table and began removing items: special earmuffs to protect my hearing and safety glasses to protect my eyes.

"This is my Walther P22," Steve said, showing it to me. "It's a gun I like to start people out on. It's ergonomic, small, and easy to shoot. Takes a little bitty bullet. Very little recoil. We'll start with that and then we'll switch to your gun. I'll show you how to load yours, get you ready to shoot it, and familiarize you with the basic techniques. Then I'll get you hitting the target. Don't worry about where you hit or how you shoot right now. This is just to get you comfortable and show you what a gun can do."

"Okay." That sounded easy enough.

"The first thing we're going to do is load the gun." Steve picked up the box of bullets and showed one of them to me. Next he picked up a rectangle-shaped item. "This is the magazine. It holds ten bullets. You pull down on this floating lever and push them in."

"So it's like a Pez dispenser," I said.

Steve laughed. "I've never had anyone say that, but yeah. I guess it is kind of like a Pez dispenser."

Next Steve showed me how to hold the gun with the webbing of my hand pressed up as high as I could against the handle. "Keep your index finger and thumb forward. Then wrap your other hand around. That's good. How does it feel?"

"Surprisingly light."

"Okay. When you're ready, go ahead and squeeze the trigger."

My heart was pounding and my fear embarrassed me. Did all women find this so difficult the first time, or was I just a complete and total wimp? I took a deep breath and squeezed.

Because of the earmuffs, it wasn't as loud as I thought it would be. I didn't feel quite as nervous when I squeezed off the next few shots. I looked at Steve and he motioned for me to go again. I emptied the magazine and used my left hand to take off my ear protection. "How did I do?"

"You did fine," he said. "How did it feel?"

"It felt okay." My confidence had already risen a bit. Now that I'd actually fired the gun, I felt like I had more control of it.

"I want you to do it again."

I emptied the magazine a second time and then looked at the target. My shots were all over the place. "I'm not very good at this."

"You're going to be even worse in a self-defense situation. You'll be under stress and you won't have time to line up anything. Keep the gun close. If you walk around with your arms straight out, they're going to get tired pretty fast. And someone could grab your gun if you let them get too close. Remember, when you're in danger, your first line of defense is your voice. I want you to yell "get back" as loud as you can. It will surprise your attacker and give you a second to prepare. If they keep coming at you and they refuse to stop, you shoot."

I exhaled and said, "Okay."

"Now, let's switch to your gun. The magazine is a bit smaller, so it will only hold six bullets. I'm going to teach you how to rack the slide in order to load the first round into the chamber. Women sometimes worry they won't be strong enough, but this is about technique, not strength."

He was right. It took me several tries, but once I got the hang of it I was able to rack it easily. Steve had me shoot, and each time I emptied the magazine, he watched as I reloaded. By the end of our session, I'd manage to improve my accuracy, and I no longer felt nervous. The gun was a machine, not a snake that would whirl around and strike me.

"You did a good job today," Steve said. "Keep practicing, okay?"

"Thanks. I will."

I left the shooting range feeling emboldened, as if I'd taken control of not only the gun, but also my life.

CHAPTER 22
BROOKS

THE HOSPITAL BED arrived at eight o'clock. I'd been sitting on the couch in the living room since six, watching the local news and checking various websites for weather, state-patrol updates, and breaking news. So far I'd determined that it was sunny and windy, there were no major accidents, and absolutely nothing of interest had taken place overnight.

I was the only one downstairs when the doorbell rang. My dad had spent most of the night trying to calm down my mom. Her breathing had suddenly become worse, which made me worry that the time she had left might be measured in weeks instead of months. There was a part of me that really didn't want to know.

Two deliverymen were standing on the front steps. "We'll need to take this door off to get it inside."

"Sure. Whatever you need to do."

Once they had the door off, one of them said, "Where do you want it?"

"Follow me."

I led them to the dining room, and when they were done setting up everything, I signed on the dotted line and the deliverymen left. My dad joined me a few minutes later. He stopped short when he saw the bed.

"Oh," he said. "I didn't even hear the door."

"They were quick."

He walked around the bed, examining it from every angle. "I guess I should see if your mother would like to move down here now. The nurse is starting today, so maybe it would be best to get your mom situated this morning. Make sure she's comfortable." He stopped walking and placed his hands on the metal rails that bordered the bed on either side. "I can't take care of her by myself anymore, Brooks. I promised her I would, but I can't." His voice caught on the last word.

"It's okay, Dad. She knows that." I wasn't lying. My mom knew exactly what was going on, and she'd never hold my dad to a promise they both knew he couldn't keep, no matter how much he wanted to. The shift in responsibility probably hurt my dad more than it hurt her.

"I have to leave for work," I said.

"Of course. Thanks for letting in the deliverymen."

I slipped my arms into my suit jacket and picked up my laptop. "I'll see you later."

I didn't really have to get to work. But there was no way I could watch my dad help my mom into the bed that everyone knew she was never going to leave until the end.

CHAPTER 23

DAISY

Kayla and I were waiting for the elevator after grabbing lunch in the hospital cafeteria when the doors opened and Brooks stepped out. It threw me for a second because I'd never expected to run into him while I was at work.

"Oh my," Kayla murmured appreciatively when she saw who I was looking at. "Someone you know?"

"Yes. Go ahead. I'll be up in a second."

After Brooks exited the elevator, he'd stood off to the side. He watched me now as I approached him.

"Hi," I said.

"Hi."

"Is it your mom?"

He nodded. "She had a feeding tube inserted today."

"Did everything go okay?"

"It went fine. She's resting now."

"The feeding tube will ease a lot of her discomfort."

"That's what the doctor said."

"What's her name? I'll look in on her before I leave tonight."

"Mary McClain. That's really nice of you. Thanks."

"Sure." I glanced at my watch. "I'd better get back to work." I pushed the button for the elevator.

"Have you taken the gun-safety class yet?" Brooks asked.

"Yes. I've had the shooting instruction, too."

"How was it?"

"It was okay. It went better than I thought it would."

"Are you busy next Tuesday? In the evening?"

I shook my head. "I work a Monday, Wednesday, Friday schedule."

"Would you like to go to the shooting range with me? Around seven?"

There weren't many places I *wouldn't* go with Brooks. "Sure. I could use some more practice."

"I'll swing by and pick you up."

"Okay," I said. "See you then."

That evening, after my shift ended, I knocked quietly on the door of Mary McClain's hospital room.

A man's voice said, "Come in."

I walked into the room and said, "My name is Daisy DiStefano. I spoke to your son earlier today and told him I'd check in on you."

The man rose and extended his hand. "I'm Theo McClain, Mary's husband. It's nice to meet you."

"It's nice to meet you, too." I walked to Mary's bedside. "I'm not one of your nurses, but I'd be happy to get you anything you might need."

Brooks's mother gave me a weak smile but didn't speak.

Theo said, "I think she has everything she needs for now, but thank you. That's very considerate."

The feeding tube was called a Percutaneous Endoscopic Gastrostomy, or PEG. A small, flexible tube would deliver nutrition, hydration, and medication via a hole in Mary's stomach. If she tolerated the tube without any problems, she'd probably be discharged in the morning. Her breathing sounded labored, which was the result of the deterioration of her diaphragm and intercostal muscles. The issue of ventilation support would soon be raised by Mary's doctors, if it hadn't been already.

I dug a piece of paper out of my pocket and handed it to Theo. "Here's my cell number. Please call me if you need anything after you get home. I'd be happy to come by."

"We have a nurse," Theo said. "She comes every day."

"Sounds like you're in good hands then."

"How do you know Brooks?" Theo asked.

"He wrote a story about the murder of my grandmother."

"I'm sorry," Theo said. "I read about that, of course."

"Brooks has been really helpful by keeping me in the loop." I gave Mary's hand a quick squeeze and turned toward Theo. "Please let me know if there's anything I can do for Mary while you're here."

"I will," Theo said. "Good night."

"Good night."

I caught up with Kayla as she was leaving the building and we walked to the parking garage together. "Is there any chance you could babysit Elliott on Tuesday night? At my place?"

"Sure. I'd be happy to watch him. Big plans?"

"I'm going out with the guy we saw earlier. The one from the elevator."

"Lucky you," she said. "If I wasn't already taken, I'd be wildly jealous." Kayla had recently gotten engaged and only had eyes for her fiancé, Brian.

"Don't be jealous. It's not a date. He's taking me to the shooting range."

Kayla was one of the few people at work who knew I'd taken the gun course. She'd been remarkably blasé about it, which made me wonder if it was a much bigger deal to me than it was to anyone else.

She laughed. "You're right. That's *not* a date."

Maybe it wasn't a date, but that didn't mean I wasn't allowed to look forward to it.

CHAPTER 24

BROOKS

I VISITED MY MOM at the hospital on my way to work the next morning. My dad had spent the night and was sitting next to my mom's bed, drinking a cup of coffee.

She was still sleeping, so I spoke softly. "Everything go okay last night?"

"The doctor said she can probably go home this afternoon," he said. "Everything looks good. No sign of infection."

"That's great," I said.

"Your friend Daisy stopped by."

"She said she'd look in on Mom."

"That was very nice of her." He took another drink of his coffee.

"How's the coffee?" I asked, pointing at the mug.

"Awful."

"You should have called me. I could have brought you some from home or stopped somewhere."

"That's okay. At least it's hot. Have you been to the lab yet?" he asked.

"My appointment's not until eight. I wanted to stop in and see Mom first."

I took a seat on the small couch near the window, browsing the news on my phone while we waited for her to wake up. A nurse came in to take her vital signs and my mother opened her eyes.

She saw me sitting there and said, "Brooks." Her voice was barely a whisper.

"Hi, Mom." As soon as the nurse left, I walked to her bedside. "How're you feeling this morning?"

"Okay," she said.

My dad reached out and patted her hand, careful to avoid the IV line. "I'm right here, Mary."

"I'm sorry I can't stay long," I said. "I have an appointment downstairs at the lab in a few minutes. It sounds like you'll be discharged today, so I'll see you when I get home from work."

"I'm sorry," she said.

Tears welled up in her eyes and my dad said, "Don't, Mary. We've been over this."

I leaned down and kissed her cheek. "It's okay, Mom. I love you and I'll see you later."

I turned to my Dad. "Call me when you and Mom get home, okay?"

"I will."

The lab was on the first floor. I pushed open the door and handed my paperwork to the woman sitting behind the desk.

"Have a seat over there," she said. "Someone will be out in a minute."

I didn't have to wait long. A nurse called my name and after she snapped on a pair of rubber gloves and tied a tourniquet on my upper arm, she took three vials of my blood.

She untied the tourniquet, applied a Band-Aid, and said, "There. You're all set. You know it will take several months to get the results back, right?"

I unrolled my sleeve and buttoned the cuff. "Yep."

*

After leaving the hospital, I stopped for breakfast at a diner not far from the newspaper. Apparently I wasn't the only one with this idea because it was packed. I could have hit the drive-through, but I really wanted food that didn't come in a Styrofoam container. I hadn't been required to fast before the blood test, but since I'd awakened to an empty house, I hadn't bothered to make anything to eat, preferring to go directly to the hospital instead. I stood in line and waited my turn.

Observing the room, I realized there was a clear hierarchy to the seating arrangements: the retired residents, the ones for whom a daily visit to the diner constituted part of their social routine, were seated in the booths that lined both walls. The tables arranged in the inner circle of the room were for families, friends meeting for breakfast, and the errant businessperson—insurance agents and realtors, mostly. The counter was where the cops and good ol' boys sat.

And reporters, apparently.

Standing next to me were three men who looked like they were around my age. Two of them were wearing Carhartt overalls with short-sleeve T-shirts underneath. The other wore camouflage pants and a sweatshirt with the arms cut off. Out of the corner of my eye, I noticed one of them staring at me.

"Do you need something?" I asked.

"Don't I know you?"

He looked vaguely like the guy who sat next to me in English Composition my senior year, the one who never read the book. I couldn't place the other two. "I think we might have gone to high school together."

"That's it," he said. "Knew I knew you from somewhere. Haven't seen you in a long time."

"I don't live here anymore. I'm just back for a visit."

"Where do you live?"

"San Francisco."

"Got a wife with you?"

"No." I turned away, hoping to stave off any more questions.

"Girlfriend?"

I turned back around. "Nope. Just me."

Half a minute passed, and I mistakenly thought our conversation was over.

"So, do you like girls?" he asked, eliciting chuckles from the peanut gallery. Encouraged by their reaction, he continued. "I mean, San Francisco? And with you dressing the way you do. No wife, no girlfriend. Well, you can't blame me for wondering."

Yes I can, you homophobic idiot.

"I do like girls. In fact, I like them a lot," I said. "And I'm certain I've had more success with them than the three of you put together." Two stools opened up at the counter and the waitress motioned to me. "If I might make a suggestion, try not buying your clothes at the same place you buy your firearms and antifreeze. And open your minds a little."

I sat down at the counter. A few seconds later, Jack Quick slid onto the stool next to me.

"Hope you weren't saving this seat," he said.

"No, but you probably pissed off the person who was next in line for it."

"Police perk," Jack said, motioning for the waitress to fill his coffee cup. "No one's gonna say anything."

"How do you stand it?" I asked.

"Stand what? Cutting in line? I love it."

"No, this town. This narrow-mindedness. I just ran into a guy I went to high school with. What, you wear a suit and tie, you're gay?"

Jack looked over at me. "Well you are kind of snazzy." He opened his menu, perused it, and closed it just as quickly. "My wife gets caught up in it more than I do. If you think the men are bad, you don't want to know what the women gossip about. I only wish I could un-hear some of that crap."

"Ever thought of moving?"

"Every damn day," he said, "but my wife's entire family lives here. We're not going anywhere, at least not until the kids head off to college, which is gonna be a while yet. My youngest is only eleven." Jack took a drink of his coffee. "If you hate it so much, why are you here?"

"My mom's sick."

Jack looked appropriately contrite. "Oh, hey. I'm sorry."

I held up my hand. "It's okay."

"How long are you going to be around?"

I looked at him and then turned away. "Until the end."

"That's rough." He took another drink of his coffee, and I opened my menu and scanned the offerings. "Tell me you've been nosing around and have something for me on Pauline Thorpe," he said.

"I've got nothing. I'm so desperate I thought about making a visit to the mobile garage sale to see what I could stir up."

Jack snorted. "Not in that suit, I hope."

"No."

"Good luck finding it," Jack said. "They're not kidding about the mobile part. We gave up trying to shut them down a long time ago. For every one we find, two more spring up in a different location. I swear they're all just stealing from each other at this point."

"For twenty bucks and a pack of smokes, my buddy down at

the Desert Tap will tell me where it is, although he seemed a bit unreliable."

"Messing with those meth heads will get you killed. No one is more paranoid than a tweaker. They'll shoot you first and ask questions later."

The waitress came by and took our breakfast orders.

"Did the crime lab ever turn up anything?"

"Not yet. We have no leads, no suspects, and no tips coming in via the hotline. Pauline Thorpe was killed by either the smartest person or the luckiest. This is so far off the record it's not even funny, by the way."

"Understood. Do you get many calls on the hotline?"

"Every mentally unbalanced person residing in San Bernardino County calls the hotline. Most of the time it has nothing to do with a case, but occasionally we get lucky. Someone shoots off their mouth in front of the wrong person and bam, we get a call that pans out. You still in touch with the granddaughter?"

"Yes."

"And?"

"Nothing. Her son hasn't said anything either."

The waitress set down our plates and we began to eat.

When we were finished, I threw some bills onto the counter, enough to cover both of our breakfasts. "I can't tell you why, but this case doesn't feel random to me."

"It doesn't feel random to me either," Jack said. "Thanks for breakfast."

CHAPTER 25
DAISY

BROOKS KNOCKED ON the door a little before seven. Kayla and Elliott were playing with Play-Doh at the kitchen table.

"Call me if you need me," I said. "Lock the door behind me and don't open it to anyone."

"I won't," she said. "Go have fun shooting at things on your non-date."

When I opened the door, I was surprised to see that Brooks was still dressed in his work clothes. "Hi," I said. Maybe this wasn't a date, but seeing him at my door sent a jolt of happiness through me. There was something so capable about Brooks, and his presence instantly put me at ease.

"Hi," Brooks said. His voice didn't sound as businesslike or as formal as it usually did. At that moment, he seemed more like a friend than a reporter.

A very handsome friend.

"Were you not able to go home first?" I asked, shutting the door behind me and waiting until I heard Kayla lock it.

"I had a few things I needed to catch up on in the newsroom."

"Have you eaten?" I asked. "You must be hungry."

"I'm fine. I'll grab something later."

It had taken me half an hour to decide what to wear, which seemed ridiculous considering the circumstances. I'd finally decided on jeans and a short-sleeve shirt with my favorite zip-front hoodie on over it. I wore my hair in its usual ponytail because I didn't want it in my eyes and besides, debuting a new hairstyle to go to the shooting range was even more ridiculous than taking a half hour to decide what to wear.

"How's your mom doing with the feeding tube?" I asked when we reached the car.

Brooks opened my door and waited until I sat down to close it, then opened the driver's side door and slid behind the wheel. "She's doing okay. It's her breathing that's gotten bad."

"I noticed she was having some trouble when I stopped by her room that night."

Brooks looked at me as he started the car.

Oh, those eyes.

"It was really nice of you to check on her," he said.

"It was no problem."

When we arrived at the shooting range, Brooks reached under the front seat and pulled out a gun case, similar in size to mine.

"You carry a gun?" I asked.

"Not usually, but I never know where I'll end up when I'm covering a story. Believe me when I tell you there are places in San Francisco you don't want to find yourself without a weapon at two a.m."

Brooks and I walked through the glass double doors of the building. An attendant sat behind a desk, typing on a computer.

"Two," Brooks said, laying down his credit card.

"Do you need ear and eye protection?" the attendant asked.

"Yes."

The guy rang us up and Brooks waved me away when I tried to give him some money.

The attendant led us down a long hallway to the last range on the left. "You've got an hour. Let me know if you want more time."

We unpacked our guns and I pulled a box of bullets from my purse.

"What did you buy?" Brooks asked.

I held it up so he could see it. "Beretta Nano."

"Wow." He took it from my hand. "That's really sleek."

"I wanted something small and easy to conceal."

"It's perfect for you." Brooks pointed at my box of bullets. "Do you need help loading the magazine?"

"You mean the Pez dispenser?" I smiled, picked up the magazine, and started loading the bullets by pushing down on the floating lever.

His face transformed. His eyes crinkled at the corners and the hard line of his mouth curved upward as he let out a short laugh, shaking his head as if I amused him. The spontaneous reaction was so different from his usual serious demeanor that all I could do was smile back. As attractive as Brooks was when he wasn't smiling, it was nothing compared to the way he looked when I finally got a glimpse of his personality.

"Hey, you smiled," I said.

He looked at me strangely. "I smile all the time."

"You smile, never."

"Yes I do."

"No you don't. You are *very* serious."

"I would like to smile more"—he paused and looked at me pointedly—"at you, but the circumstances surrounding our interactions haven't exactly called for levity."

"Oh," I said, putting the last bullet in the magazine. "Of course. But it's a really great smile just the same."

If Brooks wanted to, he could bend me to his will with that smile, and by the way he was looking at me, I would say he knew it.

After handing me my earmuffs and safety glasses he said, "Okay. Let's see what you've got."

If this were a romantic comedy, Brooks would surely be putting his hands on my hips and repositioning me by now. Maybe even asking me to spread my legs a little farther apart, which would spark awkward laughter and make me blush. But this wasn't a romantic comedy and I had bigger concerns, so I put on the earmuffs and safety glasses, approached the target, and took aim. My first two shots missed by a wide margin, but the next three got progressively closer to where they needed to be.

"Go ahead," Brooks said. "Take the last one."

When I was done, he asked, "Are you scared of the gun?"

"No. Well, maybe a little. Why? Does it show?"

"You seem hesitant. But remember, you're the one in control. Why don't you go again?"

I reloaded and this time, I tried to forget that Brooks was standing there watching me. I planted my feet and took aim, squeezing the trigger until I'd emptied the magazine.

"That was better," Brooks said. "You handle the gun well, but you need to make sure you're shooting frequently. The more secure you are in your ability, the more confidence you'll have in a self-defense situation."

I took two more turns, emptying the magazine each time. "Your turn," I said, smiling at him. "Show me what you've got."

Brooks was either very comfortable shooting a gun, very confident, or both. His accuracy was impressive.

"You're really good," I said.

"Thanks. It's been about three months since I last shot. I figured I'd better take my own advice and get some practice in."

He reloaded and shot again.

"What time is it?" he asked.

"Almost eight."

"Do you want to go again? We're paid up until eight fifteen."

"Sure."

We both took another turn and then packed our guns back into their carrying cases.

I zipped my hoodie when we got outside. The October air became chilly once the sun went down, and I shivered.

"Are you cold?" he asked.

"I'm okay."

Brooks started the car and turned on the heat, adjusting the vent so it pointed my way. On the way home he said, "When I asked you the other day if there was a guy around, you said there was, but not anymore. What happened?"

His question caught me off guard. It also sparked a flicker of hope that maybe he was asking for a reason other than mild curiosity. "Oh." I paused and then answered honestly. "Elliott and I weren't enough for him, I guess."

"I'm sorry."

"Don't be. It's better to know these things sooner rather than later. It was hard on Elliott, though."

"Hard on you, I imagine," Brooks said.

"Yeah. That, too."

Brooks drove into the parking lot of my apartment building and parked in one of the visitor spaces. "I'll walk you in."

When we reached my door, I said, "I'm glad we did this. I feel more comfortable already."

He nodded. "Keep practicing."

Knowing that Kayla would have the chain on the door, I knocked and waited for her to open it.

Brooks laid his hand on my arm. "Listen, I know I sound like I'm repeating myself, but please be careful. Call me if anything happens. If you need me, I'll come."

I had never aspired to play the role of damsel in distress, but right then it was hard not to picture Brooks sitting high up on that white horse again, ready to swoop in and save me. And really, would that be so terrible?

Kayla opened the door, and before I went inside, I turned to Brooks and said, "If I need you, I'll call."

He smiled again, and I met it with one of my own, and I was still smiling long after I closed the door.

CHAPTER 26

BROOKS

NO TWO CASES of ALS are the same, and the progression of the disease is impossible to predict. Some who are stricken have symptoms that progress slowly over a number of years, while others experience a sudden and rapid decline in their condition.

It appeared that my mom would fall into the second group.

The reason I'd stayed late in the newsroom before I picked up Daisy to go to the shooting range was because I'd started going home for an hour or two during the day when my mom was still somewhat alert and coherent. I'd ask the nurse to give us some privacy, and at my urging, my dad would finally leave Mom's bedside to take a break and have lunch. I'd sit down on the chair he vacated.

"Brooks," my mom said on the first afternoon I'd come home. I'd had to lean in close in order to catch the rest. "Did you know the sound of a child's voice is like music to its mother, no matter how old that child is? I can't speak very clearly, but there's nothing wrong with my ears."

I'd swallowed the lump in my throat and talked to her for

fifteen minutes straight. None of it was especially interesting—I mostly shared snippets about my job or reminisced with her over stories of my youth—but she hung on every word. Every day since then, I tried to come up with things to say that I knew would make her happy. She'd join in, sometimes asking questions or adding something to the conversation, but mostly she listened.

When I arrived home at noon the day after I took Daisy to the shooting range, I said, "Do you remember Daisy, the nurse who came by and introduced herself when you were in the hospital?" I took off my jacket and settled myself in the chair next to the bed.

She nodded.

"I took her to the shooting range last night."

"On a date?" Due to the weakening of the muscles that controlled her facial expressions, her smile looked more like a grimace.

Or maybe it was *meant* to be a grimace.

"If it was a date, I'd have taken her someplace nicer than the shooting range," I said. "She bought a gun for protection and I thought it would be good for her to get some practice."

"Did you have a good time?"

"We did. She's a nice girl. Smart. Very devoted to her son."

"She's beautiful, too," my mom said. This time, the grimace was definitely meant to be a smile. "I remember."

"She is." Daisy was one of those women who got prettier every time you saw them. When you finally realize they're beautiful, you wonder how you could have possibly overlooked it in the first place.

"She's alone?" my mom asked.

"Yes." A man would undoubtedly come along to replace the boyfriend who'd left.

Probably soon.

The thought of Daisy finding someone new bothered me, but my stay in Fenton was temporary and I had no right to an opinion about who she might spend her time with in the future.

Our short conversation seemed to have already tired my mom out, and her eyelids began to flutter. The last words she said to me that day took a while for her to utter. I waited patiently beside her bed, straining to hear them.

"A life without someone to love is a life not fully lived. Don't waste yours." She looked at me imploringly.

"I won't, Mom. I promise."

*

A little over a week later, Nina, the daytime nurse, called my dad and me into the kitchen as soon as I walked in the door for my afternoon visit.

"I'd like to talk to you about breathing assistance for Mary," she said. "We could begin with noninvasive assisted ventilation, which would involve the use of a portable, bedside BiPAP machine. It delivers air through a mask and will help her breathe in and out. If you're in agreement, I can reach out to Mary's physician and her respiratory team to initiate the process."

"Of course," my dad said. "Brooks?"

"Absolutely."

"The effects of underventilation can be very serious," Nina said. "I think you're being proactive by taking this step."

My dad pulled out a chair and sat down at the kitchen table. He rubbed his eyes and said, "Do you know how much time we have left with her?"

"Not a lot," Nina said. "The BiPAP will ease her symptoms, but it won't stop the progression of the disease. I'm so sorry." She squeezed my dad's shoulder on the way out of the room.

"Think I'll sit with you and your mother during your visit," he said. "Don't feel much like I need a break today."

"Sure, Dad."

The three of us spent the afternoon hours together that day, and every day afterward until the end. My dad and I took turns talking and my mom listened.

They would be the hardest and the best days we ever had as a family.

CHAPTER 27

DAISY

THOUGH I NEVER knew exactly when he would appear, I had always looked forward to Brooks's visits. They not only gave me the opportunity to receive updates about the case, but knowing that someone besides Pam and Shane was at least tangentially looking out for Elliott and me felt good.

Knowing that it was Brooks felt even better.

When a neighbor had knocked on my door recently, I was disappointed when I looked through the peephole and Brooks wasn't standing there. The night we went to the shooting range, he'd told me to call him if I needed him, but he hadn't said anything about stopping by or staying in touch; I'd come to the disappointing conclusion that I might not see Brooks again for a while. Maybe I wouldn't see him at all.

I was in the middle of trying to get my kitchen sink to drain so I could start dinner when the knock came. Trying not to get my hopes up, I dried my hands and walked toward the door. When I peered through the peephole and saw Brooks, I smiled.

I opened the door, not caring that I had a big grin on my face, and said, "Let me guess, you were in the neighborhood."

Brooks was smiling, too. "Technically this town is small enough that I'm always kind of in your neighborhood."

"That's true. But sometimes people call first instead of just dropping by," I said. Therefore giving unprepared single mothers time to ditch their ponytails and yoga pants for something a little less casual.

"Do you want me to stay out here in the hallway and call you first?" he asked.

"Do you still have my number?"

"Of course I do." The way he said it—like my phone number was information that was important to him—made my insides flip around a little. "But maybe I could come in since I'm already here."

I held the door open wide and he walked across the threshold. He stopped within a few inches of me, close enough that I could smell his cologne, fresh and slightly woodsy.

His expression was serious when he said, "But if you want me to call first, I will."

"That's okay," I said. "Mostly I find it amusing. I'd just like to point out that with a little advance notice, I can look a whole lot better than this."

He studied me, his expression quizzical. "There's nothing about the way you look right now that I don't like."

Wait.

What?

Did that mean Brooks was a fan of yoga pants and ponytails, or was this more of a general statement? Was this the first time Brooks had noticed the way I looked, or had he noticed me from the beginning? If Brooks liked girls who were low-key, would he not like the way I would look if I was all dressed up? Like if we were to go on a date? What if I wore lipstick and high heels and a dress?

I am a little bit insane right now.

I closed the door and locked it behind him, and I didn't need to look in a mirror to know that my cheeks were flushed.

"Hey, Elliott," Brooks said.

Elliott was putting together a puzzle in the living room. He smiled and waved. "Hi, Bwooks."

"Did you hear something about the case?" I asked.

"No. Not yet." His tone was briskly efficient, and instead of explaining the reason for his visit, he followed me into the kitchen where I resumed scowling at the sink.

"What's wrong?"

"The sink is backed up."

"What happened?"

"I don't know. It was working fine earlier today."

"Did you drop something down it?"

"Not that I know of."

Brooks peered into the sink. "There's no disposal and that's a fairly wide opening. If I had to guess, I'd say that something has made its way down into the pipe and gotten stuck." Brooks bent down and looked in the cupboard underneath the sink. "I can take a look at it. Can you get me a towel, a bucket, and a wrench?"

"Sure. I'll go grab them."

Brooks took off his jacket and draped it over the back of one of the kitchen chairs. He crouched down and began removing the box of dishwasher detergent tabs and the cleaning supplies I'd stored under the sink. I retrieved a towel and a small toolbox from the hallway closet and the bucket I kept Elliott's bath toys in. After turning the valve to stop the water flow, Brooks spread out the towel on the bottom of the cupboard.

"See this?" Brooks asked, pointing at a U-shaped pipe. "I bet that's where we'll find whatever's causing this."

"Is it difficult to remove?" I asked.

"Nope. Just messy." He stood, and after removing his tie, he unbuttoned his white dress shirt, starting with the cuffs and moving to the top button at his collar. Once unbuttoned, he removed the shirt and laid it and his tie on top of his suit jacket, leaving him in a white T-shirt. "First we need to get the water out of the sink. Do you have a medium-size bowl, preferably plastic?"

I reached into a cabinet for a bowl and handed it to Brooks. He used it to transfer the water from the sink to Elliott's bucket.

Once he'd gotten almost all the water out, he handed the bucket to me. "Okay, go flush this."

After I returned with the empty bucket, Brooks set it underneath the pipe and lay down on the floor, his head disappearing under the cupboard as he used the wrench to loosen the threaded caps on both ends of the pipe. He handed me the wrench and removed the pipe, which released a big gush of water. Some of it splashed onto Brooks, soaking the front of his T-shirt.

"Sorry about that."

"It's okay. Told you it was messy."

He came out from under the sink and sat up, holding the bucket. He reached his hand in and smiled. "Hey, Elliott," he called out. "C'mere."

When Elliott came charging into the room, Brooks held out a grimy, wet army man. "I think I found something that belongs to you."

"Bwooks!" Elliott grabbed his beloved toy and threw his arms around Brooks's neck, knocking him off balance. "Fank you."

Brooks patted him on the back somewhat awkwardly. "Hey, you're welcome."

"Go wash that off in the bathroom, okay?" I said to Elliott. "Make sure to turn off the water when you're done." I turned back toward Brooks. "You're a lifesaver. Elliott has been distraught over losing that toy. We've looked everywhere except, obviously, down the drain."

"It was no problem."

Noticing Brooks's wet T-shirt I said, "Let me get you another towel."

After putting the wrench and bucket away and grabbing a fresh towel from the linen closet, I walked back into the kitchen in time to see Brooks strip off his white T-shirt.

Wow.

I'd had no idea what Brooks had been hiding under those proper suits of his. Who knew he was so… defined. His broad shoulders tapered down to a narrow waist, and he had the kind of long and lean muscles I preferred over bulging biceps and a thick neck. His skin looked smooth and flawless.

Clearly he works out.

"Daisy?" Brooks held out his hand for the towel. He was trying to hide a smirk.

Stop staring at him.

"Here," I said, handing him the towel.

"Thanks."

He blotted his chest and then lay back down and put the inner workings of my sink back together.

"Would you like to have dinner with us?" I asked, holding my breath as I waited for his answer.

"Sure," he said, and if his head hadn't been shoved under the sink, he'd have seen the smile that lit up my face.

I threw Brooks's T-shirt in the washing machine and tried not to ogle him as he slipped back into his dress shirt. He left the top two buttons undone and didn't bother with the tie.

"Do you like chicken parmesan?" I asked.

"It's one of my favorites, actually."

I pulled a bottle of pinot noir from the wine rack on the kitchen counter and held it up. "Would you like a glass of wine?"

"Sure. That'd be great."

I poured two glasses and handed one to Brooks.

He took a drink and then leaned against the counter and watched as I put a pot of water on to boil and took the chicken cutlets out of the refrigerator. "Can I help you with anything?" he asked.

"I think you've helped plenty," I said. "Time for you to relax."

Elliott sat down at the kitchen table, a coloring book in one hand and a fistful of crayons in the other. After digging the army man out of his pocket, he set the toy on the table.

Brooks took his wine and sat down across from Elliott. Neither of them spoke, but Elliott shot quick, furtive glances toward Brooks, and I was almost certain that the picture Elliott was working on would be presented to Brooks upon its completion.

"So, how did your army guy fall in the sink?" Brooks asked. He lowered his voice conspiratorially. "Was he on an important mission?"

Elliott looked up from his drawing. "Yes!"

I smiled as I dipped the chicken cutlets in egg and dredged them through seasoned flour. Elliott sounded as if he was overjoyed to find someone who could relate to such a thing.

Brooks took a drink of his wine and said, "I bet his platoon is happy that he's back."

"What is a pwatoon?" Elliott asked.

"Platoon?" Brooks said.

Elliott nodded.

"It's a military unit." Brooks reached over and picked up Elliott's toy. "It's like a whole group of these army men."

"I only have this one guy. Mama never telled me about pwatoons."

What Elliott said was true. It had never occurred to me to explain anything military-related to Elliott. To me, the army man was just a toy, and Barbie dolls would always be more my speed. But a man would probably have spent hours talking about that kind of thing.

The water had finally come to a boil. I placed the spaghetti in the pot and started browning the chicken in melted butter.

"So, tell me about this mission," Brooks said.

"My army guy had to hide under the bananas 'cause a bad man come to the door. He was 'fraid the bad man would hear him."

I froze.

I set down the container of marinara sauce I'd pulled out of the fridge and listened.

Brooks was every bit as sharp as I thought he was because he said, "And then what happened?" His tone was gentle and patient.

Elliott seemed to sink down in his chair. His voice was noticeably quieter when he spoke again. "The bad man said, 'Tell me,' but Nana said, 'No. I won't.' Then he said, 'Shut up!' and Nana cried. The bad man would find Ewiott next. He would tell Ewiott to shut up and he would make Ewiott cry, so Ewiott hided and waited for Mama. Ewiott was so quiet, but he could still hear." Elliott put his hands over his ears and starting rocking back and forth.

It took mere seconds for me to reach Elliott's side, and only a few more before Brooks reached mine. Blinking back tears, I

161

pulled Elliott from the chair and into my arms, holding him close. "It's okay, honey. Mama's right here."

Brooks pulled Elliott's empty chair away from the table and guided me into it, which I greatly appreciated because my legs suddenly felt unsteady.

Once I was seated, I held Elliott tightly in my arms, rubbing his back and murmuring, "Don't be afraid. You're safe now."

Elliott lifted his head from my shoulder and looked at Brooks. "My army guy was bwave. He didn't hide. He runned across the counter to catch the bad man, but then he fell down and I couldn't find him. I wooked everywhere."

"I think you're the one who's brave," Brooks said.

Elliott adjusted his glasses. "I would wike to work on my picture now." He climbed off my lap and as soon as I stood, he sat back down in the chair, selected a crayon, and resumed coloring.

"Are you all right, buddy?" I asked.

"I'm hungry, Mama."

Clearly he did not want to talk about it anymore, and it would do no good to push him. "Okay. Dinner's almost ready."

I flipped the chicken, and when it was done, I spread marinara on the bottom of a casserole dish. After topping the chicken with thick slices of fresh mozzarella, I put the dish in the oven to melt the cheese.

"Are you hungry?" I asked Brooks. I drained the pasta and started plating the meal. All I had left to do was set the chicken on top of the spaghetti and toss the salad I'd made earlier.

"Yes," he said. "It smells wonderful. My dad and I have been living on takeout and pizza. My mom gets so tired at night. She's more alert in the morning and early afternoon, so I try to spend time with her then. It's kind of depressing in the evening because she mostly sleeps. My dad doesn't know what to do with himself. Neither do I. We eat crappy food and watch TV."

"I'm sorry. I can't imagine how hard this is on both of you. Is your dad alone tonight?"

"One of his closest friends was going to take him out for something to eat. He hasn't been out of the house in a long time. The night nurse is there, so my mom is in good hands."

Brooks must have wanted to get out of the house, too. It thrilled me that he'd come to mine.

The oven timer buzzed. "Okay," I said. "Let's eat."

Brooks got up and refilled our empty wineglasses during the meal. I couldn't remember the last time I'd felt so relaxed or so happy.

"I wike Wed Zeppwin," Elliott said—suddenly, enthusiastically, and apropos of nothing. "Me and Shane wisten to Wed Zeppwin in the car."

"Led Zeppelin. Really," Brooks said, trying to keep a straight face.

"There's no way to predict what will come out of that cute little mouth," I said, taking another sip of wine. "Other than it will probably be random and adorable."

Brooks nodded and let a small laugh escape. "I see what you mean. What else do you like, Elliott?"

"Chocwate. And fwied chicken."

"I like chocolate and fried chicken," Brooks said. "And I like Led Zeppelin. You have good taste, Elliott."

"What does that mean?"

"It means you like cool things."

Elliott smiled and took another drink of his milk, looking

adoringly at Brooks and me, as if he was having every bit as much fun as I was having, which squeezed my heart in a bittersweet way.

I wish I could give this to him every night.

"I'm full, Mama," Elliott said.

I glanced at my watch, surprised to see that it was almost seven. "Can you put on your pajamas?"

"I will put them on all by myself."

Elliott left the room, but Brooks and I remained at the table.

"This was really good," Brooks said. "You're a great cook."

His words pleased me. It was an old-fashioned way of thinking, but I liked cooking for a man, especially when he told me how much he'd enjoyed it. "Thanks. I'm glad you liked it. You're welcome to stay for a while. I'll put Elliott to bed soon." I stood and began clearing the dishes.

I didn't want him to go. I'd spent so many nights alone since my grandmother had died that I craved adult company, and so far this evening was the most enjoyable one I'd had in a very long time. I only hoped my desperation didn't show on my face.

"Are you sure?" he said, helping me carry the rest of the dishes to the sink. "You probably have to get up really early for work tomorrow."

"As long as I'm in bed by ten, I'll be fine."

"Okay, then. I'll stay."

When Elliott returned wearing his Spider-Man pajamas, I got him settled on the couch and strapped on his mask.

"What is that?" Brooks asked.

"It's a nebulizer. For his asthma. He has to have a breathing treatment every night before bed."

Elliott looked at Brooks and pulled the mask to the side. "I'm a dwagon."

"Put that back on," I said, pointing my finger at him. "The

medicine comes out in little puffs, like smoke. When he was first diagnosed, the doctor told Elliott that he would turn into a dragon for fifteen minutes every night while he took his medicine. They even have masks shaped like dragons, but so far we're doing okay just pretending."

"Nice tactic," Brooks said.

Fifteen minutes later, I clicked off the nebulizer and removed the mask from Elliott's face. "All done," I said.

"I'm not a dwagon anymore. I'm Ewiott now."

Brooks laughed.

I smoothed Elliott's hair. "Thanks for clearing that up. Bedtime, okay?" I repeated myself when Elliott pretended he hadn't heard me. "Okay?"

"'Kay," he muttered.

"Let's go brush your teeth and then I'll read."

"Good night, Elliott," Brooks said.

"Good night, Bwooks."

After I put Elliott to bed, I opened another bottle of wine and refilled our wineglasses.

"Thanks," Brooks said. He leaned forward. "Elliott said something earlier, when he was reenacting what happened the night your grandmother died. Did you catch it?"

I sat down in the chair across from where Brooks was sitting on the couch. "Yes. He said something like 'The bad man said tell me.' And then he said my grandmother said no. He's never mentioned that before."

"It immediately made me think that whoever did this came with a specific goal in mind. There was something he wanted, and your grandmother didn't want to give it to him."

"I don't know what it could have been. I saved all my grandmother's personal items. Would you like to see them?"

"Yes."

Brooks followed me into my bedroom and waited while I retrieved a box from the top of my closet. I dumped out the contents on my bed. "This is the only box that had personal items."

"What was in the other boxes?"

"Photo albums. Also her life-insurance policy and other financial records. Canceled checks and bank statements, mostly."

Brooks sat down on the edge of the bed and started sifting through my grandmother's things. He picked up the pearls and looked at me questioningly.

"They're not real," I said. "Too smooth and the color is wrong."

He ran his fingers over the earrings and put them back in the box. "Was she sentimental?" Brooks asked. "She didn't seem to have many keepsakes."

"Not really. She didn't save a lot of things. My grandmother always treasured family more than she did anything else. I suppose it's because she'd lost so many people. Elliott and I were the things she valued most."

I began putting my grandmother's meager possessions back in the box, and when I was done I said, "It's not that I want a lot of material things, because I don't, but I want the kind of life you can't possibly fit into a single box. If something should ever happen to me and people have to go through my things, I want there to be so many memories left behind that it takes a truck to move them all."

"Before she got too sick, my mom watched all our old home movies," Brooks said. "My dad had them transferred onto DVDs and she played every disc at least twice. It made me realize that memories shouldn't be something we only appreciate when we're running out of time to make more of them."

Brooks and I were sitting on my bed, which didn't seem strange when we were looking through the box but now felt strangely intimate, especially after the sentiments we'd each shared.

"That makes me want to cry, Brooks."

"I know," he said.

I placed the lid on the box and put it away in my closet.

We went back to the living room.

"Thanks for explaining about platoons to Elliott. I worry that I don't do enough of that kind of thing with him. It just doesn't occur to me like it would to a man. I don't even remember where he got that toy or why he only has one."

"He seems like a great kid. I'll be honest, I really can't wrap my head around your ex-husband not being part of his life."

"You reap what you sow as a parent. Scott's lack of participation in Elliott's life won't go unnoticed. Someday, if he ever gets clean, he may discover that Elliott doesn't want anything to do with him. I hope I raise Elliott to be a more forgiving person than that, but ultimately it will be his decision to make."

"Elliott's lucky to have a parent like you."

"I feel like I'm the lucky one. If something had happened to him the night my grandmother died, I don't know what I would have done. Someday, when he's grown, I'll make sure he leaves and finds his own way in the world. Becomes whatever he wants to be. But for now I'm holding him as close as I can."

"Is there anyone else?" Brooks asked. "Aunts, uncles, cousins?"

"My dad was an only child, but my mom had three siblings. They all had young families of their own and I guess no one was willing to take in another child. My grandmother insisted, once I was old enough to ask questions, that she stepped forward so quickly no one else had time to contemplate it. Knowing my grandmother and the kind of person she was, it's probably true. Either that or she just didn't want me to feel bad because no one wanted me. I don't have much contact with any of my relatives. They're all scattered across the country and occasionally someone will reach out to me about a family reunion on either my mom or dad's side, but I've never attended. To all of them, I'm a stranger."

"Your resiliency is amazing."

"I don't know if it's resiliency, necessarily. More like a lack of choices."

"Even so, it couldn't have been easy for you, especially when you were younger."

"There were definitely times when I felt very alone," I admitted.

I turned on the TV and switched to a satellite radio station playing today's hits, keeping the volume low. We both took a drink of our wine. "What kind of music do you like?" I asked.

"Gangsta rap, primarily."

He said it with a straight face, but I burst out laughing. "Somehow, I don't believe you."

"No," he said, smiling. "I like a little bit of everything. My iPod holds many widely divergent genres. What about you?"

"Don't laugh," I said. "And I'm only telling you this because I've had some wine, otherwise I'd probably be too embarrassed."

"I really can't wait to hear this," Brooks said. "Go on."

"I like songs that tell a story. Like 'Cat's In the Cradle' by Harry Chapin or 'In the Ghetto' by Elvis, both of which can bring me to tears, by the way. 'The Night the Lights Went Out in Georgia,' 'American Pie,' 'The River.' The list goes on and on. Pam teases me relentlessly. She thinks it's hysterical, especially because no song is too cheesy for me. In the interest of full disclosure, and because you haven't laughed at me yet, I never change the station when 'Copacabana' by Barry Manilow comes on the radio, either." I smiled at Brooks. "There's a story there."

"I would never laugh about your musical preferences, especially not after hearing the thought process behind your choices. And those are not bad songs. Except maybe 'Copacabana.'"

"That one will probably grow on you," I said.

He grinned. "No… I don't think it will."

"I was named after a song, actually."

Brooks held up his hand. "Wait. Don't tell me." It didn't take him long. "Your middle name is Jane, isn't it?"

I nodded, impressed with how quickly he'd figured it out.

"'Daisy Jane' by America," he said.

"You are very well-rounded, musically. Not everyone knows that song."

"I take it your parents were fans?"

"When I was about five or six, my grandmother told me that my mom played that album over and over when she was pregnant with me. She told my dad that if I was a girl, she wanted to name me Daisy Jane. He loved the idea. My sister's name was Danielle, so it was a good fit all around, I guess. I went through this phase in high school where I would sit in my room with the door closed, listening to the cassette repeatedly. I pictured my mom doing the same thing and it made me feel close to her. Anyway, I still love those songs."

"I can see why," Brooks said.

It was almost nine by then. Brooks's wineglass was empty, and when I asked him if he'd like a refill I expected him to say something like, "No thanks. I should really get going." But he didn't. He said, "I'll get it."

When he returned from the kitchen he picked up my glass first. "Would you like some more?"

"Just half a glass, please. I'm pretty close to my limit."

Brooks poured our wine and sat back down.

"Do you truly believe your ex-husband is responsible for the death of your grandmother?" he asked. "Because that's another thing I can't wrap my head around."

"I believe he had something to do with it. I just don't think it was as random as it seems."

"If this is too personal you don't have to tell me, but did he hurt you? Physically? Is that why you think he's involved? Because you know he's capable of violence?"

"When Scott first started using there was a lot of lying. He often made excuses for why money was missing, or why I couldn't get a hold of him on his phone. Sometimes he would become agitated and shout at me when he needed to get high and didn't have drugs or the money to buy them. But he never hit me or anything like that. Toward the end, he mostly stopped coming home at all, and I never really knew when I would see him again."

"So you didn't fear him?" Brooks asked.

I hesitated.

"Daisy, is there something you want to tell me?" Brooks asked softly.

Maybe it was a sign of how comfortable I felt with him, or maybe it was the wine, but after a moment I started to speak. "Scott showed up at the house around nine thirty one night. Elliott was asleep and I was watching TV and thinking about going to bed when he unlocked the back door and came inside. There was another man with him. I remember the hair on the back of my neck standing up, because the minute they walked into the living room, I knew something was wrong. Whether it was intuition or instinct or something else entirely, I just knew."

"Then what happened?" Brooks said. He used the same gentle and patient tone he'd used earlier with Elliott.

"Scott said he needed money. It was all very matter-of-fact. It was as if he was no longer my husband but rather some junkie who'd wandered in off the street with one goal in mind: to get high. There was no recognition in his eyes. There was no acknowledgment that I was his wife, that this was his home. No awareness that his child was asleep in his crib. He was there for one thing only, and I didn't want to give it to him. I'd already initiated divorce proceedings but hadn't moved out yet because I had hoped that Elliott and I would be able to stay and that Scott would be the one who had to leave. It was only a rental, but I had tried hard to make that house a home, and I didn't want to go. I'd gotten used to Scott not being around, so when he showed up that night, I got really angry. Why did my husband think it was okay to suddenly appear and ask for money to buy drugs? So I told him no."

I paused. "But the thing I didn't fully understand was that Scott didn't *want* money, he owed money. And someone was going to pay off that debt." I could no longer look at Brooks, so I focused on the picture that hung above the couch. Emotionally disengaged, my voice sounded distant, like I was telling Brooks a story about something that had happened to a woman who was not me.

"The man Scott had brought home with him walked up to me. He was skinny, but he was still bigger than me, and very tall. His eyes were dead, and I could smell him. Cigarettes and chemicals and filth. He reached out and ran his finger down the center of my chest. There was no doubt in my mind about what he was going to do to me. I had no way of defending myself, and I couldn't run because I would have never left Elliott behind."

"Jesus," Brooks said.

"I'd hidden some cash in an empty baby shampoo bottle. I said, 'I'll give you five hundred dollars, but as soon as I give it to you, you have to leave and you can't come back.' I was terrified that he'd take the money but… assault me anyway."

Brooks clenched and unclenched his hands and then looked away for a moment. "Did they go?"

"Yes. I had no way of knowing how much Scott owed, but meth is cheap and I'm sure there was plenty of money left over. They were probably eager to go on a binge. But before they left, the man leaned in and whispered, 'I'm not done with you.' Once they were gone, I had a bit of a breakdown. I couldn't stop shaking, couldn't stop crying, but I managed to call Pam and Shane and they came right over. It was almost ten o'clock by then, but Shane just started loading my stuff into the back of his SUV. I left the furniture behind but took all our clothes and personal items—Elliott's toys, important papers, photo albums. I knew I wouldn't be back, so I had to make sure I took everything I needed right then. When it was all packed, I carried Elliott to the car, strapped him into his car seat, and followed Pam and Shane to their house. Elliott and I moved in with my grandmother the next day, and I had Scott served with divorce papers."

"Did you tell your grandmother what happened that night?"

"No. She knew about Scott's drug problems—I was always open about that. But other than Pam and Shane, and now you, I've never told anyone about that night. It's very hard for me to talk about it. I feel so ashamed."

"Why would you feel ashamed?" Brooks sounded incredulous. "You did nothing wrong."

"I know I didn't, but it was such an act of betrayal. So barbaric. This man had stood up with me in a church in front of our family and friends and promised to love and cherish me. Instead, he was willing to stand by and let someone rape his wife."

"That disgusts me, Daisy. It really does." Brooks pressed his fingers to his temples and then looked up. "Did you by any chance mention this other man to Jack Quick?"

"I thought about saying something to him that night at the police station. But what would I have said? I'm pretty sure one of my husband's meth-head friends had horrible intentions once? What could Jack have done with that? I don't even know the guy's name."

Brooks seemed lost in thought for a moment. "Where's your computer?"

"It's on the kitchen counter."

"Can you get it? There's something I want you to look at."

I retrieved my laptop and sat down on the couch next to Brooks. After I turned it on, I handed it to him, and he typed in a web address and then entered the name "Dale Reber" in the website's search box. When a man's image filled the screen, I drew in a quick breath and my muscles tensed. I sank deeper into the cushions and pulled my knees to my chest, wrapping my arms around them.

"That's him, isn't it?" Brooks said.

"How could you possibly have known?"

"This is the man who answered the door when I went out to speak to Scott. The address you gave me is his. Dale Reber was armed when he came to the door. I'm not telling you this because I'm trying to scare you. I'm telling you this because I want you to be careful."

I'd moved a little closer to Brooks in order to see the computer screen, but now my body was pressed closer still, although I had no conscious recollection of moving toward him. Vividly aware of how safe I felt with his body next to mine, I stayed put.

So did he.

"Are you all right?" he asked.

"No," I said. "Not really."

Brooks set the computer on the table beside the couch and turned toward me. He rested his arm along the back of the couch, which wasn't quite the same as him putting his arm around me, but I still felt comforted by it.

"If it's okay with you, I'd like to let Jack know about this."

"Yes, of course."

"I'll call him in the morning." Brooks glanced at his watch. "It's ten thirty, Daisy. I shouldn't have kept you up so late."

"I'll be okay. I'll get an extra-big coffee on my way to work tomorrow. I think your T-shirt is still drying, though."

"Don't worry about it," he said. "I'll get it next time."

Next time.

Brooks slipped back into his suit coat and I walked him to the door.

"I don't know if your ex-husband or Dale Reber had anything to do with your grandmother's death, but I intend to find out. They're despicable human beings. Be careful."

Though it was a warning he'd uttered several times, this time it was accompanied by a tender expression I hadn't seen on his face before. I opened the door.

"Lock this behind me."

"I will. Good night, Brooks." After I locked the door, I checked on Elliott and turned off the lights. As I walked down the hallway the dryer buzzed, signaling the end of the cycle. I pulled out Brooks's T-shirt and folded it, but before I set it down I held it to my nose. There was no hint of his cologne, nor could I detect the smell of his skin.

The only thing I smelled was laundry detergent and fabric softener.

CHAPTER 28

BROOKS

SCOTT DISTEFANO ANSWERED the door of Dale Reber's house when I knocked on it at eight o'clock the next morning, and the sight of him filled me with rage. When he realized I was paying him another visit, he went off on me.

"This is the last time you will knock on my fucking door," he roared. "I told you I don't have anything to say about Pauline Thorpe." He puffed himself up, spoiling for a fight, but backed down almost as quickly. Maybe it was because I was bigger than him, or maybe it was the look he saw in my eyes. I was short on sleep, short on patience, and wound tight enough that I would have welcomed any excuse to knock his teeth down his throat.

"First of all, I'll knock on your door anytime I feel like it." Unlike the first time I'd paid Scott a visit, this time I was armed. "Second, I'm not here about Pauline Thorpe. I'm here to tell you that if you, or Dale Reber, ever come near Daisy again, if you scare her, or put her, or Elliott, in any kind of danger, you'll answer to me. You can count on that."

"Oh… I see." Scott smiled and leaned against the doorframe like he was settling in for a while. "I thought you said you were a reporter, but you must also be the new boyfriend. Here to stake your claim." He laughed. "You think I care that you're fucking my wife?"

Yeah, Scott. I think you would care. I think you'd care a lot.

"She's not your wife anymore. And a man that fails to protect his wife isn't much of a husband. Or a man." He started to slam the door in my face, but I reached out to stop him and said. "Dale Reber. Get him now."

"I don't have to do anything," he said. "You're a reporter, not a cop."

"That may be true," I said. "But I could call my friend Jack down at the police station and tell him I have reason to believe that there are drugs on the premises. He'd get a warrant to search the place, and God only knows what he'd find. I bet that would put a real damper on your high." I pulled out my cell phone.

"Fuck off," he said and slammed the door.

"You fuck off," I muttered.

I waited because I knew we weren't done. Dale Reber opened the door five minutes later wearing a look of pure rage, his gun stuffed down the front of his pants again. He opened his mouth, but before he could speak I cut him off. "Do not go near Daisy DiStefano ever again. Do not look at her. Do not speak to her or touch her. If you do, I'll have the police crawling up your ass so fast your head will spin."

He looked at me with those cold, dead eyes and placed his hand on his gun.

I pushed my jacket back so he could see my holster. "I wouldn't."

He didn't draw the gun, but he didn't remove his hand either. Maybe he figured a gunfight wasn't worth it, or maybe he figured it would draw too much attention if I suddenly came up missing. He spit on the ground by my feet and slammed the door.

I was halfway to my car when he opened the door again and yelled, "It's a shame she came through with the money. That would have been one *fine* piece of ass."

My first instinct was to turn around and go back, but I forced myself to keep walking because if I saw the look on his face, I was afraid I might shoot him.

Once I was in my car I took deep breaths and waited for my blood pressure to return to normal.

Daisy, you are messed up in some bad shit.

And I was getting a lot more involved than I should have, considering the temporary nature of my stay in Fenton.

I looked out over the empty yard. I'd forgotten to bring a burger for the dog, but it didn't matter because it was nowhere to be found. The collar that had been around its neck was still attached to the chain; the water bowl was overturned. Possibly they'd neglected it so badly that it died. The thought of that bothered me all the way back to town.

I called Jack Quick on the way. "Can you meet me at the diner? I need to run something by you."

"Sure. That'll work," he said. "See you in a few."

*

"I'm guessing this isn't a social call," Jack said when he sat down beside me at the counter. The waitress poured him a cup of coffee and took our orders.

"I had dinner with Daisy DiStefano last night, at her house. Her son used one of his toys to reenact what happened the night Pauline Thorpe died."

"And?"

"Whoever killed Pauline said, 'Tell me,' and Pauline said, 'No, I won't.' Daisy and I looked through Pauline's personal items again, but there still doesn't seem to be anything missing." I passed Jack the picture of Dale Reber. "I'm not so sure robbery was the motive, at least not in the sense that whoever killed Pauline Thorpe went there in search of something to steal. I think you should take a look at this guy. His name is Dale Reber."

Jack studied the picture. "What's so special about him?"

"Dale Reber owns the house where Scott DiStefano is living. Shortly before Daisy divorced Scott, she had a run-in with Dale."

Our breakfast arrived.

"Describe run-in," Jack said.

"Scott owed Dale money but was just fine with letting Daisy pay off the debt with her body."

Jack shook his head and grunted in disgust. "I could tell you stories about the things people have done in this town for drug money," he said, fork hovering over his scrambled eggs. "It's the kind of shit that keeps me from sleeping at night. Did he sexually assault her?"

"No. She had some money hidden. She told them they could have it, but then they'd have to leave."

"Smart girl." Jack took a bite of his eggs.

"Yes, but Dale told Daisy he wasn't done with her, and I'm not so sure it was a throwaway comment. He might have meant it. Daisy said she would have told you about it that night at the station, but she didn't have a name to give you and didn't think you could do anything with the information."

"She's right about that. So, what… Scott got behind in his payments again and Dale decided to see if Daisy would come through, voluntarily or involuntarily?"

"That's one possibility. Or maybe Dale needed money for

himself and decided to pay Daisy a visit. It worked for him before. In a town this size, anyone could find out where she lived. Or maybe he was in the middle of a binge and decided porn wasn't going to be quite as satisfying as the real thing. You know what meth does to a person's sex drive."

"Unfortunately, I do."

"But what Dale didn't plan on was Pauline Thorpe answering the door. Maybe his 'tell me' meant that he wanted to know where he could find Daisy."

"So why'd he kill Pauline?" Jack asked.

"Rage. Drug-fueled psychosis. Maybe he got rough with her and when she fell, she hit her head."

"I think you're reaching."

"Maybe. But I can't help but think there's a connection there."

"I can have Dale brought in for questioning," Jack said. "See where he was on the evening of Pauline Thorpe's murder. You never know. Maybe we'll get lucky."

"Well, it's not like anything else is panning out."

"Oh, that hurts McClain." Jack pretended to take a bullet to the chest, but he was smiling a little.

"Sorry. I didn't mean it like that."

"No, it's the truth," Jack said. "And breakfast is on me today."

CHAPTER 29

DAISY

THE KNOCK CAME around eight thirty. I'd just finished taking a long, hot bath and was looking forward to crawling into bed with a book. As Brooks had predicted, I was exhausted from working a twelve-hour shift after staying up with him so late the night before. All I wanted was to read for a while and then fall into restful oblivion. But hearing those three short taps on the door gave me a sudden burst of energy, and I smiled.

Does this man ever call ahead?

I surveyed my appearance and sighed. I was wearing my oldest sweats, the ones with the hole in the knee, and a long-sleeve T-shirt. I'd piled my hair on top of my head in a haphazard bun so it wouldn't get wet in the tub. If Brooks had any interest at all in seeing my glamorous side, he was going to have to give me a bit more lead time.

My smile faded when I looked through the peephole. My heart skittered and knocked around in my chest as the adrenaline started to flow.

Scott must have known how his visit would be received

because he said, "Open up, Daisy. I just want to talk to you." His voice sounded more pleading than angry, and he was alone. Regardless, I kept the chain on when I opened the door.

It had been a little over six months since I'd last seen him, and his appearance had continued to deteriorate. He'd once been a very handsome man, but now his cheekbones were craggy ridges in his gaunt face, and the skin that stretched over them looked sallow. His eyes were puffy and bloodshot; who knew how long it had been since he'd slept? My formerly clean-cut and impeccably groomed ex-husband, who'd insisted on having his hair trimmed every four weeks and rarely skipped a shave, now had at least ten days of beard growth. His hair was long and straggly, and he tucked it behind his ears repeatedly while shifting back and forth on the balls of his feet.

He was also high. I could spot the signs with ease: the fidgeting. The dilated pupils. The beads of sweat dotting his forehead.

"What do you want?" I asked.

"The cops came to my house and I got dragged down to the station and interrogated about Pauline, which I had nothing to do with. Now I got your asshole reporter boyfriend making his second visit, stakin' his claim and telling me I can't come near you. I caught all kinds of hell from my landlord because of that. He gets really pissed off when someone comes nosin' around."

"Landlord, as in Dale Reber?" I asked. He at least had the decency to flinch when I said Dale's name.

"It's private property," Scott said. "He doesn't want people thinking they can drop by whenever they want."

His words infuriated me, especially when I thought about the night he and Dale had dropped by *my* house. "I don't care what Dale Reber thinks or what pisses him off, and you can tell him

I said so. And if either one of you think I'm the same defenseless woman I was that night, you'll learn differently."

He jammed his hands into his pockets and looked down at the floor for a minute. He sounded defeated when he said, "Just tell your boyfriend not to come out to the house anymore."

I didn't bother to explain that Brooks wasn't my boyfriend because it was none of Scott's business.

I was about to shut the door when he looked up and said, "Daisy." There were tears in his eyes. "I miss you. I miss Elliott. I'll do whatever you want. Just let me come home."

"You won't do what I want. You'll do what *you* want, the way you always have. And what you want is to get high. The only thing I ever wanted was a husband who loved me and loved our son. I wanted us to be a family. What I got was a man who chose drugs over both of us."

His expression changed and hardened. "You're a bitch. You never cared about me."

We'd had countless fights that followed this pattern: anger, empty promises and remorse, anger. Arguing with an addict was pointless and futile, and I no longer had the patience for it.

"How dare you say that to me. I'm not a bitch, and all I ever did was try to help you. I suggest you rifle through your memory bank and think about every visit with Elliott that you didn't show up for. Every promise to me that you broke. You threw away every good thing in your life for your addiction. I hope it was worth it." I took a deep breath. "Don't come back here, Scott. Next time I'll call the police."

I shut the door and slid down until I was sitting on the floor, letting my head rest against it. I was proud of myself for standing my ground, but how many more times would Scott and I have to go round and round? The confrontation had only added to my exhaustion, and frustrated tears began to fall. When I finally stemmed their flow, I felt more alone than I ever had.

I wondered where Brooks was at that moment, what he was doing. Just the thought of him was enough to make me feel better, and I remembered what he'd said the night he brought me home after we went to the shooting range.

Call me. If you need me, I'll come.

I felt stupid reaching out to him now that Scott was gone. The surprise visit had left me unsettled, but I'd never been in any danger. Maybe I didn't need Brooks, but I wanted him. I dug my phone out of the pocket of my sweatpants and sent him a text. *Scott was here. I wouldn't let him in. He's gone now.*

Brooks's replied immediately. *I'm on my way.*

I closed my eyes and felt my whole body relax.

"Are you okay?" Brooks asked when I let him in.

"I'm fine. Really," I said. "I overreacted."

"You've been crying." His tone was comforting, and all I wanted was to bury my face in his chest and have him put his arms around me.

"I always cry when Scott and I fight." I locked the door and Brooks followed me into the living room and sat down next to me on the couch. He was still wearing his work clothes, but he'd loosened his tie and looked tired. He'd probably been sitting on the couch with his dad, eating or watching TV when he received my text.

"It's my fault he came here," Brooks said. "I went out there this morning,"

"He mentioned that. What did you say to him?"

"I told him if he came near you again, or if he put you or

Elliott in any kind of danger, he'd have to answer to me." Brooks ran his hands through his hair and exhaled. "I'm sorry. I should have known this was the first place he'd come."

Oh, Brooks. You did that for us? "There's no need to apologize."

"Did he raise his voice or threaten you in any way? Because if he did, I'll be going back."

"It was nothing I couldn't handle. He was high, but he was mostly a mess. He was full of bluster when he arrived, saying that Dale was furious about the cops coming out to the house. He was really mad that you'd been there twice."

"I'm sure the last thing Dale wants is to draw attention to his illegal activities. Cops and reporters probably aren't high on his list of favorite people. What else did he say?"

"He wanted me to give him another chance and he asked to see Elliott. I said no, of course. And then he called me a bitch. Because how dare I not let him come back into our lives."

Brooks shook his head. "That is *not* okay."

"I know it's not, but it's what he always says when he doesn't get his way. Don't go back there. He's not worth another visit." I laid my head against the back of the couch, closed my eyes, and sighed.

"You must be exhausted."

"I am. I just want to put this day behind me." I opened my eyes and looked over at Brooks. "I'm sorry I dragged you out of the house for nothing."

"Do you want me to stay? I can sleep on the couch if you're worried he might be back."

Yes, but not because I'm afraid.

"I'll be okay. I told Scott I'd call the police if he came back."

"Make sure everything's locked up tight. If he does come back, call the police first and then call me."

"I will." I walked him to the door but before he left, I said, "Brooks? How's your mom?"

He shook his head and looked away. "Not good."

I reached out and squeezed his hand, and when he squeezed back I felt the last remnants of our witness-reporter relationship disappear.

CHAPTER 30

BROOKS

I WAS SITTING AT my desk a few mornings later, typing up a story on vandalism in the city park, when I got the call from my dad.

"You should probably come home," he said. "Nina said she's showing some signs."

My spirits sank. I stood up and grabbed my jacket from the back of my chair, filled with dread over what was about to happen yet wanting to hurry home so I wouldn't miss the chance to say good-bye.

He met me at the front door, his eyes teary and red. For a split second I thought I might be too late, but then he said, "She doesn't want her mask on anymore. She's asking for you."

Mom's eyes were closed when I entered the room.

Nina smiled and patted my shoulder on her way out of the room. "I'll be in the kitchen if you need me."

"Brooks?"

My mom's voice had grown so weak I could barely hear her. "I'm here, Mom." I reached for her hand.

"I love you," she said.

"I love you, too."

She held on until 8:43 p.m., my dad and I at her side. Her labored breathing grew slower throughout the afternoon and evening, and she took one last gasping breath, and then her chest didn't rise again. Neither of us spoke. My dad put his head in his hands for a while and when he looked up, his face was wet with tears.

I didn't move. I didn't speak and I didn't cry. I could feel the emotion trying to find an escape route, but nothing happened. I would have welcomed a release of some kind. Anything, really, but none came. The lump in my throat grew larger.

"I'll go get Nina," I said.

After that there were phone calls to make, and a flurry of people arriving. My mother's body was taken away, and Nina gathered up her things and went home after giving my dad and me a hug.

I roamed the house, never staying in one place for very long. My head pounded as I paced the hallway between the kitchen and living room. Finally I told my dad I was going for a drive. "I need to get out of here for a little while," I said. "Will you be okay?"

My dad was sipping a fresh cup of coffee and seemed to be doing a little better. One of his closest friends had arrived and he'd brought his wife with him. She'd sprung into action, fussing over my dad, brewing coffee, and insisting that he eat a piece of the pie they'd brought.

"I'll be fine. Go," he said.

The car was no better than the house. I drove aimlessly for a while, listening to the news on the radio until the noise bothered me so much I turned it off. It wasn't until I pulled into her parking lot that I realized my destination had always been Daisy's apartment. The route I'd taken might have been circuitous, but the goal was the same.

My watch said eleven o'clock. Way too late to show up unannounced, but I knocked on her door anyway, picturing her tiptoeing quietly to look through the peephole. It took a full minute because I'd undoubtedly roused her from a sound sleep. But then she opened the door far enough for me to cross the threshold and locked it again behind me.

The apartment was dark, save for a small beam of light that spilled into the hallway from her bedroom. As my eyes adjusted, I noticed her hair. I'd never seen it down before. It fell way past her shoulders and was slightly messy, like she'd been tossing and turning in her sleep before I arrived. She wore a pair of pajama pants and a tank top with narrow straps, one of which had fallen off her shoulder.

"What is it?" she asked. "Are you okay?"

"My mom died." It felt strange to say the words out loud. My voice sounded flat, unemotional.

"I'm so sorry," she said, but she didn't say anything else.

I wanted something that would take away the empty, restless feeling inside me. Something solid and real. She was standing near enough that one step was all I needed to close the gap between us. She must have taken a shower right before she went to bed because when I plunged my hands into all that hair, grabbing fistfuls and pulling her up against me, I felt the dampness and smelled the faint traces of her shampoo.

I moved my hands to the sides of her face and cupped it. She didn't miss a beat when I pressed my lips to hers. She was probably wondering how I could possibly kiss her at a time like this, but it didn't stop her from putting her arms around me and kissing me back like it was exactly what she needed, too.

Like the steady turn of a release valve, everything that had been bottled up inside me escaped slowly through that kiss. I hadn't realized how rigidly I'd been holding my body until it slackened against hers. How tightly I'd been clenching my jaw until I relaxed it to kiss her. All the tension I'd been feeling disappeared when she opened her mouth and let me in.

It was a long, slow kiss, the kind that wasn't meant to lead to anything else and was all the more powerful because of it. When I'd finally had enough I said, "I don't know why I came. It's late. I woke you up."

"It's okay," she said softly. "I don't mind."

"Go back to bed," I whispered.

She nodded and I opened the door. "Lock this behind me," I said, and I waited in the hallway until I heard the tumble of the lock clicking into place.

I shouldn't have kissed her, because it would only send the wrong signal. Daisy deserved a man who was going to stick around for the long haul. Not someone who couldn't wait to see Fenton in his rearview mirror.

That didn't stop me from wanting to go back for another kiss.

The house was dark when I let myself in. My dad had retreated to his room. The bedroom I'd grown up in seemed the perfect place to finally let my emotions out, and when I was done I fell into a deep and exhausted sleep.

CHAPTER 31

DAISY

I DIDN'T HAVE TO work on the day of Brooks's mom's funeral. Knowing I didn't have many options for child care, Celine had told me she'd be happy to watch Elliott for an hour or two on my days off if I had an appointment or needed to run an errand alone. I'd already confirmed that it would be okay to drop off Elliott, explaining to Celine that I had a funeral to attend.

I'd read the obituary and made note of the funeral arrangements but had gone back and forth, wondering if I should go. I'd only spoken to Brooks's parents once, and I'd never met the rest of his family. There was nothing wrong with paying my respects, but I worried that the gesture might seem too forward.

But that kiss.

Though I understood Brooks had likely only been seeking comfort, you don't kiss a woman like that if you don't at least feel *something* for her.

In light of that, not attending the funeral might have seemed callous, so at a little before two o'clock, I donned a conservative black dress, dropped off Elliott at Celine's, and drove to the First United Methodist Church.

I didn't see Brooks until shortly before the service started. He was sitting off to the side, in the section specifically reserved for the immediate family members of the deceased. He wore a black suit and a somber expression. His dad was sitting next to him, dabbing his eyes occasionally. Brooks bent his head to Theo, said something, and patted him on the back. Brooks didn't seem to have a large family, and there were only about twelve people sitting in the family section.

An usher had led me to a seat at the end of a pew in a middle row. Mary McClain was younger than my grandmother, and the church filled quickly. Before my grandmother died, I had only been to one funeral. A good friend from college lost her mother when we were sophomores, and several of us drove to her hometown two hundred miles away to attend the service. I didn't let on that I hadn't spent much time in church, because everyone else seemed to know what to do and I didn't want to draw attention to myself. I'd followed the lead of my friends: signing the guest book, taking a program from the usher, reciting the Lord's Prayer at the end. The thing that had stood out the most was the organ which accompanied the hymns, rich and sorrowful and louder than I'd expected, the sound filling the church.

I'd been raised largely without religion. I'd been baptized Methodist, though not in the same church that Brooks and his family attended. I'd seen the picture of my mom standing at the altar with the pastor, holding me in her arms as my dad looked on, everyone smiling. When I was ten I asked my grandmother why we never went to church, and she said she'd stopped attending after my parents and sister died. It wasn't until many years later that I finally understood what she meant.

Scott and I got married in the same Lutheran church his parents had been married in. Considering that the ceremony had only lasted twenty minutes, it hardly counted as a religious experience. The reception had proved to be a much lengthier affair, with drinking and dancing that lasted far into the evening.

At the end of Mary's service, I stood when the usher dismissed our row and followed the line of mourners to a vestibule where coats were hung and which led to a side door. Outside, everyone gathered to wait until it was time to drive to the cemetery for the burial.

Brooks caught up with me there. "Daisy."

"Hi," I said, my voice gentle. "How are you doing?"

He gave me a solemn smile. "I'm okay." He put his hand on my arm. "I'm glad you came."

So am I.

"It was a beautiful service," I said.

I waited as a man clapped Brooks on the shoulder and offered his condolences.

After the gentleman moved on, Brooks said, "We're having a reception at the house afterward. I'd like it if you and Elliott could come."

I nodded my head. "Sure. I'll go pick him up from the sitter."

"Let me give you my address."

I dug my phone out of my purse and typed Brooks's address into my GPS app. "We should be back in an hour or so."

Someone called Brooks's name. The hearse was idling near the exit of the church parking lot and I watched as people began walking to their cars. A long black limousine waited for him and his family.

"I have to go," he said.

"Of course." I reached out, gave his hand a squeeze, and said, "I'll see you in a little while."

*

"Why do I have to wear these clothes?" Elliott asked. When I picked him up from Celine's he'd been wearing a T-shirt, tennis shoes, and a pair of jeans, all of which he would have preferred to keep wearing. Now he was dressed in khaki pants and a short-sleeved white button-down shirt with a clip-on plaid tie.

I squeezed him tight. "Because you look adorable in them. We're going to Brooks's house and we need to look our best. It's respectful."

He smiled. "I wike Bwooks. He found my army guy for me."

"That's right. So you want to look nice, don't you?"

"I guess so."

As I was combing his hair I said, "Remember when Nana went away and I told you she wasn't going to live with us anymore?"

"I did not wike that. That maked me sad."

I hugged him. "I know it did, sweetie. It made me sad, too. Brooks's mom isn't going to live with him anymore either."

"Is he sad?"

I made a minor adjustment to his tie. "He's very sad. So we're going to his house to help him feel better. There will be other people there, relatives and friends of the family. We'll tell Brooks how sorry we are, and that we're thinking of him, and then we'll come back home."

"Will there be cookies?" Elliott asked.

I smiled, ruffled his hair, and said, "I think there will probably be something you'll like."

*

When I pulled up in front of Brooks's house, I was able to find a parking spot two houses down, on the opposite side of the street. We made our way through the open front door, past groups of people talking and drinking coffee, holding plates in their hands. The hallway took us past an empty dining room and then opened into the living room area. The kitchen was off to the right.

Brooks was talking to an older woman and he excused himself when he noticed us. "Hi." He bent down to greet Elliott. "A man in a tie. I like your style."

Elliott laughed. "I'm not a man. I'm a wittle boy, remember?"

Brooks laughed, too. He was undeniably gorgeous when he smiled, but when he laughed it transported him to a different level altogether. His eyes sparkled and I noticed how white and even his teeth were when he opened his mouth. There were other things I thought of when I saw his mouth, but I told myself that this was not the time or the place to be thinking about that.

"Got your army guy with you?" Brooks asked.

Elliott reached into his pocket and pulled it out. He looked like he might have been considering giving it to Brooks, but then he quickly shoved it back in his pocket.

"Are you hungry?"

"I could eat a cookie," Elliott said.

"Will pie do?"

"I wike pie!"

"Good, because I think there's more than one to choose from." Brooks stood up and looked beyond Elliott. "Excuse me," he said.

"It looks like my aunt needs me. Please, fix a plate. Have some pie."

"Go," I said. "We'll be fine." I took Elliott by the hand and led him into the kitchen. I found a seat for him at the kitchen table and stood next to it, eating from my own plate and saying hello when people greeted me on their way to the stove or refrigerator. The kitchen seemed to be filled with women. They surrounded Brooks's dad when he entered the room, making sure his coffee cup was full and shooing him back out of the room when he tried to help.

When Elliott was done eating, I cleaned him up as best I could and we moved into the living room to free up space for someone else at the table. Theo sat in an armchair, coffee cup in hand.

"Let's go talk to Brooks's dad for a minute, Elliott."

Theo smiled as we approached.

"Hello, Mr. McClain. I'm Daisy DiStefano. We met briefly at the hospital. This is my son, Elliott. I'm so sorry for your loss."

He shook my hand and said, "Please. Call me Theo. It's nice to see you again."

"What is that, Feo?" Elliott asked, pointing to a framed picture that sat on the table next to Theo's chair. A man with longish curly hair stood beside a fish that stood at least nine feet from the spear-shaped tip of its jaw to the end of its tail.

"It's a blue marlin. I caught it in Hawaii about forty years ago. What do you think about that?"

Elliott looked mesmerized. "It's very big."

"Do you like to fish?"

Elliott shrugged. "I don't know. Nobody ever taked me fishing before."

"Would you like to go fishing with me sometime?"

"I would, I would!" Elliott said. He jumped up and down, but then his expression turned serious. "I would have to ask Mama first."

"Of course," Theo said. "She's welcome to come with us."

I smiled. "As long as I don't have to put any worms on a hook."

I hadn't seen Brooks for a while. Slowly, I searched the sea of faces and found him at the exact moment he appeared to have found me. Both of our heads had been moving as we scanned the room and they stilled simultaneously as we locked eyes. Something good, something unspoken, passed between us. He crossed the room.

"Sorry to leave you alone," he said.

"It's fine, really. You've got lots of people to talk to. I'm afraid Elliott is monopolizing your dad. They've been discussing the finer points of fishing."

We watched Theo smile as he pretended to be a shark while Elliott pretended to reel him in.

"My dad loves kids," Brooks said. "Always has."

"You must be pretty tired."

"I'm okay," he said. "You know what it's like, and you went through it alone."

"I had help. I don't know what I would have done without Pam and Shane."

"Did you and Elliott get something to eat?" he asked.

"Yes. You'll notice my son is wearing his pie on the front of his shirt."

"Ah. Cherry, I see."

I laughed. "Of course it was." It was almost six by then. "I think we're going to head out. I need to get Elliott out of his clothes and into the bathtub before he manages to transfer the pie from his shirt onto every surface of your home."

Brooks grinned. "I doubt he could do much damage."

"Never underestimate a toddler's ability to make a mess. I've learned that lesson the hard way."

"Duly noted," Brooks said. "I'll walk you out."

I offered my final condolences to Theo and peeled my son off him. When we reached the car, I unlocked it and strapped Elliott into his car seat. I moved aside so that Brooks could lean in.

"See you later, Elliott," he said.

Elliott waved. "Bye, Bwooks."

When Brooks straightened up, he said, "I'd like to take you to dinner Saturday night if you're not busy and have someone to watch Elliott."

I beamed, not making the slightest attempt to hide my happiness. "I'm not busy," I said. "I'll ask Pam if she can watch him."

"Is seven okay?"

"Sure."

We stood there, bathed in the glow of the streetlight for a moment, not talking. Was I a horrible person for wishing he would kiss me again? Was he thinking—the way I was—about what we'd done the last time we were alone?

But we weren't alone now.

There were people spilling out the front door of his house and lingering on the front lawn as they prepared to walk to their cars. Brooks didn't strike me as the public-affection type, and truth be told, I wasn't either.

"I better go," I said.

He opened my car door and I slid behind the wheel. "Bye, Brooks."

"Good-bye," he said. "Be safe."

CHAPTER 32

DAISY

PAM AND SHANE picked up Elliott at five o'clock on Saturday. Not only had they agreed to babysit, they had insisted on keeping him overnight once they heard I was going out with Brooks.

"What exactly do you think we're going to do?" I'd asked. "It's just dinner."

"I don't want you to have to worry about anything," Pam had said. "This way, you can stay out as late as you want. Besides, an overnight visit will give us a chance to practice parenting before our own precious progeny arrives."

"In that case, I will thankfully offer up my child as your guinea pig," I said. "Good luck."

Elliott was thrilled to be going on an overnight visit. He picked up the new Thomas the Tank Engine duffel bag he'd insisted we buy and gave me a hug and a kiss before marching toward the door with Pam and Shane.

"I'll be there bright and early tomorrow morning to pick you up," I said. "Be good!"

After they left, I took a long shower and poured myself a small glass of wine. I wasn't used to being alone, and the apartment was way too quiet without Elliott. I switched on the radio and thought about what I was going to wear.

I'd worn a dress to the funeral and I'd styled my hair in a loose knot, so I'd already demonstrated I was capable of something a little more put together than a ponytail and casual clothing. But I wasn't sure what to wear to dinner. For one, I hadn't asked where we were going and Brooks hadn't volunteered any information. There were a few nice restaurants in town, but none of them really qualified as "fine dining." If I pulled out all the stops, there was a very real chance I'd be overdressed. After a few minutes of contemplation, I removed a yellow dress from its padded hanger. The length was slightly above the knee and it was strapless, but I had a cropped ivory cardigan made of cashmere that I could wear over it. A pair of nude high-heeled shoes completed the outfit perfectly. Thankfully, my hair had been a no-brainer: I'd gone with loose waves and left it down. I'd gotten the impression that Brooks liked my hair down, if the way he'd run his hands through it the other night had been any indication.

Maybe I wasn't pulling out all the stops, but I did pull out my red lipstick.

Shortly after my divorce from Scott became final, a middle-aged woman in a restaurant bathroom, a complete stranger, had stood next to me while we washed our hands. When I was done, I pulled a tube of clear gloss out of my purse and applied a quick coat.

She looked over at me and said, "Honey, not every woman can pull off red lipstick. But I think you can. And I think you should." Then she'd walked out, leaving me terribly confused about why I'd been the recipient of such random and unsolicited advice.

But a month later I was walking past the makeup counter at

the outlet mall, and the woman's words came back to me. I stopped in front of the display case, gravitating toward the lipstick.

"May I help you?" the woman behind the counter asked.

"I'm looking for a new lip color," I said. "Red maybe."

She chose several, fanning them across the counter. Peering at me closely, she picked up one of them and said, "This." After she settled me on a high stool, she swiped the lipstick across the back of her hand and then dipped a tiny brush into it. Using short, feathery strokes, she applied it to my lips. "Here," she said, handing me a mirror. "What do you think?"

The lipstick transformed me in a way that made me look like someone else entirely. The woman looking back at me in the mirror was confident. She didn't look like a woman who'd spent the past year in a rapidly deteriorating marriage. She didn't look tired or frazzled or worried or anxious, or any of the other emotions I'd experienced at the hands of my ex-husband.

"Not many women can pull off red lipstick," she said.

"So I've heard."

"You can."

"Sold," I said. "In fact, I'll take two."

Now I leaned in close to the mirror, taking as much care to apply the lipstick as the woman behind the counter had. The rest of my makeup was subdued—a little mascara and eyeliner, and a barely there hint of blush to balance the red.

But my lips.

It would be hard for Brooks to miss them.

When he knocked on the door a few minutes before seven, I peered through the peephole. For the first time since I'd met him, Brooks wasn't wearing a suit. He was wearing dark jeans, a brown sport coat, and an open-collar, striped dress shirt. A leather belt and loafers. He looked like something straight out of the pages of *Esquire*.

Who dresses this man?

I opened the door. "Hi," I said.

"Hi." He studied me, taking his time. "Wow. You are stunning."

I smoothed the front of my dress and smiled. "You look pretty great, yourself."

"Are you ready to go?"

"Yes." I slipped my arms into my sweater and picked up my purse. Brooks and I stepped into the hallway, and I locked the door behind us.

"Where's Elliott?"

"He's spending the night at Pam and Shane's. She's six months pregnant, so they're using Elliott for practice. I didn't have the heart to tell them that a three-year-old is a cakewalk compared to an infant who wakes up multiple times throughout the night. Why shatter the illusion?"

Brooks laughed. "Why, indeed?"

Our dining choices were limited, but Brooks took me to one of the nicest restaurants the town had to offer, an Italian place on Main Street.

"Wine?" he asked after we'd been seated at a dark, cozy table in the corner.

"Please," I said.

"Pinot noir?"

I nodded. "Good memory."

Brooks ordered, and when the waiter came back, he poured us each a glass. Brooks took a small drink and nodded at the waiter.

"How has everything been going? Have you been sleeping okay?" I asked.

"Is that a nice way of saying I look tired?"

"No, not at all. I just had some trouble sleeping after… my grandmother. I thought you might be having trouble, too."

"I did for the first couple of days. It's better now, though."

The waiter took our order—penne with tomato cream sauce for me and chicken parmesan for Brooks.

"Again?" I asked.

"I told you, it's my favorite," he said. "How's the wine?"

"It's perfect."

Brooks took a drink from his glass and set it down. "Tomorrow would have been my parents' wedding anniversary."

"How many years?"

"Thirty-nine. I really thought she'd be able to hold on for it."

"Oh, Brooks."

"I know. Tomorrow will be rough on my dad."

"Thirty-nine years is a marriage to be proud of. The only thing that parted them was death, just like the vows say it should be. Scott and I made it a whole four years. What's that anniversary called? Oh wait, I know. Failure."

"If it makes you feel any better, mine was only marginally longer. We lasted four and a half."

"I didn't know you'd been married before. How long have you been divorced?"

Brooks thought about it for a minute. "About three years."

"What happened?"

"I worked a lot. She wanted to start a family. I was never home. She left."

"I'm sorry."

He shrugged. "As divorces go, it wasn't horrible. I learned a few things from it."

Our entrees arrived and Brooks took a bite of his chicken.

"Well?" I said.

"I've had better," he said, smiling at me.

How was it that I'd ended up with Scott when there were men like Brooks in the world? Had I not already had the worst luck in, well, everything? Had I not paid enough dues?

When we finished our entrees and the plates had been cleared, our waiter came by and said, "Did you save any room for dessert? We have cheesecake, tiramisu, a chocolate torte, cannoli, and gelato."

"What do you think?" Brooks asked.

"What flavor is the gelato?" I asked.

"We have vanilla or dark chocolate."

"Dark chocolate, please." I looked at Brooks. "Share it with me?"

He smiled at the waiter. "Two spoons."

"No problem," he said.

"How's your dad doing?" I asked after our gelato arrived and we scooted our chairs close together and dug into it like we'd been sharing desserts forever.

"He mostly wanders around the house looking for something to do."

"I'm not surprised," I said. "Being a caregiver takes an overwhelming amount of time, even with a nurse's assistance."

"It's a horrible way to die," Brooks said, taking another spoonful of gelato. "I wouldn't wish it on anyone."

"I know I've mentioned it before, but it had to be such a great comfort to your mom to have you here. Not many people would have done what you did. That says a lot about you."

Brooks set down his spoon. "I didn't want to come home," he said. "My dad called one day, clearly upset. He broke down on the phone, crying, and I just blurted it out. Said I'd come. Then later, after I thought about it, I wished I hadn't said it. What does *that* say about me?"

"It's says you're human, for one thing. It takes a lot to uproot yourself like that. And the fact that you came anyway tells me exactly what kind of person you are. Don't be so hard on yourself."

He looked into my eyes, letting the words sink in. "Thanks for that, Daisy."

"You're welcome."

"I felt bad leaving my dad tonight. He insisted he was going to be busy watching TV while I was gone. He was sitting in front of it when I left, except he'd forgotten to turn it on. I'm worried about how he's going to get along when I go back to San Francisco."

His words blindsided me.

When I go back to San Francisco.

I felt myself deflating like a balloon with a slow leak. The landscape of my future, the one I'd foolishly thought Brooks might become a part of, underwent significant changes, invisible and silent. What had I been thinking? That he'd give up his life in San Francisco? His job? Everything he'd left behind? For what? A woman he'd known for five weeks?

Of course he was going home.

I would have bet money that Brooks had feelings for me, but I had obviously misread the depth and scope of them. One great kiss and a look across a crowded room hadn't meant as much as I'd thought they had.

Stupid, stupid, stupid.

Hoping that my crushing disappointment hadn't shown on my face, I forced myself to take another bite of gelato and said, "And when is that again?"

"Sometime next week. Probably Tuesday. My boss wants me back as soon as possible."

"I'm sure you're anxious to get back home."

He studied me as if he was trying to read my thoughts. "I'm not that anxious."

I set down my spoon. "I can't eat anymore."

Brooks ate one more spoonful of gelato and pushed the dish away.

He paid the check and when we rose from the table he placed his hand on my back, guiding me as we walked toward the door. Outside, despite the chill in the air, his touch burned through my dress, the weight of his hand heavy and warm. He opened the car door for me and shut it gently after I was seated.

"Elliott must be getting excited about Halloween," Brooks said after he started the car.

Thankful for something neutral to talk about on the drive home, I said, "He's beyond excited. This is the first year he's really understood how it works. I'm taking him to the pumpkin patch tomorrow so he can pick one out for us to carve."

"Who's he going to dress up as?"

"Batman. I have a feeling we'll be working our way through the list of superheroes for the next several years."

"Every boy has to be Batman at least once. It's a rite of passage."

"Pam and Shane have invited us to go trick-or-treating in their neighborhood. There are lots of young families there."

Families. The word cut through me like a knife.

Brooks pulled into my parking lot and turned off the ignition. We walked into the building and took the stairs to the second floor.

I dug my keys out of my purse, but before I opened the door I took a deep breath and said, "I should probably just call it a night."

"Oh," he said. He didn't sound entirely surprised, but he did sound a bit disappointed. "Okay."

Initially, I had planned on inviting Brooks in. I had envisioned the evening progressing seamlessly from dinner to the "open another bottle of wine and start kissing" stage. Maybe even the "fooling around a little on the couch" stage. I'd been looking forward to the end of the date almost as much as the date itself, because the kiss Brooks and I had already shared only made me want more of them.

I could still invite him in, and we could still do all those things.

But I would only feel worse when he left.

I cleared my throat, looking down at the keys I held in my hand. "It's just that until you mentioned it at dinner, I'd forgotten you'd be leaving, which was—honestly—really stupid of me, because you said way back when you told me about your mom that this was temporary and you'd be going home. So I don't know what I was thinking. I really misread this one, so…"

"Stop," he said, placing his hand on my arm. "Don't act like you got it all wrong. You didn't. I kissed you."

I looked up at him. "I've been kissed before, Brooks. It doesn't always have to mean something."

His hand was still on my arm, and if I didn't go inside soon there was a real possibility I'd lose my resolve. "Thank you for dinner," I said. "I had a nice time tonight." It was the type of thing you said to someone at the end of a blind date that hadn't gone well, but you still wanted to be polite. It was ten times harder to say when the date had been wonderful and you never wanted it to end.

"You're welcome." His voice sounded formal, serious, the way it had when I'd first met him. "I'd like to stop by on my way out of town Tuesday to say good-bye to you and Elliott, if that's okay."

I forced myself to smile. "Sure. We should be around on Tuesday." I opened the door. "Good night, Brooks."

"Good night."

Even though he would have already been in bed if he were home, the apartment felt so empty without Elliott, and I wished he weren't staying at Pam and Shane's. I didn't bother turning on the radio or the TV. After making sure the front door was locked, I walked into my bedroom, kicking off my shoes and sending them flying. I hung the cashmere sweater back up in the closet, but I unzipped my dress and let if fall to the floor where it remained in a crumpled ball. In the bathroom, I soaked a cotton ball in makeup remover and obliterated all traces of the red lipstick. Frustrated tears filled my eyes as I washed my face, and at first I blinked them away, telling myself it was utterly ridiculous to carry on this way about a man I hadn't even slept with.

Maybe my thinking was too rigid, but I wasn't interested in being someone's long-distance girlfriend. Phone calls, e-mail, texts. Six-hour drives each way that would eat up almost two whole days per round-trip, requiring an extra day or two to be tacked on to each visit in order to make it worthwhile. Hoping I could find someone willing to watch Elliott every now and then so Brooks wouldn't be the only one making the drive. Flying was an option, I suppose. But between allowing for enough time to get to the airport, layovers if I couldn't get on one of the direct flights, and then driving from the airport to my or Brooks's place, it hardly made sense.

I didn't want any of that.

Not that Brooks had mentioned it.

I did cry then, curled up in my bed.

I cried because Brooks was a good man.

I cried for what might have been.

I cried because I wanted one damn thing in my life to work out. Just once.

I cried until I got it all out of my system, and when I was done I told myself I wouldn't cry anymore.

Eventually, I slept.

CHAPTER 33

BROOKS

I MADE THE ROUNDS at work, saying good-bye to my coworkers in the newsroom. Maggie only set down her phone long enough to shake my hand and beg me not to leave. "You do know you're abandoning me, right? I was just getting accustomed to only doing one thing at a time, and now I'm back to eating with my left hand and typing with my right. But go ahead, go back to your big newspaper and your bustling city with all its fancy crime."

I laughed. "If it's any consolation, I feel bad leaving you to report all the news by yourself."

"Eh, I'll be fine," she said and gave me a smile. "I'm a born multitasker. Seriously, though. You've been great to have around. And again, I'm so sorry about your mom."

"Thanks. Take care, Maggie."

She gave a little wave and picked up her phone. Next I stopped in Paul's office. I unclipped my badge and handed it across the desk to him. He stood and stretched out his hand. "It's been wonderful having you here," he said. "You're very well liked at the *Desert News*."

"I'm sorry I couldn't stay longer."

"It's okay. We all knew it wasn't permanent, and you did a hell of a job while you were here. Stop in and say hi next time you're in town."

"I will, Paul. Thanks again."

*

My dad helped me carry the last of my things out to the car. We'd made several trips already, similar to the way we'd unpacked the car upon my arrival five weeks ago. I slammed the rear hatch of my Jeep.

"Do you have time for a cup of coffee before you go?" my dad asked.

"Sure." I followed him back inside and took my usual seat at the kitchen table after grabbing a bottle of water from the fridge; if I actually drank another cup of coffee my heart might explode. We'd fallen into a routine in the days since Mom had died: breakfast and coffee in the kitchen, lunch—usually sandwiches—outside at a table on the back patio, and dinner in front of the TV, mostly carryout or pizza. Several breaks throughout the day, which I'd noticed had increased in frequency, sometimes making it seem as if we did nothing but sit and eat and drink. The irony was that, for all the time we spent on those activities, my dad seemed to be eating less and less, and his half-drunk coffee remained on the table until it grew cold, in which case he'd pour a fresh cup and the cycle would begin again.

But we talked, about everything and nothing. We talked more in the days following my mom's death than we had in the past ten years. They were good conversations, and at one point I said, "Would you consider moving to San Francisco?"

"That's very nice of you," he said.

"I wasn't saying it to be nice."

"If I move anywhere it'll be to the cabin." My dad owned a small cabin at Lake Tahoe, and he made several trips a year to go fishing with his buddies.

"Wouldn't you be awfully lonely there?"

"I'll be lonely wherever I go."

There was absolutely no rebuttal for that.

None.

Now, in the kitchen, my dad took a drink of his coffee and said, "I guess you'll want to get on the road soon."

I glanced at my watch. "I can stay a little longer. I told Daisy I'd stop by and say good-bye to her and Elliott on my way out of town."

"She's that pretty nurse, right?"

"Yes. Her son is the one you said you'd take fishing."

"Then I better keep my promise. She gave me her number at the hospital. I think I've still got it around here somewhere."

"I feel like I'm deserting you, Dad."

"You've got your own life to lead, and I have mine. It won't be the same without your mother by my side, but I'll get by."

"I can't imagine what this is like for you."

"No, I don't suppose you can. Until you find a woman you can't live without, it will be hard for you to imagine what it's like when she's gone. Your mother did everything in her power, every single day, to make me happy. I would have gone to the ends of the earth for her if she'd wanted me to. That's what it comes down to. When you find a woman who makes you happy, you've got to make her happy, too. And hold on to her tight, because you won't have any way of knowing how long she'll be yours. No matter how long it is, you won't feel like it's been enough when she's gone."

My dad stood up and carried his coffee cup to the sink. He

stared out the window and said, "You better get going. Especially if you still have a stop to make."

I pushed my chair back and my dad followed me out to the driveway. After we hugged, I said, "I'll be back in about a month, for Thanksgiving."

"That'll be fine. Don't feel like you have to come, though."

I knew what he was thinking: that the only reason I'd still come home for the holidays would be to lessen my feelings of guilt over him being alone. Then, after the holidays were over, he'd expect my visits to get shorter and the amount of time between them to get longer. Eventually, we might transition to phone calls instead of actual visits. It was true that my mom had been the glue that held this family together when it came to the holidays. In all the time I'd lived in San Francisco I'd only missed a few holiday dinners, and that was only because I had to work. But as I stood there in the driveway, one hand on the door of my car, I vowed not to become the kind of man who would stop spending the holidays—or time in general—with his dad, even when his dad seemed perfectly willing to give him a free pass.

"I'll be there, Dad."

He nodded and gave me another hug. "Drive safe."

*

Daisy answered the door when I knocked. Elliott was standing next to her. I felt a pang when she smiled and said, "Hi."

"Hi."

"Hi, Bwooks!" Elliott said, jumping up and down.

I ruffled his hair. "Hey, buddy."

Daisy was holding a sand bucket containing a shovel and some plastic toys in one hand and her purse in the other.

"Are you going somewhere?" I asked.

"We're heading to the park to play for a while before Elliott's nap. Would you like to come with us?"

"Sure. I'm not in any hurry."

"It's only a couple of blocks away, so we can walk." She looked at me and raised an eyebrow. "Jeans and a T-shirt? You're slipping."

I smiled. "I have a casual side. Just don't expect me to show up in a wifebeater and baggy jeans."

Daisy wrinkled her nose. "Do you even own such things?"

I gave her a look. "Please."

When we reached the park, Elliott said, "I want to dig in the sand first."

Daisy handed him his bucket. "Brooks and I will be right over there," she said, pointing at a nearby picnic table.

"Okay, Mama." Elliott walked to the sandbox ten feet away and plunked himself down, upending his bucket of toys.

"Are you packed and ready to go?" Daisy asked after we sat down on top of the picnic table so that we were facing the sandbox, our feet resting on the bench.

"Yes. I told my dad good-bye already."

"I bet that was hard," Daisy said.

"It was. I asked him to consider moving to San Francisco."

"What did he say?"

"He said no. We have a fishing cabin at Lake Tahoe. It's kind of rustic, but he loves it. He said if he moved anywhere it would be to the cabin. Speaking of which, I reminded him that he said he'd take Elliott fishing sometime."

"That's very nice, but I don't want him to feel like he has to. I can take Elliott myself."

"Honestly, he wouldn't be doing it out of a sense of obligation. He loves kids and he loves to fish."

"Okay then. Elliott would love that." Daisy set her purse

beside me. "Can you watch this? And keep an eye on Elliott for a second? I have to go to the bathroom. I never leave him unattended when we're here, so it's a rare luxury not to have to make him stop playing and come with me."

"Absolutely. Go. We'll be fine."

"Thanks. I'll be right back."

Daisy had only been gone a matter of minutes when some kid—a boy of maybe eleven or twelve—sprinted through the sandbox, weaving between the kids who were playing. Elliott, who had been squatting in the sand, lost his balance and fell backward on his butt. Remembering that I'd promised to watch Daisy's purse, I scooped it up and intercepted the boy as he turned around to make his way back through the sandbox again.

"Hey!" I said. "Did you not see the little kid you almost ran over?"

"How am I supposed to see him?"

"I don't know, maybe with your *eyes*." I led him over to Elliott. "Quit being a punk and tell him you're sorry."

"Sorry," he mumbled.

"Go," I said, pointing my finger toward the other side of the playground.

I helped Elliott to his feet. "Are you okay?"

He adjusted his glasses. "I is okay, Bwooks. That boy is mean. One time he kicked sand in my face and it stinged!"

"Then what happened?"

"Mama tooked me to the bathroom and splashed water in my eyes. Then she got mad at that boy."

Daisy walked up to us. "What happened?"

"That kid over there almost ran over Elliott."

Daisy turned to see who I was pointing at. "Oh, yes. I have to watch that one. He's here all the time."

"So I've heard. Here," I said, handing Daisy her purse. "I didn't want to leave it on the table."

"Thanks."

"I want to play with my toys," Elliott said.

"You can have ten more minutes. It's almost nap time."

I followed Daisy back to the picnic table.

After we sat down, she said, "There are so many reasons I want a house of my own someday, but one of the biggest is so that Elliott can play safely. I want a fenced-in yard with a sandbox and a swing set that's just his."

"Something tells me you'll have it," I said.

"I will," she said. "I'm getting closer every day."

Daisy's independence and resourcefulness were two of the qualities I admired the most about her. She certainly wasn't waiting around for anyone to give her the things she wanted.

"Listen, you need to go to the range and shoot, okay? Don't let too much time go by without handling your gun. You won't be as comfortable with it. Are you taking it with you when you leave the house?"

"It's in my purse right now. That's why I asked you to watch it."

"I'm worried about you and Elliott. Don't get complacent, even if you think the threat of danger has passed."

"We'll be fine," she said. She tried to sound stoic, but there was no mistaking the undertone of sadness I heard in her voice.

Daisy was a lot of things: beautiful, kind, smart, and strong. But she was a horrible actress, and the look on her face at dinner, the one she'd waited a few seconds too long to hide, told me how she really felt about my leaving. And if I'd had any doubt, she drove the point home by not asking me to come in, proving that she had a hell of a lot more self-restraint than I did. Because if she had invited me in, the first thing I would have done as soon as she closed the door was back her up against it and kiss her. I'd been desperate to feel her mouth underneath mine again, especially since I'd been staring at it all through dinner. I wanted to plunge my hands into her hair, and I wanted to touch her wherever she'd let me.

But I'd put my life on hold, and it was waiting for me to come back to it. Staying in Fenton was never supposed to be anything other than temporary. What was I supposed to do? Quit my job in San Francisco and move to Fenton?

I had to go.

However, now that my leaving was imminent and despite the fact that I loathed long-distance relationships, I couldn't bear the thought of cutting ties with her.

"My work schedule makes it hard to come back as often as I'd like, but I'll be in town for the holidays. We could get together then. In the meantime, there's always the phone. And we could e-mail and text. Whatever you want. There's a direct flight out of Ontario. I could fly you up sometime."

"That's a really nice offer," she said. "But I've been waiting so long for my life to start. To get past these roadblocks and false starts. I need to move forward, and I have Elliott to think about, too. I'm sorry."

She hardly needed to apologize, not when I was the one who was leaving.

"I'll miss you, Brooks." She hopped off the picnic table and avoided my eyes when she said, "It's time for Elliott's nap." She walked over to him and crouched down, helping him gather his sand toys.

When they began walking toward me, I met them halfway. "Here, I'll carry the bucket."

Daisy gave it to me and took Elliott by the hand, leading him across the parking lot and toward the sidewalk. Elliott reached up and put his other hand in mine, and he kept ahold of both of our hands all the way home, even as we walked, three abreast, up the stairs to the second floor.

When we reached Daisy's door, I crouched down until I was at Elliott's eye level. "I have to go now. You're an awesome kid."

He smiled at me, no idea what kind of good-bye this was. "Okay, Bwooks. Bye!"

I waited until Daisy opened the door and then I handed her Elliott's bucket.

"You better get going," she said.

"Good-bye, Daisy." I wanted to kiss her, but that's how this whole mess had gotten started.

Elliott's hand slid from my grasp as he and Daisy walked into the apartment and shut the door behind them.

His hand was small and soft and scratchy with sand, and letting go of it was almost as hard as saying good-bye to his mother.

CHAPTER 34

DAISY

IT'S TRUE THAT when it comes to men, my luck hasn't been all that great. I lost my virginity to my high school boyfriend, Curt, the night of our senior prom—right after we pledged our undying love to each other—and was unceremoniously dumped by him four months later after we left for separate colleges. He'd discovered that a smorgasbord of drunken hookups was infinitely preferable to remaining faithful to a girl who was matriculating halfway across the country.

After Curt, I started dating Joe, who was kind and thoughtful and showed me by comparison that Curt had had absolutely no idea what he was doing in bed. Joe and I dated until graduation, when he finally admitted that he couldn't see himself settling down at twenty-two and took off for an extended backpacking trip through New Zealand. The truth was, I wasn't ready to settle down either, and it was only in retrospect that I realized Joe and I hadn't been well matched in a number of significant ways, most notably his propensity for taking giant bong hits, playing video games for twenty-four hours straight, and his reluctance to "join the rat race." And by rat race he meant get a job.

Despite never having traveled much herself, my grandmother had tried her hardest to instill in me a sense of adventure, of wanderlust. "There is so much to see in this world, Daisy," she'd said. "Don't limit yourself to your own backyard."

I'd started out on the right track. I'd gone off to college at San Diego State with hardly a backward glance. I'd spent a memorable vacation in Australia with a few of my closest friends during winter break of my junior year and was looking forward to seeing a few more stamps in my passport in the not-too-distant future. There were plenty of cities in the US I'd never been to, either, and I planned to rectify that as well.

When I graduated, my classmates began to scatter themselves across the country: to New York City and Portland. Austin, Seattle, and Boston.

But not me.

I collected my BSN and came right back home to the only constant I'd ever known. I couldn't imagine my grandmother living out her final years in that small apartment all by herself, despite the fact that she'd never once acted like she minded.

I *would* travel someday.

I would leave this dying town.

I had plenty of time to start living my life. In the meantime, I settled into my job at the hospital and decided I had a lot to be happy about.

One night after seeing a movie, Pam suggested we eat at Dee's Place. The restaurant, which was owned by the family of one of our classmates and named after his mother, DeAnna, had been around for as long as I could remember. The menu focused on home cooking, and was heavy on meat and potatoes, which had never been my thing.

"Dee's Place?" I said to Pam. "Really?"

"There was a write-up about it in the paper," Pam said. "It's called DiStefano's now. Didn't you see it?"

"No, I must have missed that one." The *Desert News* included a weekly supplement to the newspaper called the *Desert Diner*. The reviewer seldom pulled any punches, and as a result the reviews were often highly entertaining.

"Apparently it's had a complete overhaul. The reviewer couldn't stop raving about everything."

"All right," I said. "Let's give it a try."

When Pam and I walked through the front door, I blinked several times. The interior had been completely gutted. The standard restaurant-issue tables and chairs—with their Formica tops and vinyl upholstery—had been replaced with cozy booths that lined the perimeter of the room and counter-height tables arranged in a line down the center. Gone were the kitschy knick-knacks, plastic-covered menus, and the old jukebox that had stopped working sometime in the early nineties. Polished, dark hardwood had replaced the old linoleum and whoever had designed the lighting was a genius. Pendants in jewel tones hung from the ceiling, giving the dining area a beautiful glow.

"Wow," I said. "This is incredible."

The woman who greeted us was at least five years older than we were and was dressed all in black: fitted turtleneck, pencil skirt, sky-high stiletto heels that click-clacked on the floor as she led us to our table. She had diamond studs in her ears and wore her hair in a tasteful bun. I would come to find out that all the women who greeted the customers—no one would dare refer to them as mere hostesses—dressed in an identical manner, like something out of a Robert Palmer video.

Pam looked down at her jeans and lightweight sweater. "I feel like a total slob," she said after we'd been seated.

I was dressed in a similar outfit. "Me, too. I'm buying a pair of black stilettos tomorrow. I have nowhere to wear them, but I must have them."

"She classes up the place, that's for sure."

Our second shock came when we perused the leather-bound menu.

"There's no meatloaf," I said.

"Or gravy," Pam said.

"Thank God," we said in unison.

"Look, they have tapas," Pam said, pointing to a section of the menu. She read the description: "A selection of small plates of food from around the world, which allows a wide variety of choices and ample time for conversation between courses."

"I see bruschetta and sautéed prawns," I said.

"And stuffed figs," Pam said. "I don't even know what that would taste like, but I'm intrigued. Should we start with two or three and go from there?"

"I'm in."

We were on our second round of tapas—duck meatballs, calamari, and mushroom and brie crostini—and halfway through a bottle of wine when I spotted Scott DiStefano across the room. He spoke to a bartender and then stopped by a booth in the corner where he spent several minutes talking to the people seated there.

I'd known Scott all my life and had, in fact, recently come across a box of keepsakes, one of which was my kindergarten class photo. In it, Scott had been missing one of his front teeth and his blond hair was so light it looked white. He was quiet, bookish, and sort of shy, and I'd never thought of him in a romantic way despite the fact that he was good-looking. He'd had the same girlfriend all through high school, a studious and quiet girl named Megan who moved here from Philadelphia in sixth grade.

"Scott DiStefano is over there," I said to Pam.

"Where?"

"He's talking to the people in that booth."

"Do you think he's the one behind all this?" Pam asked.

"Maybe." That surprised me, though, because I wouldn't have guessed that staying in Fenton had ever been on Scott's short list of goals for the future. He'd graduated in the top five percent of our class and been named "most likely to succeed" in our senior roundup. I'd assumed he'd go the investment banker route, or maybe pursue a law or medical degree.

I must have been staring because Scott caught my eye and smiled. Two minutes later, a server arrived with a much nicer bottle of wine than the one we'd been drinking. "With compliments, from Mr. DiStefano," our server said.

Scott eventually made his way to our table. "Hey," he said. "I'm glad you stopped in."

Scott at twenty-three was even more attractive then he was when I'd last seen him, which was probably the summer after we graduated high school. He'd always been tall, but he'd filled out a little and his boyish good looks had given way to features that were a bit more mature and refined.

"This is absolutely fantastic, Scott," Pam said. "I'm full, but I don't want to stop eating."

Scott smiled modestly. "I'll let the chef know." He turned to me. "What about you, Daisy? Do you like it?"

"It's incredible. And thank you for the wine."

"You're welcome."

"So, are you running the restaurant now?" Pam asked. "I thought you were at UCLA."

"I was. I graduated with a business degree last spring. But then my mom got sick and she and Dad started talking about selling the restaurant and moving to Florida."

"What's wrong with your mom?" I asked.

"Congestive heart failure."

"How old is she? Are her symptoms due to heredity or lifestyle?" I asked. "Is she responding to treatment?"

"Daisy's a nurse," Pam said. "She's not just being nosy."

"You're a nurse?" Scott asked.

"Yes. At the hospital in Barstow."

"Oh," he said. "I figured you were the type who would move away."

"Really?" Because it was just my grandmother and me, I assumed most people would think I was the type who would never leave.

"I just pictured you in a bigger city. You have that look."

What look? "I don't know about that," I said, "but I decided to stay."

"The doctor said my mom's prognosis is good, but that she had to make some changes. She can't be on her feet constantly. The strain of fourteen-hour days isn't something she can handle anymore, and my dad is just tired in general, I think. They're only in their late fifties, but they want to retire. They weren't ready to sell the restaurant, though. They asked me to consider postponing my plans for a year and asked if I'd be willing to take over."

"Well, you've done a fantastic job," I said.

"Thanks," he said. "I didn't expect to like it this much. I only agreed because I could tell they were really torn up about parting with this place. I figured I could give them a year. It helped that they told me I could make whatever changes I wanted. I hired a new chef and we put our heads together and decided to completely overhaul the menu, which was risky because I wasn't sure how customers would respond. So far, the feedback has been overwhelmingly positive."

"This is exactly what this town needed," Pam said. "Although I have to say my boyfriend, Shane, will probably miss the old menu. That boy is meat and potatoes all the way."

Scott laughed. "Well, when you come back you'll have to leave him at home and bring Daisy instead." He looked right at me when he said it, and suddenly I saw my future in a whole new light.

Scott pursued me with the same diligence and enthusiasm he poured into making the restaurant a success. He was kind, he was romantic, and he treated me like a princess. I fell for Scott DiStefano, and I fell for him hard.

"He sure is a charmer," my grandmother used to say.

I stopped thinking about leaving. Why would I? Everything I wanted was right there in front of me.

By the time I turned twenty-four, Scott and I were engaged. We were married at twenty-five and pregnant at twenty-six. Elliott came along right after my twenty-seventh birthday. Scott worked long hours and so did I, but my grandmother watched Elliott on the days I worked, and I still had four days a week to spend with him. When I wasn't working, we'd go to the restaurant for lunch and Scott would carry Elliott around, showing him off to the staff.

I had never been happier.

Eventually, the fatigue of working fourteen-hour days, seven days a week, caught up with Scott. He tried to take time off, but whenever he attempted to steal away he inevitably got called in to solve a problem or cover a shift because an employee called in sick. I convinced him to hire a general manager, but Scott was unable to turn over the reins to anyone for very long. He needed to have his hand in everything, which resulted in frequent power struggles.

The manager stormed out one day and didn't return. Scott refused to hire a replacement.

Over the next year, our household and marriage started to suffer.

Then one day Scott abruptly stopped complaining about being tired. He didn't come home, eyes red-rimmed, and announce that he was about to fall asleep on his feet. He didn't grumble when two of his waiters called in sick on the same night. He stayed at the restaurant doing inventory and organizing the back room long after the last employee had left. He was suddenly *energetic* after working for days on end. When he *was* home, he was either playing with Elliott or working on the long list of odd jobs around the house that needed attention.

I wasn't completely naïve when it came to drugs, thanks to my pot-smoking college boyfriend Joe, but when I caught Scott smoking a bowl of meth with one of his busboys, I knew I had a much more serious problem on my hands. Scott's ability to stay awake, to multitask and be superdad, had come from a source much more sinister than caffeine or energy drinks.

I cried.

I raged.

He confessed and promised he'd never do it again.

What followed was a year and a half of confrontation, threats, and watching our disposable income go straight into the coffers of the local meth dealers. When the abuse turned into full-fledged addiction and I watched all the money we'd saved for a down payment on a home disappear, I decided I could no longer save him and started making plans to leave. The night my husband stood by, idly waiting for me to pay off his drug debts with my body, was the night I realized how treacherous my environment had become. All that mattered was finding a safe place for Elliott and me.

I'd always thought Scott and I would grow old together, front porch swing and all that, but instead I signed my name on the dotted line of several legal documents, severing our union permanently.

And though I had no interest in dating right away, I found myself rebounding from Scott with Nick. He was smart, attractive, kind, and—most importantly—he hated drugs.

But it should come as a warning to all women that the first man they fall in love with after they get divorced should not be the lawyer who'd handled it for them. Especially when you later discover you are compatible in every single way except the one that matters most to him.

So all I wanted by the time Brooks came along was one good man. Someone who was smart, attractive, kind, didn't do drugs, and was on the same page as me.

Someone who would treat Elliott as his own.

I was willing to keep looking with the hope that someday a relationship would work out for me.

I chose to remain optimistic.

I *wanted* to fall in love again.

I'd never understood the notion of putting up walls or pushing away a great guy because those who'd come before him had hurt me. Wasn't that the same thing as being unhappy? Wouldn't I be just as alone?

But it wasn't only about me anymore. I had Elliott to consider.

When I told Brooks that the end of my last relationship had been hard on Elliott, it was nothing compared to what it would be like as each year passed. The older Elliott got, the more he would have to bear the loss of any man I introduced him to, without the cognitive ability necessary to fully understand it.

If I didn't have a child to consider, I would have entered into a long-distance relationship with Brooks in a heartbeat. Yes, they had their limitations, but so what?

It would have been worth every mile I put on my car.

Every phone call.

Every vacation day.

But I did have a child, and his well-being meant more to me than anything in the world.

I was getting really tired of what the universe kept throwing at me, but I held out hope that one day what the universe sent would be everything I needed.

CHAPTER 35

BROOKS

I FLIPPED ON THE lights and set down my keys and phone on the counter, loosening my tie as I walked down the hallway to my bedroom. A few of my fellow reporters had taken me out for a welcome-back beer, which turned into several after half the newsroom decided to join us. I'd stumbled my way out of the bar at one a.m. after the Features editor finally stopped ordering shots for everyone.

I'd taken the train home and now all I wanted was to trade my work clothes for a pair of sweats and a T-shirt. After I changed, I stopped in the kitchen for a big glass of water, some Motrin, and an antacid.

I'm getting too old for this shit.

At least it was Friday. I could sleep in unless there was breaking news, in which case I'd haul my tired, hungover ass out of bed to chase the story. My phone signaled an incoming text, so I grabbed it from the counter and headed to the living room, resting my feet on the coffee table after I sat down on the couch and turned on the TV.

The text was from Diana: *I heard you were back. I'm so sorry about your mom. Are you free tomorrow night?*

Diana was a pretty thirty-five-year-old brunette who worked as a broadcast journalist for one of the local news stations. We'd met many years ago when we were first starting out. She'd scooped me on a very big story—although I maintained it was only because she happened to be in the vicinity of the crime when the news broke—and I made sure it never happened again. This resulted in a mutually respectful—yet highly competitive—friendship that morphed into something else after Diana's marriage failed roughly two years after mine. Unlike me, Diana had been married to her high school sweetheart for fifteen years and had promised herself at least one year—maybe two—to sow the oats she hadn't sown when she was younger.

I'd been divorced longer than Diana, and I still hadn't figured out what I wanted. Sex? Absolutely. Commitment? Sure. If the right girl came along. In the meantime, Diana and I had a casual arrangement that included overnight visits once or twice a week and not much else. It suited us both. Occasionally I brought Diana to a wedding or other function that warranted a date, but that was about as far as it went with us. Ours was a union of convenience, mostly, and I held no illusion that I was the only guy Diana was sowing her oats with. But since we always practiced safe sex, I was hardly in a position to complain.

It's difficult for reporters to date someone outside the industry. The news waits for no one, but women aren't usually okay with the idea that you might have to randomly abandon them at a moment's notice, regardless of what you're in the middle of doing. This is especially problematic when the woman you've been dating for a few months—who you really like and could picture settling down with—suddenly reads the writing on the wall and realizes you may be gone.

A lot.

Without notice.

Which doesn't work for her.

That means a reporter either has to find a woman who doesn't mind (trust me, they all mind), or he dates another reporter. Since I have an aversion to dating my coworkers, this leaves me with an incredibly small pool of women to swim around in.

I sent a quick text back to Diana. *Thanks. Sorry. Already made plans.*

The fact that Diana and I hadn't interacted during the whole time I'd been gone didn't bother me, because it had not crossed my mind to reach out to her, either. But it did serve to highlight the emotionless quid-pro-quo nature of our relationship.

Daisy's name was right above Diana's on my text log. I clicked on it and read the text I'd written when I got back into my Jeep the day I said good-bye to her and Elliott.

I'll miss you, too.

I'd never sent it, because what purpose would it serve?

But now that I was back in San Francisco, Daisy was never far from my thoughts. On my first day back to work, I stopped at the coffee shop around the corner from my apartment. As I stood in line, I noticed the music playing on the sound system, an instrumental version of "Daisy Jane" that they'd probably played hundreds of times before. Instantly I pictured Daisy in her yellow dress, red lips curved upward in a smile. I was so lost in the memory that the barista had to say, "Sir. Sir?"

Two days later I spotted a woman beside me on the street who was walking with a child, a little boy who looked about Elliott's age. She was holding his hand and they were laughing. I slowed my pace to match theirs and watched as a man walked out of a building up ahead. He spotted them and smiled, and when the little boy broke free from his mother and ran toward the man, he swung him up into his arms. When the woman reached them he leaned down while holding the child and kissed her.

Everywhere there were things that reminded me of Daisy: chicken parmesan advertised as the daily special on a restaurant's sidewalk chalkboard, a display of pinot noir at the market, a gelato stand. It seemed that every beautiful woman I passed on the street wore her blond hair in a ponytail.

I deleted the text message and typed a new one.

I hope things are going okay. My thumb hovered over the Send button.

It was one thirty a.m. by then, and Daisy would be sleeping. The last thing I wanted was to wake her up by sending the lamest text ever, especially after she'd shot down my offer to stay in touch via phone and computer, which, in hindsight, was a little bit like the type of relationship I had with Diana in that it would cause very little disruption in my life.

Or effort on my part.

But when I closed my eyes I didn't see Diana, I saw Daisy.

I saw her face and her smile and that damn hollow at the base of her throat that I wanted to press my lips against.

I erased the text and threw my stupid phone across the room where it hit a chair and clattered onto the hardwood floor.

And even though there were no breaking-news stories overnight and I could have slept in until noon if I'd wanted to, I woke up at six a.m. because for some reason, I couldn't sleep.

CHAPTER 36
DAISY

"Hold still, Elliott. I can get you into this thing a lot faster if you quit moving around."

"Hey, Pam," Shane yelled. "Did you know Batman is in our kitchen?"

Pam came waddling around the corner. "Oh my God, look at him!"

Elliott beamed.

"Let's put your mask on so Pam and Shane can get the full effect," I said.

"Does Batman wear gwasses? If Batman doesn't wear gwasses, I don't want to wear them either."

"If Batman needed glasses to help him see, he would wear them. I know he would. And you want to be able to see, don't you?"

"I guess so," he said.

I maneuvered the bows of Elliott's glasses underneath the mask and then took several pictures of him. "You are the most adorable superhero I've ever seen."

"Will I get lots of candy?"

"Way more than you need," I said.

"Is it time to go?" he asked.

I glanced at my watch. "A few more minutes. Where's your bucket?"

"It's out there," he said, pointing to the living room.

"Why don't you grab it and we'll get ready to head out?"

Pam stayed behind to hand out candy while Shane accompanied Elliott and me as we walked around Pam and Shane's neighborhood, stopping at every house within a three-block radius until Elliott began walking slower and slower. Shane picked him up. "You gettin' tired, little guy?"

Elliott rubbed his eyes. "I'm not tired. I want to eat candy."

"You can have two pieces," I said. "But that's it."

"You got a piece of candy for me?" Shane asked.

Elliott held his bucket tightly to his chest. "I will check."

"Maybe your wife will let you steal a few pieces from her bowl."

"You want me to take candy away from a pregnant lady?" Shane's eyebrows shot up. "Are you insane?"

"I've got an extra bag in the kitchen. I'll hook you up."

"Always looking out for me, aren't you, Daze?"

I smiled. "It takes a village."

When we got back to Pam and Shane's, Elliott insisted on dumping out his candy on the living room floor so he could sort it into piles based on the color of the wrapper. Shane sat down beside him while I joined Pam on the front steps to finish handing out candy. By then it was mostly stragglers who hadn't gotten an early start. A few junior high school kids who hadn't bothered with a costume slowed down in front of the sidewalk but changed their minds and kept going when Pam glared at them.

The nighttime temperature was in the low fifties, and I pulled my jacket tighter around me to ward off the chill.

"Do you think I did the right thing with Brooks?" I asked.

"Why, are you having second thoughts? Your argument for why a long-distance relationship wouldn't work made a lot of sense to me."

"I don't know. It's just that now that a little time has gone by I wonder if my decision was a bit hasty. You know, baby, bathwater, blah, blah, blah. Outside of the whole kissing thing, I felt like we were friends. You can never have too many of those, right?"

"True. But then again, it's probably better that you put an end to things before you really fell for him."

"Yes, that would be so unfortunate," I deadpanned.

Pam looked at me with a sympathetic expression. "Oh, no," she said. "Really?"

"Well, it's just that he's so..." I made an exasperated sound. "Perfect. He's perfect, okay?" Pam started to speak, but I held my hands up and said, "You know what? Never mind. I don't want to talk about it. What's done is done and I'm not going to dwell on it. Besides, I've got plenty of things to keep me busy. I've started planning your baby shower."

"Promise me you won't melt candy bars in diapers and make us play 'guess what this is?'"

"Like you did for my baby shower?"

"Did I do that?"

"Yes. And I feel it's my duty as a friend and a mother to tell you that real baby shit does not look or smell even remotely like a Butterfinger."

"How long do think it'll be before Shane throws up?"

"He might be okay until the baby starts on solid food. After that he's on seriously borrowed time."

"That's kinda what I thought."

The screen door creaked and Shane said, "Uh, Daisy? Elliott said he doesn't feel good. I think he ate a few extra pieces of candy when I went to the bathroom."

I laughed. "Don't feel bad. He's very clever that way."

Pam and I followed Shane inside.

"Elliott? How many pieces of candy did you eat?" I asked when we reached the living room.

"Two."

I counted no fewer than five crumpled-up wrappers on the carpet. "Two, huh? Oh, Halloween," I said, sighing. "You're all fun and games until a three-year-old eats himself sick." I picked up Elliott and rubbed his back, and he laid his head on my shoulder.

"Thanks for letting us borrow your neighborhood," I said.

"You're more than welcome," Pam said. She leaned in and gave Elliott a hug. "Bye, sweetie." She turned back to me. "I wish you'd reconsider Thanksgiving."

Pam and Shane were traveling to San Diego to spend the holiday with Pam's family at her aunt and uncle's house. Not wanting Elliott and me to be alone, they'd invited us to come with them. In the past, I'd always celebrated the holiday with my grandmother and maybe one or two of the widowed ladies who lived in our building if they didn't have other plans. Scott had even enjoyed the quiet, low-key gathering, saying it was a nice change from the frantic pace of the restaurant.

"I appreciate the offer, really I do," I said. "But I have to work the next day, and with the drive we'd get home pretty late. Elliott and I are going to cook a turkey and relax on the couch. We'll watch the parade and the dog show and whatever Disney movie he wants to watch. We'll be fine." And we would, although someday

I hoped to celebrate the holidays with a slightly larger gathering of people.

"Let me know if you change your mind. You and Elliott are always welcome."

I reached out and gave Pam a one-arm hug. "Thanks." After hoisting Elliott a little higher on my hip I said, "Okay, Batman. Let's go home."

CHAPTER 37

DAISY

MY FEET WERE dragging when I left work on Friday. The insomnia that had plagued me during the rough times with Scott had returned—though I wasn't sure why—and my sleep had been coming in fits and starts. Sometimes I dropped off without any trouble but would wake up at three a.m. and never get back to sleep. Sometimes I couldn't fall asleep until after one, and since my alarm was set to go off at five fifteen, that wasn't nearly enough time to become fully rested. I was becoming seriously sleep-deprived but was hesitant to employ the use of a sleep aid, fearing that it would make me groggy in the morning or prevent me from hearing Elliott if he needed me during the night. My sleep problems didn't seem as prevalent on the weekends, so I was looking forward to catching up on my rest a little bit.

Despite telling Pam I wasn't going to dwell on my decision not to stay in touch with Brooks, I'd been unable to stop thinking about him. The more I tried to get him off my mind, the more aware I was of the loss of him. I missed his smile and I missed the way I felt when he was around. Earlier in the week, one of the doctors I worked with had asked if I might like to go to dinner some night, and I'd given him my number. He seemed like a nice man, handsome and obviously intelligent, but I didn't feel the spark I did when Brooks was around. I promised myself I would give it a chance, though. Who knew what might develop after I'd had a chance to get to know him?

I picked up Elliott at Celine's and sat him down on my bed with a book while I showered off the hospital germs and slipped into pajama pants and a tank top. Then, after a quick bedtime snack, I tucked him into bed and read to him, blinking to maintain my focus.

When I yawned, Elliott said, "Mama is tired."

"Yes. Mama is tired. And so is Elliott. Time to go to sleep." I gave him one last kiss and gently closed his bedroom door.

Lacking the energy to do anything else, I flopped down on the couch and turned on the TV. It was 8:04. If I fell asleep this early, I'd regret it later when I was staring at the ceiling at two in the morning, but I was so exhausted I really didn't care. *I'll just take a short nap*, I promised myself.

When the knock came—three short, rhythmic taps—I thought I'd only been asleep for a few minutes, but one look at the clock told me it was actually eleven thirty.

Awfully late for a visitor, especially when they were so infrequent.

An anxious, uneasy feeling spread over me and my heart rate quickened. I had no desire for a repeat of my last conversation with Scott. And what if he wasn't alone this time?

The knock came again.

The TV was still on, so whoever it was would know I was home. My door would hold, I was sure of that, but I picked up my cell phone, thumb poised over the keypad to call 911.

Silently, I made my way toward the door. I looked through the peephole and then unlocked it and opened it wide.

"I was nowhere near your neighborhood," Brooks said.

CHAPTER 38

BROOKS

DAISY'S EYES FLEW open, but she didn't have a chance to say anything because I'd already entered her apartment, closed the door, taken her face in my hands, and covered her mouth with mine. I kissed Daisy like I was dying of thirst and she was made of water. Maybe she felt the same way, because she clung to me, wrapping her arms around my neck and pressing her body against mine, our lips moving together in frantic synchronization. I moved my hands to her hips and drew her closer, losing myself in the smell of her skin.

When I finally pulled away, she took several deep breaths. "Will you be randomly showing up at my door late at night to kiss the hell out of me?"

"I'm sorry. I promise not to keep doing that."

"I think you should promise never to stop," she said, looking into my eyes.

I smiled. "I hope the knock didn't scare you."

"I'm just a little out of it. I fell asleep on the couch and didn't realize it was so late."

"I'm sorry about that, too."

She locked the door and turned around. "Is everything okay? Did something happen to your dad?"

"Everything's fine."

Daisy's forehead creased in confusion. "Then why are you here?"

"I missed you."

Her expression softened. "You drove four hundred miles to tell me you missed me? Why didn't you just call?"

"I can't kiss you over the phone. I can't touch you."

"Brooks," she whispered.

"You said a kiss didn't always have to mean something, but when I kissed you the night my mom died, I know it meant something to you because I could *feel* it. You said you'd forgotten I'd be leaving. Well, that's because I didn't act like someone who would be leaving. When I got home I realized I didn't have as much to go back to as I thought I did. Nothing in San Francisco makes me feel as good as the way I feel when I'm with you. And every time I think of you, which is roughly every ninety seconds, I remember that you're here and I'm not. So I got in the car after work and drove here to find out if you've been thinking about me as much as I've been thinking about you."

Her face crumpled. "I think about you all the time. No matter how much I try not to, you're always in my thoughts," she said. "You were the best thing to happen to me in a long time."

Listening to her say that made me realize there was so much more to life than where I lived it. The only thing that really mattered was who was living it with me.

"I want to be where you are," I said.

"You hate living in Fenton."

"You live in Fenton, and you're not planning on staying here, either. You said you were tired of waiting for your life to start. So let's start living it. Right now. You and me."

"I'm a package deal," she said, lifting her chin slightly.

"As far as I'm concerned, that kid of yours is a bonus."

She smiled and her eyes filled with tears. Seconds later, she flew into my arms and I pulled her tightly against me. We stayed that way for a while until finally she lifted her head.

"Don't break our hearts," she said.

"Never," I promised.

CHAPTER 39
BROOKS

I WAS DONE WITH the talking part of my visit, at least for now. Once again I cupped her face in my hands and pressed my lips to hers as all the longing that had been pent up inside me came pouring out. I kissed her slow and soft and hard and fast, and each kind was my favorite until we moved on to the next

At some point, I relocated us to the couch, pulling Daisy onto my lap so that she was straddling me. Reaching up, I released her hair from its ponytail and slid the hair tie onto my wrist, then ran my fingers through the strands, twisting them. Her mouth made a trail from my ear down to my neck and back again. Groaning, I pressed my lips to the hollow at her throat, dipping my tongue into it.

The concept of time ceased to exist, but after kissing for what felt like hours, I finally broke away. I was breathing hard when I said, "Don't think for one second that I don't want you, because, sweetheart, I do. But I didn't come here tonight to try to convince you to sleep with me." Sitting on my lap, I knew she could feel my desire for her. But *when* we slept together for the first time would be her call.

Daisy struggled to catch her breath. "I want you," she said. "Soon. But not tonight." She looked at the clock. "It's one a.m. You must be tired from the drive. Stay with me. Get some sleep."

"Yes," I said.

Daisy eased herself off my lap and I went downstairs to retrieve my overnight bag from the car. When I came back, I double-checked that the front door was locked while Daisy looked in on Elliott.

We took turns in the bathroom and then, in the sliver of light that came in through the window, I stood next to her bed and took off everything but my boxer briefs. Daisy inhaled sharply.

"I thought you weren't going to try to convince me to sleep with you," she said.

"I'm not. This is me being a gentleman. Usually I sleep naked." I reached out and untied the drawstring on her pajama pants, watching as they fell to the floor. "There," I said, running my fingers along the stretch of skin just below the bottom of her tank top. "That's better."

"That's not even remotely helping," she said.

"You have nothing to worry about tonight," I said. "But next time I won't be such a gentleman. And you won't be wearing anything at all."

"Stop talking, Brooks. I'm not made of willpower."

I laughed softly. *Say the word, Daisy, and this is on.*

But she didn't. She slid under the covers and I settled in beside her, pulling her close so that her head rested on my chest. I tangled my fingers in her hair.

"I can't believe you came back," she said. "It's like you knew I needed you."

"I didn't come back because you needed me. I came back because *I* needed *you*."

CHAPTER 40

BROOKS

I WOKE UP WHEN Elliott came tearing into the room.

"Mama. Let's make pancakes!"

Daisy muttered something unintelligible as I propped myself up on one arm.

"Bwooks! Hey! I got new shoes. I'll be back."

His footsteps thundered down the hall as Daisy sat up, rubbed her eyes, and smiled. "This is how we wake up on Saturday mornings."

"Should we be wearing pants?"

"Only if we don't feel like answering a thousand questions."

We threw back the covers and got out of bed. Daisy tossed me my jeans and stepped into her pajama pants. I had just zipped up when Elliott came back wearing his new shoes.

He stomped across the room and then hopped on both feet. "They wight up! Wook!"

"Those are really cool," I said.

"I know!"

"Bring it down a bit, Elliott," Daisy said.

I picked up my shirt from the floor and put it on.

"Are you gonna have pancakes wif us, Bwooks?"

"I'd love to have pancakes with you."

"Will you be okay if I take a quick shower?" Daisy asked.

"Sure. You want me to start some coffee?"

"Well, now you're just spoiling me. It's in the cupboard above the coffeemaker."

When Daisy was finished in the bathroom, I handed her a cup of coffee and took a shower. When I came out, hair wet and feet bare, Daisy was flipping pancakes and frying bacon. It had been a while since a woman had slept beside me and then made breakfast. Walking up behind her, I slid my arm around her waist and kissed her temple.

"I like sleeping with you," she said. "You don't snore and you don't try to steal all the covers."

"You do both," I said.

She turned around. "What?"

I kissed her again, this time on the mouth. "I'm kidding."

"You better be," she said, turning around to flip another pancake. "I do not snore."

I laughed and wandered out to the living room, sitting down on the couch next to Elliott who was watching TV. "Got big plans for after breakfast?" I asked as I put on my socks and shoes.

"We are gonna go to the park. You can come."

"I wish I could, but I need to go see my dad. Do you remember him? His name is Theo."

Elliott nodded. "Feo is gonna take me fishing."

"That's right."

"I will probably catch a big one."

I laughed. "I'm sure you will."

I scrolled through my e-mail and checked my phone for texts, relieved that there was nothing that needed my immediate attention. A few minutes later, Daisy called us to the table. She set down a large plate of pancakes and bacon and helped Elliott with the butter and syrup.

"Does your dad know you're here?" Daisy asked.

I shook my head as Daisy passed me the bacon. "I think it's safe to say he'll be as surprised to see me as you were."

"He may not give you the same kind of welcome I did, but I'm sure he'll be very happy."

"Oh, the things I'm remembering right now," I said. Like Daisy sitting on my lap. Daisy kissing my neck. Daisy without any pants on.

She smiled at me over the rim of her coffee cup. "Does anyone else know you're here?"

"No. And I'm lucky nothing too newsworthy has happened since I left San Francisco because I'd have a hard time explaining why I'm four hundred miles away. I'm sorry. I have to head back today."

"I understand," she said. "Just out of curiosity, what exactly is the plan?"

"Something tells me Paul probably hasn't filled my position yet, so I'll drop by the newsroom after I let my dad know that he's going to have a roommate whether he wants one or not."

"I'm sure he won't mind," Daisy said.

"No. I don't think he will. When I get back to San Francisco, I'll give my notice at work and arrange to sublet my apartment and put my things in storage. I'll shoot for being here by Thanksgiving since I planned on coming home then anyway."

Daisy set down her fork. "This is kind of crazy, isn't it?"

I grinned. "Little bit."

"Telling you I wasn't interested in a long-distance relationship wasn't some kind of power play. I hope you know that."

"I never thought it was. I'm not a big fan of long-distance relationships either."

"Any second thoughts?" she asked lightly.

Maybe she thought I'd lost my mind last night and had come to my senses in the light of day.

"None," I said.

"Okay, then," she said, smiling at me.

After we finished eating, I helped Daisy clear the table and then walked into the living room to grab my bag, which I'd left on the floor near the couch. Elliott was playing with a toy flashlight that also made noise.

"I'll see you later, Elliott. Have fun at the park."

"Bye, Bwooks," he said.

Daisy walked me to the door.

"I'm going to try to get on the road by two," I said. "I'll stop back on my way out of town."

"We'll be here."

I kissed her good-bye and as I turned to go she said, "Brooks?"

I turned back around. "Yes?"

"I just want you to know that you've made me really happy," she said. "You're turning your life upside down for me, and I'll do everything I can to make you glad you did."

At that moment, I understood what my dad meant about finding a woman who would make me happy and making her happy, too. "You already have." I kissed her again. "See you in a little while."

CHAPTER 41

DAISY

AS I'D ANTICIPATED, Theo was overjoyed that Brooks would be returning.

"He tried to downplay it," Brooks said when he came back that afternoon, "but you should have seen the look on his face. He was pretty much an open book."

"What about Paul?" I asked. "Did you talk to him, too?" I couldn't help but worry that maybe Paul *had* found someone to fill Brooks's position. There was only one newspaper in town, and I didn't know what Brooks's options were if he wasn't able to get his job back.

"Paul said I made his day. He seems very eager for me to get back to work."

"That's wonderful." I hadn't realized I'd been holding my breath until I let it out.

"Is Elliott napping?" Brooks asked.

"Yes. He was exhausted. He did a lot of running around at the park."

I hadn't mentioned to Elliott that Brooks would be returning in a more permanent capacity. It wasn't that I didn't believe Brooks or doubted his commitment—his willingness to give up his job and his apartment had cemented that. But Elliott's grasp of the situation was abstract enough that I thought it might confuse him. Better to let Elliott believe that Brooks had never left in the first place than to muddy the waters now.

"I dropped by the police station and talked to Jack Quick," Brooks said after we sat down in the living room. "They haven't brought Dale Reber in for questioning yet."

"Why not?" I asked.

"They can't find him. The person who answered the door at his place claimed he wasn't there and they didn't know where he was. The police made a few follow-up visits, but no one will come to the door now at all."

"Can't Jack get a warrant to search his home?"

"Not without probable cause. Warrants require facts, and at this point all we're really going on is a hunch."

"Oh," I said.

"Don't worry," Brooks said. "He'll turn up eventually, and when he does they'll bring him in."

"I hope so."

"What do you think about coming to my dad's for Thanksgiving? Or do you already have plans?"

"Pam and Shane invited us to join them at Pam's aunt's house, but I said no because it's a long drive and I have to work on Friday. I was going to cook Thanksgiving dinner for Elliott and me, but I can cook it at your dad's house just as easily as I can here."

Brooks looked alarmed. "I hope you don't think that's why I asked you."

"No. I'm just being practical. Besides, I'll need some help. I feel compelled to mention that I run a very tight ship in the kitchen. If you don't toe the line, I'll give you all the crap jobs like peeling potatoes and reaching your hand into the turkey for that little bag of giblets."

"Okay," he said, grinning. "You can be in charge in the kitchen." He pulled me into his arms and kissed me, slowly and deeply, leaving no question about who would be in charge elsewhere. After a few minutes he shifted his weight and moved us so that we were now lying on the couch facing each other. I brought my hands up, cupped his jaw, and kissed him back, thrilled that he was mine to touch, to kiss, to hold.

"How long until Elliott wakes up?" he asked.

"Any minute."

I might as well have said "Take me now, Brooks!" because instead of being deterred by Elliott's imminent arrival, Brooks kicked it up a notch and fluttered kisses from my ear down to my throat. When his mouth latched onto the tender skin and he began to suck and nibble and bite, I gasped. We were both breathing harder by then, and the temperature in the room felt like it had risen ten degrees.

Brooks pulled the neckline of my T-shirt to the side, trying to reach more of my skin. The limited access must have frustrated him because he abandoned that tactic and pushed the T-shirt up from the bottom, exposing my chest.

His hands were everywhere. He brought his lips back to mine and kissed me while stroking my nipple with his thumb. We both moaned when it hardened. Brooks pulled the cup of my bra to the side and traced my nipple with his tongue. I was in such a state by then that I could hardly string two cohesive thoughts together. There was something about Elliott I needed to remember.

At some point during all this, I'd wedged my thigh between Brooks's legs, and he seemed awfully pleased about it. If this went any further, one of us was going to come undone right there on the couch.

Possibly both of us.

That's when Elliott's door creaked open, which to a single mother is the equivalent of being doused with ice water. I sat up, made sure my clothing was in the right place, and said, "Hey, buddy. All done with your nap?"

His hair stuck up in back like a rooster and his eyes were sleepy. He walked over, crawled into my lap, and laid his head down on my shoulder.

I might not have missed a beat, but Brooks hadn't recovered quite so quickly. He'd managed to move to an upright position, but his eyes were still half-closed and his hair looked like a woman had been running her fingers through it. Gently, I covered his lap with a throw pillow. "I'm sorry," I whispered.

"My fault," he said. "You did tell me we were on borrowed time."

"To be continued," I promised.

Brooks smiled. "I'm counting the days."

"Are you with us yet, Elliott?" I asked.

He lifted his head from my shoulder. "Can I have some milk?"

"Sure." I settled Elliott on the couch and went to the kitchen.

When I returned, Brooks said, "I better get going. It's almost three." He looked at Elliott. "I'll see you in a couple of weeks, okay?"

"Okay," Elliott said. He turned his attention back to his milk.

I walked Brooks to the door. "Drive safe," I said. "Call me when you get there."

"I'll call you from the road." He leaned in and kissed me. "Be careful."

I reached up and smoothed his hair back into place. "I will. See you soon."

CHAPTER 42
DAISY

DESPITE THREATENING BROOKS with the task, I was the one who actually had to stick my hand inside the turkey and pull out that disgusting little bag of giblets, which I promptly threw away. My grandmother had always done something with them, and her gravy was the best I'd ever eaten, but I had no idea how she made it and no real desire to learn. We'd have to make do with gravy from a jar.

Brooks had gotten in at ten last night. He'd hired movers to bring some of his things and they'd shown up at his apartment late, which had set him back a few hours. I didn't care. I was just happy he was here.

I'd decided to prep the turkey at home and put it in the oven at Theo's. Brooks was coming over in two hours to pick us up, so after I slid the roasting pan into the refrigerator, I bathed Elliott and explained why he had to wear a pair of corduroys and a button-down shirt instead of athletic pants and a T-shirt.

"It's Thanksgiving. We need to dress nice when it's a holiday. You can watch the parade while I'm in the shower, okay?" I turned on the TV.

"Whoa," he said, pointing at the TV screen. "Snoopy is huge."

I put fresh sheets on the bed, and when I was in the shower, I paid special attention to any area that needed to be buffed, moisturized, or shaved. Afterward, wrapped in a towel, I stood in front of my dresser and selected a black lace bra-and-panty set. The outfit I'd chosen—a pair of leggings and a long sweater, with knee-high boots—was the perfect mix of dressy and casual. It needed something else, though, so I pulled a silk scarf from a hanger and looped it around my neck. I left my hair down.

Perfect.

In the two weeks leading up to Brooks's return, we had made good use of our phones and computers. I received several texts from him throughout the day, at least one e-mail, and we ended the evening on the phone. "Is there someone you're leaving behind?" I asked one night.

"You mean was I dating anyone?"

"Yes."

"There was a woman I saw fairly regularly, but we weren't exclusive. She wasn't looking for a commitment, so it was mostly a relationship of convenience. The last time I saw her was about a week before I moved home to be with my mom."

"So you haven't seen her since you moved back to San Francisco?"

"No. I kept making excuses for why I couldn't get together. You see, there was this other woman I couldn't stop thinking about."

"Aw. That's very sweet."

"I did call her the other day to tell her about you and to let her know I was moving. She wished me the best."

"Good," I said firmly.

"What about you?" he asked.

"A doctor I work with asked me if I'd like to go to dinner sometime. I told him I was no longer available."

"Be sure to let *all* the doctors know," Brooks said, laughing.

"I can't wait to see you again."

"Me, too."

"And kiss you again. You're an excellent kisser."

"Pretend that I'm kissing you right now," he said. "Your lips. Your throat. Everywhere. Does that feel good?"

"Brooks McClain, are you trying to initiate phone sex with me?"

"Well, if you have to ask I must not be doing a very good job."

"Oh no, you've definitely piqued my interest. I just wanted to make sure. I don't have any experience with this particular act."

"Hmmm, a virgin," Brooks said.

Aware that his voice had gotten softer, huskier, I matched his tone. "Well, just the phone part. When you're the mother of a three-year-old, I think it's safe to assume the virginity ship has *sailed*. But if I'd known about this in advance, I would have dressed better. Maybe lit a candle."

"Let me tell you the great thing about phone sex, sweetheart," he said. "You can pretend you're wearing whatever you want. I'll never know."

I looked down at my pajama pants and tank top. "I'm wearing a black push-up bra and matching, lacy underwear."

"I'm getting a very nice visual," he said. "Now I want you to take the bra off very slowly."

Wait. Is he serious?

It turned out that he was.

Afterward I said to him, "I wish you were here."

"Soon," he promised. "I'll be there soon."

*

And now he *was* here. He knocked on the door at eleven a.m., and I opened it wide. Once he stepped inside, he pulled me into his arms and held me tight.

"I missed you," I said.

"I missed you, too."

"Hi, Bwooks."

"Hey, buddy. Are you ready to go?"

Elliott hopped off the couch. "I need my bag of toys. Mama said I could bring them."

Once we loaded everything into Brooks's Jeep, I grabbed Elliott's car seat out of my Camry and strapped him into it.

"I wike this car," Elliott said. "I'm sitting up so high. I can see everything!"

I slid the turkey into the oven immediately upon our arrival at Theo's.

"How long does it need?" Brooks asked.

"About four hours. Maybe a little more. You don't have to start peeling those potatoes for a while yet."

"You're very funny," Brooks said. He leaned in for a long kiss. "You're also beautiful."

"You look quite handsome yourself." Brooks was wearing flat-front khakis and a tailored, navy-blue jacket with a checked, button-down shirt underneath. I'd almost become accustomed to Brooks wearing jeans since that's what he'd been wearing the last two times I'd seen him, but looking at him today reminded me how well this man could dress.

"What's next?" Brooks asked after we placed the rest of the food in the fridge.

"Nothing right now. I made green-bean casserole because Elliott loves it, but we'll need to wait on the potatoes until the turkey is closer to being done. I talked to your dad earlier this week. He insisted on taking care of everything else. I just need to figure out what time to put it all in the oven."

"It sounds like we're set for a while then."

"Did everything go okay with the move?" I asked.

"Once the movers finally showed up, it did." Brooks had brought his queen-size bed from his apartment and his leather couch and big-screen TV. "I love my dad, but if I thought I could rent my own apartment without hurting his feelings, I would."

"Now you know how I felt living with my grandmother after my divorce."

Brooks nodded. "You know what? I actually do."

"I'll tell you what I told myself back then: it won't be forever."

"That's a good way to look at it," Brooks said.

It was awfully quiet and Brooks and I had just enjoyed a nice conversation without interruptions, which meant something had caught my son's attention. "Where are Elliott and your dad?"

"They're in the backyard," Brooks said.

Elliott had cornered Theo the moment we walked in the door. I looked out the kitchen window, which faced the backyard, and spotted them. The weather was sunny and mild, and I was glad Elliott wouldn't have to be cooped up inside all afternoon. "What are they doing?" I asked Brooks.

"Get this. My dad rigged him a fishing pole with a plastic fish on the end. He's going to teach Elliott how to cast it into that bucket."

"That is the nicest thing he could have done for Elliott."

"When I told you at the funeral that he liked kids, I really meant it." Brooks looked away for a minute. "My mom loved kids, too. I feel bad that she never got to hold one of mine."

Oh, God.

"Daisy?" Brooks said. "What's wrong?"

"Nothing," I said. "I was watching Elliott. That fish is not landing anywhere near the bucket."

You should tell him now.

"He just needs a little more practice."

"Yes. That's it. How about some football?" I asked.

"Come with me," Brooks said, taking me by the hand. "You can sit on my leather couch. It doesn't remotely match the rest of the furniture, but it's comfortable as hell."

"Don't get too comfortable. You've still got some potatoes to peel."

Our dinner turned out beautifully. Brooks opened a bottle of wine shortly before we ate and kept an eye on my glass throughout the meal, which we lingered over for some time.

"How's your turkey, Elliott?" I asked.

"I wike it. And those beans you made for me. And Feo's stuffing."

"I didn't actually make the stuffing," Theo said. "I bought it."

Elliott looked at Theo. "That's okay."

"How about my potatoes?" Brooks asked.

"They are the bestest, Bwooks."

I patted Brooks's arm. "Well, I guess we know what your job will be from now on."

"I didn't think that through, did I?" he said, grinning. Brooks was adorable when he grinned.

"I'd like to propose a toast," Theo said. He stood up, holding his wineglass out in front of him. "To the memory of those who can't be with us today, and to making new memories with those who are."

Brooks and I raised our wineglasses. "Cheers," we said. Elliott raised his glass of chocolate milk and shouted, "Cheers" in a decidedly less somber tone than we had used.

I would not have been able to make that toast for fear of upsetting Theo and Brooks. Their loss was more recent than mine, and while the grief over losing my grandmother was still present, it wasn't nearly as raw as theirs had to be. Theo was either very stoic or he preferred to keep his feelings private. Either way, it was a beautiful toast.

I stood and began clearing the table. Brooks helped while Theo cut slices of pumpkin pie at the table.

"I wike pie," Elliott said as he sipped on a seemingly bottomless glass of chocolate milk, courtesy of Brooks.

"Would you like whipped cream?" Theo asked, holding up the kind you sprayed from a can.

"Yes I would," Elliott said.

Theo squirted a big mound of whipped cream onto Elliott's pie.

When Brooks tried to refill my wineglass for the third time I held up my hand and said, "No more for me. A third glass would probably put me to sleep."

"Oh, there will be none of that," Brooks said as he laughed quietly and removed my glass altogether.

After we finished dessert, Brooks and his dad sipped slowly on whiskey as we watched the end of a football game. Elliott drew a picture for Theo and played with his toys, but his eyelids started to droop around eight, and we gathered up our things and got ready to leave.

"Thank you so much for having us, Theo. I had a wonderful time."

"Thank you for everything you did. You and your son made a difficult day much easier. I know you're the main reason Brooks came back, and I'm thankful for that, too."

"You're welcome," I said, giving him a heartfelt smile.

"Bye, Feo," Elliott said.

Theo rumpled Elliott's hair. "Bye, Elliott."

"Will you be okay tonight, Dad?" Brooks asked.

Theo waved him away. "I'll be fine. I've got whiskey, your big TV, and leftovers."

"That sounds pretty good," Brooks said. "I'll see you tomorrow."

As Brooks drove us back to my apartment, it was hard not to think of those who were no longer with us. But we'd come together that afternoon, four people who knew what love and loss were, and by the end of the evening I don't think there was anyone whose heart didn't feel a little bit lighter.

CHAPTER 43

BROOKS

I WAS WAITING FOR Daisy on the couch after she put Elliott to bed. I'd already taken off my jacket and checked to make sure the door was locked. She walked into the living room, unzipped her boots, and stepped out of them. Neither of us spoke as she slowly unwound the scarf from her neck.

There was a lamp on the side table next to the couch. I switched it off and stood up, crossing the room to where she stood. I twisted my fingers in her hair and pulled her closer so that her body was pressed up against mine. Our kiss was slow and unhurried.

I shut off the remaining lights and took her by the hand. When we entered the bedroom, I said, "Is it okay if I lock the door?"

"Yes. He'll call out if he needs me."

Daisy was standing next to me, the outline of her body visible in the faint glow of the streetlight that filtered in through the window shades. I grabbed the bottom of her sweater and pulled it slowly over her head, taking a minute to admire the lacy black push-up bra before I eased her pants down over her hips. Her underwear matched the bra.

"Did you wear this for me?" I asked.

"Yes."

I was aching for her by then, and taking off the bra I'd just admired only increased my physical discomfort. Pulling her in for another kiss, I fought the urge to speed things up, reminding myself that I was not sixteen and we had all night.

When the kiss ended, Daisy reached for my wrist. She unbuttoned both cuffs and then turned her attention to the buttons that ran down the front of my shirt. Once it was hanging open, she pushed it off my shoulders and stripped off my T-shirt. The touch of her hands as she ran them down my arms and then rested them flat on my chest made me groan softly.

"Come here," I said, pulling her by the hand toward the bed. We lay down on it, Daisy on her back and me partially covering her with my body as I kissed her repeatedly. I pulled back a few inches and lowered my head. "This right here," I whispered as I placed a kiss in the hollow at the base of her throat, "drives me insane."

I lowered my mouth to her nipple and traced it with my tongue. The sound of our breathing and Daisy's soft moan filled the room. When I began to suck, she cried out and ran her hands through my hair as I paid equal attention to both breasts.

Daisy repositioned herself so that she was lying on top of me. She looked right into my eyes and then grasped my hands and held them as she began kissing my neck.

I would agree to anything this woman asked me for while she was kissing my neck.

Anything.

Daisy bit, sucked, and licked, and by then the need to be inside her was almost more than I could handle. I rolled her onto her back and hooked my thumbs in the elastic of her underwear, my hands skimming along the curves of her hips as I pulled them off. I was suddenly very happy about that streetlight because I could *see* her. Every inch of her naked body was on display for my eyes only.

"So beautiful," I said.

My pants felt two sizes too small by then, at least in the zipper area. I got up and stood next to the bed. Daisy moved to the edge of it, facing me, and reached for my belt. The relief when she eased my zipper down was instantaneous. She touched me, but I was way too close for much of that. Instead, I eased her gently onto her back and put my hands on her thighs, opening her legs to me. I touched her, feeling how aroused she was.

Maybe she was too close, too, because she said, "Do you have a condom? If not, there's one in the drawer of my nightstand."

"Yes," I said

"Get it now," she panted.

I found my pants on the floor and reached into my wallet for a condom. By then, the need to be inside her had reached epic levels. When the condom was in place, I covered her body with mine and thrust into her hard. I pulled back and entered her again, slower this time, waiting as she lifted her hips and set the rhythm, which I did my best to match even though I was half out of my mind.

"You feel incredible," I said.

She moved faster, legs wrapped around my back, increasing our pace and pulling me into her with an intensity that matched mine. "Oh my God, Brooks," Daisy said, crying out as she contracted around me.

I came seconds later, groaning from the sheer relief, breathing as hard as if I'd run a race.

Afterward, when I held her, she whispered in my ear, telling me over and over how good it had felt.

My decision to come back had been the right one, and I would never let her go again.

CHAPTER 44

DAISY

BROOKS KNOCKED ON the door a little before eight on a Monday evening in mid-December. I was still in my scrubs.

"I hope you're in the mood for Mexican," he said, leaning in to give me a kiss hello. "Hey, Elliott."

"Hi, Bwooks!"

"Carne asada?" I asked.

Brooks looked at me and winked, a move that often rendered me speechless. "And fresh guacamole."

"I'll repay you for your kindness later," I said, adding a wink of my own.

"Then let's go to bed early," he whispered in my ear.

I'd admitted that I often ate a bowl of cereal for dinner because Elliott ate at Celine's and I was usually too tired to cook for myself. Brooks had shown up the very next night with a bag full of pad Thai and skewers of chicken satay.

"You brought dinner?" I asked.

"Yes. Aren't you hungry?"

"I'm starving. And I *love* Thai food."

He'd followed me into the kitchen and set the bag on the counter as I reached into the cupboard for plates. "You are the best boyfriend *ever*."

Now we'd settled into a routine. On the days I worked, Brooks would arrive shortly after Elliott and I got home, bearing takeout that he'd picked up for us on the way over. I told him I wasn't picky and that anything he brought was better than cereal. He seemed to enjoy surprising me.

"Are you ready to eat?" he asked.

"I'm a little behind schedule because I got out of work late. I'd like to put Elliott to bed and take a shower first. You do *not* want to know about the bodily fluids I came in contact with today."

Brooks smiled and shook his head. "Not even a little bit."

"Do you mind waiting? Are you hungry?"

"Are *you* hungry?"

"Starving."

"Is there something I can do to help?"

Even though I'd been up front with Brooks about the fact that Elliott and I were a package deal, I never wanted him to feel like he had to fill any parenting shoes. Elliott was my responsibility, and I was the one who would take care of him. But if Brooks was having any qualms about dating a single mother, he sure hadn't shown it. He'd been accommodating and respectful when it came to planning activities that wouldn't exclude Elliott, and he was patient when Elliott peppered him with questions or drew him endless pictures. If either of us hoped to eat before eight thirty tonight, I'd need to take Brooks up on his offer.

"You could sit with Elliott and read him a couple of books while I take a shower. But only if you want to," I quickly added.

"Sure."

Elliott was sitting on the couch, listening to our exchange.

"Would you like Brooks to read to you while I'm in the shower?"

"Can he read my Frankwin book?"

"I'll read whatever you want," Brooks said.

Elliott ran out of the room and returned with a stack of books, several of which slid out of his grasp and fell to the floor.

"How many books do you have in that pile?" I asked.

"Four," he said. More like seven or eight.

Brooks sat down on the couch next to Elliott. "Go take a shower," he said. "We'll be fine."

"I won't be long," I said.

Elliott handed Brooks a book with a turtle on the cover. "This one."

"You got it."

I took a quick shower and put on a pair of flannel pajama pants and a T-shirt. When I walked into the living room, Brooks was still reading. Not wanting to interrupt them, I sat down on the far end of the couch and listened silently until Brooks turned the last page.

"All done?" I asked.

"He knows all the words," Brooks said. "Every single one of them."

"He's memorized them. They're his favorites."

"That was wild. I could see his lips moving, and I thought he already knew how to read."

Elliott threw his hands up in the air. "I don't know how to read. I'm only free years old."

Brooks laughed. "You crack me up, you know that?"

Elliott let out a giant belly laugh.

"I hate to break up the party, but it's time for bed," I said.

"I am ready for my snack," Elliott said.

"That might work with Brooks, but I know how you operate. And you already had a snack."

"Okay," Elliott said, sounding dejected. He started to follow me into the bathroom so I could brush his teeth but then stopped abruptly and threw his arms around Brooks. "Night, Bwooks."

Brooks hugged him tight and said, "Good night, buddy."

*

On Saturday morning, Brooks walked to the park with Elliott and me. Theo had been cleaning out the basement earlier in the week and had come across a large plastic tub of Brooks's old toys. Inside was a tiny baseball glove and ball that Theo thought Elliott would like. They were covered in red and green Velcro, which made it easy for a toddler to catch the ball.

Elliott had gone nuts.

The way his face lit up when Brooks handed him the ball and glove almost brought me to tears. Elliott had slept with the ball and glove that night and insisted on bringing it with him to Celine's. He'd actually relegated his army man to a spot on his nightstand instead of in his pocket, and I took it as a positive sign that he felt safe and secure enough to let it go.

When we reached the park, we found a grassy area and Brooks patiently threw the ball after first showing Elliott how to catch it. Elliott was concentrating so hard his tongue stuck out the side of his mouth. The Velcro mostly did its job and every time Elliott caught the ball, he yelled, "I did it! I did it!"

"You did," Brooks said. "High-five."

They smacked their palms together.

"Throw it again, Bwooks. Pwease."

"Get ready," Brooks said.

"Watch, Mama," Elliott yelled.

"I'm watching. You're doing awesome!"

When Elliott was finally ready to take a break, we walked over to the playground. I lifted him into a bucket swing and pushed him, watching the wind blow back his hair and listening to his laughter.

"Higher," he said. "Higher."

"I was thinking I could make dinner tomorrow and we could take it over to your dad's," I said, giving Elliott another push. I insisted on cooking for Brooks every weekend since he took care of dinner during the week. Brooks said he and his dad often ordered pizza or went out to grab a bite, so I figured Theo might enjoy a home-cooked meal.

"Honestly, he'd probably love that," Brooks said.

"Okay. Let's plan on it then. What does he like?"

"He'll eat anything you make, but he's kind of a meat-and-potatoes guy."

"I'll make him a roast with all the trimmings."

"He already likes you, you know," Brooks teased. "All I hear is 'Daisy this' and 'Daisy that.'"

"I like him, too," I said.

After the swings, we moved to the sandbox. I'd brought Elliott's sand toys and he busied himself, digging with a small shovel and transferring the sand to his blue bucket. Brooks and I sat on top of the picnic table in our usual spot, watching him play.

"Sitting on this table together always reminds me of the day you came to say good-bye," I said.

"Same here," Brooks said. "I think about it every time we watch Elliott dig in the sand. You probably didn't like me very much that day."

"I still liked you. That was the problem. But I'm actually glad you left."

"Why?" Brooks sounded incredulous.

"Because sometimes the only way to find out how much you want something is to walk away from it."

Brooks put his arm around me. "Not just a pretty face, are you?"

I laughed.

Elliott walked over to the picnic table. "I'm done."

"Had enough?" I asked. "Come on. Let's gather up your toys." I hopped off the picnic table and began walking toward the sandbox.

Elliott hung back, so I turned around to see what was keeping him.

"I would wike to go to Chuck E. Cheese's now," Elliott said to Brooks.

"Chuck E. Cheese's? What is that, like a restaurant?" Brooks asked.

"They have pizza there."

Brooks crouched down so that he was eye level with Elliott. "Are you hungry, buddy?"

Elliott nodded solemnly. "I'm very hungry and firsty."

"Well, okay. We can go to Chuck E. Cheese's."

"Do you pwomise?"

"Sure."

If he hadn't been so busy being manipulated by a three-year-old, Brooks might have seen me walk up behind Elliott. I was making sawing motions across my neck in the universal sign for *Stop talking right now!*

"You know the rule about Chuck E. Cheese's, Elliott," I said. "That's a special treat. And we were just there in August for your birthday."

"But he's hungry," Brooks said.

"So hungry," Elliott echoed.

Oh, give me a break. Brooks had no clue how hard he was being played.

Amateur.

"He's not hungry because he finished his lunch"—I consulted my watch—"a mere sixty-three minutes ago. He will eat exactly one tiny corner of one piece of pizza, if we're lucky. And he'll miss his nap."

"But Bwooks made a pwomise," Elliott said.

"Why don't you go pick up your sand toys while I talk to Brooks?"

"Uh-oh. I screwed myself with the promise thing, didn't I?" Brooks said as soon as Elliott was out of earshot.

"Don't be too hard on yourself. He took total advantage of you."

"We have to take him there, otherwise he won't trust me. I'll buy him some pizza and something to drink."

"Okay. But no one goes to Chuck E. Cheese's for the food."

"What do they go there for?"

"You'll see."

*

Twenty-five minutes later, we walked through the front door of Chuck E. Cheese's.

"I need your hands," the attendant said.

Brooks held out his hand. "What is this?" he asked me.

I held out my own hand, and Elliott's. "It's so we don't steal someone else's child. We can only leave with the one we brought."

"I don't know if that's comforting or alarming," he said.

The look on Brooks's face as I led him into the sheer bedlam that is Chuck E. Cheese's was priceless. For a second I thought about snapping a picture of his expression with my phone so we could laugh about it later.

"Wow," he said. "And I don't mean 'wow, cool.' I mean 'wow, this is insane.'"

"Starting to see the big picture now?"

"It's getting clearer." Brooks wrinkled his nose. "What's that smell?"

"Diapers and feet."

Brooks now appeared to be breathing through his mouth. "Yes," he said solemnly. "That's it exactly."

"You'll get used to it. By the time we leave, you won't even notice it."

The plastic tubes at Chuck E. Cheese's always reminded me of something you'd find in a hamster cage, only these tubes were large enough to hold children.

Elliott was pulling on my hand, dragging me toward them. "I wanna go in the tubes."

"Take off your shoes first," I said, stopping him in front of the shoe cubbies.

He shoved his tennis shoes into the nearest empty slot and took off. "Watch me!"

"We will."

Brooks and I managed to find a table that was close enough for us to keep an eye on Elliott. When the waitress came around, I ordered a small pepperoni pizza and a glass of lemonade.

"Is the pizza any good?" Brooks asked.

"It's not horrible. Elliott seems to like it. I'll ask for a box and he can eat it for dinner. It's doubtful he'll stop long enough to eat much while we're here."

We watched Elliott climb up into the tubes and go down the

slide, repeating the process over and over until I convinced him to take a break. He was sweating and wheezing a bit.

"You okay? Do you need your inhaler?"

"I'm okay." He took a big drink of his lemonade. "Can we go to the ball pit now?"

I cringed. I hated the ball pit, but Elliott loved it.

Well, in for a penny, in for a pound.

"Sure," I said

Brooks and I looked on as Elliott took a flying leap into a pit filled with plastic balls. The toddler next to Elliott was entertaining himself by picking up the balls, licking them, and throwing them over his shoulder.

Brooks looked horrified. "That pit can't be remotely sanitary."

"Management claims it is, but I don't believe them. Which is why Elliott is going straight into the bathtub when we get home."

Forty-five minutes later, we walked toward the exit. Elliott claimed he was too tired to walk, so Brooks was carrying him.

"You were right, Daisy. I don't even notice the smell anymore."

"This has been a very good day," Elliott said.

"It's been a great day," Brooks said.

It has been a wonderful day.

*

"Let's get you into the tub," I said to Elliott when we got home.

I ran the water and grabbed a towel from the linen closet. Once the bathtub was full, Elliott stripped down and jumped in, splashing the front of my shirt.

"Easy there," I said. I washed his hair and rinsed out the shampoo. Out of the corner of my eye, I noticed Brooks in the doorway.

"I thought I'd go pick up some wine to have with dinner," he said. "And maybe dessert."

I'd made a pan of lasagna before we went to the park, and all I had to do was bake it.

Elliott stood up. "I have pizza to eat for dinner!" He plunked himself back down in the tub, splashing me once again.

"Careful, buddy. You're soaking me."

"Sorry, Mama."

I turned my attention back to Brooks. "Wine is essential after a visit to Chuck E. Cheese's. They should really give you a bottle on your way out."

"Pinot noir, coming right up. Any special requests for dessert?"

"Chocwate," Elliott yelled, splashing and soaking me a third time.

"I give up," I said.

Brooks laughed. "I can see right through that shirt."

By the time Brooks returned, I'd changed into a dry shirt, put the lasagna in the oven, and convinced Elliott to get into his pajamas even though it was only four thirty in the afternoon.

"There's no reason to get dressed again if we're not going back out," I said. "And since you skipped your nap, you'll be going to bed early tonight."

It might have seemed boring to some, but nothing made me happier than the thought of hanging out on a Saturday night with Brooks and Elliott.

Brooks poured the wine and after I took a drink, I retrieved my laptop from the kitchen counter. "I want to show you something." After opening Excel, I clicked on my debt-reduction spreadsheet and pointed to a number. "Look at the total. It's gotten lower." I smiled. "When I get to zero, that means I've paid off every cent Scott ran up on those credit cards. Then I can start putting the money I used to pay every month toward a down payment on a house."

Brooks looked at the beginning total and whistled. "That's incredible. I am seriously impressed."

"It's going to take me a long time to save up enough, but maybe I can rent a house in the meantime. Elliott would at least have a yard to play in."

The oven timer went off, and I got up to check on the lasagna. Brooks followed me into the kitchen.

"I really don't like your ex-husband," Brooks said.

"I'm not his biggest fan, either."

I opened the oven and peered inside. Ten more minutes to let the cheese brown and the lasagna would be perfect. I set the timer and turned around. Brooks had a serious expression on his face.

"What is it?" I asked.

"I look at you and Elliott and wonder how in the world a man could just walk away from his wife. From his child. How can someone do that, plus leave so much carnage in his wake? I can't wrap my brain around it. I've tried and I can't do it."

"That's what addiction does to a person," I said. "I believe Scott loved me until the end. There may be a part of him that still loves me. I know he never stopped loving Elliott. But he loves meth more. No matter how much he doesn't want to, he just does."

"If he stopped using, would you take him back?" Brooks asked suddenly. "If he showed up here again some night, clean this time, and said he wanted another chance, that he wanted to put his family back together, would you?"

His voice sounded intense. Angry, even. But his troubled

expression showed a vulnerable side of Brooks that I hadn't seen until now.

"No." I put my arms around him and pulled him close. "He betrayed me in the worst possible way. He's used up all his chances and he doesn't get any more. He hurt me too much for that to *ever* be a possibility."

Brooks took my face in his hands and kissed me. There was something about the kiss that felt possessive, as if he was trying to assert himself as the only man who had the right to kiss me now.

I wasn't wrong, because later that night, after Brooks and I had made love and were lying entwined in each other's arms, he said, "I don't ever want him to think he can walk in here and have you again," and I didn't need to ask him who he was talking about.

CHAPTER 45

BROOKS

I WAS SITTING AT my desk typing up a story when Jack Quick called my cell phone. "One of my patrol officers just pulled over Dale Reber for speeding. They're bringing him in."

I sat up straight in my chair. "How long can you detain him?"

"Hopefully long enough for him to answer our questions. I'll call you when we're done."

"Thanks."

*

Jack called me two hours later and asked me to meet him for lunch at the diner.

"Tell me you have good news," I said when he sat down on the stool next to me.

He exhaled and rubbed his temples. "We hammered him pretty hard, but he wouldn't talk. After about an hour of him not saying anything, he informed us that the questioning was over and left the station."

"He can do that?"

Jack nodded. "Technically he can."

"I can't shake the thought that he had something to do with Pauline Thorpe's murder."

"He very well may have. But until someone talks or we catch a lucky break, there's no way to prove it. Unless we have evidence linking him to the crime, we can't arrest him and we have no grounds to hold him." Jack opened his menu. "To hell with my cholesterol. I need something fried."

"Daisy wants justice, but she wants closure, too."

"The victim's family always does," he said.

We gave our orders to the waitress—a burger and onion rings for Jack and a club sandwich for me.

"How's that going, by the way?" Jack asked.

"What? Me and Daisy?"

"Yeah."

"It's going well. I'm glad I came back."

"See? You asked me once how I could stand it here. It all comes down to a woman, McClain. They'll make you do crazy shit."

"You're a man of true wisdom, Jack."

He laughed. "Tell that to my wife."

*

That night, I arrived at Daisy's with dinner from a local barbecue restaurant. I'd sent a quick text to let her know Dale had been found and was being questioned, but she rarely had time to talk during her workday, so I hadn't been able to share the outcome. She looked so hopeful when she opened the door.

I kissed her and then shook my head. "He wouldn't talk," I said.

"At all?"

"No."

"So that's it?" Daisy asked as I followed her into the kitchen and leaned against the counter as she plated the ribs and dished up coleslaw and baked beans. "They just let him go?"

"They had to."

I grabbed two beers from the fridge, uncapped one and handed it to her. She took a drink and set down the bottle on the counter.

"Jack said somebody'll talk eventually," I said.

Daisy sighed. "I hope so. I just… I want to put this whole thing behind me."

I put my arms around her and she pressed her face to my chest. She'd had time to shower before I arrived. Her hair was wet and combed back and she was wearing her usual uniform of pajama pants and a T-shirt, long-sleeved now that it had gotten colder. She smelled incredible, like the light floral scent of the body wash she always kept a bottle of in the shower. When Daisy looked like this it was as if she was sending out a signal that she was ready for bed, and I loved taking her to bed.

"Do you know that I find you incredibly desirable right now?"

She looked up at me and smiled. "Oh?"

"Yes." I bent down to kiss her and I was still kissing her when Elliott charged into the kitchen.

"Bwooks! You is kissin' my mom." He dissolved into laughter like it was the funniest thing he'd ever seen.

"Hey, buddy. Where'd you come from?"

"I was gettin' my books. I got some new ones."

"As soon as your mom and I finish eating, I'll read them, okay?"

"Okay."

Elliott always wanted me to read to him on the nights I stayed over. Daisy was quick to point out that it wasn't my responsibility. "Please don't feel like you have to," she'd said.

"No, I want to. He seems to really like it. He looks at me like I'm a superhero or something."

"That's because to him, you are," Daisy said.

She carried our plates to the table and we sat down.

"Do you want a rib, Elliott?" I asked.

"Do I wike those, Mama?"

"I don't think you've ever tried one."

Elliott sat down in his chair while Daisy went to the cupboard and retrieved a small plate.

"Here," I said handing Elliott a small rib. "Try this."

It took less than two bites for Elliott's cheek to become smeared with barbecue sauce. He wiped his cheek with his hand instead of the napkin Daisy had given him, and before either of us could intervene, he somehow transferred the sauce to his hair.

"I'm waving the white flag," Daisy said, laughing and taking a bite of her own rib. "I'll clean him up when he's done."

"I wike these, but they are messy," Elliott said.

"You ready for your books?" I asked when we were done eating.

"He's very excited for you to read," Daisy said. "We went to the bookstore yesterday and he picked out some new Christmas books."

"Speaking of which, what do you want for Christmas, Elliott?"

"So many fings!" Elliott said. "I will have my mom wite it all down for you wike she did for Santa."

"I want you to give it to me the next time I come over, okay?"

"Okay."

Daisy was watching us with a smile on her face.

I caught her eye. "What about you? What do you want for Christmas?"

"It hardly seems fair to ask for more when I'm looking at everything I've ever wanted."

CHAPTER 46
SCOTT

SCOTT WAS SITTING on the couch watching TV when Dale walked up behind him and pressed something hard against the back of his head.

That's the barrel of a gun.

"When did you call the motherfucking police?" Dale demanded. "When!"

Thank God I'm high. He's probably going to kill me.

"I didn't call the police," Scott replied calmly, although his heart was pounding out an erratic, staccato rhythm. "I have no idea what you're talking about."

"I think you do," Dale said.

When Brandon walked into the room, Scott started to produce copious amounts of sweat. Droplets of fear gathered and multiplied rapidly at his hairline, his upper lip, the back of his neck. Brandon was ruthless as hell when it came to dealing with anyone who drew attention to his operation. He pulled up a chair in front of the couch so that he was facing Scott. One nod from Brandon and Scott was almost certain he would cease to exist in this world.

Dale removed the gun from the back of Scott's head and came around to the other side of the couch, pulling up a chair beside Brandon and pointing the gun at Scott's face.

"Well then," Dale said, and Scott hated the tone he used, knew he was just trying to appear important in front of Brandon, "you mind telling me why the cops wanted to question me about the death of Pauline Thorpe?" He kicked the frame of the couch, jarring Scott. Tim, another guy who rented a room from Dale and who was sitting right next to Scott on the couch, didn't even flinch. Nothing was interesting or alarming enough to pull his attention away from the porn on the television screen.

"I don't know why they questioned you," Scott said, which was the truth.

Dale's paranoia had reached epic levels. He insisted he was being followed whenever he drove somewhere and that DEA agents were surrounding the house at night and using infrared telescopes to spy on him. His latest claim was that the birds flying overhead had tiny cameras attached to their legs. Dale said if they wanted to continue living in his house they had to follow all sorts of bizarre rules, such as leaving the shades drawn at all times and never answering the door. Occasionally he would demand they turn off all the lights and speak in whispers.

"This Pauline Thorpe person was related to your ex-wife. Is that correct?" Brandon asked.

"Yes," Scott said.

Brandon turned to Dale. "And now the police are interested in you?" He shook his head as if he was dealing with a bunch of idiots. Brandon looked at Dale and cocked his head toward Scott. *Shoot him*, the gesture said.

"Wait," Scott said in a desperate, panicked voice.

He might have lost everything. He might have suffered

episodes of severe, crippling depression when he thought about what he'd become. But he hadn't lost his will to live.

Not yet.

And a man whose death was imminent would betray just about anyone in order to survive, including the ex-wife he still loved. "Daisy probably gave your name to the police," he said. Or maybe it was the reporter who'd given Dale's name to the police. The thought of Daisy with another man filled Scott with a white-hot rage, but right now he had bigger things to worry about.

"Why would this woman give your name to the police, Reber?" Brandon asked, leaning back in his chair.

"Because she knows he lives here," Dale said, pointing toward Scott with the gun. "They can't pin anything on him so they've moved on to me."

"Then you need to make sure she stops talking," Brandon said mildly.

Scott could breathe a little easier now that the focus had shifted from him to Daisy. Had he not been able to talk his way out of this, he was certain Dale would have followed Brandon's directive with little hesitation, if only to show his loyalty.

But it would have left Dale with a hole in his operation that he wouldn't have been able to plug very easily. Unlike Dale, whose appearance was frightening and memorable, Scott was still able to blend in. He retained just enough of his good looks and people skills to put customers at ease.

Dale loved to brag about Brandon's connection to the Mexican drug cartel, but all Scott cared about was that the cartel's meth was superior in quality to most of the crap that was sold down at the Desert Tap. He was the one who'd insisted they give away small quantities of meth for free in order to hook the customers and bring them back for more. It didn't take long for Scott to acquire a stable of regular—and eager—buyers. They followed his rules. They paid in full. Scott told them to keep their mouths shut, and if they didn't he told them to find another connection. They never talked. Scott was reliable and the meth he sold them was just too good.

Scott moved a lot of drugs for Brandon and shouldered a large portion of the risk. He was the one who sold to customers who might turn out to be undercover cops. He often carried enough drugs on his person or in his vehicle to qualify for a Possession with Intent to Deliver charge, which was a felony in the state of California. He was responsible for moving the meth quickly, and if Scott couldn't account for every cent due to Brandon, it was his ass on the line, not Dale's.

In return, Scott never had to come down unless he wanted to.

And he never wanted to.

Brandon left the room and Dale followed him like an obedient puppy. Scott exhaled, and slowly his body relaxed. The pungent scent of his sweat lingered on his skin.

When Dale came back inside, he mixed a large shot for Scott and for himself, and they tied off and slammed it.

They watched some porn.

Neither of them mentioned what had happened.

Neither of them mentioned the gun.

They were still getting high and watching porn twelve hours later.

Meth was the only thing that could make Scott forget about the danger he'd been in.

The utter hopelessness that was his life.

Meth was the only thing that kept him from feeling much of anything at all.

CHAPTER 47

BROOKS

I DROVE TO DAISY'S apartment in the late afternoon on Christmas Eve. Daisy didn't have to work and I'd met my deadline, so I'd taken off early. When I arrived, she and Elliott were in the kitchen listening to Christmas carols and baking cookies. Neat rows of frosted snowmen were lined up on waxed paper on the kitchen counter.

"We is making snowmans, Bwooks," Elliott said. "Do you want one?"

"I think *you* want one," Daisy said.

"I do!" Elliott said.

"How's it going?" I asked, bending down to kiss her.

"Other than the complete annihilation of my kitchen, it's going great. Someone didn't want to take a nap. He's *very* excited about Santa."

"I didn't want to take a nap," Elliott said, pointing to himself and smearing frosting on his shirt.

"Dad asked if we could meet him at the restaurant at six."

"Sure," Daisy said. "I'm sure I can have this disaster area cleaned up by then."

We were joining my dad for an early dinner so Daisy could get Elliott to bed on time. "I don't want Daisy to think she has to cook for us all the time," my dad had said. "I want to take everyone out for dinner on Christmas Eve."

Tomorrow Daisy was hosting a holiday gathering at her apartment. "Nothing big," she said when she first mentioned it. "Just appetizers and desserts. My place is too small for anything really fancy. Pam and Shane are going to drop by in the late afternoon. Maybe some of my friends from the hospital. I want your dad to come over in the morning. He can stay all day if he wants. I know it's not very traditional, but people are busy with their families. It'll be an open-house kind of thing."

"Sounds good to me," I'd said.

Daisy frosted a cookie, set it down on the waxed paper, and wiped her hands on a towel. "Okay. That was the last one. Go ahead and put on the sprinkles, Elliott."

"Is everything else ready?" I asked.

"Almost." She covered Elliott's ears. "I might need some help with an assembly project after Elliott goes to bed."

"Hey!" Elliott said when Daisy let go. "I could not hear just now."

Daisy laughed. "Weird."

"I'll help you with whatever you need," I said. "But right now I really want one of those cookies."

*

When we got home from dinner, I read to Elliott and then Daisy told him it was time for bed. "The faster you go to sleep, the faster it will be morning and you can see what Santa brought you."

"I will go to sleep right now," Elliott said. "I want to get up very early."

"Not too early," Daisy said. "I'll come in and get you when it's time."

"And I will be waiting."

"Good night, Elliott," I said.

He gave me a hug. "Good night, Bwooks."

"Is this the first Christmas where he understands what's going on?" I asked when Daisy walked back into the room.

"Yes. Last year he was still a little too young. I can't wait to see his face tomorrow morning."

"I opened some wine," I said.

"Good. We may need it for this." She left the room and returned with a large cardboard box.

"What's in there?"

"Rescue Heroes. The Mountain Action Command Center. Elliott is going to go ballistic. He insisted I put this at the top of his list to Santa. He even made me underline it a bunch of times." She pulled out the directions and peered at them. "Yikes."

"Let me see." I looked at the instructions Daisy handed me. "They're not too bad. But we better get started."

An hour and a glass of wine apiece later, Daisy positioned the toy under the tree. "Never again."

"Is there anything else we need to put together?"

"No. Thank God. Now we relax. More wine?"

"Yes." I gave her my glass. When she returned, I handed her a gift-wrapped box. "Why don't you open this now while it's just the two of us?"

She looked surprised. "Really?"

"Yeah."

"Okay." She set down her wine, then carefully peeled off the paper and lifted the lid. "Oh," she said. She covered her mouth with one hand.

I'd bought her a sterling silver rope chain with freshwater pearl accents. There was a silver heart pendant with an oxidized finish hanging from it. It was beautiful and delicate, just like Daisy. "Do you like it?"

"I love it." She handed me the necklace, turned around, and lifted up her hair. "Can you put it on me?"

I put the necklace around her neck and fastened the clasp.

She turned around to face me. "What do you think?"

The heart lay right in that dip in her throat. "It looks great on you. To be honest, I wasn't sure if you liked jewelry. You hardly ever wear any."

"We have a pretty strict dress code at work. I can wear a watch, but bracelets aren't allowed. A lot of nurses wear their wedding rings, but mine had a raised stone and it always got caught on my gloves, so I left it at home. Did I ever tell you that Scott pawned my wedding ring one day while I was at work?"

"You have *got* to be kidding me."

She shook her head. "He swore that I must have lost it or accidentally knocked it down the drain, but we both knew what really happened. When I turned in the claim to our insurance company, I put the money in my savings account instead of replacing the ring because I knew he'd just steal it again."

"I'm sorry," I said. "I'd make a comment about how I can't believe someone could stoop so low, but frankly I'm not that surprised."

"It hurt at the time, but I'm over it."

"Can you wear a necklace to work?"

"Yes. Lots of nurses wear short necklaces. This length is

perfect." She touched the small silver links. "I'd forgotten how nice it is to have something pretty. Thank you," she whispered.

I pulled her close and kissed the top of her head. I would buy her more, I decided. I wouldn't stop until she had a jewelry box full of pretty things.

"Just out of curiosity, what did you get Elliott?" she asked.

"I got him a three-hundred-piece toy-soldier playset. It's got all kinds of army guys and missile-launcher trucks and tanks and bombs."

"I bet you can't wait to play with that," she said.

"You mean Elliott?"

She grinned. "No. I mean you." She reached under the tree and pulled out two boxes. One was small and wrapped in navy-blue paper with a silver bow on top. The other was wrapped in red and crisscrossed with a plaid ribbon. "Here."

"Two? Which one should I open first?"

"The big one."

She'd bought me a dress shirt and tie and they were exactly my style.

"They're perfect," I said.

"Just a little something for you to wear under those dashing suits of yours," she said. "Okay. Open the other one."

I unwrapped the gift and lifted the lid to find a pair of silver cuff links. "Well, won't I look sharp in these?"

"Oh, yes." Daisy pretended to fan herself.

"Hold on, Daisy Jane. Do cuff links turn you on?"

"I just… when I see them on a man, I go a little crazy."

"A cuff link fetish. Interesting," I said.

"There are *much* weirder fetishes than cuff links."

"Do you have any of them?"

"Wouldn't you like to know?"

"Yes, I would. Right now."

"Cuff links are as freaky as it gets with me. Sorry to disappoint you."

"You have never disappointed me," I said. We were sitting on the floor. I stood up and turned off the lamp, which left only the glow of the lights on the Christmas tree. I sat down on the couch. "Come up here."

Daisy sat on my lap and straddled me. I put my hand on the back of her head and brought her lips to mine, dipping my tongue into her mouth. Her lips were soft, but her nipples hardened instantly when I ran my thumbs over them through the thin fabric of her shirt. I took it off. Tracing the lace edging on the cups of her bra as I kissed her, I slipped a finger inside one of them. After unhooking her bra, I pushed the straps off her shoulders and removed it entirely. I paused for a second to look at Daisy, naked from the waist up, wearing only the necklace I'd given her.

One of the many things I liked about Daisy was that she never said things about her breasts like "I wish they were bigger" or "You probably wish I had implants" or any of that other crap women had occasionally said to me. She owned those breasts like they were the best breasts anyone had ever seen. And to me they were: firm, perky. Small pink nipples. A perfect handful, or in this case mouthful, because by then I was tracing one of those perfect pink nipples with my tongue. Daisy sighed and ran her hands through my hair, holding my head in place. When I started to suck she began squirming around on my lap, which sent all kinds of sensations shooting through me.

"You better take me to bed before Elliott wakes up and checks to see if Santa has arrived," she said. "I don't want to traumatize him on the first Christmas he might actually remember." She climbed off my lap.

"I'll be right there." I shut off the lights and checked to make sure the front door was locked and the chain was on.

I caught up with Daisy just inside the door to her bedroom. She pulled my T-shirt over my head and I steered her toward the bed, falling onto it with her. Holding her close, skin to skin, I kissed her until I had to come up for air. Daisy's breathing sounded as ragged as mine.

I knelt between her legs and took off her jeans. Slowly I pulled down her underwear and threw them on the floor. She let out a little gasp when my fingers made contact. I pushed her legs farther apart and teased her, rubbing her slowly and circling the spot that drove her wild with my thumb. A minute later I added my tongue and she came hard, shouting my name and running her fingers through my hair.

When her shuddering subsided, she pushed me onto my back and unbuttoned my jeans. She pulled the zipper down and took them off, and just the way she was looking down at my hard-on straining at my boxer briefs was enough to push me halfway over the edge. I groaned loudly when she touched me. She applied exactly the right amount of pressure, and as good as it felt, all I really wanted was to be inside her.

"Daisy." When she stopped what she was doing and looked up at me, I said, "Condom. Now."

She reached into the nightstand for a condom, then unwrapped it and put it on me. I pulled her on top of me and she guided me inside. It felt incredible. Daisy closed her eyes and moved up and down and around, and I held her tightly by the hips and watched her.

"Think you can come again?" I asked.

"I'm certainly going to try."

"Better hurry, sweetheart. I can't hold back much longer." I reached my hand between our bodies and rubbed her.

"Oh, God. Do that again," she said.

So I did, and I watched her come for the second time, thinking she never looked more beautiful than when she let go so completely, without inhibition. I flipped her onto her back and sank into her as hard and deep as I could. That was all it took, and I groaned, saying her name over and over. My movements eventually slowed, but I didn't pull out of her. She held me tight, and I kissed her throat, tracing the necklace with my finger.

"I love this necklace," she said. "I am never taking it off, Brooks. Never."

CHAPTER 48

DAISY

"MAMA! I IS awake!"

Elliott's voice shattered the silence of the apartment, and both Brooks and I woke up rather suddenly. The clock said six a.m. I gave Brooks a quick kiss and said, "Merry Christmas," then I slipped on my robe and Brooks dressed in a pair of sweats and a T-shirt.

Elliott was standing next to his bed.

"Merry Christmas, Elliott," I said.

"I waited for you to come get me," he said, wearing a big smile.

"You sure did. Should we see if Santa's been here?"

"Yes," he said and ran out of the room, Brooks and I following closely behind.

Elliott dropped to his knees in front of the tree. "He brought the command center, Mama!"

I sat down cross-legged on the floor next to him. "I see that."

Elliott picked up the action figures I'd bought to go along with the command center and started playing and Brooks joined us. "I wuv this," Elliott said.

"Don't forget to check your stocking," I said. We didn't have a fireplace, so I'd placed it under the tree with the other gifts.

Elliott tore his attention away from the toys, picked up his stocking, and turned it over. Chocolate rained down on the carpet. There were Santas and bells and snowmen all wrapped in brightly colored foil. Elliott had one unwrapped and in his mouth in record time.

"Pace yourself," I said. "I'm going to start breakfast soon. You've got all day."

"'Kay," he said with his mouth full. I'd also included a bouncy ball that lit up, a small coloring book and crayons, bubbles, stickers, and tablets that fizzed in the bathtub. Elliott picked up everything and examined it, but he quickly turned his attention back to the command center.

Until Brooks handed Elliott the present he'd brought for him.

"What is this?" he asked.

"Open it and find out," Brooks said.

Elliott tore off the wrapping paper and a look of sheer joy spread across his face. "It's army guys. Now I has enough for a pwatoon!"

"There's enough for lots of platoons."

"What is this?" Elliott asked, holding up a tank.

"It's a tank. And here's a missile launcher." Brooks looked at Elliott and smiled. "You up for a mission?"

Elliott looked at Brooks in total wonderment. "Yeah!"

Brooks and Elliott began acting out various scenarios while I started the coffee and put cinnamon rolls in the oven. They were still at it a half hour later when I called them to the table.

After breakfast, we showered and dressed. I plugged in Crock-Pots and set out the food buffet-style on the kitchen counter and table. I planned on rotating the offerings throughout the day, starting with brunch items and transitioning to hot appetizers. I also set out platters of fudge and cookies.

Theo arrived at ten o'clock.

"Merry Christmas," I said.

"Merry Christmas, Daisy." He handed me a beautiful potted poinsettia. "This is for you."

"It's beautiful," I said, leaning in to give him a hug.

"Feo," Elliott said. "Wook at all my toys."

Theo handed Elliott a long box wrapped in green. "I brought you a little something, too."

Elliott tore off the wrapping paper. "It's a fishing pole!"

Theo and Brooks had taken Elliott fishing in Apple Valley twice. It was all he could talk about for days afterward.

"Think you're ready for Big Bear Lake?" Theo asked.

"I *am*," Elliott said.

Brooks handed his dad a cup of coffee. "I hope you're not hungry, Dad. There's nothing to eat here."

"Very funny," I said. "Help yourself, Theo."

We spent the day eating and watching Elliott play. Kayla and her fiancé, Brian, joined us for an hour. Margaret Parker and her son Robert and daughter-in-law Theresa stopped by on their way home.

"Is that the reporter who came to see me?" Margaret asked, looking over at Brooks.

"Yes. He's here a lot."

"Oh, honey. I'm so happy for you."

Shortly after my grandmother died, I'd thought about what the holidays might be like for Elliott and me this year. I'd resigned myself to the fact that Thanksgiving and Christmas would probably be bittersweet.

Maybe a little lonely.

But I looked around the room as people ate and talked and laughed, and I realized that it didn't get much better than this and that I was truly blessed.

Brooks sat down next to me on the couch and put his arm around me. "How are you doing?"

I smiled and said, "Better than I ever hoped."

Pam and Shane joined us around five o'clock. Her belly preceded her into the room.

"Wow. Should I boil some water and gather up a bunch of clean rags?" I asked.

"I would actually let you deliver this baby on your kitchen table if it meant I'd get some relief," Pam said. "I can't breathe. Or sleep. Or walk. I don't know how I'm going to get through the next three weeks." She sank down on a kitchen chair.

"Can you eat?"

"Not really, but I'm not going to let something like running out of room stop me. Bring it on," she said.

I made her a plate with a little bit of everything on it and then sat down beside her.

"Is that new?" Pam asked, reaching out to touch my necklace.

"Brooks gave it to me. I'm never taking it off."

"It's gorgeous."

"I know. I love it," I said.

I stood up to see if Shane needed anything, but Brooks had beaten me to it. He and Shane were in the living room talking to Theo, each of them holding a beer and a plate of food.

Brooks and I had gotten together with Pam and Shane a few times since Brooks had moved back. I knew Pam would like him—partly because he was not Scott and partly because it was hard not to be captivated by Brooks—but Shane and Brooks couldn't have been more different, and I wondered if they'd be able to find any common ground. Brooks enjoyed being outside, but Shane was a true outdoorsman. Brooks would always have an air of the city about him while Shane gave off a subtle small-town vibe. I needn't have worried, because Shane and Brooks had found plenty of things to talk about, including sports, cars, golf, and a shared interest in old James Bond movies. Shane was especially fascinated by some of the things Brooks had reported on, and he loved to hear Brooks recount the details of his most bizarre stories.

Pam and Shane stayed until seven. "It's time for me to go home and put my feet up," Pam said. "Maybe this baby will come early and put me out of my misery."

Theo left shortly after Pam and Shane and by seven thirty, Elliott was in his pajamas and fading fast.

He yawned and rubbed his eyes. "Can I watch my Thomas movie?"

Shane and Pam had given Elliott a Thomas the Tank Engine three-disc set and he was dying to watch it.

"Do you think you can hold your eyes open long enough to make it through the first disc?"

"Yes I can." His confidence far outweighed his energy level, but so what if he fell asleep watching it?

"Okay. Mama will clean up the kitchen while you watch your movie and then it's bedtime, okay?"

"Okay."

Brooks put the disc in the DVD player and pushed Play. I went into the kitchen and began transferring leftovers to Tupperware containers and loading the dishwasher. It appeared that I had dirtied every pot, pan, and platter I owned, so when the dishwasher was full I washed the rest by hand and wiped down the counters. When I walked into the living room to check on Brooks and Elliott, I stopped short.

Elliott was on Brooks's lap, asleep. Brooks must have turned off the room's overhead light when he started the movie, because the lamp on the side table and the glow of the TV screen and the Christmas tree provided the only illumination. Elliott had turned onto his side and had one arm wrapped around Brooks's middle. The disc had ended, but Brooks had obviously not wanted to disturb Elliott because he hadn't gotten up or called out to me.

My heart swelled. I sat down on the couch beside them.

Brooks looked at me and said, simply, "I love you."

"I love you, too."

My eyes filled with tears and something in my expression must have worried Brooks because he said, "What's wrong?"

"I have to tell you something."

A flicker of apprehension showed on Brooks's face. "Okay."

"When I had Elliott there were complications. The doctor couldn't stop my bleeding and I was pretty out of it, so Scott had to make a split-second decision about whether to let them perform an emergency hysterectomy or take a chance and hope I wouldn't bleed to death. He told them to go ahead. It was one of the last good decisions that man ever made. Nick, the guy I dated before you, really liked Elliott. But it was important to him to have a child of his own, preferably two or three. He'd spent a lot of time getting his career off the ground and he was ready to start a family. I can still have children, but I can't carry them. We'd have had to use a surrogate, which Nick didn't seem very open to. He tried to hide it, but I could tell by the look on his face that his heart wasn't in it. And to be honest, I don't know that I wanted that either. Most of the time I really feel like Elliott is enough for me. We went round and round for a while, but eventually we decided we wanted different things and we broke up. If you want a child of your own, I'll do whatever it takes to give you one, but there will be some extra steps involved. Maybe I should have told you sooner. I *know* I should have told Nick sooner. But I don't know when it's the right time to tell a man something like this."

I looked at Elliott, who was still blissfully asleep on Brooks's lap. Brooks's expression was no longer apprehensive. He was looking at me quite tenderly, actually, but he'd remained silent.

"Say something," I pleaded.

"When my mom was in the hospital having her feeding tube inserted, I had blood drawn. The doctors had discovered that her ALS had a hereditary component, which means there's a chance I could develop it. If I tested negative, I'd never have to worry. My risk is no higher than anyone else's. But they told me I could test positive and still never develop the disease. I got tested because I intended to find out the results, but over the past couple of months I've come to the realization that I don't actually want to know. I don't want to spend the rest of my life worrying about something that might not ever happen. But I don't want to have any biological children. I've asked myself if I'm being selfish. Maybe a life that ends in ALS is better than no life at all. But I can't bear the thought of watching one of my children die the way my mom did. I just can't. It's okay that you can't carry any more children, because I'm not going to have any. And I think anyone who gets to be a part of Elliott's life is pretty lucky."

I was quietly and messily bawling by then.

A gushing waterfall of tears.

Because when the universe finally throws something truly remarkable your way, it is impossible to avoid the accompanying flood of emotion, at least for me.

"So, let's do this again," Brooks said, reaching over to take my hand. "I love you."

"I love you, Brooks." I buried my face in his chest, wrapping my arm around Elliott, who was still wrapped around Brooks. He held us both and eventually my tears subsided.

"Any other cards you want to lay on the table?" Brooks asked.

"No. You?"

"I'm good," he said.

Brooks carried Elliott into his bedroom and laid him down on his bed. When he came back into the room, we shut everything off and Brooks took my hand and led me to the bedroom. I needed Brooks to hold me, and I needed to hold him. Maybe he felt the same because after we undressed and were under the covers, he pulled me into his arms, his hands moving idly through my hair, twisting the strands with his fingers.

"Are you scared?" I asked. "About the ALS?"

"Yes," he said. "Does it bother you?"

"Only in the sense that I feel powerless and want you to be around for a really long time. Life has no guarantees, though. What good is living if all you think about is dying?"

"I know we all have to die someday, but if I have any choice in the matter, I'd rather not know about it so far in advance. That's why I don't want the results of the blood test."

"I don't think I would either."

"I think we should leave Fenton," Brooks said. "I don't think it's safe to stay here. I just have a bad feeling."

It seemed unfair that Brooks should have to relocate again, especially since he hadn't been back very long and I wasn't even sure where I wanted to go. My plan had always been to finish paying off Scott's debt first and then choose a few cities where I thought I could find the best job. But I trusted Brooks's instincts.

"I agree. Maybe it's better to start fresh," I said. "No more looking over my shoulder. But there is one thing I want."

"What's that?" he asked.

"Wherever we decide to go, I want you to ask your dad to come with us."

CHAPTER 49

DAISY

THE OVERHEAD LIGHTS cast a fluorescent orange glow in the stairwell of the parking garage as I climbed the steps to the second floor of the three-level structure. It was Friday, the week after Christmas, and there was something about working a full week after being home for a few extra days for the holidays that made it especially hard to get back into the swing of things. Not only that, but I'd gotten out of work twenty minutes late and felt bad that I wouldn't be able to pick up Elliott on time. Celine knew I sometimes got held up, but I pulled out my phone to send her a quick text so she'd know I was on my way.

Brooks had started perusing job boards and I'd updated my résumé. The more I thought about leaving Fenton, the more excited I'd become. Just the idea of starting over in a new town had put me in a hopeful mood.

If I hadn't been so preoccupied with thoughts of our future plans, I might have noticed the car sooner and been able to dart back into the stairwell and out the door to the pedestrian walkway linking the hospital and the garage. There were usually a few people waiting for a friend or family member to retrieve their car from the garage and pick them up in front.

But I didn't notice and I was too far away from the stairwell by the time I became aware of several things all at once: the car coming toward me and the rate of its speed, barely more than an idle, and a man—a boy really, maybe seventeen or eighteen—who had sprung lithely from the back passenger door and was approaching me steadily and with purpose. He'd also left the door of the car open, which caused all kinds of alarm bells to go off in my brain.

I'd parked my car diagonally across from the stairwell door, and the boy stood between me and the safety of my vehicle. Mere seconds passed and my heart began to pound as I assessed the situation.

The car. White, dirty, old, big.

The slow rate of speed.

The boy.

The open door.

If I'd left work on time, I would have been walking to my car with Kayla or one of the other nurses. Maybe someone else who'd worked a twelve and was heading home. But most of the shift workers had already left and the garage was virtually empty.

The boy should not be walking toward me.

Adrenaline flooded my body as he came closer.

I had a moment of all-encompassing panic when I couldn't remember if I'd taken my gun from the safe and put it in my purse that morning, but I regained a small measure of my composure when I slipped my hand into my purse's special compartment and discovered that I had.

I wrapped my fingers around the grip of the gun, calming myself with thoughts of reaching my vehicle safely and then laughing at how paranoid I'd been. Because surely there was a plausible reason for everything that seemed to be unfolding in slow motion right in front of me.

The boy kept coming. My body vibrated with fear.

Fight or flight.

...If an assailant wants to move you to another location, do not go with him. Do not get in his vehicle. If he wants to move you, it's because he wants to do something to you that he can't in your current location, and I guarantee you it will be worse than what he's already doing. Run if you can...

Could I outrun him?

What would happen if I turned my back on him and fled? Would he tackle me from behind? My legs had turned to jelly. Could I make it back to the stairwell before the car, or the boy, caught up to me?

Fight or flight.

I carried with a bullet in the chamber, so all I had to do was draw and fire. He was only fifteen feet away when I put out my hand and yelled, "Stop." That seemed to spur him on and he sneered, his expression so cold and evil that I felt a level of fear I'd never encountered before, not even on the night Scott and Dale had come to my home looking for money.

The boy quickened his pace and the car revved its engine as it hurtled forward.

The timing seemed planned.

I drew my gun. "Stop," I yelled again, but the boy kept coming and so did the car. Instead of stopping, he lunged.

I fired, the sound louder than I could have ever imagined.

The boy went down.

The car peeled out, its tires screeching as it rounded the corner, clipping the edge of a concrete pillar, the noise like an explosion as it reverberated through the garage.

I dropped the gun on the ground, my ears ringing, and fell to my knees. I crawled to the boy, sobbing and gasping. His eyes were open and he was breathing, though it sounded shallow and labored.

There must have been people in the stairwell because a man and a woman burst through the door and ran toward me. The man told the woman to run back into the hospital and summon help. "And tell them to call the police!"

"Are you okay, lady?" the man asked. "Do you know this guy?"

My ears wouldn't work right and his voice seemed so far away. I ignored him and used the boy's jacket to apply pressure to his chest, holding my palm firmly against the wound. It wasn't until the sound of footsteps, and police sirens and voices, pierced the murky and muffled world I existed in that I stopped pressing on the boy's wound and got out of the way.

I felt as if I were outside my body, detached, watching the activity around me in complete confusion. How long had it been since I'd fired the gun?

The emergency personnel worked to save the boy. But the police soon approached, and one of the officers helped me to my feet and led me toward a waiting car. After he patted me down, he took my wrists in his hand and encircled them with the cold metal of the handcuffs. I could hardly hear due to the continued ringing in my ears, but I could hear enough to understand that he was reading me my rights.

They were arresting *me*.

I said nothing.

When we got to the police station, I was placed in a holding cell. The officer reappeared approximately a half hour later and told me I could make a call.

I wanted to call Brooks more than anything in the world, but I didn't.

I called Nick Churchill instead.

He answered on the third ring.

"It's Daisy," I said. "I've been arrested." I tried to keep my voice steady, but I started crying, and once the floodgate of tears opened, I was powerless to staunch their flow.

Nick did not ask me what I'd done; I'm not sure I could have formed the words to tell him if he had. "I need you to call someone for me. His name is Brooks McClain. Tell him to pick up Elliott at Celine's." I rattled off the number without asking if Nick had a pen and paper.

"Got it," Nick said. "I'm on my way. And Daisy? Don't say anything to anyone."

CHAPTER 50

BROOKS

I WAS IN THE car on my way to Daisy's when my phone rang. "Hello."

"Hi. Is this Brooks? This is Celine. Elliott's babysitter."

Why would Celine be calling me? "Yes, this is Brooks."

"I'm sorry to bother you, but Daisy hasn't picked up Elliott and she isn't answering her phone. She sent me a text saying she'd be late, but she still hasn't shown up. I wasn't sure who else to call. I tried the emergency contact number listed on Elliott's paperwork, but I wasn't able to reach anyone. Daisy gave me your name and phone number the day you and your dad picked up Elliott to go fishing, and I added you as someone who has been authorized to pick him up."

I silenced the stereo and looked at the clock. Daisy and Elliott should have already been home by now. Feeling the first flicker of panic, I said, "When was the last time you tried Daisy?"

"About five minutes ago. I've tried calling her three times."

The flicker grew into something much larger. "Celine, tell me your address again." When she finished giving it to me, I repeated it. Drawing on my memory of picking up Elliott the day we went fishing, I realized I was going the wrong way. I swung the car around and headed in the opposite direction. "I'll be right there."

As soon as I ended the call, I tried Daisy's phone.

Come on, Daisy.

Answer.

It went straight to voice mail. Next I called my dad. "Something's wrong. Daisy didn't pick up Elliott from the babysitter. I'm on my way now to get him and then I'm going to bring him to you, okay?"

"Sure," he said. "Keep me posted."

I tapped the police-scanner app on my phone and listened. It was mostly chatter, and there didn't appear to be anything significant going on.

Unless I'd missed it.

At Celine's, I bent down to greet Elliott. He was wearing his pajamas with his little blue jacket on over them, waiting patiently for Daisy.

"Hey, buddy."

"Bwooks! Hi! Where's my mama?"

Celine and I shared a look.

"She got caught up at work, so I told her I'd come get you and we'd go to Theo's for a while. Sound good?"

"I wike Feo's house. He always pways wif me."

"It's getting close to your bedtime though, so I'd like for you to lie down and I'll check on you in a little while. Okay?"

"Okay," he said looking a little dejected.

"Here are his things," Celine said, handing me a bag with Elliott's nebulizer and clothes. "I've got an extra car seat if you need one."

"I do," I said. "Thanks."

My phone rang before we'd even pulled out of Celine's driveway. I didn't recognize the number. "Yeah?"

"Brooks McClain?"

"Yes. Who is this?"

"My name is Nick Churchill. I'm Daisy's attorney. She asked that I call you."

"What the hell is going on? Is she okay?"

"She's been arrested."

Daisy… arrested?

"For what?" I asked.

"I don't know. I'm on my way there now. I'll know more as soon as I've talked to her. She's very worried about Elliott. Can you pick him up?"

"I just did. Tell her Elliott is with me and that I'm going to take him to my dad's. Where can I meet you?"

"She's at the San Bernardino County Jail. Wait for me in the lobby. I'll come out and get you after I've had a chance to talk to her."

"I'm on my way."

I'd no sooner hung up with Nick when my cell phone rang again. This time it was Paul.

"I need you to get over to the hospital parking garage in Barstow right away. We just got a tip that an unarmed man was shot and there's a suspect in custody."

"I'm sorry, Paul. I can't take this one."

"Why not?" he asked.

"Because I'm pretty sure that the suspect in custody is my girlfriend."

My final call was from Jack Quick. "You're calling about Daisy, aren't you?"

"Yeah," he said. "I'm not sure what went down, but you better call an attorney."

"Daisy already did," I said.

CHAPTER 51

DAISY

MY PERSONAL POSSESSIONS were taken from me and inventoried. I was photographed and fingerprinted. I didn't cry when the female guard told me to strip. Though it was degrading and I was humiliated, I didn't cry when she performed the search. When she handed me the blue polyester jail uniform, my relief at being clothed again was immeasurable. She led me back to the holding cell, which was still blissfully empty, and locked the door behind her.

A different guard came for me a while later and led me to a small room with a window in the door where Nick was waiting. He was sitting at a table and when I appeared in the doorway, he rose and met me halfway.

He pulled me into his arms and hugged me. "It's okay," he said, rubbing my back. "You did the right thing by calling me."

I did cry then, the combination of my shame and his kindness too overwhelming for me to handle. "This is not okay, Nick. None of this is okay." I pulled away and looked up him. "Elliott?"

"He's fine. Brooks picked him up and his dad is going to watch him. As soon as I get done talking to you, I'm going to meet with Brooks so I can fill him in."

"Brooks is here?"

"He's in the lobby waiting for me."

Oh, Brooks. What have I done?

"What about the boy?" I asked.

"All I know is that he's alive." Nick pulled out a chair. "Here. Sit down." He removed a notebook and pen from his briefcase. "Now, tell me what happened."

I told him the whole story, or at least as much as I could piece together. The details that had once seemed so sharp—the boy, the car, the gunshot—now seemed fuzzy, and I was no longer able to recall some of them. I also wasn't positive about the order of events.

"How can I not remember every single second of the worst thing I have ever done?" I asked.

"It's quite common, actually," Nick said. "Your brain wants to block out traumatic events. Could you see anyone inside the car? How many people were there? Did you recognize any of them?"

"It was a big white car. Four doors. Old, kind of beat-up. Everything happened so fast, but I think there were three people in it. Two in front and the boy was in the back. The car had its headlights on and they were shining right in my face, so I couldn't see well. I told the boy to stop. The car door was open and I thought that meant they wanted to take me with them." I broke down bawling. "I didn't want him to put me in that car."

"Did you give any kind of statement to the police?" Nick asked.

"No. The gunshot was so loud and my ears were ringing. I couldn't hear, and I was so confused that I didn't say anything at all."

"Good," Nick said.

"I would never have fired the gun if I didn't think my life was in imminent danger, Nick. I didn't want to shoot him. I never wanted to shoot anyone."

Nick reached across the table and squeezed my hand. "I'm sure you didn't."

"What's going to happen to me?"

"The district attorney has forty-eight hours to file charges—excluding weekends—so we're looking at Monday before anything will start to happen. I'm sorry," he said. "You'll be kept here until then. When the DA decides on the charges, you'll be arraigned and moved to a cell at the courthouse. Bail will be set. I can navigate you through the process until then, but after that you'll need a criminal defense attorney. I'll find one for you, so don't worry about that."

"Will they automatically file charges? Can't you explain why I fired the gun? With everything that's happened with my grandmother's murder, won't they take that into consideration? There is no way that what happened in that garage was random. I know the two incidents are linked in some way."

He set down his pen. "California takes its self-defense laws very seriously. The fact that this young man was unarmed will make it a bit more difficult to prove that your life was in danger. But given your lack of criminal history, the circumstances of your grandmother's unsolved murder, and the events leading up to the shooting, your chances of being exonerated are good. I think most juries would have a hard time convicting you once they've been presented with all the evidence."

I held my head in my hands. "But there's no guarantee," I said. "It could go either way."

Nick reached across the table and pulled my hands away. "It

could, but I don't think it *will*. I wouldn't tell you this if I didn't believe it. I'm going to do everything I can," he said. "It'll be okay, Daisy. I promise."

As much as I trusted Nick, a promise wasn't going to cut it. In order to be reunited with Brooks and Elliott, I'd need nothing short of a miracle.

CHAPTER 52

BROOKS

I WAS PACING THE lobby of the San Bernardino County Jail when a man wearing a suit walked up to me. He looked like he was a few years younger than me and had blond hair and a neatly trimmed moustache and goatee.

"Brooks?" he said with an outstretched hand. "Nick Churchill."

I shook his hand. "Nice to meet you. How is she?"

"She's scared. Overwhelmed."

I hated the thought that Daisy was scared and there was nothing I could do to comfort her. "Can you please tell me what happened?"

"A car approached her in the hospital parking garage. One of the passengers got out and left the door of the car open. Daisy felt very strongly that his intent was to abduct her. She told him to stop and when he kept coming, she shot him."

"Is he dead?"

"As far as I know he's alive. Obtaining his identity and information on his condition is one of my top priorities."

"Why did they even arrest her? She had a permit to carry that gun, she had the appropriate instruction, and I know she fired it in self-defense. The only reason she armed herself in the first place was because she felt she was in danger. And clearly she was."

"They arrested her because that is what will happen if you shoot someone in a parking garage in California. The police are going to act swiftly and let the courts take it from there. Daisy doesn't get a pass because she's a woman, either. She's going to spend some time in jail and she's going to be charged with a crime. But as strict as our laws are, people who shoot in justifiable self-defense—and I will argue vehemently that she did—are rarely convicted. However, she has some factors stacked against her: one, as far as I know, her assailant was unarmed. Two, she referred to him as a boy, which may make this a harder battle to fight. Juries can be particularly hard on defendants when there's a minor involved. Three, she had a gun and therefore used force unequal to her assailant."

"Have you seen her? Do you really think she'd do well in a fight? I don't care if this guy was young. I guarantee he was bigger and stronger than her."

"I'm well aware of her size, but her counsel will still have to bear the burden of proving she acted in self-defense. The state will have to prove that she didn't. This isn't over, not by a longshot. I want you to prepare yourself for what's coming. The potential for Daisy to see some real jail time absolutely exists."

His words were like a punch to the gut. "Does she know that?"

Nick rubbed his chin and exhaled. "No. She'll have to face the reality at some point, but now is not that time. I won't know exactly what we're up against until I hear from the DA."

"Talk to Jack Quick. He's a detective on the force. He knows about the danger Daisy has been in."

"Trust me. I *will* talk to him," he said. "I'll be contacting him as soon as possible."

"What happens next?" I asked.

"The DA has forty-eight hours to determine the charges and file them. After her arraignment, Daisy will more than likely be transferred to the West Valley Detention Center, which will not be pleasant. She'll be placed in a cell with other inmates."

I could hardly stomach the thought of what would lie ahead for Daisy. "What about bail?"

He hesitated. "It will be expensive. You'll have to use a bail bondsman, and you'll be required to come up with ten percent of the amount. I won't know what that amount is until the charges are filed."

"So she won't be able to go home anytime soon."

"No. I'm sorry," he said. "I know this is rough."

I had never felt more powerless in my life. "I'm just glad she called you." I massaged my temples, because I had the mother of all headaches. "How long have you known Daisy?"

"Since I handled her divorce. And look, I want you to know that even though things didn't work out between Daisy and me, I still care for her very much. I'll do everything in my power to help her."

Wait a minute.

This was the guy she dated before me? *This* was the Nick who wanted kids of his own?"

"Oh, of course. I'm sure you will."

"My expertise is in family law, so I told Daisy I'd secure a criminal attorney for her. I know of a few who would probably be willing to take the case." He took a business card out of his briefcase. "Here's my contact information. Why don't you plan on coming to my office in the morning? I'll brief you on the case and let you know what I've been able to find out overnight."

I pocketed the card. "That would be great. Thanks."

"One more thing," he said as we began to walk toward the exit. "My services will be pro bono. I'll try to get a criminal defense attorney to do the same, or at least agree to reduce his fees, but I can't promise anything."

"That's very generous of you."

"Yeah, well. I know all about Daisy's spreadsheet."

*

My dad was sitting in the living room watching TV when I got home.

"Is Elliott asleep?"

"Yes. I put him in the spare bedroom. He kept asking for Daisy. It broke my heart."

"What did you tell him?"

"I said she was working late."

"Good. That's what I'm going to tell him."

"I saw a news update on TV. Tell me what really happened."

My dad listened as I explained everything that had transpired and what Nick had told me. "This isn't as cut-and-dried as I thought it might be. It could go either way."

He nodded, looking worried. "I imagine it could."

I exhaled. "This has to turn out okay. It just does."

"No sense worrying about the outcome until we know more. For right now, let's focus on what we can do to help Daisy."

"She's strong. She may not think so right now, but she is. She'll be okay as long as she knows we're taking care of Elliott. He's going to be very confused, so we'll have to find a way to keep him calm. I'll have to lie to him. I hate that, Dad. "

"He's too young to hear the truth. Don't beat yourself up over it."

"Yeah, I suppose."

You should get some rest," he said.

"Daisy's attorney wants me to come to his office in the morning. I'll leave Elliott here with you, if that's okay."

"Course it is. We'll find something to keep ourselves occupied, so don't worry about us."

"Thanks."

I tried, I really did. I went to bed, but my eyes were still open when the first light of dawn crept across the sky.

Elliott appeared in my doorway shortly after that, and I nearly lost it when he said, "Bwooks, can you pwease help me find my mama?"

"I know exactly where she is," I said. "I talked to her last night and she told me to tell you she loves you."

"Where is she?" he asked.

We were sitting on the edge of my bed, and I was trying to pull together a coherent explanation from the foggy recesses of my sleep-deprived brain.

"She's at work. They needed extra help at the hospital, so she's going to stay there until they don't need her help anymore. She wants you to stay with Theo and me, okay?"

"Okay." He looked up at me. "But I is missing her."

"I know, buddy. She misses you, too. She'll be home just as soon as she can. I have to go out in a little while to check on something. You're going to stay here with Theo. Would you like it if he got out some more of my old toys?"

"Yes," he said, but his eyes were filled with tears.

I gave him a hug. "That's what we'll do then. Come on. Let's go get some breakfast."

*

I walked through the front door of the law firm a little before nine. Because it was Saturday, there was no one sitting behind the reception desk. I was about to pull out my phone to call Nick when he rounded the corner. "I heard the door. Come on back."

I followed him to his office, noticing he was still in the same clothes he'd been wearing the night before. "You look like you've been here all night."

"I have." He was drinking coffee from a tall Styrofoam container. He raised it to his lips and made a face. "Cold. I'll be right back."

When he returned with a fresh cup of coffee, he sat down at his desk and said, "Okay. I've talked to Jack Quick. There's quite a bit of circumstantial evidence we can use. I've also spoken to a criminal defense attorney who's standing by. He's going to do some preliminary work on the case, and as soon as we know what the charges are, he'll begin outlining Daisy's defense."

"I called a colleague of mine at the newspaper," I said. "She went to the scene and was able to speak to a bystander who hadn't initially come forward. A woman claimed she saw a young man get out of a slow-moving white car but didn't think much of it until she was halfway down the stairs and heard the gunshot."

"Do you have her name?"

"Yes." I reached into my pocket and withdrew the piece of paper with the information Maggie had given me.

"Thanks," Nick said. "That'll definitely help."

"What happens next?" I asked.

"Now we sit tight and wait for the DA. Then Daisy will be

arraigned and transferred." The phone on Nick's desk rang. "Excuse me," he said. "I need to take this. There's coffee in the lobby. Help yourself."

I took my time getting coffee in order to give Nick some privacy. I also placed a call to my dad to see how Elliott was holding up, and one to Maggie to see if she'd had any luck finding additional witnesses to interview. My dad and Elliott had been to the park, and I got Maggie's voice mail. I left her a message to call me back. Nick had just hung up the phone when I walked back into his office.

"They were able to identify the young man Daisy shot," Nick said.

"Who was he?"

"A kid who'd run away a few years back who's been living on the streets. My guess is that he was probably offered drugs or money in exchange for his help. He's young, only twenty-two, but at least he's not a minor."

"That's good news then."

Nick rubbed his eyes. "It would be if he hadn't died an hour ago. The DA will automatically file murder charges, probably by Tuesday at the latest. Bail will be set at one million dollars, if it's set at all."

His words rendered me speechless. The coffee I'd swallowed churned in my gut.

"I'm afraid I have some more bad news," he said.

"I don't know what you could possibly tell me that would be worse."

"The state of California has granted temporary emergency custody of Elliott DiStefano to Scott DiStefano."

CHAPTER 53

BROOKS

NICK HAD BEEN trying to calm me down for the past forty-five minutes.

"This is not going to happen, Churchill." I banged my fist down on his desk. "I swear to God I will take Elliott and disappear."

"In which case you'll be charged with kidnapping, and if you're caught you'll find yourself cooling your heels in jail along with Daisy, therefore *guaranteeing* that Elliott will go right back to Scott."

"He's a junkie. Daisy wanted to terminate his parental rights. You know that. You drew up the paperwork. Doesn't that count for something?"

"It would have if she had actually terminated his rights, but she didn't."

"Only because the process server wasn't able to deliver the papers. He's not fit to parent Elliott."

"I am only pointing this out to drive home how tied my hands are, but you do realize that Daisy is in jail awaiting arraignment, which severely compromises my ability to argue in front of a judge about who is the better parent. Yes, Scott is a junkie, but he has no criminal record. He's the child's father and he has joint legal custody. The best thing you can do for Elliott is comply with the court and then immediately file a complaint with social services. They'll launch an investigation and we'll have him out of there in twenty-four to forty-eight hours."

The thought of Elliott spending even one day at that run-down shithole in the desert made my skin crawl. "He'll run. That lowlife will take Elliott and run."

Nick shot me a look.

"Yes, I know what I said. But him running and me running are not even remotely the same."

"I know that. But it's illegal in both cases," Nick said. "It's the chance we'll have to take. I'm sorry." He reached into a desk drawer. "I retrieved Daisy's personal belongings early this morning. I thought you might need to get into her apartment. I'm guessing you'll need to go there now to get Elliott's things." He handed me her purse and a sealed envelope with her name scrawled on the front.

"How long do I have?" I asked.

"You have to turn him over to Scott at five p.m. I'll call you as soon as I know where Scott wants you to drop him off," Nick said.

Even though I knew none of this was Nick's fault, I didn't respond. I let the door to the law firm slam shut behind me when I walked outside.

I drove to Daisy's apartment and parked. Feeling what I thought was the outline of her keys in the envelope, I ripped it open and poured the contents into my hand.

It was the necklace I'd given her for Christmas.

I am never taking it off, Brooks.

Never.

I sat in my Jeep with her necklace clenched in my hand and my throbbing head resting on the steering wheel until I felt composed enough to get out of the car.

Daisy's keys were at the bottom of her purse. I dug them out and unlocked the door of her apartment. Once inside, I stood for a moment in the stillness, steeling myself for what I had to do. In the doorway of Elliott's room, I took in his twin-size bed and his Thomas the Tank Engine comforter. The ball and glove I'd given him sat on his nightstand; a platoon of army men surrounded the base of the lamp. His light-up shoes were on the floor by the dresser.

I sat down on the bed. Daisy was probably sitting in her jail cell, crying her eyes out. Desperately in need of her own comfort. And here I was, getting ready to hand her child over to the one person she didn't ever want him to be with.

I made myself get up and cross the room to Elliott's small closet. There was a blue Thomas the Tank Engine duffle bag, and I filled it with some of Elliott's clothes. I opened his dresser and added pajamas and bent down to grab his light-up shoes. In the bathroom, I found his Elmo toothbrush and Sesame Street toothpaste, and I almost lost it, bracing my hands on the sink when all I really wanted to do was put my fist through the mirror.

When I finished packing for Elliott I entered Daisy's bedroom, thinking of the last night I'd spent in her bed and how she liked to fall asleep with her head on my chest.

I love this woman. She is mine and I will do whatever it takes to get her and Elliott back.

I opened the closet door, scanning the shelves and pushing the clothes aside until I found what I was looking for. The two-drawer metal file cabinet was locked, but I pulled Daisy's key ring out of my pocket and searched the keys for the one I thought might fit. Hoping for my first lucky break of the day, I slid a small key into the lock and exhaled when it turned with ease and I was able to pull open the top drawer. Thumbing through the tabs, labeled alphabetically, I sent a mental thank-you to Daisy for her impressive organizational skills and then pulled out the legal-size papers held neatly together with a small binder clip.

I rolled them into a tube, shoved them into my back pocket, locked the file cabinet, and walked out of Daisy's bedroom.

*

My dad and Elliott were sitting at the kitchen table eating lunch when I returned.

"Hi, Bwooks. Me and Feo is having some mac and cheese!"

I hugged him tight. "I see that, buddy. I need to talk to Theo for a second. Keep eating, okay? We'll just be in the other room."

"Okay."

"The kid Daisy shot has died," I said as soon as we were out of earshot.

"No," my dad said.

"Yes. And Daisy's ex-husband has been awarded temporary emergency custody of Elliott."

"You've got to be kidding me." Dad sat down heavily on the couch, as if standing was suddenly too difficult. Seeing the anguish on his face only increased my feelings of helplessness. "When does he have to go?"

"I have to have him there by five. Nick is going to let me know where to take him." I sat down on the couch next to my dad and neither of us said anything for a minute. "I thought about taking off."

"I think anyone in your position would."

"It would only make things worse." I took a deep breath. "I need your help."

"Of course. Tell me what you need me to do, and I'll do it."

*

I was instructed to meet Scott in the Del Taco parking lot—his choice, not mine. I wasn't surprised that he didn't want me bringing Elliott out to Tweakerville. No need to draw attention to the fact that he lived in a house full of meth addicts. I still couldn't believe that the court would let someone have a child simply because they'd contributed half the DNA. It made no sense.

"The sooner you take him there, the sooner we can set the wheels in motion to remove him," Nick had said. Nick had better hope that's exactly how it played out, because if Elliott had to spend more than twenty-four hours with Scott, I wouldn't be able to handle it.

Before we'd left the house, I'd sat Elliott down on the couch and explained, as best I could, what was about to happen. I forced myself to keep my voice neutral, to make it sound like I was in favor of this plan. "I know you like being here with Theo and me while your mom is away, but I have to take you to meet your dad."

Confusion washed over his face. "But you is my dad," he said in a voice so soft I could barely hear him.

I took a deep breath. "I would really like to be your dad someday, but I'm not. Not yet. The man who is your dad would like to see you. Just a short visit and then you can come right back here with us."

"I don't want to go with that dad, Bwooks. I don't want to go with him!"

Elliott started to cry, and for a moment I wasn't sure I could go through with it. Despite what Nick had said, running seemed like a damn good idea.

I gathered Elliott into my arms and he clung to me. "When you see your dad, you might remember him. He hasn't seen you since you were very little, and he misses you." I reached out my hand and showed Elliott the army man in the middle of my palm, the one I'd scooped off his nightstand at the last minute. "Everything will be okay. I promise. I want you to keep this. Every time you feel it in your hand, I want you to remember that you're safe and I'm coming back to get you."

Elliott took the army man and wrapped his fingers around it.

"You is pwomising me, Bwooks."

"Yeah, buddy. I am."

*

Scott was leaning up against the side of a rusty pickup truck. I'd have bet my own vehicle that there was no car seat in it. By the looks of it, there might not have even been seatbelts. I could feel my blood pressure rising, and I forced myself to take deep, calming breaths. I turned off the engine, got out of the car, and opened Elliott's door. Leaning down so that I was eye level with him, I said, "Do you know what it means to trust someone?"

Elliott shook his head solemnly.

"It means that I need you to believe me when I say I will never let anything bad happen to you. It means that no matter what I say, or what I do, I will take care of you." I unbuckled Elliott and picked him up, slinging his bag over my shoulder.

"I wanna go home with you wight now, Bwooks," Elliott said, his fingernails digging into the side of my neck. I let the pain ground me as I walked up to Scott.

Scott looked at Elliott with a longing I might not have

recognized a few months ago. His features softened as he saw his son for the first time in over a year, his eyes traveling from the tip of Elliott's head down to the toes of his shoes, as if he was taking in everything he'd missed. Committing it to memory. He couldn't quite look Elliott in the eye, which told me he must have felt some shame and remorse for his actions. He took a step toward us and I instinctively took one back. The love Scott still felt for his child would not make what I'd come here to do any easier.

Scott turned his attention to me, a snide expression replacing the loving one he wore for his son, thrilled to finally have the upper hand. "Looks like I finally got my kid back," he said. "Guess you won't be sleepin' with my wife anymore either."

Then he laughed.

The asshole *laughed*.

"She's not your wife," I said through clenched teeth. I hadn't really slept in twenty-four hours. My head was pounding and my eyes were stinging. If I hadn't been holding Elliott in my arms I would have dropped Scott with one punch and pummeled him until my fury subsided.

"Where's his stuff?" Scott asked.

I handed him a bag. Not the Thomas the Tank Engine bag, but another one. Plain brown.

Scott looked inside. "What the hell is this shit?"

I let him hang, waiting for his brain to make the connection. Taking note of the look of hunger on his face I said, "You could probably get pretty far on ten grand."

And if that wasn't enough, I had another five thousand in an envelope tucked inside the pocket of my jacket. I was by no means a wealthy man and probably never would be, but I earned a good income, had only myself to support, and was particularly diligent about saving. Like Daisy, I'd been setting money aside for a down payment of my own, and I'd managed to accrue a considerable sum. But fifty-five hundred was all I'd been able to access on a Saturday afternoon when the banks were closed. My debit card only allowed me to withdraw five hundred dollars per day, but I'd been able to get cash advances on two credit cards in the amount of $2,500 apiece. My dad had come through with the rest. "Got a little cash tucked away in my safe," he'd said when I asked him for his help. "You're welcome to it."

"I want my kid," Scott said, thrusting the bag of money at me. His voice had lost a bit of its swagger and conviction. A less observant man might have missed it, but I didn't.

"Sure, here you go." I handed Elliott over to Scott along with the bag containing his belongings.

Elliott began to wail, and the sound—high-pitched, keening—was like nothing I'd ever heard before. Elliott tried to scramble out of Scott's grasp, and he reached out for me, wrapping his arms around my neck so tight that I could hardly pry them off me. When I was free, I turned and walked away, my heart nearly exploding out of fear.

I got halfway to the car before he said it: "Wait." Overwhelmed with relief, I turned around and walked back to them.

"I can't take him when he's crying like this. Make him stop."

"You make him stop. He's your son."

"Yeah, well, maybe I don't have time for this shit." He thrust Elliott into my arms, and Elliott pressed his face to my shirt, his body trembling as he sobbed.

"He's supposed to go with you," I said, holding the bag of money so he could clearly see it.

"I'm not ready. I didn't get enough notice."

"That's really not my problem," I said.

"Give me the money and you can have him as long as you want."

Though I'd expected Scott to choose the money, had been desperately counting on the fact that he would, I hid my revulsion because there was one more thing I needed him to do.

"Sounds fair. But I'll need you to sign these," I said, thrusting some papers and a pen under Scott's nose.

He scanned the sheets and shoved them back toward me. "I'm not fucking signing anything," he roared.

"If you don't sign the papers, you don't get the money. You have one minute to decide," I replied, worrying suddenly that I'd pushed too far and that he'd take Elliott after all.

Neither of us spoke or moved. Elliott's breath hitched between his cries. A trickle of sweat ran slowly down the back of my neck as Scott and I glared at each other. Finally, when time was almost up, he reached out and grabbed the papers, signing away all legal rights to his child. When I was satisfied I had every signature necessary, I handed the money to him.

He laughed, an evil patronizing sound. "You think you're pretty fucking smart, don't you? Think you're better than me?"

"Make no mistake, I *am* better than you."

"Yeah, well, I'd have taken less."

"And I would have paid more."

Scott took his bag full of money and jumped into his rusty pickup. His tires squealed as he tore out of the parking lot. I took deep breaths and willed my heart rate to return to normal.

"You was gonna give me to that man, Bwooks!" Elliott said.

I hugged Elliott close, hoping he was young enough that the incident wouldn't leave permanent scars and that Daisy would understand why I'd done what I did. Any damage this caused Elliott was mine to fix.

"I was never going to give you to him, Elliott. But there was only one way I could make sure he would give you to *me*. And now that he has, I will never let you go."

I buckled Elliott into his car seat and we drove to Nick's office. Nick was working around the clock on Daisy's behalf and would be meeting with the criminal defense attorney in the morning. The door to the law firm was locked, but Nick heard my banging and let me in.

"He didn't show?" Nick asked when he noticed Elliott standing beside me, holding my hand.

"No, he did. I tried to get him to take Elliott, but I guess he decided he couldn't handle the responsibility because he took off. Good luck to anyone who tries to find him."

I followed Nick into his office and laid the papers down on his desk. "I need you to file these as soon as possible. They're signed but they're not notarized," I said. "Will that be a problem?"

Nick picked up the papers and glanced at the names on them. His expression didn't change. "Not at all," he said. "Consider it done."

"Thanks, Nick," I said. "For everything."

CHAPTER 54

SCOTT

THE FIRST THING Scott had done when he left Del Taco was drive across town to the home of his old dealer, a short, wiry man in his early forties who went by the name of Miller. Whether that was his first or last name, Scott didn't know or care.

Miller had always been good to him. He wasn't paranoid and he treated his dealing like an actual business, with inventory you could count on. But Miller didn't front drugs to anyone, which meant Scott could only buy what he could afford.

And he had never been able to afford *enough*.

As successful as it had become, the restaurant had been a drain on their finances. DiStefano's brought in a considerable amount of revenue, but almost as much went back out to cover expenses: payroll, taxes, food, liquor, rent, utilities, and repairs. There was always something that needed to be paid, and Scott wondered how his parents had ever turned a profit.

He drew a modest salary and sometimes didn't pay himself at all, like the time one of his freezers conked out in July. Before he started using, Daisy had been supportive of the restaurant, especially since it was her salary and money management skills that kept them afloat when things started to get tight. She'd always told him how proud she was of him and what he'd done with the place.

He vowed to work more. Work harder.

He would turn things around.

Meth was cheap, he reasoned, especially compared to cocaine and heroin. So what if he took a little of their disposable income and used it to buy something that would give him the energy he needed to make it through ninety-hour workweeks? Was that so awful? Why couldn't Daisy see that everything he was doing was for her?

Gradually, as his habit increased, he spent more and more of their disposable income until what he was spending was no longer disposable. It was the money earmarked for groceries, utilities, and rent. After that, Scott started dipping into their savings, telling Daisy he needed to replace the heating and cooling system at the restaurant or that someone had broken in overnight and stolen the cash that was to be deposited at the bank the next morning. Scott would never be so foolish as to leave a large sum of cash at the restaurant, and Daisy knew it. But by then she was fed up and worn out and could no longer be bothered to confront him.

When Miller refused to let Scott slide on payment, Scott had been forced to look for another source, and it didn't take more than a day or two of nosing around down at the Tap before he connected with Dale.

Unlike Miller, Dale didn't have the capital to come up with the inventory he'd need to start dealing, but he'd been using so long he knew the name, phone number, and location of everyone in town who was. He charged nothing for his services, but he skimmed off the top of every bag, which most customers were willing to overlook because Dale had a knack for finding dealers who were open to more creative payment methods. If cash wasn't available, they'd be willing to accept merchandise instead, as long as it was something that could be pawned or traded at the garage sale. They might be willing to float you a day or two as long as Dale promised you were good for it.

These dealers might have been more open to extending credit than Miller, but that didn't mean they'd allow anyone to get away without paying, whether that meant rounding up a few people who wouldn't mind doing the collecting for them in exchange for drugs, or finding other, more jaded ways of clearing the debt.

Scott hated the games Dale played, but by the time Daisy divorced him he was homeless, penniless, and in too deep to get out on his own. And when Brandon came into the picture, he'd become Dale's pawn, at the mercy of whatever Dale wanted him to do so that the drugs would never stop coming his way.

Until now.

Scott had enough cash to buy more meth than he'd ever dreamed of. But there was one thing that was still more important to him than meth, although marginally so, and that was freedom.

He could go somewhere far away. Blend in and start over. If he was careful with the money, if he bought only cheap food and stayed in budget motels, he could make it last and have plenty to start up an operation of his own once he got settled.

Who was he kidding?

It's not like he'd bother with eating or sleeping at all.

He was supposed to be out doing his rounds instead of sitting in Miller's living room, forking over stacks of twenties. Dale never topped off his high until he returned for the night, and by the time Scott walked into the house he was always desperate for a hit. Scott's phone—provided by Brandon—had an app, which would allow Dale to pinpoint his location. Dale wouldn't bother checking the app until Scott failed to return at his usual time, and by then he'd be long gone. He'd hit the highway and just start driving, maybe stop in Vegas first. Get lost in a sea of people and then figure it out from there.

"These sacks fat?" he asked Miller.

Miller shot him a look, clearly insulted.

"Sorry, man," Scott said. "You got any rigs?"

Miller nodded and threw a few syringes in the bag. Then he handed the bag to Scott and placed the money in a lockbox.

"See you around," Scott said, walking quickly out to his truck because he wanted—no, *needed*—to get high immediately. The only way to erase the image of his son's face was to get high and stay that way.

Once he was in his vehicle, he drove to an abandoned parking lot and efficiently and methodically went through the steps of preparing the hit, worrying less about being seen than he should have. He tied off and jammed the needle home, feeling the rush, the euphoria.

But he couldn't forget his son's face.

The sound of his cries.

For the first time ever, Scott couldn't get high enough to make his problems go away.

He slumped against the window of his truck as his own tears started to fall. He knew he would never see his son again, and he doubled over in pain as if someone had punched him in the stomach. His head hit the steering wheel as sobs wracked his body. His self-loathing was massive, vast.

When his crying subsided, he mixed himself another shot.

More meth was what he needed.

It was fully dark by then, and as he pulled out of the parking lot, an idea hit him hard. He couldn't believe he hadn't thought of it sooner.

What better way to guarantee he'd be free of Dale forever?

He thought of all the times Dale had made him beg for a hit. Remembered the night Dale had pulled the gun on him, showing off in front of Brandon. Scott threw his head back and laughed, sticking his head out the window and letting the cold night air blow the hair back from his face.

"Fuck you, Dale," he screamed.

He pulled into a gas station and used the browser on his phone to look up the number. He scrawled it on a napkin and filled his tank. After climbing back into his truck, he dialed the number and when the person on the other end answered, he said, "You might want to grab a pen and some paper. I have some information I think you'll be very interested in hearing."

When he was done speaking, he chucked the phone in a garbage can and got the hell out of Dodge, because when this shit went down, he didn't want to be anywhere near it.

CHAPTER 55

BROOKS

THERE ARE SEVERAL hoops to jump through if you want to visit someone in jail. Visits are only allowed Wednesday through Sunday, and the appointment has to be made one day in advance. Luckily, Nick had given me the heads-up in time, and my request had squeaked in under the wire. I had to arrive thirty minutes early to be searched. Cell phones, cameras, and recording devices of any kind were prohibited. I was required to dress appropriately and show a valid form of photo identification.

I was up at six o'clock on Sunday morning, pacing the floor and drinking too much coffee. My appointment to see Daisy wasn't until eleven thirty, and I had no idea what I was going to do with myself until then.

Nick was meeting with the attorney he'd found for Daisy at ten. "The DA will file either murder or manslaughter charges Monday morning. I'm expecting him to file the more serious charge, so be prepared," he said.

Prepared.

How did one go about preparing for something like this? How would Daisy? Though I wanted to have faith in the legal system, I couldn't stop turning over worst-case scenarios in my mind. I'd done some research on the computer and wished I hadn't. California had some of the toughest gun-control laws in the country, and Daisy's attorney would have his work cut out for him.

The padding of little feet interrupted my thoughts. I set down my coffee cup and turned around. Elliott was standing in the doorway.

"Hey, buddy. How are you?"

He didn't answer. He walked over to me and when I picked him up he laid his head on my shoulder. "I is missin' my mom again."

"Yeah, I miss her, too. She'll be home soon, though." With one hand, I pulled a carton of milk out of the refrigerator and poured some into a cup. I sat down at the kitchen table with Elliott on my lap. "I've got to go out for a little while later this morning. Theo told me he was going to take you fishing today. Would you like that?"

He nodded. "I would wike that." He might have answered in the affirmative, but I could tell by the tone of his voice that there was nothing I could offer him that would ease his pain.

"All right," I said. "Let's get you some breakfast."

*

My dad and Elliott left for the lake and I drove to the jail.

"You'll be separated by glass," a guard said after I'd shown the proper identification and been patted down. "Just pick up the phone on the wall to talk. We'll let you know when your time is up." He pointed to a row of plastic chairs. "Wait here until we call your name."

The minutes crawled by as I waited for my name to be called.

Daisy had now spent two nights in jail. Had she eaten anything? Could she sleep? Her body temperature ran cold and she was always reaching for a sweater or hoodie. She probably hadn't been warm since she'd been arrested.

Fifteen minutes later, a guard said, "Brooks McClain."

I followed him through a labyrinth of hallways, the stone walls painted a dull, dreary gray. He opened the door to a room with six chairs facing a wall of glass, each separated from the other by a low partition. Though she was looking down, I spotted her blond hair immediately and hurried forward to occupy the chair facing her.

I picked up the phone. She wouldn't look at me. Her shoulders were shaking and I knew she was crying. I'd been warned not to tap on the glass, so I waited, willing her to pick up the phone on her side. To set aside her shame and talk to me. Finally, she reached for the phone with a shaking hand and held it to her ear.

"Look at me, Daisy Jane."

She lifted her chin. Her face was streaked with tears and the black circles beneath her bloodshot eyes were truly frightening. It was quite possible that she hadn't slept at all. The bones of her face, prominent and sharp as glass, indicated she hadn't been eating, either.

"I love you," I said. "I love you and I will do whatever it takes to get you out of here. I know why you're doing it, but please don't shut me out. There is nothing you could ever do that would make me walk away from you, especially when you need me the most. Do you understand?"

She nodded, the tears falling rapidly. "How is Elliott?" she asked. Her voice was so faint that I only knew what she'd asked by reading her lips as she formed the words.

"Elliott is fine. He misses you, but he's safe and he's doing great with Dad and me."

"I'm so afraid," she said. "Nick's trying to protect me, but I know what I'm up against. What if no one believes me?"

"The criminal attorney Nick found is doing everything he can to build a strong case. But I need you to have faith, sweetheart. This isn't over yet, not by a long shot, so you can't give up now. Try to sleep and make sure you eat. I need you to fight with me, okay?"

She nodded, but the look in her eyes told me she was barely hanging on. A guard appeared at my side, telling me to wrap it up.

"I have to go. I'll come back as often as they'll let me. I love you."

"I love you, too," she said.

Though the sun was shining brightly when I walked out of that jail, I'd never been more depressed in my life.

CHAPTER 56

BROOKS

WE WERE SITTING at the table eating lunch the next day when my cell phone rang. A glance at the display told me it was Jack. I shot my dad a look that said I didn't want to take the call in front of Elliott and walked out of the kitchen.

"Hey," I said.

"You are not going to believe what I'm about to tell you," Jack said. "And keep it under your hat, because it's big. I'm not telling you this as a cop, so you can't act like a reporter. This is so far off the record the record doesn't exist, okay?"

I felt the first stirring of hope. "Agreed. I'm listening."

"We received some information via the tip line last night."

"I thought you said people who called the tip line were crazy."

"Most of the time they are. But in this case I feel confident that it's worth checking out because the man who called it in knew a lot of things he couldn't possibly have known unless he was a part of it."

I started pacing. "Like?"

"Like Dale Reber giving some street kid an ounce of meth to intercept Daisy in that parking garage."

I sat down on the arm of the couch, but I had too much nervous energy flowing through me to sit, so I stood back up and resumed pacing. "What else?"

"Like an old white sedan that's registered to someone named Jim Watson."

I paced faster, my body vibrating as if all that energy was now looking for a way out. "I'd call that one hell of a tip."

"So would I."

"You're going to bring him in, aren't you? Today. Right now."

"You know better than most that we can't rush in, guns blazing, without a little due diligence. A tip, no matter how good it is, is still just a tip. We're moving as swiftly as we can, obtaining warrants and assembling a team. The earliest we'll be able to do anything is tomorrow morning. We'll bring Dale in first and round up anyone else who's out at the house. I'll send the CSI team to track down and impound the vehicle."

"Then what?"

"Then we lean on them. See who talks first. And listen, the chief will have my *ass* if anyone from the newspaper shows up out there tomorrow. It's too risky. Who knows what we'll be walking into?"

"Will you be able to make an arrest?" I asked.

"Hard to say. I'll know a lot more after tomorrow."

"What about Daisy's attorney? Can I let him know?"

"That's your call. But I think I'd wait to see what happens tomorrow. No use getting anyone's hopes up until we know more."

"Scott DiStefano called it in, didn't he?"

"The tip was left anonymously, but if I were a betting man, that's who I'd put my money on."

I stopped pacing because I thought I should sit down before I asked my next question. "Did Scott say what would happen to Daisy after they grabbed her?"

Jack didn't respond. Finally he said, "Come on. You don't want to hear that."

"Probably not, but tell me anyway."

There was silence on the other end, but then Jack started to speak.

He was right. I shouldn't have asked.

Because the things Jack told me that day would bother me for the rest of my life.

*

On Monday morning I wanted to drive out to Tweakerville and watch from the sidelines as the police hauled Dale and other assorted losers out of the house. I wouldn't, though, because Jack had been good to me and the best way to help him was to stay out of his way.

In light of what was going on in my personal life, Paul had told me to take the week off, which I felt bad about because I certainly hadn't earned the time. If I could contribute in a way that would help Jack and also benefit the newspaper, maybe I wouldn't feel so guilty.

I decided to do a little research on the owner of the vehicle that the crime scene investigators would be locating and impounding. Jack said his name was Jim Watson. Because it was a common name, I had to access three different databases to track down his address, and even then I wasn't sure I had the right guy. I was even less sure the car would be there. Maybe Jack and his team would get lucky and find Jim—and his car—at Dale Reber's.

Two meth heads, one stone.

After plugging the address into the GPS app on my phone, I went looking for my dad and Elliott and found them in the backyard playing catch.

"I need to run out for a minute," I said. "There's something I want to check on."

"Go ahead," Dad said. "We'll be fine."

Jack hadn't mentioned anything about staying out of the crime scene investigators' way, so I decided there was no harm in taking a little drive out to Jim's house, just to see if anything interesting was happening.

*

The house was located near the freeway, in a depressed neighborhood comprised of chain-link fences, litter that blew along the streets like tumbleweeds, random outbuildings, and sandy yards dotted with brush. The structure itself was severely neglected. The paint appeared to be white, but so much of it had peeled off I couldn't be sure. The area was fairly deserted, so I parked at the end of the street and set out on foot, deciding I'd approach from the backyard a few houses down and then double back.

I scaled the fence, landing lightly on my feet. Snooping was a whole lot easier in jeans and tennis shoes than it was in a suit and wingtips. I kept to the back perimeter of the yards, hoping no one would look out their window and wonder what the tall, dark-haired stranger was doing. I scaled another fence, which put me next door to Jim's house.

The one that had a tarp thrown over a large, car-shaped object in its carport.

Seriously.

At least this would make the CSI's job easier. Feeling somewhat confident that this was the last place anyone connected with the crime would want to be, I quickly approached the house and then crept alongside it toward the carport. I would look under the tarp and when I spotted the car—because I was almost certain it would be there—I'd snap a few pictures for the newspaper and then hang out for a while and wait for the investigators to show up.

To say that the gunshot took me by surprise would be a gross understatement, especially given the fact that it was accompanied by a shower of glass. The bullet splintered one of the carport beams behind me, just above my head, which meant that the shooter was inside the house and hadn't bothered opening the window before he pulled the trigger.

What these idiots lacked in common sense, they more than made up for in firepower.

Then again, I was the one being shot at. And my gun was resting comfortably in its case under the front seat of my Jeep.

I scrambled under the tarp and hurried around to the opposite side, putting the car between the shooter and me. Trying to calm my galloping heart, I took a few deep breaths and pulled my cell phone out of my pocket. My thumb scrolled through the log of my recent calls, and I jabbed unsteadily at Jack Quick's name.

Come on, come on, come on.

I heard the click of his voice mail picking up and then the sound of his voice inviting me to leave a message at the beep.

Okay, plan B.

I hit the button for 911, just in case a friendly neighbor hadn't already called in to report a gunshot in the neighborhood. Lowering the volume considerably so as not to announce my location to the person who had shot at me, I listened as the dispatcher said, "Nine one one, what is your emergency?" I remained silent, hoping the dispatcher would follow normal protocol, be able to trace the call successfully, and send an officer to the scene. The fact that I was outdoors weighed heavily in my favor. As long as my cell phone's GPS connected with a satellite or cell tower, the dispatcher would be able to pinpoint my location.

At least I hoped so.

I peered out from underneath the bottom of the tarp to get my bearings. I had a straight shot into the backyard, but I'd have to be crazy to run out into the open like that. The odds of a gunman hitting you when you're running are supposed to be quite low, but I wasn't feeling especially lucky at the moment. I wouldn't be leaving anytime soon and would have to rely on my hearing for the sound of approaching footsteps, which would alert me to the fact that the shooter had come outside to look for me. My only hope was that the police would arrive soon and take this mess I'd stumbled into off my hands before someone got shot, namely me. I resigned myself to staying put until they did.

I would have gladly stuck to that plan had I not seen a man silently creeping along the fence line toward the house next door. And once I realized it was Dale Reber, there was no way I could remain hidden. If he managed to leave the area, Scott's tip would be for nothing and Daisy would be no better off than she was now. Feeling extremely nervous about the possibility that the shooter was not Dale and was instead someone who was waiting inside for me to show myself so he could pick me off, I left the safety of the tarp and started running.

Dale hadn't been running very fast when I first began to chase him, but when he looked back to see where the loud, pounding footsteps were coming from, he took off like a shot and scaled the fence. And just to make it more interesting, the crack of a gunshot behind me told me that my theory about the shooter capitalizing on my being out in the open was alarmingly accurate. On a positive note, Dale and I were quickly putting distance between us and the house, and the shooter didn't seem to be as fast on his feet as we were. I hated to admit it, but Dale was really hauling ass and I'd need to step it up a little if I was going to catch him. I called upon my anger, my absolute fury at what this man had tried to do to Daisy—what he would have done if he'd been successful in abducting her—and I gained some ground, closing the gap a little more. He scaled another fence, taking a second to look over his shoulder. I scaled it, too. My chest burned and I gulped at the air.

I might not have caught him, but then he made another of his many bad decisions. He turned around and pulled his gun, but he'd been running so fast that when he slowed down he was off center, with no control over his stance or his aim. He fired and the shot went wide, coming nowhere near me. His second shot came closer, and I swear I heard something go whizzing by my ear. When he realized I was closing in fast, he abandoned trying to line up a third shot and took off again.

He wasn't fast enough this time. I had momentum on my side, and I plowed into him, taking us both down to the ground. I landed on top of him and was trying to figure out where the gun was when Dale threw some kind of meth-fueled super punch, which landed squarely between my eyes.

Everything got a little hazy after that. I remember finally getting a good grip on Dale and slamming him repeatedly into the dirt.

The sound of police sirens in the distance.

The yelling and thunder of many footsteps. I didn't snap out of it until two police officers pulled me off Dale, and Jack Quick's face suddenly appeared in front of me.

"I need a paramedic over here," he yelled.

"I don't need a paramedic," I said and then promptly sank to my knees. I wasn't sure if it was the lack of oxygen from running so fast, the effects of the punch, or the aftermath of a massive adrenaline dump, but all I knew was that I really preferred to be closer to the ground. None of that stopped me from digging my phone out of my pocket, though, and snapping a picture of a policeman slapping handcuffs on Dale. It would take more than a teeth-rattling punch to the face—and possibly my impending shock—to make me miss a photo op.

"Let me guess," I said, gasping. "No one was home at Tweakerville."

Jack crouched down beside me and smiled. "Let's just say no one came to the door when we knocked and leave it at that."

"You got here fast," I said, taking deep breaths. I would never take air for granted again. Never.

"We were already en route when you called my phone and left your cryptic non-message. Then the 911 dispatcher sent out an alert. I connected the dots."

"That's probably why you're a detective." My head throbbed and I squinted through my rapidly narrowing field of vision. "There was another guy. He had a gun."

"Jim Watson. He's already in the back of a squad car."

"Asshole shot at me. They *both* shot at me."

"You can tell me all about it later. Right now this nice paramedic is going to make sure you're not seeing two of me."

"I'm having trouble seeing one of you, Jack."

"Exactly."

CHAPTER 57

DAISY

I WAS CURLED INTO a ball on the top bunk of my cell on Tuesday afternoon, trying to stay warm. I dozed in fits and starts, my body jerking me awake every few minutes. I hadn't been able to stay asleep long enough to rest sufficiently, and the exhaustion was taking its toll. Brooks had told me to eat, but food was still out of the question.

My roommate, a middle-aged woman named Polly who had about four teeth and who'd been busted for drug possession, was snoring softly on the bottom bunk. She told me she hadn't had any meth in over fourteen hours and was going to take a nap while she waited for her boyfriend to scrape up the money to bail her out.

"Good luck to them guards if they think they can wake me up in the meantime," she'd said.

I could have done much worse considering the woman in the next cell hadn't stopped screaming and swearing since they'd put her in it the night before. She sounded big and she sounded mean, and I was grateful there was a brick wall between us.

I was waiting for the guard to come get me, which would mean that Nick had heard from the DA's office. Part of me wanted to see him and part of me didn't. Until I sat down across the table from him and he told me that I'd officially been charged, I could pretend that this was just a bad dream. Words like murderer and defendant wouldn't be attached to my name.

I missed Elliott so much that I ached. I'd have given anything to feel his hand in mine or the weight of his body on my lap. The next time Brooks came, I was going to ask him to bring me a picture of Elliott. Even if they wouldn't let me keep it, Brooks could hold it up to the glass. Thinking about Elliott and how much I missed him made my eyes fill with tears.

After today there could be no more crying. I would also need to start sleeping and eating, because once I was charged Nick said they would move me, and it would take strength—both physical and mental—to survive in a women's prison. I would allow myself to remain here on this bunk, feeling hopeless, until Nick came. Then I would prepare for the fight of my life and hope that justice would be served.

That didn't stop the massive jolt of anxiety that caused my heart to start hammering in my chest when the guard appeared twenty minutes later.

He unlocked the door and said, "Your attorney is here."

The guard led me to the small room where Nick and I had conversed last time. Nick gave me a hug.

"Have the charges been filed?" I asked as I lowered myself into a chair and looked him in the eye.

Nick smiled and shook his head. "No."

There was no reason for Nick to be smiling, unless… "Why not?"

"On Saturday night the police received a tip via the hotline. Yesterday they acted on it and two suspects were taken into custody. Dale Reber was one of them. The other was a man named Jim Watson."

I sat up straight, every nerve in my body on high alert.

"It took the police most of yesterday and into the night, but the detectives are very good at what they do. In exchange for leniency, Jim Watson finally broke down and gave them a detailed account of what was supposed to happen in the parking garage and why. The police were able to impound the car used in the abduction attempt and a witness has verified that it was the car she saw that night."

My hopes soared. "What does this mean, Nick?"

Nick smiled and nodded. "It means that the DA will not be filing any charges, and as soon as they finish processing your paperwork, you'll be out of here."

In the dark days after the shooting, I had not let myself ponder such a miraculous outcome. Wishful thinking, I'd told myself. Better not get your hopes up. But now I basked in the news Nick had given me, and I cried giant heartfelt tears of gratitude.

"Brooks played a significant role in all this," Nick said. "He went to Jim's house, hoping to be on site when the investigators impounded the car. He got there a little earlier than everyone else and walked into an ambush of sorts when shots were fired."

I stood up so fast my thighs banged into the edge of the table. "What? Oh my God, is he okay?"

Nick reached across the table and placed his hands gently on my shoulders. "He's fine. He does have two rather impressive black eyes from tussling with Dale, but if Brooks hadn't gotten there when he did, Dale and Jim would have been long gone and the DA would have filed the charges."

"When can I see him?" I asked.

Nick laughed. "What a coincidence. That's the same thing he asked me about you."

*

It took two more hours of listening to Polly's snoring before the guard returned. Two hours of turning over in my mind the fact that I would soon be reunited with Brooks and Elliott. I couldn't stop smiling.

This time, the guard led me to a small, windowless room with a lock on the door. "Here are your clothes," he said, handing me a plastic bag containing the scrubs and shoes I'd been wearing the night of the shooting."

I dressed as fast as I could and opened the door. The guard led me to a window where a woman slid several forms toward me, asking me to verify the information on the discharge paperwork and sign my name. She didn't have to ask me twice.

A buzzing sound accompanied the opening of a large steel door, and I followed the guard through a hallway that twisted and turned before opening into a large room.

And then I saw Brooks.

I'm not sure how he could see me with his eyes almost swollen shut, but he did. Before I even knew what was happening, he'd pulled me into his arms. He didn't say anything, but he squeezed me so tight I could hardly breathe. Clinging to him, I inhaled the smell of his skin.

Finally, I pulled away and looked at Brooks's face. The skin around his eyes was stretched tight and an alarming shade of purple. "Oh, Brooks."

"I'm okay. Just let me hold you." When he finally let me go, he took my hand. "Come on," he said, leading me toward the door. "I brought you something."

Brooks had parked at the far end of the lot where there weren't many cars. I figured out why when I spotted Theo and Elliott standing beside the Jeep. As we got closer, Elliott recognized me and his face lit up.

"Go," Brooks said.

Theo must have given Elliott the same directive because as I ran toward him—tears streaming down my face—he ran toward me as fast as his little legs would carry him. I scooped him up and squeezed him every bit as tight as Brooks had squeezed me.

"Mama! Mama! You is back!"

"I'm back," I said. "And I'm never going to be away from you again. I've missed you so much, Elliott." I kissed his face and I ran my hands through his hair.

As I held my child in my arms, I'd never felt so grateful to be alive and free.

*

Brooks sat in the backseat with Elliott and me while Theo drove. "Is it okay if we stay at Dad's?" Brooks asked. "Most of Elliott's things are there and I thought you might not want to bother with relocating. I went to your apartment and packed a bag for you."

"It's more than okay. As long as I have you and Elliott, I don't care where we stay."

On the way home, I rolled down the window and breathed in the fresh air. If things had worked out differently, it might have been years before I would have ridden in a car again. Known what it was like to do things when I wanted to do them instead of when someone told me to.

When we got home, I snuggled on the couch with Elliott until I'd had my fill, and then I excused myself to take a shower. I could detect the faint antiseptic smell of the county jail's soap on my skin and in my hair, and I was eager to wash away all traces of my stay. I found the bag in Brooks's bedroom that contained the toiletries, clothes, and pajamas he'd retrieved from my apartment.

In the bathroom, I brushed my teeth and then undressed and stepped under the shower spray, adjusting the water temperature until it ran as hot as I could stand. I must have been running on adrenaline because once I started washing my hair, the fatigue set in, and I felt the weariness clear down to my bones. After I rinsed my hair, I flipped open the cap of my shower gel and inhaled the clean scent. Soaping my body from head to toe had never felt so good. Once I'd stepped out of the shower and patted myself dry, I slipped into a pair of leggings and an oversize, long-sleeve T-shirt.

Brooks was waiting for me in the bedroom. "How do you feel?"

"I feel incredible. You thought of everything."

"You're missing one thing," he said. "Turn around."

Brooks fastened the necklace he'd given me for Christmas around my neck. I turned back around, clutching the silver heart in my hand. "Do you know how hopeless I felt when they took this away? I was afraid it was a sign that I'd never be with you and Elliott again."

I sat down on the edge of the bed and Brooks sat down beside me. I laid my head on his shoulder.

"I ended someone's life, Brooks. I always said that if anyone threatened my child I wouldn't hesitate to pull the trigger. But I wasn't defending my child. I was only defending myself."

"Do you think your life is somehow not as important? A mother can't protect her child at all if she's not around." Brooks put his arm around me and pressed a kiss to my temple. "I can't tell you how to feel about this, Daisy. I'll help you get through it any way I can. But if you're able, I want you to celebrate the fact that you're alive, and that you're here with Elliott, and with me. Because I sure as hell am going to."

"You're right. This could have turned out so differently." I squeezed his hand and looked into his eyes, searching. "Do you believe in miracles?"

He shook his head. "I didn't. Not really. But I do now."

Later that night, after Pam and Shane had come and gone and I'd eaten two helpings of Thai takeout and read to Elliott and kissed him at least fifty times, I put him to bed and changed into my pajamas.

Then Brooks put *me* to bed. He turned down the covers and before I slipped underneath them, he kissed me—a long, lingering kiss. I fell asleep seconds after my head hit the pillow.

CHAPTER 58

BROOKS

ELLIOTT CAME INTO the bedroom at eight the next morning. I smiled because he had dressed himself in a red-and-green argyle sweater, which was too small, and a pair of blue athletic shorts that were too big. It was a lot less amusing when I remembered that I was the one who'd packed most of his clothes.

"I want Mama," Elliott said.

As bad as I felt about keeping him from her, I knew Daisy was exhausted and probably needed more sleep. "Let's let Mama sleep a little longer," I whispered. "We can go get donuts."

"Really?" he said, his eyes growing wide. "Mama said donuts is bad for me."

Oh, shit. *I am horrible at this.*

"I bet she'd say they're okay once in a while."

Elliott nodded his head and gave me an earnest look. "She would."

I grabbed some sweatpants and a T-shirt and hustled him out of the bedroom before our voices woke up Daisy. After brushing our teeth, we went in search of my dad. We found him sitting at the kitchen table.

"Feo! We is going to get donuts."

"Donuts, huh?" Dad pushed his bowl away. "That sounds a lot better than heart-healthy oatmeal. I'm in."

"Good," I said, handing him my keys. I jammed a ball cap onto my head and reached for a pair of sunglasses to cover my blackened eyes. "I still can't see well enough to drive."

After I strapped Elliott into his car seat, Dad drove us to the bakery. Elliott picked out a dozen donuts, all of which were chocolate frosted and covered with sprinkles.

"Boy likes his chocolate," my dad said.

When we got home, my dad poured a fresh cup of coffee, brought it to the table, and sat down. After careful consideration, he selected a donut with rainbow sprinkles.

I poured Elliott a glass of milk, handed him the box, and said, "Knock yourself out, buddy. But no more than two, okay?"

Elliott picked up a donut, took a giant bite, and sprayed crumbs all over the table when he said, "Okay."

After breakfast, I convinced Elliott that we should lounge on the couch for a little while. I was enjoying the nostalgia of Scooby-Doo when Daisy walked into the room at nine thirty, yawning and rubbing her eyes.

"I can't believe I slept so long," she said, sitting down on my lap. Elliott launched himself at Daisy and she caught him with an "Oompf" and hugged him. "Hi, baby."

"I not a baby."

"You'll always be my baby." She studied him. "What are you wearing? Is that last year's Christmas sweater?"

"Bwooks gived me donuts!" Elliott yelled.

She looked at me and smiled. "That explains a lot."

"For distraction purposes only," I said, putting my arms around her and Elliott to hold them steady on my lap. "I wanted to make sure you got enough sleep."

She leaned down to give me a kiss. "I never realized how much I took the simple things for granted. I feel like a new woman."

"Good morning, Daisy," my dad said when he walked into the room.

"Good morning," she said, smiling at him.

"You look like you got a good night's sleep."

"I did. I feel absolutely wonderful."

"I promised Elliott we'd go fishing if that's all right with you. We won't be gone long. I know you probably want to spend time with him."

"Would you like to go fishing with Theo?" Daisy asked Elliott.

"Yes! Me and Feo is getting really good at it."

Daisy sighed dramatically. "I can probably survive without you for a little while." She pulled Elliott closer and gave him a loud, smacking kiss on the cheek. "But I'll sure miss you while you're gone."

Daisy packed some snacks and drinks for them to take to the lake. We waved good-bye and after they drove away, Daisy and I walked back inside.

"I need to tell you something," I said. I hadn't brought it up yesterday, partly because she was so happy and I didn't want to take anything away from that, and partly because I knew she was exhausted. We hadn't had much privacy, either, and this was certainly something I didn't want to talk about in front of Elliott. If I was being honest with myself, I wasn't looking forward to telling her what I'd done. But my conscience was screaming at me, and I couldn't wait any longer.

She looked up at me, forehead creased. "What is it?"

I thought it was best to just rip off the Band-Aid. "The state of California tried to give temporary emergency custody of Elliott to Scott."

Her eyes grew wide. "What! You have got to be kidding me, Brooks."

"Nick said it was Scott's legal right as a parent. Because you hadn't terminated his rights, the courts would automatically try to place Elliott with him."

Daisy started pacing. "Oh, God. Are you going to tell me Elliott was with Scott while I was in jail?"

"No, because he wasn't. But I need to tell you what I did."

I started at the beginning. I told her about getting the cash together and how I'd dangled it like a carrot in front of Scott. I told her about Elliott crying and digging his fingernails into my neck, and the sound he made when I put him in his father's arms and walked away. "It's a sound I'll never forget."

She sat down on the couch and put her hand over her mouth.

I took a deep breath. "Are you upset with me?"

Tears rolled down her cheeks as she shook her head. "Of course not."

"But what if it caused irreversible damage?"

Daisy held her hand out to me, and I took it and sat down on the couch beside her.

"I have no doubt he was terrified, and that's hard for me to hear." She wiped a tear from the corner of her eye. "Really, really hard. But if it meant that he'd be safe, I have to focus on the greater good. As a mother, I would beg, steal, or worse in order to protect my child." She looked over at me. "That's what a parent does. The fact that Elliott hasn't mentioned it to me yet tells me he's already put it behind him. Children are remarkably resilient. They also know when they're loved and cared for. That's all that matters to them."

"I found those papers in your file cabinet. The ones you tried to serve Scott with to sever his parental rights. I... coerced him into signing them and then gave them to Nick. I knew all this would be hard on Elliott, and I almost talked myself out of it, but in the end I did what I thought was right."

Daisy held my hand tighter. "Everything we do in life requires us to make a choice, Brooks. Scott made his. I love you even more for yours," she said, sounding choked up. "Elliott is very blessed. Scott may not have been willing to be a part of his life, but there are many other people—wonderful people like you and your dad—who are."

"Just remember that I'm still learning. I bribed Elliott with donuts this morning so you could sleep."

She smiled. "Now that's a universally sanctioned parenting move if I ever saw one. Don't worry. You've got this."

*

Daisy's phone rang as we were getting ready to sit down to dinner. She picked it up and glanced at the screen. "It's Nick," she said. She motioned for me to come with her and I followed her out of the kitchen and into the living room.

"Hi, Nick," she said.

We sat down on the couch. After she greeted him, she didn't say much at all. I assumed he was advising her of any remaining legal red tape she might have to deal with. Statements or depositions she'd have to give.

After a few more minutes of silence she said, "Thanks for letting me know."

"Remember all the evidence the crime scene investigators

collected from my grandmother's apartment?" she asked after she hung up the phone.

"Yes, of course."

"They lifted fingerprints from the inside doorknob of the apartment but didn't receive a match when they ran them through the national database."

I knew immediately what she was going to tell me. "Dale Reber had never been arrested," I said, "so his prints weren't stored anywhere."

Daisy nodded. "Jack asked the CSI to check. Dale's prints were a perfect match."

"So he *was* looking for you that night," I said. "Not something to steal. Just you."

"It looks that way," she said. "He said, 'Tell me,' because he wanted my grandmother to tell him where I was, or maybe when I would be home. She protected me and she protected Elliott, but she paid with her life. She's dead because of me."

"It's not your fault," I said. "There were too many other factors that played a part in this. And Dale wouldn't have come after you again if I hadn't convinced Jack to bring him in for questioning. I'm the one who made things worse for you."

"But you were right," she said. "And who knows if Dale would have ever been brought to justice without your help? I wanted the person who killed my grandmother to pay for it, and because of you, he will. I finally have the closure I was hoping for. My heart breaks when I think about my grandmother and all she endured, but I'm alive and Dale is behind bars. I have you and I have Elliott. And I'm ready to start living my life."

*

Three days later, we were still at my dad's house.

"Either he's a really good actor, or he actually likes having us around," Daisy said.

"Trust me, I can read him like a book. He might not admit it, but he likes having us here, especially Elliott. Is it okay with you that we haven't gone back to your apartment?"

"Yes," Daisy said. "I don't know what it is, but I feel very comfortable here."

"Good."

She'd had bouts of sadness. There were times she wanted to be alone and there were times I'd come upon her and Elliott playing down on the floor in the spare bedroom. I'd sensed that she needed to spend time with him—just the two of them—and I'd let her be. I'd slept with her in my arms every night, aching to do more than just hold her, but after all she'd been through, it was her decision to make. She'd let me know when she was ready.

*

After I read to Elliott and Daisy put him to bed in the spare bedroom, she joined me in my room. I was lying on the bed and Daisy walked over and stretched out on top of me. She kissed me and it was a different kind of kiss than the ones we'd been sharing.

"I want you," she said.

I put my arms around her. "I want you, too."

"How many girls have been in this room before me?"

"So many," I said. "There was practically a revolving door on it when I was in high school."

"Well. That's to be expected. You *are* gorgeous," she said.

"Actually, my parents never left me alone long enough to sneak a girl up here. You're my first."

She slid her hands under my shirt. "Then I promise to make it memorable."

Gently, she pressed her lips to the corner of my right eye, which was still swollen shut. Thankfully, my left eye had opened up enough so that I wasn't walking into walls, but I'd need three or four more days before I'd be back to twenty-twenty.

"Your poor eyes," she said. "Will you be able to see anything once my clothes are off?"

"God, I hope so," I said, rolling over on top of her and pinning her arms above her head. "But it may require getting up close and *very* personal, which won't exactly be a hardship, sweetheart." I brought my mouth down to hers. Her lips were soft, and her tongue met mine. I kissed her neck and worked my way down to the hollow that drove me nuts, biting and sucking.

Daisy nudged me off of her and rolled back on top. Then she sat up, her legs straddling me, and took off her shirt and bra.

"Can you see me?" she asked, waving her hand back and forth in front of my eyes.

I flipped her onto her back, my head hovering a half inch or so over her nipples. "Oh, I can see you just fine," I said, drawing one into my mouth.

"I'm going to pretend your dad can't hear all the bouncing around we're doing up here."

"Yeah, me too." I also didn't mention that my bedroom door didn't have a lock. It was a little late to be worrying about it now, but I hoped like hell Elliott wouldn't walk in on us. All the lights were on and we weren't under the covers, so the chance of Elliott seeing something he shouldn't was extremely high. I pushed the thought from my mind and unsnapped Daisy's jeans. "Let's get these out of the way." I pulled her jeans and underwear down and she kicked them off the bed.

It actually *was* kind of hard to see her, so I decided to utilize two of my other senses—touch, followed closely by taste. Daisy whispered words of praise when I touched her, and then, when my mouth made contact, she slammed a pillow over her face to muffle the sounds that started coming out of hers. When her body finally stilled and the shuddering subsided, she sat up and helped me out of my clothes.

"Oh, my. Look at you." She reached out a hand to touch me.

"My high school self is so incredibly jealous of my adult self."

"Your high school self is about to have his mind blown," she said. "Or something blown, anyway."

I laughed, twisting her hair loosely around my fingers after she bent her head. "You are amazing."

I tried not to think about anything but how good it felt. When I sensed I was getting too close, I stopped her. "I need to be inside you."

After Daisy told me she couldn't get pregnant, I'd asked if we still needed to use condoms. Since my divorce, I'd always practiced safe sex. Daisy had too, and she'd also been tested for STDs three times in the past eighteen months because she said she couldn't be sure Scott hadn't done something sketchy in exchange for drugs. "My doctor said there was no reason for a fourth test. Actually, he said there was no reason for a third," she said. "But I wanted to be sure."

I figured if she'd been tested it was only fair that I be tested, too. What was one more blood test? I'd taken care of it the week after Christmas. I certainly wasn't anti-condom, but I knew how good it felt not to wear one.

I flipped onto my back because hey, what was one more squeak of the bedsprings when there were about to be a lot more? and pulled Daisy over on top of me. I tried—and failed—to suppress a groan when she sank down onto me.

Now I *did* wish I could see her better. There was nothing I liked more than watching her move around on top of me.

Except for maybe *feeling* her move around on top of me.

I held her hips and she moved a little faster as she found her rhythm. Since I couldn't really see anyway, I closed my eyes—eye—whatever. I listened to our breathing and the sounds Daisy was trying not to make. She trailed her fingers across my chest as she ground our bodies together in a way that told me it wouldn't be long for her. And when she came, I felt every pulse of it. A minute or two later, I joined her.

Afterward, we lay tangled together—me still worrying a little about the unlocked door—trying to catch our breath.

"I love you so much," Daisy said.

I kissed her forehead. "I love you, too."

"I wish we could stay like this forever."

"In my childhood bedroom?"

She propped herself up on her elbow and grinned down at me. "Maybe not that. But somewhere soothing and uncomplicated. I have so many things I still need to take care of. I can't hide my head in the sand forever. I need to call Celine. I need to call my supervisor. When Nick called the other day, he said to expect some additional paperwork. It's overwhelming." She exhaled. "I don't know if I can go back to the hospital. I'd like to think I'm strong enough to ignore the whispers and the stares, but I'm not sure I want the stress that will come with it. I know we've barely scratched the surface on our plans to relocate, but what do you think about expediting everything? Because if the time has ever been right for a fresh start, it's now."

"You don't know how happy I am to hear you say that, because there's something I want to run by you."

"Really?" It was hard to miss how hopeful she sounded. "Hold that thought," she said. "I want to give you my full attention, but I really need to go to the bathroom first." She pulled on her clothes and when she reached the door she turned the knob and said, "Oh my God. Did we forget to lock this?"

I laughed. "Yeah. Let's go with that."

EPILOGUE

DAISY

THE BACKDROP OF Lake Tahoe is made up of stunning vistas: lush, green forests of evergreens and pines that reach toward the clear blue sky, the snowcapped Sierra Nevada Mountains, and the dazzling, cobalt water of its namesake lake. The air is cool and crisp and smells cleaner than I could have ever imagined.

I'm more accustomed to the dust and hot wind, and the shrubs and bushes of the Southern California desert, but I've adapted to my new surroundings with minimal effort. It's not that difficult a task when you live in such a beautiful, breathtaking place.

I didn't have to think it over for very long when Brooks ran the idea by me that night in his bedroom. As we sat up talking for hours, I started mentally packing my bags when I realized how perfect this location would be for all of us.

"And did you really mean it when you said you wanted my dad to come?" Brooks asked. "We have a fishing cabin up there—which my dad will insist on living in—so it's not like we'd be sharing a place with him or anything."

I'd laughed. "After all the racket we made up here tonight,

your dad will probably be grateful that he has another option. And as someone who was raised by her grandmother, you kind of hit the jackpot with me in that regard. I would love for Elliott to experience a little of what I had growing up. And your dad seems so happy to have you in his life again. I really can't imagine leaving him behind."

Brooks loves San Francisco, so it surprised me when he said he wasn't interested in moving back there.

"San Francisco is a wonderful city, but it's an incredibly expensive—and cramped—place to live," Brooks said. "It's highly doubtful our housing budget would stretch far enough to give us the space we'd need. A higher cost of living means more work, and a more frenetic lifestyle. If we moved to Tahoe, we could buy a house and have a lot more space than we would in San Francisco. I did some checking, and there are a couple of different newspapers and a hospital, so cross your fingers that they're hiring. If you're okay with this idea, I could contact a realty company and have them start putting together a list of properties for us to look at."

"I don't have a lot of cash, Brooks. I always assumed that when I finally moved away I'd rent first, and when I had enough saved up for a down payment, I'd buy. I can easily pay my share of the mortgage payment and household expenses, provided I can find a job. But I only have about fifteen hundred in my savings account, and that's only because I had to have something set aside in case of an emergency. Anything left over after I pay my living expenses goes to paying off Scott's debt."

"Don't worry about it. I can swing the down payment."

"That hardly seems fair," I said, looking away. *Especially since Elliott and I have already cost you ten thousand dollars.*

Brooks put his hand on my chin and turned my face back to him. "Listen, I've been saving for a down payment of my own for quite some time, so I have the money. We're going to need someplace to live, and it makes more sense to buy."

"I know. You're right."

He put his arms around me and gave me a squeeze. "Let's get the ball rolling here and then take a drive up there and find ourselves a house, okay?"

I took a deep breath, smiled, and said, "Okay."

*

The house we bought is on the south shore, close to the Nevada border. It's a spacious log-cabin-style home. There are three bedrooms, and upstairs there's a large loft where Elliott can spread out all his toys and play when the weather is too cold or rainy to be outside. In back, there's a fully fenced yard with a swing set, a sandbox, and an absolutely gorgeous view of the surrounding meadow.

It was a bit of a fixer-upper. When the realtor showed it to us, we agreed that it was solidly built, with good bones. It didn't need any major repairs, but it was in dire need of some updating. The previous owners had lived in the house since 1973, and it showed. Theo insisted he needed something to keep him busy and has thrown himself headfirst into the renovation project. He can often be found tearing out or ripping up something for us. Brooks is rather handy in his own right, but Theo clearly has him beat in the home-improvement department, and our home has undergone a remarkable transformation.

Elliott is almost five now. On the days I work, he spends the morning at preschool and the afternoon with Theo, fishing for trout. When we first moved to Tahoe, he fell in love with skiing and begged us constantly to take him to the "swopes." I've no doubt that by the time he's seven, he'll be skiing circles around both of us. Hiking has replaced our trips to the park, and Elliott squeals with delight at the chipmunks and squirrels we encounter on the trail. If we ever see a bear, I'll be the one squealing, and not in a good way.

Jack Quick stopped by my apartment a few days before we left Southern California. Once Brooks and I had decided to leave Fenton, we'd quickly put our plan into action. We'd quit our jobs and were packing up the last of my things.

"Hey," Brooks said when he answered the door. "Daisy was just saying we needed to take you out for dinner before we left."

Jack glanced at Elliott, who was sitting at the kitchen table, coloring. "I, uh, have something to tell you."

The serious look on Jack's face made me tremble slightly. "Elliott?" I said. "Can you go into your bedroom for a second and make sure all your toys are packed the way you want them? I want to make sure we're not forgetting anything."

He got down from his chair. "Okay, Mama."

Jack sat down in the living room, across from Brooks and me. "We put out an APB on Scott DiStefano when Dale Reber and Jim Watson were taken into custody. We wanted to ask him some questions that might help the case and see if he was aware of Dale's involvement in the murder of your grandmother. We haven't had any luck in tracking him down, but I got a call this morning from the Las Vegas Police Department. They found a truck registered to Scott DiStefano in a parking lot. There was a body inside that appeared to have been there for a day or two. They're waiting on dental records, but we're reasonably certain it's your ex-husband."

I couldn't speak.

Regardless of all the heartache Scott had caused me, I'd never wanted anything bad to happen to him. I'd always hoped that one day he'd get clean. Get a brand-new lease on life. Maybe even work his way toward a relationship with Elliott. Images of Scott flashed before my eyes like a slideshow. I recalled the words he'd said to me the night Pam and I ran into him at the restaurant. I thought of the way he used to smile at me and how he'd tell me how happy he was that I was his wife. How he would hold me and tell me he loved me. The hardest, most bittersweet thing for me to remember was the night Elliott was born.

Scott had looked at me with tears in his eyes. "I have a son," he said. He held our swaddled child so tight that no one would have been able to pry him out of Scott's arms.

Someday, when Elliott is older and starts asking questions, I'll call upon that memory and I'll describe it to him in vivid detail. That's all he ever really needs to know about his dad.

"Do they know how he died?" Brooks asked.

"Preliminary reports indicate an overdose. There were drugs and paraphernalia in the vehicle."

After Jack left, Brooks turned to me and said, "I might as well have killed him myself, Daisy. Instead of the money, I should have just given him a loaded gun and told him to put it in his mouth. I may have despised him, but I'm not so heartless that I wished him dead."

I pulled Brooks into my arms. "You didn't kill him," I said. "He made his choice a long time ago."

Later that night, I found Brooks working his way through a bottle of wine on my tiny balcony. I could assure him over and over that it wasn't his fault, but I understood that this was something he'd have to get through on his own.

Our move to Northern California wasn't without its challenges. Both Brooks and I struggled to find jobs. I had to start out part-time, and it was almost five months before a full-time nursing position opened up at the hospital. Brooks fared even worse since many newspapers were trimming staff and offering buyout packages to some of their long-term employees. He had hoped to get hired on as a reporter at the *Tahoe Daily Tribune*, but it was eight months before he was able to make it happen. In the meantime, he worked for a much smaller newspaper and did some freelance photojournalism on the side. Neither of these career setbacks affected our financial situation too much since we were both responsible when it came to spending money, but Brooks felt unsettled for a while.

I made the last payment on my spreadsheet a few months after our job situation worked itself out. Brooks had long since offered to pay off the balance for me, but I was vehemently opposed to accepting any more of his money, and thankfully he didn't push. I rewarded myself for the accomplishment by taking Brooks out for a fancy dinner.

We celebrated our one-year anniversary, which we loosely calculated as "a couple of weeks before Thanksgiving," about nine months after we moved to Tahoe." Elliott was spending the night with Theo, so we got dressed up and went to Cafe Fiore.

"This reminds me a little bit of the first time you took me out to dinner," I said after we were seated at a small table in the corner. "Italian food, intimate setting."

"I hope this doesn't mean you're going to shoot me down at the end of the evening," Brooks said.

"Hey," I said, playfully punching him on the shoulder. "I didn't invite you in because you crushed me by announcing you were moving back to San Francisco."

The waitress stopped at our table and Brooks ordered a bottle of wine.

When she left, he said, "Well, I soon discovered the error of my ways and returned, so I certainly hope you'll be a bit more accommodating tonight."

I pretended to be interested in my menu. "Maybe, now that I'm reasonably certain you're going to stick around."

Brooks looked at me and smiled.

We went to bed as soon as we got home. Brooks was already under the covers when I joined him. After I slid in next to him, he reached for my left hand and placed a diamond ring on my finger.

"Restaurant proposals are so cliché," he said.

I can't say that I was shocked, or even surprised. I already felt that Brooks was every bit as committed to me, and to Elliott, as we were to him, and a piece of paper wasn't going to make much of a difference. But I wanted that man to be my husband more than I'd wanted anything in a long time, so when he added, "Daisy Jane, will you do me the honor of becoming my wife?" I said yes.

Rather loudly and excitedly.

After Brooks got me calmed down, he said, "What do you think about me adopting Elliott?"

I was so choked up I couldn't speak, so I nodded and Brooks said, "Okay, then."

The next day, when Theo brought Elliott home, we told them the news. Elliott didn't really understand, but he seemed excited nonetheless.

"I have a very serious question to ask you," Brooks said.

"I will answer you very serious," Elliott said.

"I want your mom to be my wife, but I also want you to be my son. That doesn't mean you have to call me Dad if you don't want to. You can still call me Brooks. It's your decision to make, and you may not be ready to make it yet. But your last name would be McClain, like mine. What do you think about that?"

Elliott's face lit up. "I would wike to be Ewiott McCwain!"

Brooks's face lit up, too.

"When's the wedding?" Theo asked.

"We were thinking about June," I said. Brooks and I had talked about it a little and agreed that we wanted something small with just a few close friends.

"As long as you don't cheat me out of seeing you in a wedding dress," Brooks said.

"I wouldn't dream of it." I had always thought there couldn't be anything more handsome than Brooks in a suit, but I thought I might change my mind when I saw him in a tux.

And cuff links.

When June rolled around, we were more than ready to make our union official. "We can't let your mom be the only one in this house who's not a McClain, can we?" Brooks asked Elliott.

"No! I want her to be a McClain like us!"

Brooks turned to me and laughed. "It's almost a shame he can pronounce his Ls now, isn't it?"

"Thankfully I captured it extensively on videotape," I said.

We'd sailed through the adoption process with ease. We'd been prepared for it to take up to a year, but it had come through a few days before the wedding.

I can't wait to see what the future holds for us. I've tried my best to leave the past behind, and the world we've built for ourselves here is as close to idyllic as I can imagine. I'm still healing, but thanks to therapy and the support of Brooks, I've come a long way. They say that women do better than men when it comes to dealing with the emotional aftermath of a self-defense shooting, but anyone who thinks that taking a human life will not leave scars behind is wrong. It's something I'll live with for the rest of my life, and not a day goes by that I don't think about it. Replay it over and over in my mind.

It's part of who I am now.

Brooks and I have discussed it at length. Could I have done something differently? Should I not have drawn my gun that day? Should I have tried to run? Brooks says no, emphatically so, but that's because there are things Jack told Brooks that Brooks refuses to talk about. I could press him for the details, ask him to tell me on the grounds that I deserve to know, but I won't.

Because I don't *want* to know.

Sometimes the young man I killed appears in my dreams. In them he is chasing me, and I wake up trembling right after he catches me. Brooks always holds me until I drift back to sleep.

I'm thankful for Brooks and for Theo, and most of all for Elliott. We live a simple, fulfilling life. And maybe ours is not the typical family dynamic, but a family can be made in so many different ways.

And I'm blessed to have finally found the one I've been searching for all my life.

THE END

ACKNOWLEDGMENTS

I am deeply grateful for the contributions, assistance, and support of the following individuals:

My husband, David, because his encouragement means more to me than he'll ever know.

My children, Matthew and Lauren. Thank you for being patient—again!—while Mom spent all that time with her laptop. I love you both.

Elisa Abner-Taschwer, Stacy Elliott Alvarez, Tammara Webber, and Colleen Hoover. Thank you for your encouragement and for helping me to see what I could not.

Peggy Hildebrandt. You have put in almost as many hours on this manuscript as I have. Your insight, encouragement, and enthusiasm for this project means more to me than you'll ever know.

Sarah Hansen at Okay Creations. I love that I can send you a semi-coherent message about what I'd like my book cover image to convey, and you nail it on the first try. Your talent is truly amazing.

Anne Victory of Victory Editing. Thank you for your eagle eye and your words of encouragement. You helped me in more ways than one.

Amy Gulbranson. Thank you for taking one last look.

Jane Dystel, Miriam Goderich, and Lauren Abramo. You are truly the trifecta of literary-agent awesomeness.

Cherie Dreier and David Dreier. Thank you for opening up your home and your private shooting range in the name of friendship (and research). What a wonderful day that was! Let's do it again soon.

Steve Hensyel, Hawkeye Firearms Instruction. I would have had no idea what I was talking about when it came to firearms if not for your patient instruction.

Gail Drier-Hensyel, Assistant Instructor, Hawkeye Firearms Instruction. Your input on the female perspective of carrying concealed is greatly appreciated.

Krista Reha. Thank you for answering all my questions about nursing and hospitals. Your firsthand knowledge made it easier to write the character of Daisy DiStefano.

To Maggie O'Brien, Tom Alex, and Stan Finger. Thank you for sharing your knowledge of investigative reporting with me and answering all of my many questions. I would not have been able to write the character of Brooks McClain without you. PS: All three of you told me slightly different things, so I mashed it all together to come up with a fictional version.

John Aquilina. Thank you for your input regarding the California criminal process.

Regina Ochoa and Shane Geschiere. Thank you for your help in naming two of the characters in *Every Time I Think of You*.

A special thank you to Sergeant Jack Beardsley of the Des Moines Police Department. You are a wealth of knowledge and I could not have written the scenes involving detective Jack Quick without your expert guidance. Bonus points for also being my awesome cousin.

The book bloggers who have been so instrumental in my

ability to reach readers. You work tirelessly every day to spread the word about books and the writing community is a better place because of you.

Autumn Hull and Andrea Thompson of Wordsmith Publicity. Thank you for making my job easier. The amount of time you've saved me is immeasurable and I know I'm in great hands when the two of you are in charge.

The booksellers who hand-sell my books and the librarians who put them on their shelves.

My heartfelt thanks go out to all of you for helping to make *Every Time I Think of You* the book I hoped it would be. Words cannot express how truly blessed I am to have such wonderful and enthusiastic people in my life.

And last, but certainly not least, my readers. Without you, none of this would be possible.

ABOUT THE AUTHOR

Tracey Garvis Graves is the *New York Times* bestselling author of three full-length novels and two novellas. She lives in a suburb of Des Moines, Iowa, with her husband and two children. She can be found on Facebook at https://www.facebook.com/tgarvisgraves and Twitter at https://twitter.com/tgarvisgraves or you can visit her website at http://traceygarvisgraves.com She would love to hear from you!

OTHER BOOKS BY TRACEY GARVIS GRAVES

On the Island
Uncharted
Covet
Cherish (Covet, 1.5) coming 10/28/14

Printed in Great Britain
by Amazon